TRUCK STOP
TRYST

KRISSY DANIELS

TRUCK STOP
TRYST

For all the knife wielding, ass kicking,

stiletto wearing ladies of the world.

Stay soft. Stay strong.

PROLOGUE

"AIDA, PRINCESS. YOU ARE not supposed to be here."

My spine stiffened at the gruff, irritated rasp. I turned to face my best friend, knowing he'd have my back despite his ire.

Jaw set tight, he flashed me a warning glare that held little conviction.

"I missed your ugly mug," I teased, planting a kiss on his scratchy cheek.

"Yeah, yeah," Tito grumbled, pushing me away. "Your pops is gonna rearrange my mug if I let you step one foot closer to that ring."

My father would skin me alive, after he'd disemboweled my bodyguards for letting me give them the slip.

Ever since the word *pregnant* appeared on that damn Clearblue digital stick, Dad had forbidden me to attend, or come within a three-thousand-mile radius of his fights.

Crappy for me, because I loved everything about the violent gatherings—muscles, egos, blood, and bruises.

Adding salt to my wound, my banishment from the underground scene had created the perfect opportunity for Rafael, my soon-to-be-ex, to wander. And wander he did.

Straight into the arms of a beautiful blonde. What I couldn't figure out, was why he had put zero effort into hiding his extra-whore-icular activities.

Too bad I had to take him out. Rafael Turner was an impressive fighter, but his real talent was in the bedroom. The man was an orgasm-inducing wonder.

"Listen." Tito wrapped his thick fingers around my upper arm. "Don't start anything. My bullshit bucket is full. I don't have time to mop up another one of your messes. You have to behave."

"Aw." I pursed my lips at my lifelong partner in crime. "Don't spoil my fun tonight."

"Aida," he warned. "Swear to fuck, you start anything, there will be hell to pay."

"You and I both know Rafael Turner is double-dipping that legendary cock of his. He should've considered the consequences. I'm carrying his child. Am I supposed to give him a free pass?"

"Let your father handle it, Aida." He pointed a finger at my face. "Hell, let me handle it. I've been itching to put that guy in his place."

"No, Tits." I'd given Tito his nickname, Tits, in sixth grade, after I'd caught him feeling up Olivia Fields. He'd said, "I can't help it. I'm a tit man." The name stuck. I was the only human on Earth who could get away with calling him Tits.

Demon-like fury flashed in his eyes, crimson and terrifying. Damn, Tito was a scary fucker when he was pissed.

He gripped my shoulders. "This is what's gonna happen. You sit here like a good little girl until I get back. Fold those hands in your lap. Bow your head. Pray to God your father doesn't see you. When the fight is over, I'll drive you home. We've got seven figures riding on this match-up. Turner is a key player. We need his head in the game. Got me? Until then, no trouble."

I leaned forward and planted a kiss on Tito's cheek. "I promise, no trouble."

We both knew I was lying. But what could he do? Hogtie a pregnant woman?

Tito pulled a crate behind me. "Sit. I'll be right back."

Most would cower under the heavy weight of his command. I simply rolled my eyes.

"Sure thing, Tits." I perched my ass on the wood box and watched while he stormed down the hallway, then blurred into the crowd.

Too easy.

I found Rafael in a matter of minutes. Wasn't hard. Empty hall. No bodyguards, no posse, no managers. No hype.

I didn't bother to knock on the heavy wood door before peeking my head in the dimly lit room. Chanel No. 5 overpowered the usual scent of sweat, leather, and the musty tang of a building well past its prime. I listened before venturing farther inside.

A woman's giggle. The shuffle of feet. The buzz of florescent lighting.

A breathy voice said, "I thought you weren't supposed to fuck before a fight."

"Doesn't matter, baby," came a deep, throaty reply. "This one's in the bag. Dixon will go down in the fourth. All I gotta do is put on a good show."

"Rafi," she whined. "Please tell me you didn't make a deal with Voltolini."

Rafi? Dear God, she'd given him a pet name.

"I'll tell you whatever you wanna hear, doll, as long as you're on your knees. You've promised that mouth for days. We've got twenty minutes. Work your magic."

A low moan followed a sensual giggle. "Oh, sweet Jesus, you're huge."

Perfect. Caught in the act. Made retribution all the sweeter.

I stepped out of the shadows. There was no arguing, Rafael's cock was a thing of beauty, which, to be honest, was my favorite thing about him. Despite the fact I was finished with the bastard, I had no desire to see his meat in someone else's mouth.

I sauntered around the corner, every inch of my body vibrating with venomous wrath. "Sorry to break up your little party." I pounded my palm to my forehead. "Wait. Not sorry. Not sorry at all."

"Aida, shit," Rafael sputtered, leaning forward and scrambling to pull himself away from the woman's busy tongue. "What? Who let...? I mean. What the hell are you doing here? You're not allowed anywhere near the fucking fights."

"Oh, honey. That's no way to talk to the mother of your child." I dropped my gaze to the woman on the floor. Rafael's erection deflated in blondie's hand, and I decided I'd been wrong. The dipshit's twiddle-stick wasn't all that impressive.

The young woman scrambled to her feet. "You said she couldn't come here. Goddammit, Rafi." Her wild eyes searched the room, landing everywhere but on me. "Are you trying to get me killed?"

Rafael fumbled with the drawstring of his pants. I smiled and dropped the blades from their holders in my sleeves, hiding them in the palms of my hands.

"So, *Rafi*." I poured plenty of sticky sweet syrup into his name. "Am I correct in assuming that you've been stuffing your cock in other holes the whole time you were proclaiming your undying love to me? That's bold, albeit terribly stupid, using me to weasel into my father's good graces."

A sheen of sweat glistened on the dark skin of his forehead. "You and me, Princess? We're not over, if that's what you're getting at. You're wearing my ring. Carrying my child. That makes you mine. No matter who I choose to fuck."

Fatally arrogant twat.

"Oh, but you see, I'm not wearing the ring. I've yet to give you an answer." Moving closer, I admired his thick chest for the last time. I would miss his muscles almost as much as his dick. The rest of him, not so much. "Aside from knocking me up, then getting caught..." I dropped my glare to his groin, then met his green eyes again. "With your pants down ... you only made one mistake."

"I don't make mistakes," he said, confident as all dumbfuck.

"Au contraire, love." Ignoring the woman fumbling to put her shirt on behind me, I stepped closer and poked a finger between his pecs, lowering my other hand to his crotch. "One. Fatal. Miscalculation."

A haughty smirk played across his face as he looked down his nose at me. "Okay, baby. I'll bite."

I thrust my knife upward into the soft flesh between his legs. His mouth formed an O in a silent scream, his lips working like a fish out of water. "You underestimated me." I pulled the knife out and struck again.

Rafael raised a fist, but before he could aim, I slashed my other blade across his wrist. This time, his scream reached my ears. As did the woman's high-pitched, "Oh my God! Oh my God!"

Blondie ran to his side and followed him to the floor as he folded and fell, writhing in pain.

I wiped my blades on the crisp, white towels stacked in a neat pile next to his boxing trunks

"I'll kill you. I'll kill you, crazy bitch!" he cried, floundering in the smears of blood on the floor. "I don't give a shit who your father is."

"Aw. Rafael. You'll be fine. They're only flesh wounds," I reassured him as I tucked away my blades. "Unfortunately, you'll have to forfeit the fight. Afraid you can't put on a good show in that condition. My father will not be pleased."

Papa Voltolini would have no choice but to dispose of him.

"You know what that means, right?" I made my way to the door. "The deal you made with my father is off." Pausing in the threshold, I tapped a fingernail on the frame and looked over my shoulder. "And so is any chance of a wedding, obviously."

Rafael pushed from the floor and charged, hatred contorting his face. I twisted to dodge his assault at the same time someone grabbed me from behind and swung me backward, pulling me out of harm's way.

Idiots had no clue I was the dangerous one.

Tito and two other fighters dragged Rafael, kicking and cussing from the dressing room, down the dark corridor, and through the back exit.

I laughed, satisfied, and to my surprise, relieved, until a deep voice startled me from behind. "Aida."

I turned to face the wrath of Luciano Voltolini. Under the flickering bulbs lighting the dark hallway, Dad looked considerably older than his fifty-some years—his wrinkles more pronounced, the dark shadows under his whiskey-colored eyes deeper, darker, and deadlier than I'd ever seen.

I crossed my arms in defiance, daring him to wax poetic the new ways in which I'd broken his heart and disappointed him.

For the first time in my life, he didn't lecture. Lips pursed, he waited for an explanation.

When I didn't give one, he gestured to his bodyguard. Sebastian handed my father his favorite knife.

"Thank you, Sebi," Dad said, admiring his weapon. "Take care of the girl. Then help Tito secure Rafael. I'll be there shortly." He pulled a polishing cloth from his pocket and rubbed the blade, raising one eyebrow, inviting me to explain myself.

"I won't apologize. He used me to get closer to you."

"You think I'm a fool?" His lip curled in disgust, a rare show of emotion. "I own that man. It's my business to know his every move. He played you from the beginning. I had no intention of allowing a marriage. I only needed time to figure out his end game."

That stung. "You knew he was playing me?"

His head remained down, but his eyes lifted to mine. "I know everything."

Sucker-punch straight to the throat. "And you let it happen? At what cost? My heart? Your empire is more important than your only daughter?" The pressure was building too fast. "I'm fucking pregnant," I screamed and raised my hand to strike. I had never, ever in my twenty-five years, raised a hand to my father.

Dad caught my wrist. Eyes dark as midnight, he hissed, "Love has no place in our world. I taught you better than that." A dark curl fell across his forehead, and he released my arm to swipe the loose hair back into place.

Dad rarely lost composure. Standing before me, father to defiant daughter, he was dangerously close to revealing his true colors. "Princess. I'm sorry it has to be this way. Yes, the child was a surprise. I can't take the blame for that irresponsible turn of events. You should've protected yourself. You and I both know you were never in love with Turner."

"I did protect myself. You didn't raise an idiot."

It hadn't taken long after I'd missed my first period to realize Rafael had messed with my birth control. Reason number one for choosing to target his baby makers.

"He'll suffer for using you. Give me your knives."

"No."

"Aida. They're evidence. They need to disappear." A man like my father didn't care about evidence. Taking away my babies was his way of punishing me for my lapse in judgment and self-control.

"Dad. No. Not my knives."

"You can hand them to me, or Sebi can disarm you. Your choice."

Sebastian was one of only a few men I'd yet to take down on the training mats. One of the only people on the planet I feared.

I pulled up my sleeves, unfastened my wrist sheaths, and surrendered my favorite accessories. With a deep breath and a regretful twinge of shame, I pulled the large diamond engagement ring out of my pocket and dropped it into my father's hand. "Make him choke on it."

His lip twitched, threatening to lift in a smirk. "Aida. Princess."

A loud, pained scream echoed through the hallway.

My father's deadly mask fell back into place. "I understand your rage, and I share it with you, but you've gone too far this time. You have no idea what you've done."

CHAPTER 1

I PLOPPED MY ASS onto a stool and watched my sister float across the black and white checkered tile, in the arms of her best friend, and, as of today, her fiancé. It'd been three hours since Tango popped the question in my sister's newly remodeled diner, The Truck Stop, and we'd all watched from behind the scenes.

She hadn't stopped smiling since.

I strained to keep my gaze on the happy couple and away from the raven-haired sex-goddess laughing and dancing with the other men at the party. Christ, she was a beauty. Eighty percent curves, twenty percent doe-eyes. One hundred percent feminine wiles.

Aida Voltolini had the best laugh. Raspy and deep. Paired with her wicked smile, the woman was downright bewitching.

My nephew, Rocky, squealed. Out of the corner of my eye, I watched Aida scoop him into her arms and spin. The little tyke had fallen under her spell, too.

"No. That's not how you do it," he said, giggling.

Curiosity got the best of me, and I turned their way, giving them my full attention.

Rocky pulled Aida's hand into his and held his arm out straight. "Like this, see?"

"Oh. Yes. That's much better." Aida straightened her back and spun, raising up on her toes, then dipping low, laughing, and kissing the little lady-killer on the cheek.

Tango, breathless from dancing, and still wearing a cheesy grin, set one elbow on the counter next to me and leaned close. "Thanks for helping me arrange this shindig."

Sometimes I hated the guy for taking away my family. Sometimes I wanted to hug him for putting that fucking brilliant smile on my sister's face.

"No problem," I said, unable to peel my eyes off the mob princess and my nephew.

Tango leaned close, so only I could hear him ask, "The house ready?"

"Good to go." I pulled a set of keys from my pocket and handed them back to the grinning man. "Slade doesn't know yet?"

"Doesn't have a clue."

My sister's home had burned to the ground a little over a month ago. She and my nephew had been staying with me until their new house was move-in ready. Unbeknownst to Slade, Tango had hired a crew to speed up the process. He was about to surprise her and their son with their newly remodeled abode. Thank God. I couldn't wait to head to my condo and get reacquainted with my king-size. The couch had been a killer on my back.

I waved a hand to shoo him off. "Take your dancing queen to her new castle. I'll help Charlie clean up the mess here and lock up."

"Do you mind bringing Aida home later?"

Hell yeah, I minded.

"Not at all." The smile I forced was painful. Last thing I needed was to be alone with the only woman who'd stirred the blood in my cock in years. "She all moved in?"

"Yeah. Furniture was delivered day before yesterday. Tito helped her settle in last night. He said she only grumbled for the first three or four hours. Can't blame her. It's got to be hard, moving from a castle to a nine hundred square foot basement apartment."

"Poor spoiled princess," I huffed.

"You have no idea." With a hard clap to my shoulder, Tango said goodbye. I watched the happy family make their exit. As Tango lifted Rocky to his shoulders and tucked Slade under his arm, my chest ached.

I had watched over my sister and nephew for years. Now that they had Tango, I wasn't sure what to do with my spare time. And the damn hole in my chest only seemed to get bigger. I itched for a hunt. Yeah. That sounded good. I'd hunt. After dropping the mob princess at home.

Mom, Dad, and the rest of the partygoers said their farewells and made their way out the door.

Tango's cousin, Tito Moretti, wrapped a beefy arm around my shoulder. "I'm off. Got a plane to catch. Keep in touch, Tuck. Ever want to visit the Big Apple, I'm your man." The guy was all beef and smooth talk, layered over a deadly confidence. He nodded toward Aida who was saying goodbye to Tango's father. "Keep an eye on my girl over there. She's got a heart bigger than Texas. Just gotta shovel through a valley of bullshit to find it."

"My eyes aren't going anywhere near that vixen." Let alone any of my other body parts.

"Aw. She isn't so bad, once you dust off the gunpowder." Tito strutted toward the door and pulled Aida into a tight embrace, his hands on her hips, his mouth on her cheek, whispering words that made her smile and blush.

I curled my fingers into my palm and headed to the kitchen for a trash bag. Damn. I didn't like seeing Tito's arms around her. Not one bit. More disturbing, was the fact that their intimacy bothered me. I shook that thought off real quick.

The girl was trouble. Not a chance in hell I was getting close to that. Aida was Tango's problem, not mine.

I lived a carefully designed, drama-free life. Work. Gym. Eat. Hunt. Sleep.

No girlfriend.

No worries.

I made quick work of helping Charlie tidy the kitchen before heading back to the dining area where Aida would no doubt be waiting, all doe-eyes, moist red lips, and attitude. I pushed through the swinging stainless steel doors and damn near fell to my knees at the sight of her, bending over, heart-shaped ass in the air, fiddling with the hem of her gown.

At the sound of the doors clunking, she stood up and looked over her bare shoulder. The diamond earrings she wore caught the light just right, flashing a bright sparkle across her olive skin.

"Oh, hey Tuck." She gripped the sides of her bustier and adjusted her breasts. "What can I do to help?"

Christ, that voice. Soft and deep. Seductive. So damn intoxicating. The suit pants I wore were insufficient to hide my growing erection. Thank God, I'd untucked my shirt earlier.

After clearing the lust from my throat, I pointed to a stool. "Nothing. I've got it, Charlie's got the kitchen, you relax. Can I get you something to drink?"

Aida quirked a brow at me and rubbed a hand over her small belly. "I'm pregnant. Not helpless."

And ... that took care of the boner problem.

Aida was off-limits. Pregnant. Under the protection of Tango, my soon to be brother-in-law. Not to mention, the only daughter of one of America's most elusive criminals, Luciano Voltolini.

Yep. Definitely off-limits.

"Didn't say you were helpless. Just thought you might need a breather after all that dancing." I plucked red plastic cups off the bar and dropped them into the trash bag.

Aida sauntered around the corner, grabbed a bottle of spray cleaner and a towel, and proceeded to wipe down the counter as I cleared it of debris.

"There," she said after we finished. "Good as new."

By the time I'd dumped the trash bag in the bin behind the diner, and returned with the push broom, Aida had made herself comfortable on the new, red leather couch in Slade's office.

Feet perched on a pillow, she smiled up at me and wiggled her bare feet. "You were right. This feels good."

I proceeded to sweep, counting my strokes to keep my mind off those naked legs and perfectly manicured toes.

The day couldn't end soon enough. A few more hours and I'd be home free. Back to my simple, single life.

Aida

Single life was not working for me. I hated being alone. In Whisper Springs, my options for male companionship were slim to one. The *one* being the only single man I'd met since being sent to my small-town hell.

Tucker Slade was not my type. Not even close. My type wore Armani suits, drove Ferrari's or Porsche's. My type bloodied faces in their spare time, in the underground fights controlled by my father. Slick. Shiny. Beautiful. Dangerous.

Tucker Slade was rough, burly, and unpolished. He wore his suit like a peacock in a beige leotard. Damn thing choked the very life and personality right out of him. Thick, unkempt brows, two-day stubble, not a lick of styling product in his wavy hair. Quiet. Brooding.

Not my type.

Then why, after every time his gaze fell on me, did I feel like a woman claimed, owned, wanted? Why did my skin heat, my heart race, my body ache to the bone?

Pregnancy hormones. The only logical explanation.

My fascination with the man definitely had nothing to do with the way he smelled like leather and pine, or those denim-colored eyes, or the way he looked at me like I was the only woman on the planet. Most men looked at me that way. Perhaps the fact that Tucker hadn't acted on the obvious attraction was what had my brain jumbled.

I rubbed my small baby bump. Wasn't even a bump yet. Swell? Puff? Whatever. I knew it was there. I knew what was coming, or who, rather. "Mama's losing it, little one. It's all your fault."

Pre-pregnancy, my life was all about sex.

Stressed? Call the trainer, work out in bed.

Angry? Fighter's rage fucked like nobody's business.

Celebrating? Hit the clubs with private rooms.

Getting to know the enemy? Seduce them. Most men fuck the same way they conduct business.

Lonely? My little black book had been upgraded from notebook to novel years ago.

I was sexually frustrated, to say the least. It'd been months. Now all I could think about was climbing and conquering Mount Tucker. I laughed to myself. Not a chance in hell a man with his manners and rugged, country boy charm would want to bang a knocked-up single girl with a knife fetish and ties to the mafia.

Nope. Wasn't gonna happen. I needed a distraction. Scratch that. I needed an industrial strength vibrator.

Unfortunately, I'd been whisked off to my temporary prison with little time to pack, and tragically, every one of my BOBs had been left in the dust.

I heard the smack of Tucker's flip-flops before he entered the office. Flip-flops were ridiculous creations, and I'd only ever worn them to the salon, but they'd been required for this engagement party, so we all donned a brand-new pair. Who was I to judge? I had a knife fetish. Apparently, Slade had a rubber footwear fetish. Whatever floats your boat.

"All done here, ready to head home?" He braced his arms on the doorframe above his head. The way he filled the space, all muscles and white teeth, made my head spin and heat swirl through my insides.

I sat up, tucked my legs underneath me, and patted the cushion. "No. Not yet. Lets give Tango and Slade time alone in their new home."

Tucker dropped his head low and moaned.

Ouch. That stung.

Back home, men threw themselves at me. Kissed my ass, too, and yes, it was because my last name was Voltolini. Didn't matter. I gobbled the attention, demanded it, rather. In Whisper Springs, Idaho, Aida was a nobody.

I wasn't ready to retreat to my basement apartment below the new Rossi love-shack. The last thing I needed was to hear the lovebirds and their happy family dancing over my head. However, it was clear by the scowl on Tucker's face that he had no interest in keeping me company.

I had a battle on my hands.

I patted the cushion. "Come on, Cowboy. Please. We can fire up Slade's new television."

He quirked a brow. "Cowboy?"

I offered him the remote. "I'll even let you pick the show." Tango had recently remodeled The Truck Stop Diner for Slade, restoring it to its nineteen fifties retro vibe. The office, however, was designed with his son Rocky in mind, complete with a play area, pint-sized homework desk, couch, and flat-screen television. Slade's desk was hardly noticeable, tucked in the far corner.

"I've got an early day tomorrow. I should head home." He rubbed a hand through the mess of hair on top of his head.

"Please. Just an hour. Please. I'll slit my throat if I have to watch another second of their happy, love crap."

"Aida. You have a separate apartment downstairs. You don't have to see them if you don't want to."

"Oh. You must be referring to my dark and gloomy underground prison. Yeah. That's something to look forward to." I batted my lashes and patted the cushion one more time. "You have any idea what that cave will do to my healthy glow? You want me to be hideous and pale?"

Tucker closed the distance between us in four long strides and dropped next to me with a loud sigh, throwing his heat, and his welcoming scent around me like a rainy day wool sweater. He quirked a brow and grabbed the remote from my hand. "What did you do to earn this banishment? Had to be bad if Luciano Voltolini sent his only daughter away."

Out of habit, I rubbed at the bare spot on my left forearm where my knife holder had once lived like a second skin. I missed my babies.

No use lying. Aside from Slade, Tango, and Tango's father, Carlos, Tucker was the only other person in town who knew my real identity. I was introduced to everyone else as Tango's cousin, Aida Suarez. "I stabbed the father of my baby. In the balls." I held up two fingers. "Twice."

His jaw dropped before he caught it and lifted his lips into a nervous smirk. "That's a good one. Seriously, what'd you do? Or are you not allowed to talk about it?"

"I'm telling the truth. The asshole cheated on me. I caught him in the act. Stabbed him twice."

Tucker's face paled.

Shoot. Should've lied. No way his dick would come anywhere near me now. I was doomed to serve my sentence as a celibate—horny, and growing less attractive by the day.

Tucker didn't ask me to elaborate, but I did, because it felt good to talk to someone who wasn't being paid to appease me. "I've never had unprotected sex in my life. I've always used birth control and condoms. Faithfully. Rafael figured if he knocked me up, he'd have an in. Access to my father. Not sure how he did it. Damn sure wasn't going to let him get away with using me. Seems Dad had a plan of his own, though. One I wasn't privy to. Apparently, I caused a ton of trouble for Dad, pissed off the wrong people. Now, I'm hiding here, in Butt-Fuck-Idaho until Dad mops up my mess." I slumped into the buttery soft leather.

Tucker loosened his tie and undid the top two buttons of his shirt before scooting deeper into the cushions himself, hands at his sides, knees spread wide. "So, you're kind of a badass, then?" He clicked the power button on the remote and chuckled. "Princess Badass. Nice."

Wasn't the reaction I'd expected. Most men would run for the hills, cupping their junk. Tucker seemed to find my twisted idea of justice amusing. Okay, so maybe there was hope for the guy. Of course, if anything of the sexual variety were to happen between the two of us, it could only be a fling. A dalliance. My father would send for me soon.

Until then, Tucker could be a beautiful and much-needed distraction. Tucker Slade and his brilliant blue eyes.

Tucker

Those damn doe-eyes. All liquid chocolate framed with long lashes. Sucked me right in. Deceiving as hell.

Princess Voltolini was dark and dangerous. I needed to remember that.

I shifted, praying she wouldn't notice the bulge swelling behind the fly of my ridiculous suit pants. I hadn't worn a suit since Nicki's funeral. Everything about the expensive get-up felt off. Scratchy, ill-fitting, and pompous.

Aida was nervous. The click of her red nails made that a no-brainer. Was she worried her little confession would scare me off?

It should have.

"What should we watch?" I asked, changing the subject, no longer eager to head home. Matter of fact, little miss knife fetish had become all the more tantalizing.

"Really?" She blinked at me. "Anything. I'll watch anything. Just don't take me to that prison yet."

"Alrighty then." I pressed the channel change button at a steady pace, acutely aware, from scalp to toes, of the warm, sensual heat seated next to me.

Aida continued to tap her nails together.

Click. Click. Click.

Damn, that was annoying. Kinda cute. Mostly annoying.

I stopped channel surfing when a familiar image caught my eye. A rest stop on Highway 12 near the Idaho-Montana border. The title on the screen read *Rest Area Reaper Claims Another Victim*. Corny? Yes. Accurate? Hell, yes.

The attacks were occurring more and more frequently and were no longer confined to the Pacific Northwest. Was

I concerned? No. Every headline failed to report the most important fact about the *psychopath* targeting truck drivers. The specifics everyone in the trucking industry knew. A dirty little secret nobody talked about. Every trucker who had been attacked by the Rest Area Reaper had been fishing for underage companionship, under the cover of night, in the sleazy underbelly of my chosen profession. The victims didn't talk to the authorities, for fear of prison, or their families discovering their illegal proclivities. The *working* girls didn't talk for fear of losing their livelihood. The pimps, well, they stayed hidden.

I wasn't concerned. Our drivers were screened, drug tested, road tested, screened again. Our trucks had cameras running twenty-four-seven, inside and outside the cab, to ensure no illegal exchanges took place on our clock.

Most victims of the Reaper were private contractors. Every one of them had narrowly escaped with their lives, beaten to a pulp. Not a single one could identify the person or persons who'd assaulted them.

I changed the channel again, before Aida could process, or, God forbid, question me about the Reaper story, and landed on an image of a man in waders, hip deep in crystal clear water, demonstrating a brilliant river load cast.

"Fishing? Really?" she asked with a huff.

"It's relaxing." I glanced at her hands. "You should try it sometime. I've never seen a girl wound so tight."

"I have good reason." She studied the screen.

"I suppose you do."

It took unfathomable will power not to laugh as she shifted and squirmed next to me, clearly agitated, but trying hard to keep her trap shut. Sweet Mother of Mercy, she smelled good.

Her patience only lasted two minutes. "So, this is what you do to relax? Watch men in rivers play with their skinny rods?"

I melted deeper into the couch and laced my fingers behind my head. "When I need to relax, I hit the gym. Sometimes I go fishing."

"You like to play with your rod, too?" *Click. Click. Click.* "Sounds fun."

I glanced her way in time to catch an eye roll.

The mob princess could throw an attitude. Damn, I wanted to tame that fiery spirit. Or throw some gasoline on it and see how hot she could burn. I could've continued to banter. Instead, I asked, "What do you do to relax?"

"Sex," she said without hesitation. Then her eyes widened, and she slapped a hand to her mouth. "Sorry. I mean. Um. Oh God. That sounded awful."

Yeah. Her confession was too good to let slide. "So, I'm in the company of a nymphomaniac, testicle-carving, mob princess. I can't for the life of me understand why any man would let you slip through his fingers."

She searched my face, gaze falling on my mouth, darting to my eyes, then dropping back to my lips. Her forehead wrinkled, eyes pinching together as if she couldn't comprehend what I'd just said.

Fuck me, but I wanted to devour those plump red kissers. "Stabbing him wasn't enough, you know. Any guy who cheats deserves to have his nuts cracked, chopped, and slow-roasted over a campfire."

And there it was—Aida's deep, raspy, laugh.

No better sound in the world. I did that. And quick as a snap, I was addicted. Obsessed. Committed to making her laugh every day.

For the tenth or sixtieth time since meeting her, my cock swelled. Before I had time to adjust my hips and hide my arousal, Aida sprung across the couch and crashed her mouth to mine. Her bare arms coiled around my neck. Straddling my lap, she settled her full, soft ass on my thighs. With tongue, lips, and soft moans, she attacked. A full-frontal assault.

It'd been too long since I'd kissed a woman. Instinct urged me to back off and slow things down. Protect myself. But with her breasts rubbing against my chest, her warm thighs bracing my hips, and the sweet, cotton candy scent of her skin, I was helpless, mindless, selfish, and I gave in to basic human need. I slid my hands down the silky fabric of her gown and cupped her ass, pulling her closer, tighter against my erection.

Sweet hell, I'd forgotten what a pair of breasts and soft skin could do to short circuit a man's dignity.

I had to stop. Before I couldn't.

Aida tangled her delicate fingers in my hair and pulled. Fire seared my veins. When I drew in a sharp breath, she yanked my head, forcing it against the back of the couch. Rising on her knees, she crashed her mouth to mine.

The girl was strong, and she held me tight and still during the attack. It wasn't a kiss. It was mouth fucking. Dirty. Raw. Painful. And the hottest damn sexual experience of my life.

I let her have her way with me, on the couch in my sister's office, until my dick threatened to erupt. Curling my fingers into her hips, I urged her back down into my lap.

Immediately she began to grind against me. Moaning, kissing, biting.

Shit. Too many layers of fabric separated us. As if reading my mind, Aida sat back on my thighs and pulled the bodice of her dress down, exposing her full, heavy breasts, and their enticing rose colored buds. I needed a taste.

First, I needed to slow the bump and grind before something embarrassing happened.

Fuck. I needed to stop touching her.

And I would.

After a taste. One taste.

I lifted her off my lap and laid her on the couch. She reached for my belt buckle. I swatted her hands away.

Her eyes darkened, and she reached for me again. I grabbed both of her wrists and pinned them above her head, causing her breasts to wiggle and bounce in an erotic tease.

One taste. Then I'd stop.

Ducking my head, I pulled the taut skin of one nipple between my teeth. She was salty and sweet, tight, and responsive. When I rolled my tongue across the bud, Aida bucked beneath me. I adjusted my position, to gain better access of her exposed skin, planting one foot on the ground and one knee between her legs.

One more taste. I had to have one more.

I moved to the left breast. When I nibbled on the hard peak, Aida arched and slid her body down the couch, finding purchase on my leg. She wrestled one hand out of my grip and slapped it hard on the back of my head, digging in, pulling me tighter to her bosom.

I sucked, drawing long, slow pulls of her breast. Aida ground her pussy against my thigh, writhing, riding, getting off. It'd be a lie if I said she wasn't driving me insane. My dick throbbed, screaming for attention, but the beauty beneath me was once again running the show. Her death grip held me steady physically, her moans held me captive mentally. I toyed with her breast. She worked herself against me.

My angry erection remained untouched, but that didn't stifle my oncoming orgasm. I had to end our heavy petting before I made a mess of my new suit, or worse, a fool of myself. I pulled the tip of her pebbled flesh between my teeth and flicked my tongue across the top.

Aida's head flew back into the cushions, her hips tilted, rocking harder against my leg, and she came with a string of gorgeous, ecstasy-tainted profanities, her thighs clenching tight around my leg, her body twisting, her hands fisting my hair, painful and thrilling, and scrambling my brain.

Fucking hell. I'd never experienced anything so carnal. Never had I witnessed a woman come undone with such wild abandon.

I did that.

Aida

I had never done that. Holy shit. What just happened? Never had a man made me come just by playing with my breasts. If making out with Tucker was that good, I couldn't wait to get to the real action.

Mindless bliss, my drug of choice. I sighed and opened my eyes, eager to continue, beyond excited about my new discovery, my new toy.

Tucker hovered over me, shit-eating grin on his face, chest rising and falling in rapid bursts. His tongue appeared in a slow drag across his bottom lip. "You relaxed now?"

I realized I was still gripping the back of his head and let my arm fall to my side. "I am so fucking relaxed," I said, wiggling my fingers so he would release my other hand.

Before letting me go, he dropped a hard kiss on my lips. Then, much to my dismay, he tugged my dress back over my boobs. "It's a shame we need to cover those up. Prettiest damn things I've ever seen."

Heard that before. However, until those words fell from his lips, I'd never felt the power they held. The need fueling his gaze, the way he stared into me and not at my breasts, each word pierced me through and through.

I couldn't wait to reciprocate. "We're not done," I said, reaching for his crotch. "It's your turn."

A sad smile cracked his face before he leaned down to kiss my nose. "Nah. I'm good."

"What?" He had to be joking. Men didn't get women off just to get women off. A man got a woman off so he could bury his dick in one of her holes and feel like a king.

"I said, I'm good."

"Yeah, right." I grabbed him anyway. Good Lord, he was hard and huge in my hand. When I squeezed, he jerked back and jumped off the couch like I'd electrocuted him.

"Time to head home," he mumbled, avoiding my gaze while offering a hand to help me up.

"Are you fucking serious?" I swatted him away and propped my arms behind me. "Did I do something wrong? Is it the baby?" I looked down at my stomach. "I knew it. It's a turn-off. Jesus, men are so shallow—"

"Aida. Shut up," he half-shouted, half-growled.

"No. No. It's okay." I straightened my shoulders and pushed off the couch, bumping the big lug out of my way in the process. "I get it." I hadn't had many conversations with Tucker since coming to Whisper Springs, three maybe, in total, but I had watched him, studied him, and early on, had decided that he was the epitome of small town, American good ol' boy. Man. Whatever. He was too wholesome for the likes of me.

"It's not you. I mean. It is you." He scratched the stubble under his chin before squeezing his eyes closed and shaking his head. "You are perfect. And that mouth? Seriously. Didn't know it was possible to kiss like that."

"But I'm trouble," I interjected.

"What? No."

"Listen," I adjusted my breasts, straightened my skirt. "You're a good guy. I can see that. You need a sweet girl to warm your bed, not a cock-stabbing criminal—"

Tucker attacked, clamping an arm around my waist. He slammed me against his chest, and our mouths collided in a hard, desperate kiss. When he came up for air, I was speechless.

"Let's get one thing straight, Aida. I want nothing more than to rip off that ridiculous dress and take you in every corner of this room. But you're right. I'm a good guy. And that's exactly why I'm shutting this down before it gets out of hand. I don't have time in my life for a relationship, romantic or otherwise, and I refuse to lead you on just to get my rocks off."

Tucker reached around me and pulled the door open, pausing before allowing me through. "And the fact that you're carrying a baby? Not a turn off. Nothing sexier in this world than a woman with child."

My lips, hell, the whole area surrounding my mouth, burned from the scratch of his stubble. My insides were on fire, perhaps from the heat of his gaze, or maybe it was his words that torched me. Either way, I wasn't about to let him know he'd singed me with his rebuff.

A sharp sting bit my backside as I passed him. My insides heated another gazillion degrees. I turned on my heel and shoved a palm into his chest. "Don't ever slap my ass like that again. And, for the record, I don't want a relationship, romantic or otherwise, either. Especially with some backwoods hick who doesn't seem to own a razor."

I turned and stormed toward the back exit before running my mouth more than necessary, before he could read the disappointment on my face, or hear the anguish behind my words. Rejection fucking sucked.

When I passed the wall of knives in the kitchen, I yanked one off the magnetic holder and pitched it across the room, landing it with precision into the wall above the prep sink. Damn, that felt good. At least the pregnancy crap hadn't messed with my aim.

I pushed through the door and waited for Tucker by his Jeep.

Thankfully, the drive home was less than three minutes, seeing as my new apartment, in the basement of Tango's new home, was just up the hill from The Truck Stop.

I shoved the door open before he put the vehicle in park. I hopped to the ground and headed straight for my private entrance around the back of the house before realizing I had left my keys and my handbag at the diner. Great. Now I'd have to go bother Tango.

"Looking for this?" Tucker dangled a key over my shoulder.

"Thank you," I mumbled, snatching it from his hand. His heat warmed my back as I slid the metal teeth into the lock. Not a chance in hell I was going to turn around. The evening had been an epic, embarrassing mess. I was going to keep it, and him, where they belonged, behind me.

Pushing open the door, I steeled my spine, sucked in a breath, and pushed through the threshold into my empty, lonely, temporary home.

"See ya, Bambi." Tucker chuckled, before smacking my ass, hard, and retreating to the safety of his vehicle.

CHAPTER 2

Aida

"AIDA, HI!" SLADE BEAMED, all blonde hair, blue eyes, and angelic glow, from behind the counter. She nodded toward the table in the corner of the dining room. "I'll be there in a sec."

I made my way, as instructed, to the corner booth, and shimmied into my favorite seat, at the table boasting the best view of the lake. The dining room was full. It always was, because The Truck Stop had Charlie Lincoln behind the grill, flipping the best damn burgers I'd ever tasted. My mouth watered in anticipation.

Slade set down a strawberry lemonade and fell into the seat across from me. "Hey, chubby. How you feeling?"

Seriously, Slade was the only person on the planet who could get away with calling me *chubby*. Anyone else tried that, their tongue would be removed, deep fried, and fed to their mother. She used the nickname because of my growing belly, and the fact that I'd come in for the burger basket every day since The Truck Stop diner had reopened over two weeks ago. To be honest, I kind of loved the endearment. It was far better than *Princess*, which had been my nickname from birth. I hated *Princess*.

"I'm feeling good. Hungry. Bored out of my mind." What an understatement. I'd watched every movie on Netflix, abused Slade's library card, and even stooped so low as kidnapping Rocky, just to have someone to talk to.

"Hey. We're having a welcome home dinner for Tuck tonight. Come upstairs and eat with us."

"Welcome home?" I lifted the lemonade to my lips and took a quick sip. "Was he gone?"

"Yeah. Hitched a ride with one of his drivers to New Mexico, I think. Said something about securing new accounts. He left right after the engagement party."

"Oh." And here I thought he'd been avoiding me. I pretended not to care, ignoring the warm, albeit annoying, tingles that graced my body, inside and out. "I hadn't realized. Does he do that often?"

"He mostly helps our dad manage the company from his home office. Securing accounts, and routes, and whatnot. Hitches rides every couple of months. Gets to know his drivers better, calls it performance audits, or something like that." Slade leaned closer, elbows on the table, butt off her seat. "Between you and me, I don't think he likes the trucks. He always seems so sad when he comes back from a run. Looks like he'd survived a trip to hell and back. He never wants to talk about it, though." She fell back into her seat. "Have you heard the news stories, about the psychopath who's attacking truckers? God, it makes me a nervous wreck every time Tuck is on a run."

"Yeah. I've seen it on the news. Creepy." To be honest, I hadn't paid much attention. Shit like that happened all the time in my world. If the family business wasn't directly affected, I couldn't waste my energy worrying about it.

"So? Dinner tonight?" Slade asked, eyes bright and willing me to say *yes*.

"Oh, I don't know. Sounds like a family thing. I'll probably hunker down with a good book and a frozen pizza tonight."

"Aida," Slade said with a pout. "Come on. You never leave the apartment except to eat at the diner. Please. Have dinner with us."

"I'll think about it." I was so done with Whisper Springs and its sweet, happy personalities. "Did Tango mention if he'd heard from my father?"

"No. I'm sorry." She pulled my drink to her side of the table and took a sip. "You miss home, don't you?"

"A bit." I missed the luxuries of home. I missed being surrounded by people. Even knowing they were only around me because my father paid them to be. "I miss the noise, most of all. The busyness. The constant buzz of energy."

"You're not much good at relaxing, are you?"

No. Because I could never let my guard down. "Is it that obvious?"

Slade's waitress, Margie, brought our food. "Here you go. Extra pickles for Aida, extra ketchup for the boss lady." She winked and made her way to the next table.

Slade shoved two fries in her mouth.

"How the hell do you stay so thin?" I asked, half-laughing, but mostly jealous of her lean, long figure. "You eat burgers with me every day, and I swear you've lost five pounds since last week."

"Ha," she said with a mouthful of potato. "It's in my genes. Plus, I walk everywhere. Walking makes me happy."

Back home, I wasn't allowed in public without a posse. Nope. Drivers and military trained bodyguards escorted me everywhere. Made walking a nuisance. Luciano Voltolini's daughter traveled in style, safely hidden behind the shield of ballistic nylon, leaded glass, and polycarbonate reinforced vehicles.

"This is the most I've ever walked," I told Slade in-between bites. "Up and down the hill to the diner."

"Well. It's a start. You must be going stir crazy. I'm sorry I've been working so much and haven't had time to hang out. Hey. I have an idea. Why don't you come and work with me? Tango said you have a business degree. We've been busier since the remodel, and I'm needed on the floor more, since I'm down a waitress. You could take care of the back end, help me get my finances in order. I've fallen behind with all that's happened the past few months."

Slade Mason hadn't fallen behind. Slade worked her ass off for the diner. Always with a spring in her step. She was offering me a lifeline. A way out of the doldrums of my stint in exile. Working at a diner wasn't what I'd envisioned for myself, but it beat sitting in a dark apartment, watching my stomach grow, waiting for the call that my father was sending his private jet to bring me home. I had spent much of my childhood in the seedy kitchens of my father's restaurants, so I was familiar with the ins and outs of the industry.

"I know what you're doing. And thank you. I mean it. I'm going insane with nothing to do. I'd love to come and help, however I can."

I hadn't thought it possible, but Slade's mile-wide grin spread even further. At first I thought it was because I'd accepted her offer, then I realized she was looking over my shoulder.

No need to turn around to see who'd caught her attention. The air shifted, alerting me to *his* presence.

Tucker slid into the seat next to his sister and planted a kiss on her cheek. "Ladies," he said, popping a fry into his mouth. He nodded my way and smirked. "Looking lovely as ever."

Had my gut been given wings, it would've been halfway to the moon. I sucked in a sharp breath, surprised by the rush of blood pounding through my ears.

"Didn't think I'd see you until tonight." Slade wrapped both arms around his neck and pulled him close. "Successful trip?"

"Sure." He shot a glance my way, then wrestled free of Slade's hug. "Secured three new accounts."

"That's great, Tuck." Slade slid her plate in front of her brother and pushed from her seat. "We'll celebrate tonight. I need to get back to work. Finish this for me?" She came around the table and kissed my cheek. "So, dinner at six. You'll be there, right?"

Before I could swallow my food and decline her offer, Slade was out of earshot, leaving me alone with Farmer Fred and his delicious dimples.

"Welcome home," I said, forcing a confidence I didn't feel at all.

"Did you miss me?" he asked, face full of mischief and charm.

"I hadn't realized you were gone until Slade mentioned it five minutes ago, so I guess that would be a no." Why did I feel the need to lie? Self-preservation. Wounded ego, perhaps. Truth was, I hadn't been able to shake the memory of his lips and the way my body had responded to them.

Dammit. My erratic heartbeat was pissing me off. Heat blasted my cheeks, and I dropped my chin, pretending to study my burger, hoping to hide the blush.

Tucker

Christ. That blush spread so fast across her cheeks I almost jumped across the table to check her pulse.

"You okay?" I asked, stifling my amusement at her sudden shyness.

"I'm fine, why?" Aida lifted her bun, pulled a pickle from under the lettuce, and popped it between those beautiful, red lips.

Lips I'd been more than eager to see again, despite the blaring sirens in my head warning me away from the sexy, doe-eyed firecracker.

"You're a little flushed," I teased.

"Hot flash. Happens all the time. These damn hormones are a killer." Aida fanned her face with a dessert menu. "Whew. Are you hot? It's hot in here, isn't it?"

Hot flash? Right. I bit my lip to keep from laughing.

"Well. I should get going. Got a busy day today," Aida said, pushing her plate to the edge of the table.

Busy day, my ass. She wanted to avoid me. Smart girl. Too bad I wasn't ready to say goodbye. "You didn't finish your lunch."

"I'm full," she said, an obvious lie.

"Don't go." Fuck. That sounded like begging.

Her big mocha eyes sizzled with amusement. "Are you one of those people who can't stand to eat alone in a restaurant?"

"Yes," I fibbed. "Please. Stay with me. It would be irresponsible to let this food go to waste. Besides, you need to feed the baby."

She quirked her brow at me, looking a little confused, but mostly amused.

I had her. "Do it for the baby."

Aida pulled her burger basket back in front of her. "Who am I doing it for? *My* baby or the one sitting across the table from me?"

"Good one," I said, pointing a fry at her. I sat back, sinking into my chair, stretching my legs under the table.

Aida curled her delicate fingers around her glass. Her nails were painted black. Last time I'd seen her, they were red. I liked the black. It suited her.

"Slade told me you were on a run," Aida said, interrupting my musings.

I nodded. A run, of sorts.

She waited for me to speak. When I didn't, she asked, "Don't you go crazy on those long drives?"

"No. I love the open road." Not the driving, not the trucks, but the hunting. I lived for the hunt.

She picked at her fries, pulled out the largest one, and dragged it through her squirt of mustard, then the blob of ketchup. "That why you don't have a wife or girlfriend?"

"What?"

She took a bite. Chewed. Stared me down. Swallowed. "Seems like it would be hard to maintain a relationship if you're taking off for weeks at a time." She slammed her palms on the table, eyes wide. "Oh my God, please don't tell me you're one of those slime-bags who picks up hookers at the truck stops."

I wasn't about to answer that question. The vixen was trying to rile me. Probably still pissed that I'd rejected her after our insane make-out session. If she only knew I'd spent the past few weeks trying to shake her from my skin.

Her red lips continued to move, but I didn't hear a word that came through them. I had thought that leaving would clear my head. Last thing I needed was a fling, no matter how short lived, but I couldn't stop thinking about how perfect she fit against me, how I craved the sound of her laugh, or the way she destroyed me with those damn lips. I'd spent weeks jerking off in crappy hotel rooms to the memories of Aida writhing and moaning, coming undone beneath me.

"Well?" She snapped her fingers in my face. "Have you?"

"I'm sorry," I said, blinking away my lust haze. "Have I what?"

"Ever fucked a lot lizard?" She stared at me like I was the star attraction at Freak-Du-Soleil.

"No. God, no." I crumpled a napkin. I hated that term, *lot lizard.*

Aida leaned forward, crossing her arms on the table. "Have you been approached by any?"

"Sure. It happens." The girl was striking too close to home. What the hell did she know about lot lizards anyway?

"Ever been tempted?" she asked.

Heat crept up my neck, landed on my cheeks. "No. And what's your fascination with truck stop whores?" I winced. *Whores.* I hated that term, too. Victims would be more accurate.

Her lips parted slightly and her eyes seemed to lose focus. "I was just curious. Seems you'd get lonely out there on the road."

"What's this really about?"

"Nothing." She waved a hand and sat back in her chair.

"Aida. You can't lie for shit. What's eating you?"

She cocked her head. "The truth?"

"That would be good." Her lips on mine would be better. For obvious reasons, I didn't voice my thoughts.

"You're too nice. I'm trying to find the flaw."

I had my share of defects. Wasn't letting her anywhere near them. "I'm an open book, Bambi. What you see is what you get." I stretched my arms wide and shot her a wink.

Her eyes brightened, gaze dropping to my chest. Then her blush returned, boosting my ego to the moon. I wanted to flex my pecs, but that might have been overkill.

With a challenging glower, she stood. "Oh, Tucker. If there's one thing I know, it's trouble. And you are a shit-storm wrapped in a pretty package." She plucked the butter knife off the table and twirled it between her fingers. "I'm bored, and that makes me dangerous." She tossed the utensil in the air and caught it by the handle, her glare never leaving mine. "I'm going to enjoy unearthing your secrets."

"A challenge, then." I stood, too, and caught a whiff of her cotton candy scent, sending my thoughts straight down the gutter. "Bring it on, Bambi."

The knife to my throat was a surprise. Not because there was a knife to my throat—it was only a butter knife after all—but because she'd moved so fast.

"Call me Bambi again, and I'll go backwoods hunter all over your pretty face." She blinked her doe eyes at me and flashed a soul-gutting smile before patting my cheek. "You shaved. Looks good."

Aida set the knife on the table, turned, and sauntered toward the door.

It was a damn good thing she was leaving town soon, because after that morbid display of affection, I wanted nothing more than to drag her home and tame that feisty ass.

I absolutely did not need the complication.

But damn, how I wanted Aida Voltolini.

I caught up with her halfway through the parking lot. She wore a sheer, billowy black tank top, black shorts, and lace up boots that accentuated her tan, shapely legs.

A black, sixty-five Impala turned into the lot, catching my eye. Instead of slowing, the driver sped up, throwing dust and gravel, missing Aida by only a few feet. She stumbled backward. I caught her before her ass hit the ground.

"Jesus. Fucking. Christ," I hissed. "You okay?" I set her back on her feet.

"I'll kill that fucker." Aida took off toward the now parked car. I wrenched an arm around her waist. "Whoa, there. I got this. Stay here."

I reached the car as the man stepped out. Buzz cut, beard, combat boots. Swastika tat on his neck. Shit. I'd seen a group of kids with the same ink running around town. Brainless fuckers were nothing but trouble.

"Hey, man." He greeted me with a chin nod.

Not a good time for pleasantries. "You almost ran over a pregnant woman."

He shot a glance at Aida then back to me. "That spic bitch?"

Fist to temple I struck, acting on instinct and rage, and dropped the shit-head to the ground. "Get the fuck up," I ordered. "Get in your car, drive away, and never come back. You've got ten seconds before I tear those tats from your skin with my teeth."

The kid scrambled to his feet and spit blood at my boots. I shoved him backward into the car and slammed the door. No doubt, had he not been alone, I'd have a bloody fight on my hands. He revved the engine and tore out of the lot faster than he'd come in.

"With your teeth?" Aida stood, arms crossed, mild amusement in her eyes. "Not very sanitary."

She wore a killer smirk. Swear to my Maker, there was a new twinkle in her eye.

"Yeah. Well, I made my point." I wrapped an arm around her shoulders and headed toward the hill. "I'll walk you home."

I could've driven her the short jaunt, but I needed to cool my jets.

Aida shrugged off my arm. "Nice right hook. You a fighter?"

"No." Not in the traditional sense of the word.

"Too bad."

"Why?" I stepped in front of her and stopped, gripping her shoulders, and dipping my head to get a good look at those damn eyes. "Would that turn you on?"

"God, no." Again, and more aggressively than the last time, she shook free of my touch, but not before I caught a glimpse of humor in the pull of her lips.

"Liar."

Aida

"Liar!" I shouted into the computer, slamming my hands against the oak desk. "Tell the truth, Tits, or I swear to God, I'll cut out your tongue and tie it in a neat little bow around those hairy balls of yours." I couldn't believe what he was telling me.

The bastard only laughed, feigning humor that didn't reach his eyes. "I've missed you, Princess." I heard a bang. Tito's face disappeared for a second, then came back into view. "Aida, baby. I'm sorry. That's all the info I've got for you. Looks like you're stuck in Idaho indefinitely." I heard two pops, and Tito jumped. "Shit. I gotta go."

"Wait. Were those gunshots?" I grabbed the edges of my laptop, shaking it as if it'd bring the black screen back to life. "Tits, answer me."

I heaved my computer across the room, leaving a hefty dent in the wall. My arms trembled, my head swelled with rage. "I am not having my baby in this shitty town!" I screamed, and took out my frustrations on a stack of library books, throwing some, ripping pages from others. Then I made my way to the kitchen, rifling through my drawer of silver ware, dropping forks and spoons to the floor until I found what I was looking for. A steak knife. Cheap and factory made, but it would do.

"Fuck you, Daddy," I growled, throwing the knife at the white wall. Its tip stuck for a split second before falling to the floor. I grabbed the piece of shit off the tile and threw again, harder this time. The blade fell short of my mark and ricocheted off the refrigerator, missing my leg by an inch. "Fuck!"

I needed my blades.

I retrieved the knife and threw again, targeting the front door. The blade stuck, the door opened, and Tango barreled through.

He plucked the knife from the wood. "What the hell?"

"What do you want?"

"I heard screaming." He glanced around the torn-up room. "What's happening, Princess?"

"I just ended a Skype call with Tito. Did you know?" I planted fisted hands on my hips.

Tucker slithered in behind Tango. "Everything okay down here?"

Hard as it was, I refused to look his way, aiming my anger straight at Tango. "When were you planning on telling me? After the baby?"

"I don't know what the hell you're talking about."

"Dad went underground. Shut down all communication. I'm stuck here for God knows how long. Don't pretend you didn't know."

"Aida. Have I ever lied to you? This is the first I'm hearing of it. Did Tito give you any details?"

Tango never lied. His honesty, however brutal, was one of the few things in my life I could one hundred percent count on.

I drew a deep breath, attempting to calm my vibrating nerves. "No. Just that he'd be out of touch for a while, and I needed to stay put." I squinted my face to hold back the threatening tears. "I heard gunshots, Tango. Right before he ended the call."

"Hey." He stepped closer and grabbed my shoulders. "I'll get a hold of Tito, see what I can find out." He kissed my cheek. "There are worse places you could be stuck. So please, for the baby, try not to worry."

I nodded and leaned into the comfort of his arms. His tension didn't go unnoticed.

When I looked up, Tucker was gone.

"Come on." He urged me toward the door. "Dinner is ready."

I followed my reluctant babysitter upstairs. Slade, Tucker, and Rocky were seated at the table. Tango fell into the chair next to Slade, leaving me no choice but to sit next to the burly blond.

"Hey, chubby." Slade smiled, passing me an overfilled plate of lasagna, salad, and bread. "Hope you're hungry."

Tucker's head snapped my direction and our eyes met. He smirked and mouthed, "Chubby?" at me, then made quick work of filling his plate.

"Auntie Aida, Auntie Aida," Rocky said, bouncing in his seat. "I start school in two days." He held up two fingers. "I got a new backpack and crayons and new shoes, and I can run really fast in them."

His excitement was infectious, and I couldn't help but feel happy right along with him. "That's great, Rocky. Can I see your new stuff after dinner?"

"Yeah." He shoved a forkful of meaty sauce into his mouth.

Dinner was pleasant, despite my turbulent state of mind. Given the company, I should've enjoyed myself. Instead, I struggled to make it through the meal without collapsing into full nuclear meltdown.

Dad was in trouble. I felt it in my gut, buzzing and churning like a shaken beehive. I wasn't naive. Most people didn't live long in the life I'd been raised. Although I was under constant protection, Dad had never shielded me from the ugly underbelly of his business. In fact, he had groomed me for survival. That instinct he had honed was telling me things were going to get worse before they got better.

God, I needed my knives.

After dinner, I said my goodbyes and snuck downstairs while Tucker was wrestling on the floor with his nephew. I fell into the overstuffed couch and rubbed my stomach, the weight of the world pressing me deeper into the cushions. I wasn't cut out to be a mother, yet there I sat, knocked up, with no baby-daddy to support me through the scary plight. For the first time in my life, I was terrified.

A soft knock saved me from what was sure to be an epic pity party.

Tucker greeted me when I opened the door, all smiles, wrinkled T-shirt, and rumpled hair. Arms crossed, he leaned against the wall. "Chubby, huh?"

I mimicked his pose. "What?"

"Slade gets to call you Chubby. Tango calls you Princess. I get a knife to my throat for calling you Bambi."

I stepped back and gestured for him to come in. Always the gentleman, Tucker waited for me to go first, then closed and locked the door behind him.

"Bambi? I mean, come on. Sounds like a seventies porn star."

His head jerked back with a disgusted chuckle. "Porn? Really? That's where your mind goes? I'm thinking Disney, you're thinking *Debbie Does Dallas*?"

I knew hundreds of porn stars. A few, I even liked. Dad had a thing for them. They had a thing for his money. I learned everything there was to know about makeup art from three of the "actresses" he had dated over the years.

"I've never seen a Disney movie," I grumbled. Settling back into my favorite spot on the couch, I patted the cushion. "Make yourself comfortable."

He fell into the love seat across from me, feet planted on the floor, knees falling wide, hands clasped behind his head.

I swallowed the extra saliva in my mouth.

The man was downright edible.

Tucker

"What's eating you, Aida?" I strained not to stare at her perfect breasts.

"What do you mean?" she asked, coy and unconvincing.

"You were unusually docile during dinner." Every other time I'd seen her in public, her fake smile was set like stone, her gregarious mask set to high-watt.

"Is that why you're here?"

"I figured you needed someone to dump on. It's not good to hold all that shit in."

The little beauty shifted in her seat, tucking one leg underneath her butt. "What would you know about my shit?"

"I heard your exchange with Tango. I also get the feeling you don't want to dump any more pressure on him. You need someone to talk to. So, here I am."

Click, click, click.

"I'm fine. Really. Wanna watch a movie?"

Click, click, click.

Again with those damn nails.

I crossed my arms over my chest. "Not much in the mood for a movie."

"I'm not much in the mood for talking. So, I guess we're done here. You can let yourself out." She reached for the television remote and pushed the power button. "Thanks for stopping by."

It took everything I had not to yank that device out of her hand. Something about her defiance made my blood run hotter, and incidentally, straight to my cock. I wasn't leaving. Call it stubborn. Call it stupid. Hell, I wasn't even sure why I'd hopped down the stairs to her apartment instead of going home to my bed.

"Okay. Fine. Maybe *I* need someone to talk to," I lied.

"Nice try." She winked at me, offering a sardonic grin.

She flipped through the channels, paying no mind to the selection.

"I mean it." I leaned forward. "We have something in common, you know."

Her gaze drifted from the screen to me. "What would that be?"

"Neither of us has any friends in town. I moved to Whisper Springs to take care of my sister and Rocky. I never bothered with the social scene. Now that they have Tango, I got nothin'. You want to stay out of their way, not be a burden, but you're lonely."

"And?" She quirked a brow. "Your point would be?"

"Let's be friends. Hang out."

"Tucker." She hit the power button and dropped the control. "I've never been friends with a guy. Ever."

Found that hard to believe. "What about Tango?"

"Nope. He was good in the sack. When that fizzled, he only came around to rescue me."

"Tito?"

"He's like a brother. Tits doesn't count." Those doe eyes softened. "I pretty much live to make his life miserable."

Damn, that made me happy to hear.

"Listen, I know what you're trying to do. But you need to understand something about me. I don't have friends. People use me to get to my father, whether their intentions are good or bad. If a man is in my life, it's for sex. I love sex. Thrive on it. So, unless you're game for a purely casual, full-on fuck fest with a pregnant girl, I'm not interested. You're a great guy. It's a shame I'm built the way I am, but that's how it's got to be."

"That's the biggest line of bullshit I've ever heard. Everybody needs somebody. Besides, I'm not asking for feelings. We don't even have to call it friendship. How about companions. Movie buddies. Hell. I don't know." Why the fuck was I begging for this?

"Okay. You want to be my friend? Prove it."

"Prove it? Are you kidding me?"

"You made it clear you don't want to fuck me, so I need a vibrator."

Well, hmm. The conversation skyrocketed from irritating to exciting. "Go buy one. I hear all the liberated ladies are doing it."

"I'm in hiding. I can't very well use my credit cards, now can I? And I sure as hell am not asking Tango or Slade to make a trip to the sex-store on my behalf."

"So, you're asking me to buy you a vibrator, for the privilege of hanging out with you?"

"That's what I'm asking."

"You're a little bit insane. You know that, right?"

"Last guy who called me crazy ended up with punctured balls."

I winced, playing it up, hoping to crack her layer of ice. "I'll keep that in mind."

Her lips twitched. Almost cracked into a smile. "So, will you do it?"

"Hell no."

"Well, you're of no use to me then." She flicked her delicate hand at me. "Off with you, prude."

Now she was just making fun of me. At least the nail clicking had stopped.

"Okay, how about this. I'll consider buying you a dildo if you do something for me."

Crossing arms and legs simultaneously, she said, "You've piqued my interest. What?"

"I promised Rocky I'd take him to the county fair. It's our thing. We go every year. Come with us."

"To the fair? Isn't it dirty?" She looked ten years younger when she scrunched her nose in disgust. Damn, the woman was a work of art.

"Yeah. It's dirty. It's also fun. Oh, God. Please don't tell me you've never been to a fair."

Aida shook her head. "Never. Not interested, either. Besides, I've got nothing to wear." She gestured to her baby bump, which was hardly a bump at all. "I'm growing out of all my clothes."

My gaze raised to her chest. That damn shirt was pulled nice and tight across the swell of her breasts. Was it too small? Hell if I cared. Made those beauties even more tempting.

Shit. I needed to leave before I ravished her on the couch. "Not a problem. I'll pick you up at ten tomorrow. We'll hit the mall, buy you some proper fair attire, then, if you're a good girl, we'll stop by the porn store."

I showed myself out before she could protest. It wasn't until I'd pulled out of the driveway that I pounded my steering wheel and cursed my brain-numbing boner. What the hell was wrong with me? I hated shopping.

CHAPTER 3

Aida

"THIS CANNOT BE SAFE," I protested, backing away from the line of sticky-faced kids and frazzled parents.

Rocky's hands pressed against my butt, holding me in place. "You promised. You can't break a promise." He pushed, inching me back to my place behind Tucker. "It's only the Ferris wheel."

"Fine." I threw up my hands in protest. "But this is it. Then you can ride all the creaky metal death traps you want. I'm going back to look at the sweet little bunnies and baby pigs."

Tucker chuckled in front of me, his shoulders bobbing. If Rocky hadn't secured a tight hold on my pinky finger, I would've swatted his uncle in the back of the head.

Like the gentleman he was, when our turn came, Tucker helped me into the seat, then stepped to the side, smiling wide, having way too much fun at my expense. Rocky settled next to me. The young man manning the controls, who couldn't have been older than seventeen—which was way too young in my opinion to be operating the giant wheel—slammed the metal bar into place.

The wheel creaked and lurched, pulling us forward, then stopped to load more passengers. The process was slow, and my stomach dropped lower in my abdomen with every ascent and pause. Rocky rattled on and on about his roller coaster ride with Tucker, all the while wiggling in his seat, rocking the tin contraption. I white-knuckled the bar and pretended I could hear what the little munchkin was saying.

By the time we'd reached the top, I'd relaxed enough to enjoy my surroundings. The view simply took my breath away. Past the fairgrounds and highways, I had a clear perspective of the vast mountain ranges surrounding us. I'd never felt so small and insignificant in my life.

When I found the courage to look down, I found Tucker immediately. He blended well with the general population—jeans, boots, and plaid flannel, but he didn't get lost in the crowd. His stature, his brilliant smile, his aura, they parted the crowd, and every person around him seemed to fade and blur into the background.

By the time the ride was over, my cheeks hurt from smiling.

Hours later, after we'd shuffled through throngs of people to find a seat on the worn wooden bleachers of the stadium, I watched my first rodeo. I had also sampled my first corn dog, elephant ear, and buffalo burger.

And for the first time, and I prayed to God it would be my last, I used a porta-potty.

An hour after the sun had set, Rocky finally, *finally*, ran out of steam. With his nephew on his shoulders, Tucker held my hand and helped me navigate the terrain of the dark parking lot, leading us safely back to his Jeep.

I opened my door and was about to climb in, as Tucker buckled the sleepy boy into his car seat. I watched in awe, jealous of the ease in which he accomplished such common tasks. I knew nothing about taking care of another human being. I hadn't considered car seats, diaper bags, cribs, or strollers. I hadn't considered doctor's appointments, or maternity clothes, bottles, or bedtime stories.

From the moment I had discovered I'd be a mother, I had not put any thought or planning into anything other than revenge. After that, I had been sent away, and then my thoughts were consumed with returning home to Dad, the man who took care of everything, or at least had a staff that would take care of everything. I was screwed. I was jobless, pregnant, without a home, without my only parent, and one hundred percent without a fucking clue.

"Hey. Whoa. Aida. What is it?" Tucker's thick arms closed around me, tucking me against his dusty shirt.

Oh, crap. Tears. Out of nowhere. I was not a crybaby. I hated seeing women cry. Yet, there I was, bawling into Tucker's chest.

Without questioning, hushing, or giving me the good old, *there, there*, he held me tight and let me leak my unchecked emotions. When I peeled my face off his chest, he reached into his glovebox and pulled out a mini box of tissues, then proceeded to dab my face and wipe my nose.

"I'm sorry," I mumbled. "I don't know what happened."

"Don't worry about it." He helped me into my seat. "I remember my first fair like it was yesterday. I cried when it was time to leave, too. It's a lot to take in—the cows, the sheep, the quilts, and giant squash. Overwhelming for a newbie." He winked before closing my door.

When we pulled out of the fairgrounds and hit the highway, I turned around to look at Rocky. His neck was bent in an awkward position, his jaw slack, and drool glistened on his chin. So sweet and innocent in his sleep. So vulnerable.

"I'm scared," I confessed, settling into my seat. "Okay, not scared. Terrified."

Tucker shot me a curious glance.

"I don't know anything about taking care of a child. I don't have a nurturing bone in my body. I'm going to ruin this kid."

"You'll do fine. I've seen you with Rocky. He adores you."

"You don't understand. I've never held a baby. I don't know how to change a diaper. And breastfeeding?" A shiver ran through me. "Ouch and eww."

"Where is Rafael now?" he asked without a lick of judgment in his tone.

"Don't know. Don't care. Dad handled the situation."

"But he's the father of your child. That has to count for something."

"It should, you're right. But he's gone now."

"Did you love him?"

The air we shared seemed to thicken. "Does it matter?"

"I'm just trying to figure you out."

"I'm an open book, Cowboy," I said, throwing his words back at him. "What you see is what you get."

Falling in love was a fool's luxury. Loving someone meant trusting them. Trust in another human being was a crap shoot. I'd trusted a handful of men in my lifetime. My father, because trusting Dad meant survival. Tango, who had never lied to me, even when the truth hurt like hell. And Tito, who, from the time we could speak, had helped me lie my way out of countless sticky situations, most of which he had helped me get into in the first place.

Was Tucker trustworthy? I studied his profile. Strong jaw, the straight blade of his nose, a full mouth that curled up in one corner in a devilish semi-smirk, like he knew the world's best secret and couldn't wait to tell everyone.

Good manners.

Great with kids.

Killer right hook.

Too good to be true.

I knew better than anyone that appearances could be deceiving. Yeah, he seemed trustworthy enough, but Tucker Slade was hiding something dark behind that country boy facade.

I knew it in my bones.

Damn if that knowledge wasn't giving me a lady-boner.

Tucker

Damn, I couldn't wait to get home and take care of my boner. I carried Rocky into the house and handed the little tyke off to his dad like a hot potato. Waving over my shoulder, I let myself out, jogged down the porch steps, and headed to my car.

Much to my surprise, Aida had waited, arms crossed, hip propped against my Jeep. With her dark makeup, black sweater, leggings, and moto boots, the girl looked one hundred percent kick-ass-and-take-names-later trouble.

Thank fuck it was dark. Thank double-fuck my jacket covered my crotch.

"Hey," she said as I approached, flashing those enormous, liquid chocolate eyes up at me.

"Everything all right?" I asked.

"Yeah. I just wanted to say thanks." She pushed off my car and stepped closer.

"So, you had fun, despite the dirt." I brushed a smudge of dust off her cheek with my thumb.

Her head tilted into my touch. "Dirty isn't so bad."

Not yet ready to lose the skin to skin connection, I rubbed at another smear that wasn't there. "Everyone needs to get dirty occasionally."

Aida closed her eyes and stepped away. "Want to come down for a drink, or a shower maybe?"

God, how I wanted to say *yes*. "I can't tonight." I followed her to the back of the house and down the cement steps to her door. "Maybe next time?"

"Sure." She shoved her key into the lock.

I fought the urge to brush her hair to the side and plant a kiss on her neck. Instead, I adjusted my swelling cock and said, "I'm glad you came with us."

"I really did have fun." Aida turned and lifted on her toes, landing a kiss on my cheek. "Don't get to do that very often. Have fun, I mean."

Fuck. That was sweet. "Now, why did you have to go and do a thing like that?"

"Like what?" she asked with a grin full of sin and mockery.

Little vixen knew exactly what she was doing. "Get close. Press those breasts against me. Tease me with those lips. You're making it awful hard for me to turn around and walk away."

"Then don't."

"I have to."

"Why?"

"Friends, remember?"

"Oh, yeah. Right." She turned back around and opened the door before looking over her shoulder and making a tsk sound. "Damn. Whose idea was that again?"

"Goodnight, Aida. Make sure you lock the door."

"Night, Tuck."

I listened for the lock to click, then made my way home.

One hot shower later, my cock got his much-needed relief. After washing the fairground grime from my body, I stood naked in front of my bedroom mirror and forced myself to look at the scars on my abdomen.

Sure, they were grotesque, jagged reminders of the wreck I'd survived. But it was what they represented, the internal damage, that left me undesirable. I traced the blemish that led up my shaft, the skin that was stretched, and pocked ... and ugly. So damn ugly.

What girl would want to fuck this? Certainly not a woman like Aida Voltolini. Not that it mattered. She would return to New York soon. I'd be nothing but a pleasant memory. Even if she wasn't repulsed by my defect, a big city girl could never settle into the small-town life. It wasn't in the stars for us. But damn, when I was with her, I felt bigger than the universe.

I settled into bed and stared through the darkness at nothing.

Funny. A few weeks ago, I couldn't wait to have my king-size back. Tonight, the mattress was too large. No matter how tight I wrapped the blankets around myself, or how hard I hugged the pillows, the vast, empty bed sucked me deeper into its cold, empty folds.

I was about to give up and head for the couch when my phone dinged.

Aida's name didn't pop up on the screen, but I had memorized the number the same day Tango had given it to me.

Aida: U awake?
Me: Am now.
Aida: I can't sleep.
Me: Why?
Aida: Indigestion.
Me: I warned u to stop after one corn dog.
Aida: Ha ha. The baby was hungry. I blame the baby.
Me: Or u can admit u love fair food. It's ok. I won't tell a soul.

Aida: I admit nothing.
Me: U loved the ferris wheel.
Aida: Meh
Me: I saw ur face. U loved it.
Aida: I saw ur face. U were waiting for me to freak.
Me: I admit nothing
Aida: Thanks again. Fun day.
Me: Anytime, Bambi.
Aida: I warned u about calling me Bambi. Better sleep with one eye open. Night, Cowboy.
Me: Sweet dreams.
Me: Bambi

I woke the next morning with my phone still in my hand.

Aida

"Hand it over, big guy." I stretched my arm across the cutting board and wiggled my fingers in a *give it now* gesture.

Charlie, The Truck Stop's famed chef, continued to chop onions and merely shook his head. "Nobody touches my Bob Kramer. Not even pretty ladies. This beauty was designed for my hand and my hand only. So, don't even bother with those fat, puppy-dog eyes."

"I'm not just anyone," I said, throwing a low growl into my voice. "I can handle a blade."

"I'm sure you can," he countered my growl with an impressive scowl. "But nobody touches her. Waited four-and-a-half years for this beauty. She goes home with me at night, stays in my fingers or locked up when I'm at work."

"Fine. Can I at least help? I'm not ready to go home yet. I need something to do." I needed a distraction, to get the jolly blond giant out of my head. Tucker and his too-pretty smile, those impressive muscles, and that damn outdoorsy scent that followed him everywhere was doing a number on my libido, and my psyche.

Charlie shot a glance through the service window and drew a deep breath. "Fine. But if you cut yourself, I'm not taking the blame. I'm telling boss lady you forced me."

He rolled his eyes, stepped in front of the magnetic knife rack, and reached for one of his store-bought chef's knives.

I crossed my arms. "Uh-uh. No way. I want one of the good ones. The Shuns you have hiding in that secret drawer over there."

His cheeks darkened three shades. Much to my surprise, he turned and popped open the hidden drawer.

"Fine," he harrumphed. "Grab a hairnet. They're on the shelf behind you."

I did as ordered. My heart palpitated when he handed me the gorgeous blade with its charcoal and crimson wood handle. It was a little heavy in my small hand, but it would do. Sweet Jesus, it would do. God, it felt good to hold a real knife.

"Okay, Chef. How do you want them? Sliced, diced, julienned, minced?"

Charlie quirked a brow at me. "Chopped for chili. Half-inch. Fill that bucket."

I got to chopping and Charlie paused a few times to watch me work. I wasn't as fast as he was with the onions, only because I had to keep wiping my eyes, but I kicked his ass when it came time to julienne the carrots for the chicken soup.

Charlie was a genius in the kitchen. Prepping food, flipping burgers, dipping fries, moving fluidly from one end of the room to the other in a beautiful ballet. The man was funny. And true to chef legend, he had a dirty mouth, and an arsenal of filthy jokes. When he learned I'd grown up in the kitchens of my dad's many restaurants, and after I dropped the f-bomb a few times, he relaxed and stopped hovering.

Time flew by, and before long, there wasn't a vegetable left to cut. I offered to debone chickens but Charlie gave me a firm *hell no,* and shooed me out of his domain. I finished cleaning up and headed for the employee bathroom.

My knees wobbled and nearly gave out when I looked up to find Tucker leaning against the wall in the hallway, wearing a gray thermal that molded to his chest, and dark jeans that hugged his thick thighs. Seriously, I'd never been so out of sorts around a man. My unusual lack of grace was beginning to piss me off.

"Have fun in there?"

"Fuck yeah." I said, walking past and pushing into the bathroom.

Tucker caught the door before it closed. "I've never seen you smile so much."

"Were you watching me?"

"Not for long. Heard you laughing, came to see what was up. Couldn't bring myself to interrupt your fun."

"I like to cut things," I whispered, wiggling my brows at him.

"So I've heard." He flashed me that ridiculously sexy smirk.

"Need to pee, so unless you're into that kinky shit, you might want to give me a minute."

Tucker winked and closed the door.

When I came out, he was waiting. For some odd reason, I liked finding him there.

"Go for a walk?" he asked, offering his arm.

"Well, I had a fun-filled afternoon planned with my new vibrator, but I suppose that can wait." I hooked my arm through his and waved to Slade as we headed toward the exit.

"Wait." I shouted, digging my heels into the checkered tile. "Let me tell Charlie goodbye." I turned and scurried back into the kitchen.

"Thanks for letting me help today, Chef." I kissed his cheek. A little thrill ran through me at the sight of his blush. "I'll see you tomorrow. What time do I start, five AM?"

"Start?" he asked, planting his palms on the counter and tilting his head.

"I got the job, right? Come on. There's no arguing, I'm a genius with chopping. And the beauty of it is, you only have to pay me in burgers."

Charlie started to speak, but a loud crash from the dining area startled us both. Through the partition, I could see Tucker surrounded by three men. One I recognized as the guy from the parking lot who almost ran me over the other day. His friends wore the same swastika tattoos on their necks. Tucker must have knocked one of them to the ground, because with a bloodied face, the guy scrambled to get off the floor.

"Fuck me," I mumbled, turning to grab a knife. I picked up the Shun, then laid it back down. Wouldn't be right to defile such beautiful steel. I yanked two slicers off the magnetic holder and pushed through the double doors.

Tucker had managed to wrestle his attackers outside and away from the customers, and seemed to be holding his own. Another customer jumped in to help, but didn't stand a chance against the brass knuckles that struck his temple. The jackass wearing the weapon raised his fist to strike again.

I didn't miss a beat. Stalking forward, I forced one blade into the dipshit's right buttock, pulled it out, and stabbed the back of his thigh. Before he could fall to the ground, I drug the other blade across his knuckles, right along the top of the steel, opening his flesh to the bone, ensuring it would be a long time before he could strike anyone with that hand.

Tucker took punch after punch but hadn't fallen yet. His attackers didn't see me coming. The larger of the three raised his fist to strike. With the tip of my blade, I opened his arm from wrist to elbow. He squealed, reminding me of the pigs at the fair, and turned to retaliate.

He paused, no doubt thrown that a woman had cut him. I used that opportunity to sink the tip of my blade into the skin at his throat. "How about you sit this out, let it be a fair fight," I said, nodding over my shoulder to Tucker and the remaining assailant.

Baldy sunk to the ground, tucking his arm into himself, trying to stop the flow of blood. I wanted to watch the fight. But I didn't dare turn my back on the douchebags I'd rendered useless.

I smiled wide when Charlie barreled through the door with a shotgun. He fired into the air. "Get the fuck away from my restaurant," he shouted.

The bloodied assailants scrambled to their car, cursing, spitting, and promising our certain deaths.

Sucking in a soul-cleansing breath, I winked at Charlie.

Judging by the pinch of his brows, he wasn't too happy to see me wielding his cooking utensils. I held the knives, tips up, and shrugged my shoulders. "I'll buy you new knives."

He only shook his head and chuckled.

Tucker coughed behind me. When I turned, he was on his ass, Slade kneeling beside him, asking, "You okay? Do I need to call an ambulance?"

Shameful, really, but the sight of Tucker, bloody and bruised, made me weak in the knees. When he looked up at me and smiled, teeth full of crimson, something in my chest cracked.

"I'm good. Nothing some ice won't fix." He pushed to his feet with a grunt.

Wide-eyed, Slade looked at me. "What the hell was that?" She gestured to the blades still in my hands. "Jesus, Aida. You're pregnant. You can't do shit like that anymore."

I tightened my grip and enjoyed my weapons for one more second before dropping them to the ground.

Slade retrieved them and stood face to face with me. I'd expected to see disappointment in her eyes. What I found could only be described as awe.

"Someday, I want to hear how you learned to do that," she whispered, before turning to Tucker. "You okay to drive?"

He spit and nodded yes.

"Good. The cops are on their way. Aida can't be here. Take her home. She can ice your face." She winked at me and threw an arm over my shoulder. "I think we're going to be best friends."

Tucker

"I think this friendship thing is going to be fun." Aida laughed, dabbing antibacterial goo on my lip with a cotton swab.

I'd never seen her so animated. It was inspiring, in a perverted way, listening to her babble about dicing onions and slicing skinheads, like they were normal, everyday tasks.

"Think I'll need stitches?" I managed to mumble through my swollen lip.

I was seated on her bathroom toilet. Aida scooted between my knees, cupped my jaw and tilted my head up, inspecting the wound below my eye. "It's iffy. If you don't mind a kick-ass scar on your pretty mug, I'd say, no, it's not necessary."

Still holding my face, she studied my mouth. "It'll scar either way, but your call. It's clean. I've got skin adhesive we could use."

It was hard to focus with her breasts in my face. I dug my nails into my thighs to keep from wrapping my arms around her hips and pulling her closer.

"Do what you gotta do, Doc," I mumbled.

She stared down at me with those enormous brown eyes, and swear to Christ, she wanted to kiss me. I wanted her to kiss me. I wanted to taste those lips she'd been licking and biting for the past fifteen minutes.

A lip-lock was out of the question in my current physical condition, so instead I asked, "Do I want to know why you have skin adhesive at your disposal?"

To which she replied, "No."

"You're good at this."

"What?" she asked, eyes squinty, focused on my face.

"Taking care of wounds. You've done this a lot?"

"More times than I care to count."

"Because you dated fighters?"

She sighed and rolled her eyes. "Because I'm the daughter of a gangster. There," she said, stepping back to inspect her work, "good as new. Now, let's get some ice on that lip, shall we?"

I avoided the mirror as I exited the bathroom. Judging by the throbbing pain and blurred vision, I wouldn't have liked my reflection.

"Sit," she ordered, pointing to the couch.

I eased my ass into the cushion, sinking deep. Damn, her sofa was much softer than mine.

Aida tossed me a bag of crushed ice. "I need to change. Be right back."

I watched her sway down the hall with that gorgeous, confident swing of her hips. I listened to her pull open a drawer, then slam it shut. I closed my eyes and imagined her pulling the shirt over her head, wiggling out of her leggings, exposing that heart-shaped ass. My fingers curled at the memory of holding that plump flesh.

The front door flew open with a loud crack. I sprang to my feet, poised to kill.

"Aida!" Tango shouted, searching the room. "Where is she?" He stormed past me and headed straight for the bedroom.

Oh, fuck no.

I caught him before he entered her room. "She's changing. Give her a minute."

Tango shrugged me off, and damn if I didn't see red.

"What the fuck were you thinking?" he hollered into her half-open door.

I shoved past and stood in the threshold, blocking his view. Not a chance in hell he was laying eyes on her naked body. "I said, she's changing."

"It's all right, Tucker. Nothing he hasn't seen before." Aida patted my back in a *there, there* gesture.

Tango's chest rose and fell in angry thrusts. He glared over my shoulder into her room.

I knew they had history. Slade had told me they'd dated briefly when Tango had lived in New York. Still didn't make his behavior acceptable.

Grabbing his shirt collar, and putting my full body weight into the action, I forced Tango backward and clear of her door.

"Jesus, Tuck!" Aida yelled. "I'm dressed. I'm dressed." She shoved past me. "Down, boy. Down."

Tango shoved my hands away, never taking his eyes off Aida. "If anything happens to you, Princess, it's not only me on the hook, it's my family, and that's fucking unacceptable. While you're here, you don't touch a fucking knife. You don't go looking for trouble. You see trouble, you run the opposite direction. You put yourself or that baby of yours in danger again, it's lockdown. Got me?"

"Yeah, pretty boy. I hear you." Aida mumbled cuss words and stormed down the hall.

Tango roughed a hand through his dark hair and released a long breath, finally meeting me eye to eye. "These racist fucks gonna be a problem?"

"I had an altercation with one in the parking lot the other day. Made it clear he wasn't welcome at The Stop. Guess he didn't like that. Probably thought if he brought his brothers he could teach me a lesson. It was nothing more than a pissing contest."

Arms crossed, Tango leaned against the wall. "I thought that Aryan organization moved out of the area years ago."

"Looks like they're back."

"What's with you going all bulldog over Aida?" he asked, the frustration in his eyes morphing into an expression of mirth. "Something you need to tell me?"

"Don't like seeing ladies disrespected, T. That's all."

"Right," he chuckled, rubbing his chin. "Well, good luck with that. You're in for one hell of a ride." He cupped my shoulder and headed into the living room.

When I caught up, he and Aida were standing toe to toe, arms crossed, eyes narrowed. Damn, I had to respect the way she stood up to him.

"You don't go anywhere alone. Not even down the hill to The Stop. You need anything, need to get somewhere, call me. Oh," he said, pulling an envelope out of his suit jacket.

"Tito sent your new ID, social security card, insurance papers, everything you need."

"So, he's okay?" Aida practically cried.

"Appears so." Tango bared a small grin. "Also, you've got an appointment with an OB/GYN tomorrow. I'll pick you up at noon." He looked over his shoulder at me, evil intent blazing in the crinkle of his eyes. "Unless you want Tuck to escort you."

Fucker.

Her gaze jetted from Tango to me, then dropped to the floor. "No, it's fine, you—"

"I'll take her," I blurted. Not sure where that came from, but the idea of Tango sitting in the waiting room with Aida filled me with rage I didn't understand, but welcomed nonetheless.

Aida pulled her new ID out of the envelope and quirked a brow. "Aida Suarez. Suarez is such a common name," she said, rolling her eyes. "Couldn't you have come up with something better?"

Clearly a dig. The girl wanted to fight.

Tango didn't take the bait.

"Wasn't my call. Got a complaint, take it up with your father. And don't knock it. Suarez was my mother's maiden name."

I watched as something shifted in her gaze. With a quick glance my way, her shoulders relaxed, and her hands moved to her stomach in a delicate rub. My chest ached at that beautiful, unconscious gesture.

"Thanks, Tango. I'll try to stay out of trouble." She landed a kiss on his cheek and headed back toward her room.

Tango scrubbed his hands over his face. "She doesn't know how to stay out of trouble. I'll hire a few men to keep an eye on The Truck Stop. Those idiots will be back after they lick their wounds. Probably bring an army next time." He turned to leave, stopped with his hand on the knob, and laughed. "I don't understand. Why didn't you take them out? Looks like they beat the shit out of you."

"It was three against one."

He turned, stepping close, and lowered his voice. "It was three against *you*."

"What the hell is that supposed to mean?"

His charming smile made my blood boil. "Don't worry. Your secret is safe with me. I'm honored to be in your presence, and I'm not too proud to admit that you're better equipped to protect Aida than I am."

I planted my hands on my hips and released a few of my own profanities. Of course, he had looked into my past. I couldn't be mad at him. I had done the same the minute I'd discovered he was Rocky's father. "Who found it? Tito?"

Tango clapped my shoulder. "There's nothing Tito Moretti can't hack. Not even the Department of Defense."

CHAPTER 4

Tucker

THE WAITING ROOM SHRUNK around me while the fish tank that divided the play area from the private seating seemed to expand. Aida had been with the doctor for over an hour. I watched a blue and yellow fish float through the water while Dory's voice from *Finding Nemo* played on repeat in my head: *Just keep swimming. Just keep swimming.* Rocky and I had watched that movie so many times, I could recite the entire script by heart.

A tall drink of water poked her head through the frosted glass door that led to the exam rooms. "Mr. Slade?"

I jumped to my feet. "Yeah. That's me."

Her warm smile and soft voice matched the decor of the office with its muted colors and tranquil music. "Aida would like you to join her."

My ticker dropped to my toes. "Everything all right?"

"Yeah. Yeah." She shot a glance down the hall, then back to me. "She's just a little overwhelmed." The woman opened the door wider, gesturing for me to follow with a nod of her head. "It happens."

Something in my gut shifted, like I'd eaten a bad burrito, or too many burritos. I heard sobs coming from the far end of the hall, and my legs grew heavier with each step. Before

64

opening the door, the nurse laid a hand on my arm. "Take your time."

Aida sat on the exam table, fully dressed, holding a small piece of paper to her chest. A box of tissues sat next to her, along with a crumpled paper gown. Tears flowed like a river, carving black trails of makeup down her face.

When she noticed me, her sobs grew louder.

"Aida," I said, inching closer. "Everything okay with the baby?"

With a loud sniff, she handed me the photo. "She's a perfect baby girl. Oh my God, she's real and moving and has feet and fingers, and I'm going to be a mom. Oh shit." She wrapped her arms around her middle. "What was I thinking? I can't do this. I'm not built for this."

I caged Aida between my arms and pulled her head to my chest. I had no comforting words to offer, but I had strength, and I held her through the tremors, binding her together as she fell apart.

Curling her fingers into my shirt, she gripped tight and cried. My heart shattered hearing her pain. With each violent tremble, she exposed her fear, bared her vulnerability. Trusted me to carry her load.

In her moment of despair, of shedding her wall, she unwittingly chipped a crack in my armor, too, revealing a sliver of the man I used to be. The part of me I had buried after the accident.

Aida was stuck with a baby she never wanted.

I mourned the children I could never have.

The little green monster was a nasty bitch, sneaking up on me, sinking her gnarly claws deep.

Fucked up as it was, Aida's meltdown angered me. The spoiled girl had everything I'd always wanted. Yet, there I stood comforting *her*. For what? Because her cush life had been disrupted? Because she would grow out of her designer clothes for nine months? Or maybe because her champagne and caviar nightclub lifestyle had to be put on hold. Fucking spoiled brat.

Despite my shameful jealousy, I held Aida. Gave her what she needed. Minutes passed, maybe five, before she drew a deep, ragged breath and let go of my shirt. I helped her off the table, grabbed her hand, and led her through the back exit.

I tucked her into the Jeep and headed toward her temporary home.

Unspoken words thickened the air between us. I rolled down the windows, hoping the rush of cool air would soothe my unjustified agitation.

"Thank you." Her voice, scratchy and raw, filled the small space.

I rubbed the pain in my temple. "For what?"

"For being my friend," was her simple reply.

And that's all I would ever be. To her, to any woman. Friend. Fuck buddy.

Husband and father? Not in the cards for me. I'd accepted that truth years ago. Thought I'd been okay with it. Until that moment.

Damn her for putting that chink in my armor.

I didn't want to be mad at her. I didn't want to envy her ability to create life. But to watch her dissolve the way she had, over seeing her child for the first time, it downright pissed me off. That was supposed to be a joyous moment. A celebration. Not a nuclear meltdown. I was angry not only for me, but for the innocent life growing inside Aida, for the child who deserved to be celebrated.

"Tucker. What's wrong?"

"Not a damn thing, Princess."

"Bullshit. You just called me Princess. You've never called me Princess."

"Okay. Truth?" I pulled to the side of the road and slammed the Jeep into park. My cheeks burned, fingers trembled. "I'm so fucking pissed at you right now I can't see straight. You have this miracle growing inside you. A fucking miracle. And all I've ever heard you do is pout about it."

"Pout about it?" she shouted, doe eyes narrowing to dark pinpricks of death. "Is that what you thought I was doing?"

"That is exactly what you were doing. *I can't do this. I wasn't built for this. I'm scared.* You're a fucking spoiled rich kid whose perfect life has been disrupted. And it pisses me off because you don't realize what a blessing this baby is."

Aida turned in her seat, brows pinched, holy fire darkening her cheeks.

I already regretted my outburst.

"Let's get one thing straight, you self-righteous, judgmental fuck. For the first time in my life, I love somebody more than myself. I love this baby. I would die to protect this baby. And if you were any kind of a *friend*, you would see that I'm a fish out of fucking water."

She leaned closer. "I didn't have a mother. I was raised by a criminal. Was I spoiled? Yes. Material things were all my father had to offer. He doesn't know how to love. He knows how to survive. He knows how to kill. His idea of bonding was sharing his obsession with carving human flesh. I learned how to throw a knife when I was six. You think I was raised wearing tutus and tiaras? Try hooker heels and knife straps. I love this baby. That's why I'm terrified. She deserves a better life than I can offer, but I love her too much to ever let her go."

Aida's vehemence hit me with brute force, each word pounding iron fists at my wall.

She didn't wait for me to respond. "I didn't choose this life. My baby didn't choose the life. We're stuck in it, and I'm terrified of losing her to this hell I'm living."

What a jackass. My fingers tightened around the steering wheel. I banged my head against the headrest. "Fuck, Aida. I'm sorry."

Aida

I wasn't sorry for vomiting my emotions all over Tucker. Purging felt good. I would've continued, but when he said he was sorry, there was no doubt he meant it. I'd heard thousands of sorries in my life. Spurted even more. It was easy to tell the difference between a genuine, heartfelt expression of regret and blurted words meant only to appease.

My stomach growled, echoing in the cabin of the vehicle, breaking the thick tension. I rubbed my baby bump and sucked in a deep, calming breath before saying, "I accept your apology. Can I buy you a burger?"

Tucker's steely eyes liquefied as the corners of his mouth turned up. Just like that, all was forgiven.

"We should probably clean up your face first." He lifted his hand to cup my cheek, and rubbed a thumb under my eye. "It looks like a Rorschach test upchucked on your face."

"Seriously. If you want to be my friend, don't ever say that to me again. I mean it. Not cool."

"There are baby wipes in the glove box, next to the tissues. Slade says they work wonders on cosmetic mishaps."

"Baby wipes?" I asked, raising a brow.

Tucker rolled his eyes. "I keep them in the car for Rocky. You know, to wipe his hands and shit." Tucker reached up and pulled his visor mirror open for me, then yanked open his glove box and pulled out the packet labeled "natural care."

"Oh," I said, looking at my reflection. "You weren't exaggerating. This is bad." I got busy cleaning my face. Those funny smelling cloths worked better than any of my expensive eye-makeup removers. Unfortunately, it took half his supply to undo the damage I'd done with my meltdown in the doctor's office. With the way my eyeballs had been springing leaks the past few weeks, I'd have to invest in waterproof mascara.

"Sorry," I said, holding up my wad of used towelettes. "I'll need to replenish your supply."

Tucker looked my way. His eyes softened when they fell on mine. "Aida," he breathed, and brushed a strand of hair off my forehead. "You are so fucking beautiful. Why do you hide behind all that shit?"

"What?" was the only response I could squeeze past the lump in my throat.

"Don't get me wrong. You're hot as hell with the face art. But damn. Look at you."

I didn't want to look at myself. I wanted to enjoy the way Tucker looked at me. There was something so pure and honest in his expression, and the warmth behind his smile was infectious, filling my fevered body with foreign emotions, and, like a neglected puppy, I wanted to roll on my back, expose my belly, and beg for more of his attention.

I didn't roll over for anyone.

If he continued to look at me that way, I probably would have whimpered and licked his face. My stomach rumbled again, begging for food.

"We better feed that baby, she's getting angry," he said, shifting the gear into drive and checking the road before pulling back onto the street.

I studied Tucker, his square jawline, those thick arms, his strong hands. My body warmed, my insides tingled. I forced my eyes closed and drew a deep breath, his airy, woodsy scent a lullaby to my frantic nerves. My limbs grew heavy. I inhaled again, absorbing his aroma, greedy for his warmth, and melted into the seat, relaxing more with each rock and bounce of the Jeep.

"Aida." Warm fingers grazed my cheek. "Sleeping Beauty. Wake up. We're here."

Tucker's white teeth slowly came into focus. Then his dazzling baby blues.

I couldn't help but smile back at him. "Did I fall asleep?"

"Out like a hibernating bear."

"Is that cooking grease I smell?"

Tucker held up a paper bag. "Burgers and fries. Not Charlie's. Hope that's okay. I didn't want to wake you."

"How long was I out?"

"About forty-five minutes."

"Where are we?" I asked, eyeing the paper bag.

"The mall." Tucker pulled out a burger, unwrapped it, then handed it to me.

"The mall? You hate shopping."

"You need things."

"You don't have to do this." I took a bite, and moaned as the flavor exploded in my mouth.

"I know."

Tucker finished eating before me, but waited patiently while I enjoyed my bacon double cheeseburger.

When I finished, Tucker reached for his glovebox and retrieved, once again, his stash of baby wipes. "Here. They're great for greasy fingers, too."

We strolled through the mall's main entrance. Like a man on a mission, Tucker beelined for the baby store, leading me straight to the furniture department. He talked in great detail about crib safety, testing the latches and hardware on every model. We moved on to car seats, then strollers.

Somewhere along the way, he'd picked up a shopping cart and proceeded to fill it with diapers of different sizes, baby wipes, bottles, pacifiers, and something called changing pads.

The cart was overflowing by the time we rolled up to the check-out stand.

Tucker ordered me to head to the clothing store next door while he ran his purchases out to the Jeep. I walked the short jaunt through the mall between shops and no less than five different people either smiled at or said hello to me. Kids ran free, screaming and laughing, and nobody seemed to mind. A group of elderly women wearing matching pink T-shirts, power-walked around me, their conversation as lively as their pace. A security officer nodded at me as I passed, then continued his conversation with a group of twenty-somethings.

A feeling of dread blanketed me.

I was surrounded by people, friendly people, yet I'd never felt so alone, so out of my element. A foreigner in a land of happy-go-lucky strangers.

I had just found the maternity department when Tucker caught up with me. "Hey," he said, a bit breathy, his gaze raking the length of me. "Go crazy. Do your girl thing." He plopped his butt down on the velour green couch stationed outside the fitting room and shoed me off with his hand. "I know it's not the designer labels you're used to, but we're not leaving empty-handed. You need clothes that will stretch over that beer belly, and this is the best Whisper Springs has to offer."

Beer belly? I looked down at my expanding waistline. He'd pay for that little dig.

A sales lady must have overheard our conversation and bounced over to greet us, studying me with adoring eyes. "Hi. Oh wow. Look at you. Glowing." She turned and winked at Tucker. "What a lucky man you are."

Tucker sat back in his seat, crossing one leg over the other, ankle to knee. He folded his arms, tilted his head, and pretended to inspect me. "Yeah. She'll do. Think I'll keep this one."

The girl laughed and turned back to me. "I'm Linda. What can I help you find?"

"Everything," Tucker interjected. "She needs everything, from underwear to a winter coat."

Linda and I raised our brows simultaneously.

"Well, this is going to be fun." She rubbed her hands together and shooed me into a fitting room. "You get comfortable. I'll be right back."

Tucker

"My back is killing me," Aida complained as I helped her into the Jeep.

Her hair brushed across my face, and I inhaled deeply, savoring the sweet scent. My hands lingered on her hip longer than necessary, and I hoped to hell she hadn't noticed.

Shopping had been torture. But watching how Aida had interacted with the sales girl, softening to her, laughing with her, had made the painful excursion all worthwhile. Before we left, Aida shocked me by pulling Linda in for a hug.

I drove her home, texted Tango one more time, letting him know we were back, and unloaded her bags.

Aida had already fallen into the couch and propped her feet on the coffee table. Phone in one hand, she thumbed the screen. With her free hand, she started the *click, click, click* of her nails.

"What's wrong?" I asked, parking my ass next to hers.

"No word from Tito." She dropped the phone and turned to me. "I'm worried." *Click, click, click.* "Did Tango say if he'd heard from anyone?"

I shook my head no, pulling her hand into mine, straightening her fingers to stop the nervous tick. "I'm sure we'll hear from him soon."

"We won't. I can feel it in my gut." She pushed from the couch and paced the living room, rubbing frantic circles over her stomach. "It's my father. Something's happened. I knew this day would come. I've always known. I just didn't expect it to happen so soon."

She stopped in her tracks and looked down at me, eyes liquid, face crumpling. "What if I did this? What if this is my fault? He told me the night I stabbed Rafael that I'd gone too far. That I had no idea what I'd done. Oh. Tuck. What if it's my fault that he's dead?"

"Whoa. Whoa. Whoa." I jumped to my feet and skirted the coffee table to meet her toe to toe. "Who said anything about him being dead? Jesus, Aida. Stop worrying yourself." I rubbed my hands up and down her shoulders.

She wrenched free of my grip. "Can you take me to The Stop? Now. I need to go now."

"Maybe we should stay here."

"Tucker. God dammit. Either you drive, or I'm walking."

Five minutes later, I followed Aida into the kitchen of The Truck Stop. I watched from the corner as she twisted her hair into a bun and covered it with a little black net.

"Move, Charlie," she grunted, pushing past the gentle giant and pulling a knife out of a drawer I'd never noticed before.

Charlie shot me a *what the hell* glance.

I held out a palm, gesturing for him to back away.

"I need to chop. Charlie, what can I chop?"

"Choppin' is done, Aida. It's about closing time."

Her gaze bounced around the room. "Then give me a chicken. Give me a goddamned chicken or a slab of meat, Charlie, or swear to Christ, I'll go Freddie Krueger on your ass."

Slade burst through the doors. "What the heck is going on back here?"

"She needs to chop," I said, shrugging my shoulders. "Or de-bone."

"This isn't funny," Aida yelled, yanking the cooler door open and sticking her head inside. "Where do you keep the poultry, Charlie?"

Charlie's face reddened. If there was one thing I'd learned about my sister's famed chef over the years, it was that nobody, not even hot-blooded, sexy, knife-wielding mafia princesses called the shots in his kitchen.

Voice deeper than I'd ever heard come out of his mouth, Charlie warned, "Back away from the meat locker, little lady, or so help me, I'll throw you over my knee and—"

The knife Aida had been holding stuck into the wall above Charlie's head, mere inches from his balding scalp.

"And what?" she asked, voice low and threatening.

Audible gasps filled the room before Charlie exploded in a cataclysmic kaleidoscope of profanities.

When he charged, Slade and I simultaneously jumped into the line of fire. I pushed Aida behind me. Slade threw herself in front of Charlie, arms outstretched, palms slamming into his chest. Charlie stalked forward, promising, with a colorful vocabulary, to spank some manners and respect into Aida. Slade's Chucks squeaked, trying to find purchase against the tile floor as he pushed her backward.

Fuck. I needed to defuse the situation. And fast. Aida reached around me for another knife.

I snagged her around the waist, swinging her away from the weapons and out the door. I pulled her across the hall and into the office, slammed and locked the door behind me.

The second she found her footing, she threw a punch, clocking my left cheek, hard enough that my vision blurred.

"Mother fucker," I grunted, clapping a hand to my face and shaking the stars from my vision. Shit, the little spitfire knew how to hit.

"Ow," she cried, stumbling backward and rubbing her right hand.

"What the hell was that for?"

"I just wanted to chop some fucking vegetables. I need my knives. I'm losing my mind," she yelled, ripping the net from her hair.

"Yeah, I get it. But you need to pull your shit together."

"I can't. I'm scared. What if I killed him? What if Dad is gone because of me?"

I slammed my arms around her, squeezing tight. "Stop. Just stop. I hate seeing you like this."

"I don't have anybody else. I can't lose him. He's my only family."

"That's not true." I pressed a hand on the side of her abdomen, spread my fingers across the swell. "You have her, Aida. You have your daughter, and she needs you to keep your shit together."

Aida lifted her doe eyes to mine, cracking that damn armor again.

And you have me, I wanted to say. My jaw clenched tight, holding the words where they belonged—in my head.

Aida pushed up on her toes and crashed her lips to mine. Sliding her hands around my neck, she tangled her fingers in my hair and pulled me tighter against her assault, holding me steady, holding me captive.

I knew what she wanted, what she thought she needed. It wasn't me. It was relief. It was escape from the worry. She could get that from any man. She could go home and get it from her new vibrator. But fuck me and my selfish pride, I wanted to be the only one easing her frustration.

I had no right.

If I gave in to her desire, there would be no going back.

A true gentleman would not take advantage of the situation.

Then again, a real man would not let her leave the room unsatisfied.

Aida

Satisfied that he'd gotten my not-so-subtle hint, I released my death grip on Tucker and wiggled free of his embrace. If I couldn't chop, dice, or slice my frustrations away, I'd fuck them to dust.

"We gonna do this?"

"Slade could walk in," he mumbled, shaking his head in a less than convincing *no*.

"I need this. For the baby," I said, hitting him in his soft spot. I took a slow step back, lifting the hem of my shirt.

"For the baby? Or so you don't go back out there and murder Charlie?" Tucker stalked forward, licking his bottom lip.

I yanked the shirt over my head, thankful that I'd put on my white, lace bustier that morning. Its stretch made it easily removable. I made a slow-go of peeling it over my head, excited beyond measure at the blush of Tucker's cheeks, the lust in his eyes. "Right. For Charlie, then."

I toed off my ballet flats and kicked them aside.

Nostrils flaring, Tucker's gaze dropped to my breasts, then lower to my round belly. He pulled me against him so fast and hard it stole my breath. Before I could think straight, he cupped my ass and lifted me off my feet, urging me to wrap my legs around his waist.

Damn, he was strong.

His kiss was hard and commanding. His body vibrated against mine. When he lowered me to the couch, his hands traveled without haste to the button of my jeans. With surprising skill, he slid them off my hips and down my thighs, tossing them to the floor.

Kneeling between my shamefully open legs, he studied me. His chest rose and fell while he gnawed his lower lip. Oh God. He was going to bail. I could see the angel on his shoulder fighting with the devil in his ear. He didn't want me.

I needed him.

I would not give up without a fight. I cupped my breasts, massaging the ache, teasing and tempting him, silently begging, *don't leave.*

Tucker dropped his chin to his chest, shook his head, and mumbled, "Fuck it." Raising his tempestuous eyes to mine, he pulled his shirt over his head.

Mother of Mercy, the man was built. Virile. Thick. Layered with proof that he'd clocked countless hours at the gym. Blond hair dusted his stacked chest, formed a trail down his ripped abs, and disappeared behind the waistband of his jeans.

Mmm ... I couldn't wait to see what else was hiding behind that denim.

I reached for the button, biting my bottom lip to stifle a moan. When my fingers brushed his waist, he sucked in a sharp breath, captured my wrists, and pinned them above my head.

Leaning forward, he pulled an earlobe between his teeth, nipping hard before trailing his lips down my neck and over my shoulder, sending bone-chilling tremors through my body.

"I'm running this show, Bambi," he said with a thick rasp. "I say if, or when, my jeans come off."

I turned my head, searching for his mouth—a kiss, a lick, a bite, anything. Anything that was more. More flesh, more heat, more Tucker.

He brushed his lips softly against mine, then ducked lower, releasing my arms to balance himself mindfully and gracefully over me.

His scent made my head spin, filling me with dizzying want. Sweat and warm, musky spice. He was raw, calloused, hard-working, all-American grit from head to toe. No frills, no fancy cologne. No polished shoes or fake tan.

Tucker took his time tasting, exploring, inch by agonizing inch. My breasts ached. My clit throbbed. I writhed and arched beneath him, biting my lip, fighting the urge to scream in frustration, or beg for his cock. I had never begged, but oh, how I needed to feel him inside me.

He moved from breast to breast, teasing each nipple into a painful peak. I flittered between anger and need. Anger because I had no control. Need, because his control was flawless, working me slow and steady in an upward spiral, pulse racing, muscles trembling, skin vibrating, tensing, melting under his touch.

Moving down my body, he dropped soft kisses on my stomach, dancing his fingers in a delicate pattern over the stretched skin. Something shifted, deep inside me, a place untouched, unexplored, protected. As I watched him worship my body, admiring with his lips and tongue and fingers, not only me, but my child, I knew, what I needed from him was no longer about sexual gratification. I was exploring that dangerous territory that I had never dared cross into. Freely giving all of myself, not just flesh, but *all* of me—emotional, physical, spiritual.

Surrender.

And there was no question whether I could cross that line. It was done. He'd carried me over. And when he lifted his eyes to mine, his melty, possessive gaze, offering reassurance, acceptance, gratitude, I knew beyond doubt or reason that I would never be the same.

There was something so incredibly freeing in that realization.

Tears sprung free, and as Tucker lowered his head between my legs, as he stroked a finger over the lace of my panties, as his hot breath warmed my swollen clit, I closed my eyes and surrendered.

"Fuck me," I begged. "I need you. Please."

I had never felt more vulnerable, or more powerful.

Tucker crawled back over me, kissing me softly before whispering, "I can't fuck you, beautiful. I don't have any condoms." He reached between us and skimmed a finger over the sensitive throb between my legs, sending delicious shivers through me. "Don't worry. I know what you need. I'll take care of you."

I cupped his face, pulling him closer. "You're going to fuck me, Cowboy. Here. Now. I'm clean. Tell me you're clean, Tucker. Tell me and I'll believe you." God, I'd never acted so desperate and mindless. But if there was one thing I knew about this man, it was that he wouldn't lie, or put me or my child at risk.

He studied my face, his battle of conscience evident by the set of his jaw, the wrinkle between his brows, the tempest brewing in the ocean of his eyes. He dipped his head and caught my gaze, holding it for a long spell, as if giving me time to change my mind, or perhaps trying to find permission in my eyes. And then he kissed me. Long and soft and sweet. My hands wandered to his waistband, and his body tensed, his kiss growing harder, his need stronger.

Tucker reached between us, locking his fingers with mine. "No. I'm not fucking you today. Not like this." He guided my palm over the thick mound of his erection, then raised my arms back over my head and pressed his lips to mine, settling his hips between my thighs. I wanted to look. I needed to touch, but Tucker kissed me dizzy—my mouth, my jaw, my neck.

"Don't worry sweet girl, I'll take care of you," he whispered with a strained gravel against my ear.

Sweet girl. Nobody had ever called me sweet.

Whimpering against his cheek, I brought both hands around his neck, arched as much as his heavy body would allow, and ground against his cock, begging him to fill me. "I want you. Please."

His body trembled, and he breathed, "Fuck, fuck, fuck," into my neck.

Tucking one hand under my head, he curled his fingers in my hair. His other hand skimmed my side and gripped my hip, tilting me, rubbing himself harder between my legs.

When he slid back down my body, nestled his shoulders between my knees, and kissed where I needed it most, I closed my eyes and gave myself fully to the sensation. I refrained from trying to control my orgasm. I didn't care if I came. I was lost in all that was Tucker—his scent, his labored breaths, his heat, and hardness. His strength.

For the first time in my life, I submitted beneath a man, my body pliant, trusting him to take me where I needed to go. He pulled my panties to the side and worked me slow and steady, licking, biting, sucking. His muscles coiled and bunched beneath the rake of my fingernails. When I slid my hands into his hair, pulling tight, he trembled, moaning, working me more frantically.

He lifted his head, molten eyes meeting mine, and whispered, "Jesus, Aida. You're perfect."

I didn't know if it was the words, or the way he spoke them, or the way he prowled up my body to claim my lips, pressing his erection again between my legs, or maybe it was the way he possessed me with his kiss, but I came. There was no slow build-up. It was fast and hard. And when I cried into his kiss, Tucker came, too, his hips locking against mine, his body going rigid. Sticky moisture warmed my lower abdomen.

I curled my arms around his neck, my legs around his hips, and I squeezed. I never wanted to let go. I wanted this man on top of me, inside me, by my side, forever.

Tucker drew a deep breath, then rolled off, leaving me warm and liquid on the couch. With his back to me, he looked down, mumbled, "shit" and righted his jeans. He scooped his shirt off the floor, and pulled it over his head.

I couldn't move.

Tucker couldn't move fast enough.

Silent and stiff, he grabbed tissues off Slade's desk and wiped my stomach and then his own. Then he retrieved my clothes and helped me dress. After brushing hair off my face, his hand lingering on my cheek, he dropped his forehead to mine, squeezed his eyes shut, and whispered, "You relaxed now?"

I shivered at the cold bite to his tone, and rubbed my arms up and over his shoulders, hoping I was reading him wrong. "I'm so fucking relaxed." I lifted my chin, seeking his lips.

"Aida. Listen," he said, stepping back, dropping his gaze to the floor, and scrubbing the top of his head. "I, uh. I gotta go. I'll have Slade drive you home."

Without so much as a glance my way, he slipped out the door.

CHAPTER 5

"PLEASE, CHARLIE. I SAID I'm sorry. I promise, it won't happen again." I slunk deep into his personal space, close as I could get without violating him, and craned my neck, tilting at an odd angle to challenge his angry, stubborn pout.

Slade butted in, "I thought you wanted to help with the books."

"I hate numbers," I confessed, not taking my eyes off the giant, spatula-wielding, burger genius. "Just a few hours in the morning? Prep. Please?"

New wrinkles formed on his forehead above where his brows met in the middle of his red face. "No."

I steepled my fingers. Batted my lashes. Pursed my lips. Charlie shook his head *no*.

I'd had it with Whisper Springs. Mostly the men of Whisper Springs, who seemed to get off on rejecting me. I was about to voice my thoughts when Slade pushed between us, nudging me toward the door. "Aida, give Charlie and me a minute, will ya?"

Deflated, but not defeated, I made my way toward the ladies' room, pausing when I heard Rocky's giggle coming from the office. I poked my head through the half-opened door.

Father and son sat on the couch. Rocky was tucked under his dad's arm, holding an open book, sounding out words one consonant at a time.

"Hey, boys." I crouched as Mini Tango shimmied off the seat and barreled at me, full speed ahead.

"Aida. Guess what?" he shouted, throwing his arms around me.

"What?" I asked, struggling to stay upright.

He wiggled free before I could enjoy a full squeeze. Bouncing on his toes, he exclaimed, "Uncle Tuck is taking me to see Grandma and Grandpa next weekend."

"Yeah?" I asked, trying to keep my voice steady at the mention of Tucker's name. "That's great."

"He's picking up his girlfriend."

My heart shriveled. "Girlfriend? Tucker has a girlfriend? You sure?"

The boy nodded. "And I get to ride her."

"Ride her?" I reached behind me and gripped the wall for balance. Did he mean, ride *with* her? Was Tucker's girlfriend a truck driver?

"Yeah." He leaned closer and whispered, "She's really big, but she's not scary."

I didn't dare look at Tango, for fear of revealing my utter, devastating disappointment.

"You wanna come?" Rocky asked, back to bouncing.

"Oh, no. I can't." Nor would I want to. I hadn't seen Tucker since he'd left me, alone and confused, in the very same room I was currently standing in, over a week ago.

Girlfriend.

Girlfriend?

Huh.

That would explain his reluctance to fuck me, and his need to flee the moment our mutual orgasms had occurred. Damn. Where were my knives when I needed them?

"Okay," Rocky shrugged, flashing his killer green eyes at me and skipping out the door.

I struggled to stand. Tango watched from his spot on the couch, smirk on his face.

"What's so funny?" I asked, faking a smile.

"You. All fat and shit." His gaze travelled the length of me before resting on my baby bump.

"Shut your mouth, pretty boy." I dropped my butt next to his and pretended I wasn't stewing over the girlfriend comment. Why was this the first I'd heard of her? And why the hell did my insides feel like pâté. "I'm gorgeous, and you're jealous because I'm prettier than you."

"Yeah," he said, wrapping an arm around my shoulder. "We all know you're gorgeous. It's fun watching you expand. You should slow down on the burgers, though. That ass gets any bigger, we'll have to hire a tent maker for your next wardrobe upgrade."

"Low blow." I reached over and gave his nipple a twist. "Have you forgotten? I can snap my fingers and make you disappear."

"Yeah, yeah," he said, smacking my hand away. He dropped a kiss to the top of my head. "How you holding up?"

I drew a cleansing breath and relaxed into his warm embrace. Tango, in all his pretty-boy glory, had gradually become a salve to my ever-blistering burn. "I'm going out of my mind. Have you heard from Tits?"

"No. And we need to stay off radar. Can't reach out, Princess. You know that as well as I do."

"I know," I sighed. He was right. Without knowing which enemy we were fighting, we couldn't risk exposure. "Tango, what if he's gone?"

His thoughts hung in the air between us, unvocalized, but blaring nonetheless.

We'd known this was coming.

"Are you ready for that? If it happens?"

I'd never been eager to take the helm, but I'd always been prepared. "I used to think I was. Now?" I rubbed my stomach. "I'm not so sure."

Tango cleared his throat. "You have options."

"Do I?" I'd been born into the dark underbelly of society. Raised to fight, scheme, thrive, at any cost. Stay two steps ahead of the game. Trust no one. Kill or be killed. "If I don't step up, claim my throne, I lose everything. Everything Dad has spent his life building. My home. Our investments. The vultures will swoop in and devour all of it."

With a huff, he let go of me and leaned forward, forearms resting on his thighs. "It's only money."

When he tilted his head to look at me, I could see the worry in his eyes.

"It's my future. Her future," I said, tasting the sour bite of those words before they left my lips. God. What kind of mother wanted that destiny for her child?

"Aida. You're one of the most resourceful people I've ever met. Luciano didn't raise a fool. You can build your own damn empire if that's what you want. Or? Hell. Wash your hands of that world. Start fresh and clean, here with us."

"I don't know how to exist in your world."

With a cocked brow, he argued, "You're doing fine so far."

"I'm hiding."

"True. But you're adapting, too. I can see it. Even Slade has noticed."

I didn't want to acclimate. I wanted to go home.

"Doesn't matter. Eventually, I'll need to go back, whether it be to snuff the torch or burn Dad's enemies to the ground."

We sat in silence, because really, what more was there to say? When my exile was over, whatever the outcome, I had no choice but to return home. I didn't belong in Idaho. I belonged in New York, where I was heir to a dark and bloody throne.

"What was Rocky whispering to you over there?" Tango asked, snapping me out of my dismal thoughts.

Damn. Bile rose in my throat. "He was telling me about his trip with Tucker." I almost choked on *his* name.

"Right. Tuck's bringing Frankie home. Haven't had the pleasure yet. Hear she's a beauty."

The room shrunk around me. My lungs failed, collapsing under the weight of vile remorse and degradation. Never had I let a man make me feel that way. I pushed to my feet and headed for the door.

"You okay?" Tango asked, hopping up, and coming my way.

I wasn't okay. I was pissed. And hurt. Mostly pissed because it hurt. I'd known he had a secret. I hadn't expected it to devastate me. "Why is this the first I'm hearing of his girlfriend?" I turned around and crossed my arms, pinching my lips tight to hide the quiver.

Tango's brows drew tight. He sucked in a breath. Looked at the ceiling. Planted his hands on his hips. Then he laughed. "You've got to be kidding me."

"What?"

The door flew open, hitting my backside and knocking me into Tango.

"Oh God. I'm sorry." Slade closed the door behind her. "Jeez. Sorry. I was just so excited to tell you that I talked Charlie into letting you help in the kitchen."

"He agreed?" I asked, unable to hide my glee, despite the pain in my shoulder.

"Yep. Well. I didn't give him a choice, really. I am the boss after all."

And a damn good boss she was. "You bribed him, didn't you?"

"I'll never tell." Her smirk told me all I needed to know.

"That's my girl." I pulled her in for a hug. I was starting to like hugs. "So, I can start tomorrow?" I asked, peeling a chunk of her blonde hair out of my lipstick.

"Tomorrow. Six AM sharp." She pressed her lip to my ear and whispered, "Only for a few hours a day, though. Tango will kill me if I work you too hard." She stepped away from me and into Tango's arms.

A few hours a day, with knives, slicing things. I could handle that. Especially if I pretended Tucker's dick was on the chopping block. "I'm going to go tell Charlie thank you."

"No. No. No." Slade held up a palm, shaking her finger. "I wouldn't go in there if I were you. When I walked out, he was still crying."

Tucker

"Mom, are you crying?" I asked, when her sniffle registered through the speaker.

Mom cleared her throat. Paused for a deep breath. "I'm sorry. Deep down I was hoping you would move back home. You know. Now that Tango is there to take care of your sister."

Mom hated that I had moved away, despite knowing I'd relocated for Slade and Rocky. Truth be told, my sister had never needed me. I'd used her single-parent status as an excuse to relocate. I'd had no choice. I couldn't keep explaining to my mother, who used to stop by my apartment unannounced at least three times a week, my whereabouts on the nights I'd been out hunting. Living a state away from my parents gave me freedom to come and go as I pleased. Cell phones gave me the freedom to let Mom believe I was home, rather than waiting in a dark lot for the perfect girl to creep out of the shadows. "Love it here, Mom. Whisper Springs is home now. Didn't Dad tell you? I found some property, gonna make on offer." Billings held too many dark memories, I left unsaid.

"He told me. I'm happy for you, I am. It's just, part of me hoped you'd want to go back to work with the FBI."

"Can't do that." Too many rules. Too many eyes. I worked better on my own.

Another huff came through the speaker. "I'll see you Friday. Love you."

"Love you too, Mom."

I tossed my phone on the nightstand, crossed my arms behind my head, and closed my eyes, struggling to find peace amidst the chaos playing in my mind. As had happened every night this past week, Aida's breasts, her flawless olive skin, her sweet voice begging me to make love to her, played like an amateur porno on the insides of my lids.

The palm of my hand was a horrible substitute for the real thing, but it was all I had. Sleep never came until I allowed the movie to play to the end. Until I came all over my fist to the memory of Aida crying my name, her body trembling, then melting beneath me. As had become routine, I fell asleep hearing her laughter, picturing her smile. I woke every morning wearing a big ass grin but feeling empty all the same.

I'd acted the jackass the last time I was with her. After she'd come undone, and clung to me like I was a fucking lifeline, I had lost my shit. Her vulnerability had hit me hard, in the gut, and in the chest.

By her own admission, sex was her way to relax. Like a fool, in the heat of the moment, I had convinced myself that

I was merely giving her an outlet. Truth was, my motivations were shameful and selfish. I'd wanted to fuck her senseless from the very moment I'd laid eyes on those luscious curves, those wicked, seductive eyes, that damn dirty mouth. I'd seen the opportunity, and I had jumped her like a rabid dog in heat. Who in the hell took advantage of a pregnant woman like that?

Aida deserved better than to be dry-humped on an office couch.

I didn't want to live like I'd been living the past weeks. I hated how she weaseled her way into every thought. How I woke in the morning, eager to see her face. How sleep only came after I'd jerked-off to the fantasy of her naked body. How I craved her laughter.

I despised the fact that I wanted Aida more than I wanted to hunt girls.

I didn't want to need somebody.

Aida woke something in me. Hunger. Desire. Hope. Damn if that didn't make me vulnerable. Damn her for popping my self-imposed bubble.

I'd avoided her for over a week. Giving the whole *out of sight, out of mind* theory another shot. Avoidance only made my cravings worse.

I needed to man up. Tell Aida the truth. Expose my scars. Explain to her why I'd bailed. She deserved nothing less. To move forward, I'd have to come clean.

I had to see her, regardless of what the future held.

I'd intended on heading to Aida's early, but when I stepped out of the shower and heard my work phone ringing, my high hopes shattered and crumbled at my feet.

Rollover accident. West of Missoula on Interstate 90. One of our senior drivers, Bob Riggins, twenty years on the road. Minor injuries, no fatalities, thank God. Thirty thousand worth of merchandise damage. A truck worth over a hundred grand, headed for the scrapyard.

What a shit storm.

I thumbed through my cell, hovering over Aida's number, then shot her a quick text.

Need to see you, Bambi. Dinner tonight?

I hunkered down at my desk to tackle the list of phone calls I didn't want to make. First Dad, then the hospital to check on Bob, and on to the blood suckers. My head was ready to explode after talking to our insurance company. My suspicions were confirmed when the Montana Highway Patrol informed me the accident was caused by a driver who was most likely looking to cash in on an insurance claim, purposely trying to force Bob into rear-ending him. I fielded calls from reporters and spent hours sweet-talking our clients, ensuring we wouldn't lose one of our oldest accounts.

At six, I'd had enough, and shut down the computer. Aida hadn't responded to my message. I expected no less than a tongue lashing. I'd have taken anything. Even a simple *go to hell.*

My stomach rumbled, protesting its neglected state. Wasn't much in the mood for cooking so I headed to The Stop for dinner. When properly nourished and hydrated, I'd be in better shape to swing by Aida's and grovel. I couldn't let another day pass without seeing her. Tomorrow, Rocky and I were off to Billings and I couldn't leave before at least attempting to fix what I'd broken.

I pulled around to the back of The Stop, anxious and amped, my blood pumping harder, my tunnel vision directing me toward the diner, knowing I'd see my Bambi soon. That was probably why I hadn't paid any mind to the truck parked in the dark corner of the lot, or why I chose to ignore the crunch of heavy boots pounding the gravel behind me.

The putrid stench of tobacco hit my nose a mere blink before the first strike hit my head. Survival mode kicked in. My senses came into focus—the scent of surrounding pines, the cold bite of fall, soft waves lapping against the rocky shore of the beach just below the parking lot. The heavy breaths of three—no, four—men.

I twisted, raising my left arm to block another blow, striking the assailant in the temple with my right fist, hard enough to render him unconscious. Maybe brain dead. It was a fine line, and it was safe to say I was off my game.

The glint of a blade flashed to my right, and I ducked, throwing a punch to the man's throat. He stumbled backward, knife still in hand, and fell on his ass, struggling for breath.

A gun cocked to my left. "Let me kill this traitor. We'll get the spic bitch later."

The voice was too close.

Lucky for me.

Shitty for the idiot holding the glock.

I whirled, grabbed the barrel with my left hand, and cracked the man in the nose with my right. Warm liquid hit my face, and he flew back, shrieking in pain,

"There will be no killing today, boys." Another gun cocked over my right shoulder. "Pick up your trash. Run like hell. You have until the count of three."

I risked a glance to my side. Officer Roger Caldwell stood a step behind me, gun raised, looking every bit the badass street thug in his black gear and beanie.

"One." He stepped in front of me.

Face still hidden, the remaining assailant bent and scooped his unconscious friend off the ground, dragging him away.

"Two."

Throat-punch helped broken-nose off the ground, and they stumbled after their friend.

"Roger," I said, taking a breath and shaking the tension from my arms.

The battered men piled into their truck, moaning, cursing, and promising my certain death.

"You good?" he asked over his shoulder, weapon still pointed toward my attackers.

"Yeah. Thanks for that."

We watched the old Chevy roll out of the parking lot. Only after it disappeared did Roger lower his arms.

"What the hell was that?" he asked, tucking his lady into his hip holster.

"It appears I've made some enemies." *We'll get the spic bitch later.*

He gave me a one-sided eyebrow raise. "I'm not talking about those incompetent inbreds. I'm talkin' 'bout you taking three of them down, blind. Shit. I saw them coming for you and barely had time to sprint over here before you'd taken care of business."

"Got lucky, I guess." Wasn't about to share my history. "You're not in uniform. You moonlighting for Tango?"

He shrugged his shoulders. "Can't raise a family on an officer's salary."

Tango had hired a security crew. Off-duty cops, apparently. Good call. I started for my Jeep.

Roger stopped me with a hand to my chest. "Watch your back, Tuck. Don't know what you did to piss off those boys, but you're on their radar now. They're not the smartest bastards, but once you've been targeted, they are relentless."

Kill this traitor ... we'll get the spic bitch later.

They weren't just coming for me. I patted Roger on the shoulder. "Thanks again, Rog."

I ran to my car and dialed Tango. He answered on the third ring.

"You home?"

"Yeah," he grunted. Rocky squealed in the background.

"We've got a problem. I'll be there in five."

I tossed my cell on the passenger seat and released my frustrations on the steering wheel.

Boom. Boom. Boom.

Aida

Boom. Boom. Boom.

I cranked the shower knob to OFF and quickly patted myself dry.

Boom. Boom. Boom.

"I'm coming. I'm coming!" I shouted, certain nobody could hear me from the far corner of my apartment. I'd barely tied the towel around my chest and cleared the back end of the hallway when the front door flew open, smashed into the wall behind it, and swung back to the closed position.

A deep voice shouted, "Fuck," from behind the door just before the knob turned and the door opened again.

Tucker and Tango bumped shoulders, fighting to get through the entryway first, both shouting my name before realizing they were standing right in front of my half-naked ass.

Had the situation not been so ridiculous, I might have been scared. Had I not recently engaged in a marathon session with my new vibrator, courtesy of Tucker, I might have dropped my towel and taken advantage of the two insanely beautiful men standing in my living room, all heavy breaths and twitching muscles.

When they noticed my naked state, Tango rolled his eyes, then dropped his gaze. Tucker damn near tackled me, blocking Tango's view and pushing me toward my bedroom.

"Get dressed. We need to talk."

I took my time, irked that my privacy had been so dismissively violated, pissed that Tucker thought it cool to bark orders.

When I emerged, fully dressed, Tucker stopped his pacing, and Tango rose from the couch.

"All right," I said, "Here I am. What's up?"

"Your little stint with the knives and the skinheads has come back to bite you in the ass," Tango said, crossing his arms, narrowing his eyes.

I couldn't help the curl of my lips while reliving the thrill of parting skin with a blade.

"I'm taking you with me. On my trip," Tucker blurted. "Pack some things. We're leaving tonight."

Like hell. "No."

"What do you mean, no? It wasn't a question."

"No is pretty self-explanatory."

"Aida," Tango said with a huff. "Those men are gunning for you. You humiliated them. They want to save face by making you pay. You've got limited choices here. You can either go with Tucker, or I can lock you in this house, where you don't step foot outside, not even to grab the morning paper. No more Truck Stop, no more burgers, no more sunshine. I'd rather not put you through that. Honestly, I don't want to put my family through that."

"Lockdown it is. I'm not going with Tucker to pick up his damn girlfriend. Not after...." Shit. No way was I going to admit to Tango that I'd begged Tucker to make love to me. Or that I'd experienced the two best orgasms of my life, in The Truck Stop Diner, of all places, thanks to some magnificent lip skills.

"After what?" Tango asked, dragging a hand over his face.

Tucker huffed behind me, his feet shuffling on the carpet. "Girlfriend?"

Tango slipped a quick glance over my shoulder, a glint of humor in his eye. "Frankie." He studied my face, biting back a smile. "Aida here, for reasons I can't wrap my head around, is miffed that nobody mentioned you had a girlfriend."

My core temperature hit the boiling mark. He thought my situation was funny. He wouldn't think it funny if he knew Tucker had been cheating on his girlfriend. With me. In the diner, no less.

I stamped my rage down the best I could. "My father ordered *you* to watch over me." I jabbed a finger into Tango's chest, then used that same finger to point at Tucker. "Not some dumbass cowboy who can't even hold his own in a fight."

"Jesus Christ," Tucker mumbled, raking his hands through his messy hair before storming away.

I stood my ground with Tango. "They would've beaten Tucker to death in that parking lot if I hadn't disabled two of them. My father will kill you if he knows you're leaving me in Tuck's incapable hands."

A drawer slammed. Then another. Then another. When I reached my room, Tucker was shoving underwear into my suitcase.

"What are you doing?" I shrilled.

"We're leaving. End of discussion." He closed the lid and heaved it off the bed.

"I'm not going anywhere with you." I speed-walked to the bathroom and locked the door. Obviously, arguing would do me no good. I'd wait them out. Safely behind the locked door. I made myself comfortable on the edge of the bathtub. Listened to footsteps stomp up and down my hallway.

A car door slammed. More stomping. Rocky was yelling, then crying upstairs. My stomach rumbled. More footsteps, this time pausing outside the bathroom door.

I wrapped my arms protectively around my middle. "Don't worry, sweet pea. Mommy's got this."

"Aida." Tango knocked softly. "This is for the best. It's only for a few days, until I can take care of those Aryan fuckers."

I knew damn good and well what was best. A long drive, alone with Tucker, was definitely not healthy, or safe, for anyone. "Think I'll stay. Don't worry, I won't leave the apartment, I promise."

"Fuck this shit," Tucker rumbled, fury fueling his words.

He only kicked once, and the wood below the handle exploded into shards. I watched, in disgust, and awe, as the door surrendered and slowly creaked open.

A few months ago, had anyone displayed such aggression toward me, I would've taken them down. Taught them some respect. With the baby on board, I'd gone soft. Or maybe it was Tucker's unnecessary display of male brute force. Either way, I didn't attack. Instead, I inquired, "What's with all the dramatics? You could've asked nicely. I would've let you in."

Without a word, Tucker was on me, or under me, rather, scooping me off the tub, and carrying me through my apartment like a damn child.

He tucked me into the Jeep and just like that, we were on our way. Tango shook his head and jogged up his back porch toward the door. No goodbyes. No apologetic glances my way.

Like a racer's baton, I'd been passed off.

And because life wasn't messy enough, I was whisked into the dark of night, by the man I'd developed a terrible crush on, to meet his girlfriend.

Tucker

"So, about my girlfriend," I said, frustrated, and uncomfortable, with the silent routine coming from the opposite side of the cab.

Aida whispered under her breath, scooted deeper into her seat, and turned to look out the passenger side window. "I don't want to hear about her. I'm stuck with your miserable, cheating ass for God knows how many miles. I've got murder on my mind, so it's best we don't discuss your immoral tendencies right now."

I could've let her off the hook. I didn't. "Are you jealous? Is that a hint of jealousy I hear in your voice?" Yeah, I was teasing, egging her on, but damn, I'd missed her fiery tongue and she deserved some ribbing after her *dumbass cowboy who can't hold his own in a fight* remark earlier.

Snapping her head my direction, she mumbled, "I don't like you. I'd have to like you to be jealous of your fat girlfriend."

"Fat? Now she's fat?" I asked, struggling to stifle my laugh.

"Your nephew squealed like a little piggy. Didn't know you were into big girls. Of course, that would explain why you couldn't keep your hands off me and my, what did you call it? Oh yeah, my beer belly. Well, sorry, Cowboy. I'm not fat. I'm pregnant, so you're outta luck. And damn lucky I haven't stabbed you in the balls yet."

Fuck me, but jealous Aida was cute as hell. "You about finished?"

Aida loosened her seatbelt and leaned my way. "I'm only getting started. By the time I'm finished, you'll be on hands and knees begging … Oh my God." She grabbed my chin and wrenched my face her way. "Is that blood on your face?"

"It's not mine." Shit. In my rush to get her away, I'd forgotten to clean up. I yanked free of her grip and swerved, mere inches from sideswiping a minivan.

"Whose blood is it?"

"The dip-shit skinheads jumped me outside The Stop. Don't worry, though, I held my own."

Aida reached into the glove box and pulled out the recently replenished supply of baby wipes. "Hope these work on blood splatter."

She handed me one cloth after another, prodding me to clean my face. Not an easy task to accomplish while driving. After a good five minutes, Aida gave me a thumbs up and tucked my supply of magic cleansing cloths away.

"For the record, the first time they jumped me, I didn't fight back because I was trying to lead them out of the diner. I didn't want anyone to get hurt. I sure as hell didn't need help. That being said, it was a turn on, knowing you'd had my back. It proves, despite your earlier comment, that you do indeed like me."

I braved a glance her way, in time to catch her eye roll.

"Who had your back this time?" she asked. "Another clueless woman you're stringing along?"

"Listen. This isn't a joke, Aida. There were four of them this time. One was carrying a gun. They weren't only after me. They were waiting for you, too."

Her hands fell to her belly, fingers spreading as if to comfort the life growing inside her. "It's not your job to protect me. Last I checked, Tango was crowned my guardian and savior." Spiteful poison laced her words.

Protecting her wasn't my job. But I would be the one keeping her safe. "And Tango is going to take care of those bastards while I keep you out of the line of fire. This is a good thing. Think of it as a vacation. Stress-free. Dark, gloomy, apartment-free. Your only responsibility for the next few days is to feed that baby."

Aida dropped her head back against the seat, closed her eyes, and sighed. Damn, she was delicious. Thick lashes, high cheekbones, plump, taunting lips.

"Where are we going?" she asked, shifting in her seat, turning away from me once again.

"My house. I need to grab my suitcase. Then we're off to see my parents."

Aida didn't respond, only stared out the window into the dark night. It was a jackass move, but I couldn't resist poking the bear. "After that, you, me, and Frankie are taking a little road trip. She's coming home with me. You two should get to know each other."

CHAPTER 6

Aida

THREE IN THE MORNING used to be the time I'd consider falling into bed. Pre-pregnancy, anyway. Post-preggo? Well, let's just say, three AM and Aida Voltolini, I mean, Aida Suarez, were not compatible. As we pulled up to the front of the Slades' farm-style home, it took every ounce of composure and self-control I could muster not to fall into a fit of exhausted rage.

I'd slept most of the trip, or had at least pretended to sleep, to avoid ripping Tucker a new asshole for being a lying, adulterous kidnapper. My ankles were swollen, my back ached, and I had a brain-pinching kink in my neck.

Tucker helped me out of the Jeep, and somehow, even after driving for seven hours, managed to display his devilish smile. It was unnerving the way that grin made my insides warm. Had I not been so tired, I might've done something to remove his smug expression.

I followed him up the steps onto the wraparound porch. The door flew open, and James Slade greeted us with open arms and bright eyes.

We shuffled inside, and Tucker's mother, Leticia, wrapped me in a warm embrace. "Aida, sweetie, it's so wonderful to see you again."

I hugged her back, unable to stifle a yawn as I said, "Good to see you, too."

Lettie pulled back and studied my face, empathy flashing in her silver eyes. "You must be exhausted. Let's get you right to bed. We can catch up in the morning." She released me and turned to give her son a squeeze. "Tucker wasn't supposed to come until Friday so I didn't have time to get both rooms ready. I'll put you in Tuck's bed. He can have the couch. Tomorrow, we'll have the guest room ready for you. It's full of boxes right now. I repainted the office and didn't have time to move everything back in yet."

"Thanks, Mom." Tucker kissed his mother's cheek. "I'll show her where to go."

"Thanks, Mr. and Mrs. Slade. I'll see you in the morning, or later in the morning."

"Please, Lettie and Bruce," Tucker's dad corrected me.

"Goodnight, Lettie and Bruce." I waved and watched them shuffle into what I assumed was their bedroom, then turned and followed Tucker down the hall.

"The bathroom is there." He pointed to his left and then turned into the room on his right. "Hold on a sec," he ordered, dropping the suitcases and shuffling through the darkness to find the bedside lamp. "There we go. Come on. Let's get you to bed."

He laid my suitcase on a chair in the corner. "If you need anything, I'll just be down the hall."

Dark circles framed his eyes; of course, the sparse light might've been to blame. Regardless, I couldn't help but appreciate his features, and a warmth swirled through me, first comforting, then aggravating. I couldn't allow myself that kind of reaction. Not when he was taken.

Which reminded me...

I slapped him. Swift and hard.

His head moved, only a fraction, but enough that I could see the muscles in his jaw tense, then relax. He licked his bottom lip, eyes down, before the left side of his mouth lifted. "Mind telling me what that was for?"

"For not telling me you had a girlfriend."

I slapped him again, to rid his face of that annoying smirk. "And that was for not calling me for a week after giving me a mind-blowing orgasm in your sister's office, for the second time."

I swung to strike again. He caught my wrist. I punched him hard in the gut with my free hand.

A satisfying, "oof," left his lips, and he doubled over. Yeah, I could throw a punch as well as I could throw a knife. Could take one, too. Kudos to Dad's unorthodox parenting.

I bent at the waist and kissed his cheek. "Goodnight, Tuck," I whispered in a breathy tease, slapping his ass before making my way to the bathroom.

When I returned, Tucker was stretched across the foot of the bed, ankles crossed, one hand behind his head, the other sprawled over his chest. Sound asleep. Snoring.

Too tired to complain, I shimmied under the heavy blankets and gave in to the unyielding pull of exhaustion.

When I woke, alone, and well-rested, an eery silence amplified the worrisome voices in my head. My father had to be okay. We'd have heard something by now if he wasn't. I rolled out of bed, shook off the sudden chill, and dug through the suitcase for warmer clothes.

I laughed when I found my new vibrator tucked in the folds of my wool cardigan. How disturbingly thoughtful.

Unless it was Tucker's idea of a bad joke, in which case, I'd make sure the man was looking over his shoulder for the rest of his life.

Sweet Papa, I was in a mood.

I took in my surroundings. The dark blue walls made the large room look smaller than it was. Framed photos of Tucker, mostly glossy five-by-sevens with cheesy brass frames, hung above a wall of shelves boasting trophies of various sizes and colors. Some sort of martial arts, judging by the poses of the gold-plated figures. Medals hung floor to ceiling on the opposite wall. Every one of them gold or first place.

Part of me felt cheated, having never heard of Tucker's achievements, and I fought the urge to snoop and unearth more of his secrets. Then I remembered that I didn't care about the unfaithful douche.

A shower was in order. If Tucker was forcing me to meet his girlfriend, I would do it like the queen I was, with grace and dignity. Of course, in his rush to pack my clothes, he hadn't grabbed anything with a price point above the thirty-dollar mark, meaning I would meet my competition dressed like nothing more than your average, middle-income, stay at home mom. Not that there was anything wrong with that. At least I had my cosmetic bag.

My heart dropped ten inches. *Oh, please. Let him have remembered to grab my makeup.* I rifled through the disorderly pile of garments. Then threw everything on top of the bed. No cosmetic bag. No beauty products. No mascara. No lipstick.

On a normal day, I might have thrown a nuclear tizzy. I mean, seriously. Who met the girlfriend of the man they'd been hoping to bang with no makeup and off-the-rack clothing? Not Aida Voltolini.

Deep breath in. Deep breath out.

Good thing I was no longer Aida Voltolini, heir of the East Coast's largest crime syndicate. I was Aida Suarez. Soon-to-be single mom.

I could handle anything.

I tiptoed across the hall. Every step caused the weathered hardwood to creak in protest. The bathroom was small and quaint, painted white. The only color in the room came from the floral accents in the shower curtain and on the framed wall art, also floral. Pedestal sink. Toilet. Cast iron, clawfoot tub. Clean pink towels had been set on the toilet lid. On top, sat a lady's razor and a small bar of jasmine scented soap shaped like a flower.

I showered efficiently, towel dried, then finger brushed my hair. As I crossed the hall, my blood ran cold at the sound coming from Tucker's bedroom. Grunting, and a faint squeak mixed with a disgusting sloshing sound. I stepped closer to the door, heart racing, cringing at the thought of what could make a noise so off-putting. My first and only conclusion? Dirty, hardcore, haven't-seen-you-in-ages fucking.

Tucker's girlfriend must have come over early. Probably thought he had time for a quickie while I was in the shower. My cheeks heated, my fists clenched, and I reached for knives that weren't on my wrists.

I wanted to catch him in the act. I wanted to ruin their moment. I wanted to be the one underneath him.

Dammit.

No I didn't.

Tucker was not my type.

I considered my baby, for a moment, before the rage took over, and I threw the door open with a loud bang.

A black-haired beast stood bedside with puppy dog eyes and a giant cock in her mouth.

"Ohmygodohmygod. Nonononono!"

Tucker

"Oh my God, Mom. No. No. No. No. No." I waved my hand in front of her. "I mean, yes. She's gorgeous. And funny. But she can't wait to get back to New York and far away from—"

Thunder rolled through the house—in the shape of my one hundred and ten pound Rottweiler named Lola—with an electric pink hunk of latex hanging from her mouth. Following behind, a string of profanities rising from the most beautiful, hot-blooded, pregnant woman I'd ever laid eyes on.

"No! Come back here," Aida yelled as Lola rumbled through the kitchen and toward the mud room. "Drop it. Give that back, you shit." She skidded around the kitchen island, her socks slipping and sliding on the tile.

Using the counter for purchase, she paused, only long enough to shoot death lasers my way and find her footing before following a very happy dog out of the kitchen.

"Was that? Oh dear Lord." Mom slapped one hand over her mouth and one on my shoulder. "Tucker, go help her."

A crash. Cuss words, some in Italian, I think. A thud.

I ran toward the commotion and found Aida on her ass in the laundry room engaging in a game of tug-o-war with my dog. Aida held the head of her brand-new vibrator in both hands. Lola held the other end in her vice like jaws. With a playful growl and hearty head shake, Lola wiggled the toy free of Aida's grip and disappeared around the corner.

Aida leaned back on her arms, chest heaving, eyes narrowed. "This is not happening. This is not fucking happening." She tried to stand, but her belly got in the way.

Slapping my offered hand away, Aida rolled to her side and pushed to her feet.

I heard Mom gasp from the kitchen, then command Lola to release. Her laughter set me over the edge, and I lost my composure.

"Oh, it's happening," I bellowed, wiping tears from my eyes.

"What's all the racket?" Dad bellowed.

Mom mumbled something inaudible, and Dad joined in on the chuckling.

Aida's doe eyes met mine, wet, fiery, and proud. Raising her chin, she turned on her heels. "I'm a queen, dammit." She tossed wet hair over her shoulder and headed toward the kitchen.

Dad turned his back when we entered, shoulders bobbing. Mom held the vibrator in her hand, cheeks red, lips pursed. "Lose something?"

I had to give my mother credit. She managed a straight face as Aida snatched the now-useless dildo away from her and tossed it in the trash.

"They sure don't make them like they used to," Mom said, pulling Aida in for a hug. "You hungry?"

I watched Aida stiffen, then relax against my mother. They exchanged words I couldn't hear, and soon, Aida was laughing, too.

Sweet Lord, that laugh. Travelled from my ears straight to my chest, tightening the loose parts, loosening the tight.

Damn.

I struggled through our morning meal, watching Aida interact with my parents, fighting the itch to pull her close, absorb her heat, keep a respectful distance when all I could think about was how soft and pliant her body became when tucked against mine.

It didn't matter that she ignored me through most of the meal. Aida was a proud woman. I'd dragged her away from her comfort zone, in the middle of the night, with zero say in the matter, yet she exuded charm and grace with my parents.

And if she never spoke a word to me again, I had the sound of her laughter to hold on to, and that was enough to carry me through a lifetime.

So, when she turned to me, finally, and asked, "Who in the world keeps a black bear for a pet?" she may as well have offered me the world.

"Lola?" I asked, almost choking on my bacon. "She's no bear."

"She's as big as a bear," Aida retorted, shooting her pert little nose in the air.

God damn she was beautiful.

"You ever seen a bear up close?" I challenged.

She quickly countered with a glare and a, "Yes. I just wrestled one."

"You just wrestled a teddy bear." I pointed my fork her direction. "Teddy bears who lick you to death don't count."

Lola must've heard her name, because sure enough, she trotted around the corner, butt wiggling frantically. She pushed her snout right into Aida's lap, sniffed, then settled her head between the baby bump and the table, offering herself for a pat.

"A teddy bear with no table manners," Aida cooed, scratching Lola behind the ear.

Fire. Desire. Contentment. I was full.

Aida, with her mask off, her shields down, baby-talking to my dog.

I wanted *this*. I wanted her. I wanted what I couldn't have.

Because when I took what I desired, I gave everything. My everything wouldn't be enough for Aida. She would leave too soon. Leaving me empty.

Aida had been right. She was a queen. *My queen.*

I was royally fucked.

After Aida offered to help Mom clean the breakfast mess, I excused myself, eager to get away from unrequited emotions, and reacquainted with Frankie, the only girl who would never break me.

Aida

Tucker was trying to break me.

Had he not figured out that I was made of steel?

After one morning with his family, any normal girl would crack, as I was sure he had planned. Probably to soften the blow of his girlfriend situation. And I could see the appeal.

Love. Laughter. A gentle, caring family.

Who wouldn't want a lifetime of that?

Me, that's who. Because instead of family, I had an empire.

Although, now that I'd had a taste of small-town Americana, my life back home had lost its luster. Money. Power. Respect. I had those things and more, but they left me wanting. Longing for Tucker's sweet, laid back version of normal.

I wanted him.

Well, the him who didn't cheat on his girlfriend, anyway.

Damn. I'd have to meet his girlfriend soon. And play nice. Aida Voltolini didn't play nice. Lucky for Tucker, I adored his parents. I kind of liked his dog, too. Payback could wait until we returned to Whisper Springs, and oh, was he going to pay.

After helping Leticia with the dishes, she offered a tour of the property. Lola followed us across the lawn, bumping my thigh every so often, always watching me with playful, wise eyes.

"Lola is always wary around strangers. Very protective of the family. I'm surprised she took to you so fast." Lettie bent to scruff Lola's face before planting a kiss on her nose. "Dogs are the best judges of character, you know."

Tucker's mother was surprisingly petite, considering the size of her son. We were close to the same height, her being a pinch shorter than me. Her graying hair was pulled back in a low pony, and her silvery eyes sparkled against her smooth, flawless skin.

"I wouldn't know. My father never let me have pets."

We walked toward the rear of the house, across the back lawn, and through a weathered, wooden gate. The field, overgrown with tall grass, stretched forever toward the backdrop of the vast blue sky and mountain ranges.

"Was this a ranch?" I asked, admiring the way Lettie's silver hair caught the light.

"At one time, yes. Cattle. Way before we bought the property."

"It's beautiful here. The air feels different. My hair, my skin. Everything feels different." My soul, too, I left unsaid. Maybe it was the crisp, fresh air, or maybe it was the quiet peacefulness surrounding me. I suspected, much to my surprise, that it was the people, rather than the elements, lifting my spirits. A calm, airy light seeped into my bones and filled the dark, hollow places.

If James and Lettie knew what I was capable of, what my future held, would they welcome me with the same trusting, wide-open arms?

Lettie's phone rang, and she retrieved it from the pocket of her wool coat. "Dr. Slade speaking. Hi, sweetie. How far apart? Oh my. Looks like we're having a baby today. Yep.

On my way. See you soon." She tucked her phone away and grabbed my hand. "I'm sorry to cut our tour short. Got a baby to welcome into the world. Tucker is in the barn warming up Frankie. I know he's excited for you to meet her. Do you mind telling him goodbye for me?"

Nodding yes, I pulled my cardigan tighter around my body and studied the large, red structure up ahead. *She* was in there. The woman who had Tucker's heart. A wave of nausea crashed through me, jealousy and trepidation leading the charge.

Shooing Lettie off with a forced smile, I choked down the bile, alongside my violent urges. *I can do this.* I'd faced deadlier adversaries. I'd argued weapons and self-defense over lunches with drug lords. I'd fought off angry strippers, comforted jilted porn stars, and had successfully managed Dad's high-maintenance prostitutes. One harmless girlfriend was nothing. I was Aida Voltolini, mob princess. *I can fucking do this.*

"Okay, little one." I rubbed my stomach. "No knives. I'll kill her with kindness." With Lola by my side, I marched toward the barn, the loud boom between my ears matching each step.

Like ripping off a bandage, I would go in, introduce myself, pretend I didn't want to murder the bitch, then find a place to hide in the house where I could read a book, or learn to knit, or find some other normal-people-shit to keep me busy.

I reached the door, pausing to catch my breath. The barn had been farther away than it looked. Lola's wet nose tickled my fingers before she offered a reassuring lick.

Music played. A song I didn't recognize. A man with a raspy tenor singing about lovers named Frankie and Johnny, and hearts awaiting dreams. I reached for the handle and stopped when Tucker's voice paired with the lyrics. Beautiful. Rich. Deep. Passion and tenderness stitching the lyrics into a beautiful tapestry.

He was singing to *her*.

Never had a man sung to me. Not once. Not even my father.

Oh God, I can't do this. Hot liquid burned my eyes. My fingers trembled. My soul ached.

Why did it hurt?

I was the woman who broke hearts. My heart was cast iron wrapped in adamantium. Un-fucking-destructible.

"Like a bandage," I whispered before yanking open the door, blinking moisture from my eyes, and forcing my lips to spread and not purse. "Hey, Tuck."

Wearing ripped and dirty jeans, thick-soled boots, and a button-up, red flannel, Tucker sat in the cab of a shiny, gigantic, semi-tractor, with the door wide open. The brilliant blue and polished-chrome beast was beautiful.

Leaning back in his seat, arms crossed behind his head, Tucker sang along to the soulful lyrics. He hadn't heard me come in.

I glanced around the massive barn. The place was clean—one large open space. Tools hung neatly organized on the far wall. Rolled hoses hung above stacks of tires along the back wall. The large, sliding barn doors were closed, allowing only a crack of light through. No sign of a girlfriend anywhere.

I stepped closer, smiling at the emotion backing Tucker's vocals. Warming at the peaceful set of his face.

Tucker hit an impossibly high note and rolled his head my way. When he caught sight of me, he jumped up and reached forward to end the music.

The space seemed emptier, somehow, without the haunting melody. Until he climbed down from his high perch and strode my way, filling all that empty with his larger than life confidence.

"Aida," he said, voice breathy, eyes molten.

Warm, strong arms reached for me, and oh, sweet Papa, how I wanted to fall into them. Instead, I steeled my spine and took a step back.

"Where is she?" I would not cry. I would not murder or maim. "Where's your girlfriend? I'm excited to meet her."

My lip quivered at the lie, and I turned my head to hide the shameful display of weakness.

Tucker

In a shameful display of weakness, I lunged forward, halting her retreat, and claimed those thick, full lips, parting them with my tongue, delving deep, quenching a voracious thirst.

I held her close, one hand at the base of her skull, the other at the curve of her spine, fingers stretching toward that sweet, full ass. Aida would not leave this barn without knowing and feeling with one hundred percent certainty, how deeply I wanted her.

Her hard, round stomach pressed between us, and I couldn't hold back a moan. Fucking hell, there was nothing sexier than a woman with child.

Aida broke the kiss, frantically searching my eyes, hands trembling against my chest. Her brows furrowed, and she shook her head, slowly, disbelieving. "Why would you do that? How can you be so cruel?"

"Cruel?"

"How dare you kiss me like that, like you want me, like I'm special. You are the last person I'd have expected to be a cheating bastard."

Shit. I couldn't torture her a second longer. "Bambi." I stepped behind her, gripped her shoulders, and turned her toward my ride. "Meet Frankie."

Her chest rose on a deep inhale. One. Two. Three times. "Your truck?"

"My truck."

"You let me believe … I. I." Her body tensed under my hands. "Your girlfriend is a fucking hunk of metal on wheels?" Aida whipped around and slammed her palms into my chest, hard enough to knock the breath out of me.

I stood my ground. "No. My girlfriend is a fiery, doe-eyed, mob princess."

"What did you say?" She lashed out again, this time with a punch to the gut.

I let her have that one. What was I going to do, wrestle a pregnant woman? Sweet Jesus, she was gorgeous, all red cheeks and fists of fury.

Palms raised in mock surrender, I backed up. "Whoa, Bambi. Take it easy," I chuckled. "Violence is not good for the baby."

"This is not funny. I've been so angry with you." Her voice raised an octave. "And I am not your girlfriend."

"Oh, I beg to differ. You must be my girlfriend. Friends don't kiss like you just kissed me."

Raising a shaky finger to her lips, her eyes seemed to lose focus for a moment before she raised her chin to glare at me. "We're just friends."

"Friends don't get jealous of nonexistent girlfriends." I retreated another two steps.

Aida stalked forward then paused.

"We're just…" Her hands smoothed over her belly. "I mean. We can't. I'm not good for…" She shook her head. "I mean. I wasn't jealous."

"You were jealous." I planted my feet firmly on the dusty floor.

"I thought I was the other woman. I hate cheaters. That's all."

"So do I. See? We're a perfect pair." I stepped closer, daring her to strike again. Hoping she would give me an excuse to touch that body. "And Bambi, you are not the other woman. You are the only woman."

"You said you don't have time for a relationship."

"I made time."

"But—"

"No buts." I gripped her upper arms, tight enough to let her know I wasn't playing around. "We're doing this. I'm doing this, for as long as I have you. Understand? I'm done fighting fate."

"Fighting? What?" Brows pinched, her gaze bounced from my mouth to my eyes.

"Whatever the reason, life brought us together. There's no denying the attraction. I'm running with it. You can run with me, or I can chase you. Either way, it'll be one helluva ride."

"I just wanted a fuck buddy," she mumbled.

I leaned close, pressed my lips to her ear, and whispered, "Liar."

She jerked back, pulling free. "I have responsibilities back home that you can't possibly understand."

My whole body vibrated with unbridled need. "You're not at home. Right now, you're with me."

"Tucker." Aida shook her head, her attentions now on the cement floor beneath our feet.

"Aida. Stop fighting this. I feel how you melt against me. You surrender. You're not the type of girl to yield to anyone, yet you do every time you're in my arms. That means something."

"We shared a few moments of weakness, a couple of trysts at The Truck Stop. It didn't mean anything."

My chest crumpled, pained by her lie.

"Tryst?" I raked a hand over the top of my head, scratching away the irritation. "A fucking tryst? Jesus. You know it was more than that."

Every time I had touched her, especially at the diner, most definitely the first time, my world had shifted on its axis. And the way she had reacted, there was no denying hers had shifted, too.

It was clear she was only trying to protect her heart, and I couldn't be angry for that.

"Don't sell yourself short, Aida. Everything you do means something. Every breath, every sigh, every thought, desire, touch, moan. It means everything. Every fucking second you give, I cherish. And I'm done trying to pretend I don't want you. I want you, Aida. Not just that ridiculous, perfect body. I want you. Your heart, your words, your tears, your insanely strong punches. And your fucking sexy laugh. I want it all. The only thing I don't want are excuses why this can't happen."

"No, Tucker," came from her lips, barely a whisper, but her eyes, in their liquid state, her body language, the way she leaned closer, fingers curling into my arms, everything about her, aside from those two words, begged, *yes, yes, yes*.

So, I kissed her. Again. Holding her head between my hands, holding her steady, tilting her face, her mouth, to the perfect angle. When she parted her lips, I couldn't hold back my pleasure, and I moaned, delving deep, tongues colliding, exploring, experiencing, acquainting.

Sure enough, her body fell closer, tighter against me. Delicate fingers slid under my shirt, raking, teasing my bare skin, setting me on fire.

"That's what I thought," I mumbled against her mouth before taking more of my fill.

I wanted to kiss her dry, devour, gorge myself on the flavor of her lips, burn in the heady explosion of heavy breaths and racing pulses. I wanted to take her against my tractor, or maybe in the cab, hell, the floor of the barn. I wanted to take her. Pound into her, make her beg for more, beg for me.

I wanted Aida so crazed with lust, so blinded by need, that my flaws, my scars, wouldn't be visible, wouldn't matter. Wouldn't disgust or scare her away.

For the first time in years, I was ready to expose my whole self, willing to risk my pride, my heart, and fuck, for Aida, my soul.

CHAPTER 7

SWEET MOTHER OF MERCY, my ass was huge. I looked over the other shoulder, hoping a different angle might help. Nope. Wider for sure. Everything had expanded. Waistline. Gone. My formerly voluptuous breasts. Gargantuan.

I leaned closer to the full-length mirror, aka, the closet door, in my new, temporary room. My skin had never looked better. So, there was that. Yay, for the pregnancy glow.

I squeezed my massive boobs together, lifting, testing their weight. Ugh. Sore and heavy.

A small flutter beat through my abdomen, reminding me of the reason I was ever-expanding. My heart palpitated at the sensation. I rubbed my belly and took two steps back to plop my butt on the fluffy bed. "I know, I know, sweet pea. You're worth the extra pounds."

My insides fluttered again, and I closed my eyes, absorbing the sensation, the goosebumps, the elation, holding tight to the exhilaration for as long as I could. I tried to imagine what her tiny body looked like as it wiggled inside me. It was insane, and terrifying, and so fucking beautiful to feel a love so deep, so pure, that you couldn't fathom how you'd ever existed without it.

I had loved few people in my life. Dad, of course. Feared him. Respected him. But I could survive without him, physically and emotionally. He'd made sure of that. I loved Tito, in a brotherly way. I'd suffer deeply if anything ever happened to him, but it wouldn't paralyze me.

My baby? My heart was so full, I feared it might explode. That's how much I loved her already. How would I ever survive meeting her? I rubbed at the ache in my chest. I might die in the delivery room. Love overdose, or something ridiculous.

All the warm and fuzzy, happy, lighthearted emotion pumping through my spirit made my eyes leak, and with a whispered, "fuck," I wiped the dampness from my cheeks. It frustrated me beyond measure to be so out of control of my emotions, so uncomfortable with the peace surrounding me.

Power, deception, seduction, violence. Those things I knew what to do with. That was the reality I'd learned to navigate.

In Tucker's world, oddly enough, all the calm and quiet terrified me.

I rose to my feet, and glared at my reflection. Another tear slipped down my face, catching above my lip. My lip still swollen from Tucker's kisses. Oh, those kisses. I'd never felt so wanted. So desirable. So ... feminine.

I'd wanted to fuck him hard on the dirty floor of the barn. Only, his kisses, his touch, the way he held me, it was every bit as satisfying as any orgasm, and when he'd broken the kiss and sent me on my way, I hadn't felt discarded or rejected. I'd felt ... hopeful.

The door creaked behind me, and through the reflection, I watched Tucker approach, tall and confident, commanding the space around him, shrinking the room around me.

My chest erupted in a flurry of erratic rhythms. My cheeks heated. When he pressed his chest to my back, lowered his chin to my shoulder and wrapped his arms around me, I tried to stamp down the emotion. But when he spread his hands wide, encasing my baby bump in his protective grip, sharing an intimacy I'd never experienced, I stopped fighting the tears, and melted against him.

For the first time in my life, I wanted a man for reasons having nothing to do with sex, power, or the adrenaline rush. I wanted Tucker for his heart, his smile, his never-failing arms, his crazy way of centering me, of lifting me up, and making me feel deeper than the surface level of my vain existence.

"Why the tears?" he asked, lips tickling the outline of my ear.

"I just realized that my ass is as big as your truck," I lied, unsure how to voice my newfound feelings.

"Your ass is perfect, and you know it. Seriously, what's making you cry?"

"Truth?"

"Please. Never give me anything but the truth, Aida."

I placed my hands over his and caught his gaze in the mirror. His devilish smile amped those electric blue eyes by a million watts.

"I think I'm happy."

"And that's a bad thing?"

"Not bad. Unsettling. There's happy, like, *yay, I just bought a one-of-a-kind Hermès bag.* Then there's happy, like, *I just carved-up a scumbag who roughed up one of Dad's girls.* But this is different, like a permanent happy. Bone deep. Maybe happy isn't the right word. Content? Whatever it is, it's overwhelming, that's all. And I'm pretty sure pregnancy is messing with my plumbing system, because my eyes have never leaked this much."

He chuckled, then landed a kiss on top of my head. A simple gesture that made me feel cherished.

"Can I tell you something?" I asked.

"Of course."

"I'm scared of getting soft. I can't be soft when I go home. But here, I … I think I like it. I like not having to stay sharp, or watch my back. I want to be soft, Tucker. And that scares me. It seems like a luxury, you know? One I can't afford."

"Aida. Women are supposed to be soft, yes. But your razor-sharp edge is one of the most attractive things about you. You won't lose that. You can't lose something that's part of your DNA. Don't get me wrong. When you're soft, it's the most beautiful thing I've ever seen. But when you ignite, that wicked spark is downright sexy."

Tucker liked my dark side.

"I'll tell you something." He grabbed my hand, turning me to face him, then sat on the edge of the bed and pulled me close, hands on my hips, holding tight. "This baby is damn lucky to have both sides of you. You're going to be a fierce, protective mother, and you're going to be her cushion to fall into. Her safe place. So, let yourself be soft. Embrace it."

I stared down into his beautiful, masculine face, absorbing his words, feeding off his encouragement. My heart broke a little, knowing I'd inevitably have to leave. Knowing I had no choice but to return home. I didn't know how much time I had, but I wanted to enjoy every moment, every heartbeat with Tucker. I wanted to explore happiness, no matter how short-lived.

I cupped a hand over his cheek. God, he was so warm, and rough, and perfect, and I decided that I'd been wrong all these years. My type wasn't sharp suits, polished shoes, and million-dollar cars. My type was flannel shirts, scuffed boots, and eighteen-wheelers.

"Tucker," I whispered, leaning closer, craving another taste of his mouth. "You're a good man. And under different circumstances, I would most definitely be your girlfriend."

His eyes darkened and seemed to lose focus. Tilting his head into my palm, he lowered his lids, and sucked in a breath. "Aida. There are things you need to know about me."

The front door of the house slammed and James called out, "Anyone home?"

"Back here, Dad. Just getting Aida settled." Tucker released a nervous breath. "I want to tell you everything. Just not here. Not now."

My insides fluttered again. "Should I worry?"

"No, Bambi. Not with me. Never with me."

I believed him. Hell, I trusted him. With my heart, with my life. Another truth I found difficult to digest. "Okay, then. Another time."

"Soon," he rasped, squeezing my ass and pressing his lips to my stomach. "When we're alone."

I combed my fingers through his hair, trying to ignore the shiver tearing through me. Again, the moment was intimate. Too much so. Had he not been holding me, I might have floated away. I stepped back, freeing myself from his grip, shaking off the overwhelming urge to jump him, and stood at the end of the bed.

"This room okay?" Tucker asked, lifting the last of his mom's boxes off the floor. "The bed is bigger and softer than mine."

"It's perfect. My expanding backside thanks you." I smoothed my hand over the soft, ivory bedspread, stopping to admire the embroidered wildflowers. The room was bright, airy, and comfortable. Soft white walls, blue and gold accents throughout.

"I'm quite fond of that backside. Need to keep her comfortable." He winked and slipped through the open door, but not before saying, "Fuck the circumstances. You are my girlfriend."

I turned to follow when I heard the buzz of my cell phone. The phone that hadn't seen any action in days.

Oh God. It had to be news about my father. *Please be okay. Please be safe.*

I rifled through the suitcase, hands trembling, and, assuming it was Tango, answered before looking at the number. "Is it Dad? Is he okay?"

"Aida. Princess."

That voice. That fucking smug, silky smooth voice.

"How's our baby?"

Tucker

"How's that baby doing?" Mom asked, making herself comfortable next to Aida on the couch.

Aida blanched, her hands moving instinctively to her stomach. Her eyes darted to me, then back to Mom.

Something was off.

She'd been quiet all through dinner, and her hands had trembled every time she'd reached for her fork or glass.

We hadn't had a moment alone all evening, leaving me zero opportunity to probe.

"She's perfect," was Aida's unconvincing reply.

"And you're feeling okay?" Mom must've sensed something off, too.

Gotta love a mother's magical intuition.

Aida shot me another nervous glance then met my mother in the eye, forcing a smile, then faking a yawn. "Oh, yes. I feel good. Sleepy though. Think I'll call it a night."

I stood, offering a hand to help her off the couch.

"Good night, Lettie." She nodded to Mom, then turned to Dad. "Night, James."

I followed her down the hall and into her room, closing the door behind me.

"Spill it, Bambi," I said, grabbing her hand and turning her to face me.

Shit. She was pale.

"I got a call, just before dinner."

"Tango?" I asked.

"No."

I waited for her to elaborate. When she offered nothing but a vacant stare, I probed. "Who, then?"

"Rafael." The name left her lips in a choked rasp.

Painful raps knocked against my rib cage. "You sure?"

"Five hundred percent sure."

"Fuck. How the fuck did he get the number?"

"I don't have a clue. He asked how his baby was. When I didn't respond, he said I couldn't hide forever."

I watched her glassy eyes fill with worry. It pained me to see her shaken.

"Tucker. I thought my father had taken care of him."

"Where's the phone?"

She pointed to the nightstand. I snatched the cell and headed to my room, Aida hot on my heels.

"How dangerous is this Rafael?" I asked her over my shoulder, bringing up the call history.

"He was a dumb jock with a trust fund. Another one of Dad's pretty boy fighters. I won't bring this shit anywhere near Tango or his family. I won't do that. I need to go back to New York. I need to find out what the hell is going on."

I choked on the dry lump in my throat. "That's not going to happen."

"You don't understand. Dad would not abandon me. He wouldn't. Neither would Tito. It's been too long without any word. Something terrible has happened. I can feel it in my bones."

"Aida. Stop. Sit down and breathe for a sec."

"Tucker. I know he's a criminal. I know he's done terrible things, but he's my father. What if he needs me?"

"Aida." I grabbed her shoulders and nudged her toward the bed. "Calm the hell down. Your father has a damn army protecting him."

She sucked in a long breath, then released it nice and slow.

Click. Click. Click.

Click. Click. Click.

Aw, shit. Not the nails.

I pulled my cell out and dialed Tango.

He answered on the first ring. "Hey, Tuck."

"Aida's burner has been compromised."

"What do you mean, compromised?" I heard footsteps, then a door slam.

"She got a call from her ex."

"Rafael Turner? Tito told me that fucker had been terminated."

I ignored the *terminated* comment for the time being. "What do you know about him?"

"He was an up-and-comer in the fight circuit. I fought him a few times. Guy was good. Something was off, though. I always suspected he was holding back. Voltolini had a boner for him. Never understood why."

"Is the phone traceable?" I asked.

"No."

"Okay. Okay. That's good. I'm trashing it anyway."

"Tucker. Bring her back. I've got this. You shouldn't get involved."

"I am involved. You said it yourself; she's safer with me."

Silence. A few heavy breaths. "This shit is not sitting well. Still haven't heard a word from Tito. It's not like him."

Tango was as concerned as Aida. He couldn't hide the emotion in his voice.

"You worry about your cousin. I'll worry about Aida. We'll be off the grid for a few days."

With a sigh, Tango conceded. "Sorry you were pulled into this, brother."

I wasn't sorry. Not in the slightest.

"Any word on the guys who jumped me outside the diner?"

Tango huffed. Papers shuffled. "Roger Caldwell ran their license plate. Owner of the truck is Jonas Carver. His father, Jeremy Carver, heads a church out of Hatfield. White supremacist posing as a Christian leader. They have a small following. Jonas has been in and out of the system, small things—vandalism, trespassing. As of last year, aggravated assault and battery. Charges didn't stick."

"His violence is escalating."

"Roger and two of his guys paid a visit to Jonas's trailer home about thirty miles north of town. The place had been emptied like he'd left in a hurry. Haven't seen them around. Not sure what that means, but I've hired a few extra men to keep an eye out. I don't think they'll be back, Tuck. They're punk kids with misdirected anger issues. That being said, I've amped security at The Stop and the house anyway."

"Good. Good." I glanced over my shoulder. Aida watched me with wary eyes.

Click. Click. Click.

"I'll be in touch in a couple days." I ended the call and turned to face the worried woman sitting on my bed.

Squatting at her feet, I pulled her frantically working hands apart to hold them in my own. I'd always thought Aida's eyes were the most deceiving part of her. I realized then, her hands held more deception. Small, delicate, soft. No one would ever suspect how strong they were. How capable. How deadly. No one would know until they cowered beneath the power of those ten slender, perfectly manicured fingers.

I knew.

I loved her hands.

I loved that, despite the power, strength, and skill she possessed, knowing Aida could take care of herself, and then some, knowing she'd been raised to out-think, out-maneuver, out-fight any adversary, she yielded so freely to me.

Aida Voltolini had been born into a life that would break most.

Unbendable as she was, I sensed that she wanted to break free.

She didn't want the same life for her child.

I suspected that maybe, just maybe, given enough time in my world, Aida would see—no, Aida would *choose* another life, my life, over the dark and dismal that awaited her back home.

Her soul and the soul of her child depended on her separation from all things Voltolini. Damn, how I wanted to be the man who drew her out of the dark.

As I kissed her delicate knuckles, and helped her to her feet, and led her back to the guest room, a peace fell over me.

I had a new purpose. A new mission. Aida.

I knew what I had to do.

Aida

I knew what I had to do. Unfortunately, I couldn't do anything until Tucker went to sleep. As much as I loved that he'd kicked off his shoes and settled next to me on the bed—him on top of the comforter, me tucked tightly underneath—as much as I coveted the warmth of his body, the musk of fresh air and motor oil that clung to his skin, as much as I enjoyed the soothing rasp of his voice while he read some ridiculous pregnancy book to me, courtesy of his mother, I could not bring myself to relax.

A call from Rafael, but no word from Tito or my father, meant my family was in trouble. Trouble I had most likely caused. I had to right my wrong.

I needed to leave.

I'd scoped out every possible escape route in the house. *Thanks, Dad, for drilling that skill into my brain.* I'd taken note of the household vehicles, where the keys were kept, which set belonged to which car. I knew the front door opened quietly, while the back door stuck in the left corner, squeaking every time it opened. I knew I would not fit through the bathroom window. Tucker's bedroom window had been painted shut.

Tucker's Jeep had a tracker, one that had been modified, so I couldn't risk stealing his car. Lettie's truck was the best option, being as James's Ford was tucked nice and safe behind a garage door that was entirely too loud when it lifted.

Tucker read to me, about what was happening to my body and what to expect in the second trimester. I faked a yawn, rolled to my side, and pretended to fall asleep. He continued to read. For crying out loud, the guy was into the baby-brewing shit. He hadn't even noticed I'd fake passed out. Soon, his dreamy voice, along with the boring script, lulled me to slumber.

I woke with a start. A large hand caressed my stomach. Warm lips pressed against my left temple.

"Good night, Bambi," Tucker whispered before rolling off his side of the bed. "I'll take care of everything, I promise."

He landed another kiss on my cheek, and it took all my will power not to turn around and pull him on top of me.

He wanted to take care of me. Problem was, only I could take care of me. And I didn't want Tucker pulled any closer to my ugly life.

I listened to his footsteps and waited for his bedroom door to close. Fighting the pull of exhaustion, I set my alarm for one hour.

It beeped all too soon.

My foggy head begged for more sleep. My guilty conscience forced me upright.

The house was dead silent, and the only thing I could hear was my own heartbeat tapping a warning against my chest, *don't do this, don't do this.*

I had no choice.

I'd fallen asleep in my clothes, so I grabbed my suitcase and my shoes, and tiptoed out the door and down the long hallway. Lettie's car keys would be in her purse, which I'd noted earlier that evening had been left on a chair between the front door and the coat closet. I rifled through her private belongings, searching for the keys. When I found them, I mumbled a *thank you, thank you, thank you,* to no one in particular.

My stomach soured. God, I hated abusing her trust—their trust—that way.

I didn't slip my shoes on until I'd reached the last step of the front porch. Heart in my throat, I dashed to her truck. I heaved my things, then myself into the massive vehicle and put the keys in the ignition. I started the engine and rolled down the long driveway, praying I hadn't woken anyone.

I drove into the darkness, and it wasn't long before I found highway signs leading me east.

Leading me home.

CHAPTER 8

Tucker

WHILE MOST PEOPLE SLUMBERED peacefully in warm houses, under warm blankets and soft pillows, young girls, desperate for the temporary warmth of a cab, or their next fix, offered themselves for dirty money they'd never get to spend. Beautiful girls made ugly, so fat, balding pedophiles, selfish and loathsome, could blow their loads, and pretend their lives hadn't gone to shit.

If I hadn't a moral compass, I'd kill them all.

For the time being, Carl, as the man had introduced himself over the radio wave, would have to take the brunt of my rage. I hit him one more time, for good measure, tied and gagged him, then dropped him like the piece of shit he was, into the tall grass behind his Lonestar.

I climbed behind the driver's seat and settled in. The evening air held a nasty bite, yet the prowlers came out anyway, dressed in low-cut blouses, heels, and jeans that never fit right.

Pulling the lid of my cap lower, I hunkered deeper into my seat, hugged my jacket tighter around myself, and waited, watching.

The right girl would show. She'd be easy to recognize. Young. Awkward. Eyes vacant and hopeless.

I thought of Aida. Ached to be in bed with her. Imagined her naked and underneath me. Fuck, I needed to hold her.

But the call had been too strong. Before I could wholly commit to Aida, I needed to hunt.

One more girl, I told myself.

Get them out of my system. Purge the venom. Be clean for the beauty waiting for me at home.

As if hearing my silent plea, a small brunette, wearing leather boots, a mini-skirt, and a ratty, faux fur coat buttoned tight around her neck, hobbled out from behind a blue minivan.

When she hesitated, eyes darting from one truck to another, I knew she was the one. The one "Carl" had called for. My hopes were confirmed when another girl gave her a firm push from behind, pointing into the lot and barking directions in her ear.

A virgin.

Before another fucker could lay claim, I flashed my lights, signaling for her to come my way. The woman pushed her again before retreating to the passenger side of her vehicle.

I watched the child place one foot in front of the other, slow, hesitant, and not convincing in the slightest. Knobby knees, wobbly ankles, and hunched shoulders betrayed her age. I guessed fourteen.

Definitely a virgin.

My scars tingled with painful pinpricks. I shifted, adjusting my cock to relieve the ghost pains. When she approached, I rolled down my window.

"Hi." Her voice, so soft and timid, made my blood boil. "Carl?"

When she leaned closer, placing a trembling hand on my door, I damn near lost my shit. So young. So soft and pink, and fucking innocent.

"I. Um. You want—"

No time to waste. The poor thing was terrified.

"What's your name?" I asked, forcing a ton of calm and cool into my voice.

"Misty," she replied with a quiver.

"You pick that name, or did they give it to you?" I nodded toward the van that had moved deeper into the shadows of the lot.

"I, uh. I picked. I mean." She swallowed hard and shook her head. "That's my name."

"Get in." I popped the latch on my door, and she moved to the side while it swung open. I hopped down, offering my friendliest smile and gesturing for her to climb in.

Misty looked over her shoulder, toward where the minivan had been waiting, before hoisting herself up.

Her captors had driven deeper into the lot, out of sight, but I couldn't shake the feeling we were being watched.

As she stepped up, a bare pussy flashed from underneath her sorry excuse for a skirt. *Fuck.* I bit my lip to keep from shouting profanities and climbed in behind her.

She sat, knees pinched together, arms tucked tightly against her sides, fingers curled into the edge of the passenger seat. I turned my bucket seat to face her, then turned her chair, bringing us face to face, and lifted her chin to meet my gaze.

"This your first time? I want the truth, not what they told you to say. It's okay."

"Yes," she mumbled.

Thank God. I wanted to smile, but I held it together for Misty's sake.

"You carrying a weapon? A gun. Knife. Taser. Anything?"

"No," she said, licking her lips and clutching her purse.

"Mind if I check?"

She pulled the handbag tighter to her chest. "Why?"

Now was the time to inject some real fear into her. I stood and slid my jeans and underwear down past my hips, lifted my shirt and jacket, and held my flaccid penis out of the way. "This happened when I didn't check a girl first."

She leaned closer, eyes widening and filling with tears at the sight of my scars. Misty backed into the door behind her, shaking her head. "I have pepper spray, but I promise, I don't want to hurt you." She reached behind her for the door handle.

It wouldn't open. I'd jimmied the locks earlier.

I had to work fast. The fucking driver I'd beaten unconscious would wake soon. "We don't have much time," I said, dropping back into my seat. "They're watching us." I pointed out the window. "They'll keep an eye on you. Only, it's not you they care about, Misty. I could do horrible, vile things to you right now, and no one would come to your rescue. I could make you suck my mutilated cock, I could fuck you hard, until you're bleeding and sore, or I could just beat the shit out of you. You could scream, and cry, and beg for help, but no one would come. They only care about the money."

Tears poured down her face, her cheap mascara drawing creepy lines down her cheeks.

I hated spouting such ugly words at a child, but I'd learned early on that cold, hard truth was what these babies needed most. No coddling.

Fear was the most reliable and effective motivator.

I lifted my syringe from the dash. "Now tell me, Misty, how old are you?"

"Fifteen," she cried. "I'm fifteen. They made me say I was fourteen. You asked for a fourteen-year-old. I didn't want to lie, but they said they'd kill my mom and baby sister if I messed up." Her gaze darted back and forth, from the syringe to my face, and finally landed on the needle. "Please don't hurt me. Please."

"Shh. Shh." I wrapped my fist around her skinny arm and pulled her toward me.

Although the cab was cloaked in darkness, I couldn't be sure if they were watching from the van. It was important to make it look as though Misty was performing as directed.

"Get on your knees."

"No. Let me out. I want to go. I don't want to do this."

Bile rose in my throat as I gripped her shoulders and forced her to the floor. "This will all be over before you know it."

Good for her, I thought as she fought against me. Her lanky frame was scarcely a challenge, but she put up a good fight, and the fighters had often proved to be the most rewarding.

I yearned to hug, comfort, and tell her everything was going to be okay.

Instead, I drove the needle into her thigh and pushed the plunger.

Misty struggled for freedom, slapping my hands away. As the sedative took hold, she collapsed, temporarily at peace. I guided her head into my lap and brushed tangled hair off her face. "I'm sorry, sweet girl," I whispered.

A heavy guilt blanketed me, causing me to question my actions. I shrugged the emotion away, scooped the unconscious child off the floor, and laid her in the small bed in the back of the cab.

Aida

So, as it turned out, sneaking away in the middle of the night while pregnant, wasn't the wisest of plans. Such was my nature. Acting on impulse. The very thing that had landed me in my unfortunate predicament.

I had to pee like nobody's business. I was exhausted. As much as I wanted to put distance between me and Tucker, as much as I needed to get back to my father, I knew that if I didn't pull over and catch some sleep, I'd be a danger to myself, and anyone I shared the road with.

That's how I ended up at the Lovelace Truck Stop, off Interstate 94, sixty-something miles east of Billings.

I pulled into the line of pumps and filled the tank. I used the facilities, which, to my horror, were not much more pleasant than the porta-potties at the fair. After scrubbing my hands twice, I pulled Lettie's truck around back to where at least twenty semi-trucks were parked, and found a spot in the far corner of the lot, out of sight.

I'd snuggled in and had been about to close my eyes, when I caught a sight that disturbed even me.

A young girl climbed out of a light blue minivan. Short skirt, high heeled boots that she'd yet to master, and a horrible, synthetic fur jacket. She was scared. Terrified even. When she hesitated, another girl came up behind her and pushed her forward.

Curling my fingers around the steering wheel, I squeezed tight, forcing my anger into the plastic.

Sure, it was hypocritical of me to be angry. I had, after all, taken care of my father's escorts for years. However, Dad's women were just that—women. Not girls. Not innocents like this child being forced into the cold night, apparently against her will, by another child who couldn't have been much older.

Instinctively, I felt for my knives, an unholy rage churning in my guts.

Up ahead, parked in the dark shadows much like myself, a large sleeper cab flashed its lights. The girl headed that direction, struggling to remain composed, and upright.

I watched, whispering to myself, "Don't do it. Please. Turn around and run." Bile rose in my throat. Blood pounded a daunting rhythm in my head. I had to stop her. I had to do something.

I gripped the key, still in the ignition, unsure of my next step, knowing only that if she were my daughter, I'd want someone to help. I was about to start the engine, when the truck door opened and a tall, shapely man wearing a baseball cap stepped down. Red flannel jacket. Faded jeans. Heavy boots. A silhouette too familiar.

I leaned closer, squinting to get a better look—as if that would help in the dark. At the same time, the man turned his head my direction, and I caught sight of his face.

A face I knew all too well.

The face of a man I had left behind a little over an hour ago. Or so I'd thought.

My stomach cramped. The truck was all at once too hot and too small.

No. No way. It couldn't be him.

Dumbstruck, I watched as he climbed into his cab behind her. I couldn't discern their features, but the outline of their bodies told a vivid story. Sickening as it was, I couldn't turn away.

After a short conversation, or transaction, as it appeared, Tucker stood and freed his cock from his pants. The girl, clearly not excited about giving head, backed away.

Tucker sat back down, forced her to the floor, and although I couldn't see what was happening below the dash, I knew what came next.

My body vibrated with disgust, heartache, and vile, vile rage.

I knew he'd been hiding something.

I didn't know it would destroy me.

Fucking pedophile perverts. Fucking lot lizards. Fuck me for caring.

I barely made it out of the truck before I vomited something fierce. When the heaving stopped, I searched Lettie's vehicle for a weapon. Found nothing. So, I picked up the largest rock I could hold in my hand and headed toward the cab, hell-bent on bashing his fucking skull.

I'd covered half the distance between us when Tucker's Jeep pulled out from behind the cluster of pine trees directly behind the eighteen-wheeler. When he passed under a street light, I could see his face clear as day. The girl was slumped in the passenger seat, head resting against the window. "Fuck!" I screamed. What the hell was he doing?

I ran back to the truck, turned the ignition, and followed behind.

I'd trusted that man. I'd given more of myself to him than I'd given anyone.

I'd never experienced an ache so deep. In my flesh. In my bones. Soul-deep and unbearable. It was only putrid anger that kept me from crumpling into a blubbering heap of pathetic female emotion.

I didn't want to believe what I'd seen, or admit I could've been wrong in trusting Tucker. I didn't want to live with this ... heartbreak.

Oh God. I'd turned into a girl. I'd gone soft. Aida from six months ago wouldn't have hesitated. She would've stormed into that cab and sliced the child rapist to pieces, no hesitation, no questioning what she'd witnessed with her own eyes.

So, when Tucker's Jeep turned onto the on-ramp heading west, back toward Billings, I stepped on the brake, and paused to consider my options. Should I head east toward home, to the familiar, or west, to pain, to answers, to saving a kid who wasn't my responsibility?

Shit. The girl.

I couldn't abandon an innocent, helpless child.

I followed them west, knowing that when I caught up, I might have to murder the very man I'd almost lost my heart to.

Good thing I hadn't fallen in love with Tucker.

Love was bullshit.

Tucker

"You're bullshitting me."

"No, son. Your mother's truck is gone. Lola was going ballistic, woke us up scratching to get outside. You weren't in your room. Aida wasn't in hers. Where the hell are you?"

"Took a drive. Had some thinking to do."

"And Aida?"

"Not sure, Dad. But I'll find out. Don't worry. Tell Mom I'll get her truck back."

Fucking Aida. Fucking hell.

I should've known she'd bolt. Damn. Not what I needed at the moment. I regretted smashing her cell phone. I regretted leaving her bed.

I did not regret Misty, though.

She was the last, or so I told myself, which made it imperative I finished what I'd started.

I was done with the girls. No matter how many nights I hunted, how many innocents I plucked from the dark shadows, how many times I held them and told them it would be okay, it did nothing to ease the heavy burden of guilt. They weren't Nicki. They couldn't erase the stain she'd left on my soul.

I had to let her go. Let them go. Move on.

I pulled up the long, dark drive leading to the Compton estate. The willows that lined the path were hauntingly beautiful in the dark, and as I neared the three-story home, my nerves tingled, and I winced at the flood of memories that struck hard every time I delivered my offerings to the couple whose daughter I had killed.

I hadn't alerted Christopher that I was coming, so his state of undress, disturbing as it was, didn't surprise me. Long, plaid robe. White wife beater stretched over a hard, round belly. Boxers that hung crooked over skinny white legs. White hair that stuck straight up on one side. Shotgun raised, butt to his shoulder, nuzzle to my face.

"Tucker." He lowered the weapon, scratched his head, and peeked out the door, checking the property to the left and then the right. "Shit. Wasn't expecting you. What time is it?"

"Don't suppose you have any vacancies?"

"Of course I do. Always prepared for these beautiful babies." He moved to the side, opening the door to make room, eyes widening at the sight of the still unconscious girl in my arms. "She's a young one, isn't she?"

"Fifteen. Scared as hell. Still a virgin, far as I can tell."

"Kill the perp?" He asked me the same question every damn time.

I always gave him the same answer. "No."

"You should have."

He gave "Misty" another once-over before closing the door. "Good catch, Tuck. Good catch. Mama will be thrilled."

"Don't think they've shot her up with anything yet," I added, following Christopher down the long, narrow hallway and toward the short stairwell leading to what once, lifetimes ago, were servants' quarters. "No track marks, eyes were bright, but I'd like the doc to give her a quick check as soon as possible. Don't think she's a flight risk, but stick to protocol on this one, Chris."

He opened a door, and I carried Misty inside and laid her down on the full-size bed. Drawing a deep breath, I reached down to brush tangled hair off her face.

God. She was beautiful. Like Nicki. Before they'd destroyed her.

Pressing a kiss to Misty's forehead, I closed my eyes and whispered, "Take care of yourself, baby girl. You're one of the lucky ones."

I stood and headed out of the room with Christopher hot on my heels. When he closed the door, I turned to face his warm, hazel eyes. "I'm done," I grunted. "She's my last."

Christopher cupped my shoulder with a hearty smack. "You said that after the last one, and the one before that." He dropped his hand, tilted his head, and studied my face. "Although, something in your eyes tells me you mean it this time." He scratched his chin, smirked, turned and headed up the stairwell. "You never did have the stomach for it. And that's okay. You've atoned for sins that were never yours. You've done a good thing here. And if you never carry another girl through these doors, know that Mama and I will be okay."

I heard the familiar shuffle of slipper-clad feet coming our way. Marleen "Mama" Compton barreled toward me with arms spread wide and a large bosom that bounced beneath the loose fabric of her nightgown. No modesty. Didn't matter. Mama was the kind of woman you loved regardless. And no one on Earth gave better hugs. Made me almost forget that she once gave me a shiner for leaving a hickey on her daughter's neck.

"Tucker. Why didn't you call? I would've had your room ready. Were you hunting, or just on a run?"

"Wasn't planned. Kind of just happened. Snatched a good one. You'll like her. She'll be awake soon. I'd stay, but Dad just called, got a problem at home, need to run."

"Oh." Her smile faltered, only for a second before she righted it. "Well. I hope everything is okay. I better head downstairs then."

Every time Mama looked at me with those deep brown eyes, whether smiling or sad, my heart bled. Aside from the grey hair, and the twenty pounds of curves she'd earned since the accident, she was the spitting image of Nicki.

My hands trembled as I pulled Mama close and kissed the top of her head. I hated leaving almost as much as I hated the memories that plucked my nerves when I walked through the old house.

"I'll walk you out," Christopher said, curling his fingers around the back of my neck. I avoided looking at the eight-by-ten portrait of Nicki perched on the fireplace mantle. Guilt would strangle me, as it always did, and I'd have no choice but to head back into the night and hunt for another child.

When we reached the front door, I gave Christopher's hand a shake, then pulled him in for a hearty hug.

I wanted to tell them about Aida. I ached to share my joy with them. But it seemed a betrayal, as much as logic told me it wasn't. I'd killed their daughter. The girl I'd once thought I'd marry. Her death was on my hands, burrowed into my conscience, despite their protests to the contrary.

So as much as I wanted to share the news, that I'd allowed myself to move on, that another woman had pierced my shell, I pressed my lips together. With a smile in my heart, but absent my face, I headed into the foyer.

Eyes forward, one step at a time.

Toward a new future, a new purpose, a new me.

To Aida. Wherever the hell she was.

"Where the hell is the girl?"

For the second time that night, I found myself staring down the nuzzle of Christopher's rifle. Only this time, a goddamned five-foot-two, doe-eyed, and by the looks of her, pissed off mafia princess was holding the gun.

I'd never been so turned on in my life.

Aida

I'd never been so disgusted in my life. That was saying a lot considering my history.

I'd followed Tucker to the large white house and watched him carry the unconscious child inside with some half-naked, geriatric perv.

Naturally, I had followed, considering I now had two men to murder and one girl to save. Idiots had left the front door unlocked, not that it mattered because I could bypass any lock. So, I let myself in, surprised to find a gorgeous, well-kept home. Also, a loaded rifle. Which came in handy.

Tucker didn't seem surprised by my break-in. In fact, the asshole seemed pleased, judging by the depth of his dimples.

"Where's the fucking kid?" My arms shook, vibrating with rage.

"Aida." Tucker huffed. "What the hell are you doing here?"

The old man stepped back, snapping his hands up in surrender, unconsciously exposing himself, his flaccid dick peeking through the opening of his loose hanging boxers.

The scene distracted me enough to allow Tuck an opening. He lunged my way, reaching for the barrel. I dodged, shifting my hold on the Arrieta and swinging the butt, hitting my mark with a sickening crack.

Tucker stumbled backward, then fell on his ass, shaking the walls and floor of the old home.

I righted the gun at my shoulder, aiming at Grandpa. "Where the fuck is the girl?"

Holding his head, and struggling to find his bearings, Tucker shouted, "Jesus, Bambi. Put the gun down." He tried to stand, but only made it to hands and knees, grimacing. A trickle of blood trailed down the side of his face.

"You make a move, Tucker, Grandpa gets a hole in his skull."

"Tuck," Grandpa said, a bit of humor in his voice. "Mind telling me what's going on here?"

Tucker mumbled a few *fucks* combined with other colorful words, and slowly rose to his feet.

My heart raced a million miles a second. "Sit down, Tucker. I swear to God, I'll shoot this man, then I'll rip your fucking heart out with my bare hands."

Tucker ignored my command, rising to full height, his cheeks, hell, his whole face as red as the wool of his jacket. "Christopher. I'd like you to meet my..." His gaze darted to me, then dropped to the floor. With a huff and a head shake, he mumbled, "This is my girlfriend."

The old man started to laugh. Tucker joined in.

So, I shot him.

And because I was being punished by the gods of mindless bimbos, because I had my head stuck up my ass over a fucking man of all things, I missed my target.

Okay. I missed on purpose, leaving a nasty mess in the bookshelf behind the laughing bastard.

Shut him up, though. The old Aida would've put a hole in his gut, most likely the area south of his navel. Instead, I stood there like a dumbass, while two child molesters treated me like the joke of the day.

Crazy part? Neither one of them flinched. Although, Old Man Limp Dick did slap his hands over his ears.

"Aida, lower the gun. This is all a huge misunderstanding."

"I'm not moving until you bring me that girl."

"I can't do that."

"You can. You will." I sucked in a breath, trying to make sense of the chaos. "And tell Grandpa to hide his sausage; it's distracting."

Christopher righted his Fruit of the Looms like it was nothing.

The shuffle of feet echoed through the hallway. "Christopher. For the love of all that's holy, what did I tell you about that damn rifle? You okay? Did you break a hip chasing that damn 'coon again?" A tall woman came around the corner. Long silver hair, silk robe over a too-tiny chemise, frilly pink slippers. Worry wrinkling her brown eyes. Beautiful. Not at all someone I'd expect to be involved in a child sex ring. She stopped dead when her eyes found mine. "Oh."

"Mama," Christopher spit through new fits of laughter. "This is Tucker's girlfriend, Aida."

"Girlfriend?" she said, popping a huge grin.

"I'm not his girlfriend. Someone tell me what the hell is going on here. Where's the girl?"

"What girl?" the woman asked, not at all convincing with her feigning ignorance.

I turned toward a chuckling Tucker. "The girl I watched you fuck in that truck. The girl I watched you drive away with and carry into this house." That put an abrupt halt to the laughing.

"Aida. What you saw..." He cleared his throat, scratched the top of his head. "What I did with. Wait. What the hell were you doing at The Lovelace?"

"Never mind that. The girl?"

Tucker planted his hands on his hips. "Chris, Mama, you mind giving us a minute?"

"Nobody's moving a muscle until I see that girl with my own two eyes."

Chris and Mama completely ignored me and scampered off, disappearing behind a door at the other end of the room.

Tucker charged, hellfire in his eyes, moving faster than I'd ever seen, disarming me, leaving me empty-handed, and dizzy. Before I could make sense of what had happened, my cheeks were captured between his massive palms, and he smashed his lips against mine. I tried, in vain, to pull away.

Tucker held me tight, kissing my mouth, my nose, my forehead. "First of all, hello. Nice to see you. Second, don't ever hit me again. And third, you're wrong about everything." Dropping his hands, he stepped back, giving me space. "This is a safe house. I know what you think you saw, and I understand why that would upset you. I had to make it look like I was using her, in case the fuckers that threw her to the wolves were watching. How the hell could you think I'd do something like that?"

I dodged his question completely. "Safe house?"

"Yeah. Christopher and Mama ... um, Marleen, run an underground shelter. Nobody knows about our operation, not my parents, not Slade, no one."

"This is what you do when you disappear for weeks?"

"Mostly."

"I don't understand. Why keep it a secret?"

"Because the girls we help don't always want to be found, and what the Comptons do here, although successful, is not legal."

I pondered his simple explanation, my head swimming with questions—too many for me to form into any coherent order. I wanted to believe him. God, I wanted his explanation to be truth, but anger and adrenaline still pumped through me with vicious resolve. My hands trembled, heat blasted my cheeks, and I still had the rancid taste of vomit in my mouth.

"I need to see her, Tucker. I need to see she's okay. Please. I've never been so angry, just let me see with my own eyes that the girl is safe."

"You don't trust me." His chin dropped low, shoulders slumped on a long sigh. "Fine. We have to ask Mama first. Her house. Her rules. She's very protective of the girls."

Tucker

"I'm protective of you, too, Tuck." Mama Compton peeked her head around the corner. "That's why I insist you sleep here tonight. It's too late to drive home. You can take the big room." She came my way and planted a dry towel and a frozen bag of peas in my hand.

I wasn't surprised she'd eavesdropped on our conversation. The mother-hen was notorious for knowing everyone's business.

"My house is only ten miles away," I reminded her, wrapping the bag in the towel, then pressing it to the throbbing bump on my head.

"Shush." She silenced me with a wave of her hand. "You head upstairs, get washed up, and I'll take Aida downstairs to see Misty."

I wasn't about to let Aida out of my sight. "How 'bout I come down with you."

Fists to hips, she scolded me, "You know the rules. You drop 'em off … they don't see your face again."

Arguing with Maureen was never a wise idea. However, I'd rather suffer a Mama rebuke than give Bambi the chance to split again. "I'll wait in the hall."

Aida cussed under her breath before stating, "He wants to keep an eye on me."

Smart girl.

"Fine." Mama flapped a hand in the air, shaking her head as if she'd had enough of us already, and headed downstairs. "Christopher told me this was your last rescue, Tuck. He thinks you mean it this time."

"I do. I'm done," I said, following close behind the ladies.

"That's good." She reached over and grabbed Aida's hand, giving it a squeeze, pretending she needed help navigating the narrow steps.

I knew what she was up to. Forming an alliance. Damn woman had been pushing me to move on for years.

"It's time you live your life. We've got plenty to keep us busy around here. Remember Santana?"

"Course I do." I remembered every girl I brought to the Comptons.

"She brought two sweethearts in last month. One of them was even clean."

Mama stopped and turned on her heels, hands cupped over her heart. "And they're such good girls, Tuck. So beautiful, so grateful, and happy to be off the street. One of 'em is back with her family, safe and sound. The other, well, we didn't catch her in time. Poor thing has been through hell the past year. We'll get her clean, start therapy. No one's looking for her, far as we can tell.

"So, then what?" Aida asked. "What if they have nowhere to go?"

"We take them in. Get them clean, first. That's always the biggest obstacle. Then? Give them a new start, a new chance at life."

"And if they don't want to get clean?" Aida asked.

"We don't give them a choice, dear. We don't give them a choice."

Aida shot a look at me over her shoulder, brows raised in understanding.

For all intents and purposes, I was kidnapping the girls from their kidnappers. The Comptons and their team of professionals worked hard to get the girls clean of their drug habits, willing or not, and helped them get home, if they had a safe home to return to.

"Here we are," Mama said, slipping a key into the lock. She waved me back, away from the door.

I rested a shoulder against the wall, pulled my cell out of my pocket, and pretended to be otherwise occupied while Aida and Mama slipped into Misty's new room. My stomach twisted when I heard Mama say in her soothing voice, "Oh, good. She's awake," before shutting the door behind her.

I texted Dad, let him know I was with Aida and that we'd be home in the morning. I checked my work emails, paced the wood floor. Then I got busy researching Rafael Turner, disappointed, but not surprised to find that he didn't exist in Google world.

The last thing I wanted to do was call in a favor, but I didn't have a choice. I needed to know how big a threat Turner posed. I sat in the stairwell, out of earshot, and made a call I'd never thought I'd have to make.

I ended my convo as Aida came out of Misty's room, eyes red and soggy.

"So?" I asked, eager for her reaction, standing back and tucking my phone into my pocket so as not to seem overly enthusiastic.

"So. I owe you an apology." The tough little shit fought hard not to lose composure, chewing her lip, blinking rapidly.

"No. You don't. I would've jumped to the same conclusion had I been in your shoes." I grabbed her hand. "C'mon. Let's get some shut-eye." I led her up two flights of stairs and toward our room for the night.

The large boudoir boasted a four-poster bed, a floor-to-ceiling window that overlooked the Comptons' fifteen acres of land, pristine hardwood floors, and its own master bathroom. Framed art Mama had collected over the years decorated the walls. She loved to support local artists. This room, in particular, housed pieces from her favorite landscape artists, the colors on the canvas blending perfectly with the gold and mauve tones of the wallpaper and fabrics.

I watched Aida make her way around the boudoir, studying the paintings, feeling the heavy fabric of the drapes, peering through the window into the dark night. Avoiding me while I stood, helpless do anything but drink her in head to toe. Black silky hair, sinful curves, and that damn heart-shaped ass that taunted me with every step she took. God. The things I wanted to do to her.

"I'd love to know why you were sneaking off in the middle of the night."

Aida turned to face me, one hand still holding the gold jacquard curtain, the other resting on her stomach. "You're smart, Cowboy. Pretty sure you've figured it out by now."

"Tell me one thing." I closed the distance between us, braced my hands on the window behind her, and caged the petite firecracker between my arms. "Were you running from me, or toward home?"

Slow and hesitant, her doe eyes lifted to meet mine. Those fucking sexy lips parted on a soft exhale. Face to face, I absorbed the pelts of her soft breaths against my skin. Her cotton candy scent invaded my senses. My heart beat quickened, roaring through my veins, amplifying the pain in head, causing a ruckus behind the fly of my jeans.

Aida Voltolini. All hard edges, and soft, gooey middle. I'd make her mine. I'd make her see that I was where she needed to run—always.

I leaned closer, savoring the heat of her breath on my lips, craving a taste. Her eyes glazed, and I was about to take my fill when her mouth opened on a loud yawn.

"Oh my God, I'm sorry. Shit." She laughed, clapping a hand over her mouth. "Talk about ruining the moment.

Yeah. That was our cue. "C'mon. Let's get you to bed."

"Wait." She pressed a palm to my chest. "Don't you have something you want to say?"

I had so many words. Not one of them appropriate. "Like what?"

"Come on, Cowboy. Throw it at me," she said as I tugged her toward the large bed.

"Throw what?"

"The lecture. The guilt trip."

"We're both too tired for a heavy convo like that." I threw back the down comforter, revealing soft gold, inviting sheets. "Let's sleep. We can talk in the morning. Left side is mine, unless you have a preference."

"Um." Aida sucked her lips between her teeth and contemplated the bed.

"Well?"

"I guess not." Sleepy eyes met mine, and she shrugged. "I usually sleep dead center."

"Works for me." The closer the better.

"You're really not going to chastise me for sneaking away in the middle of the night? For stealing your mother's truck?"

"No. I get it."

"You do?"

"You're worried about your father. You don't like feeling helpless. You hate being out of the loop. You're used to getting your way. I get it. Thing is, Bambi, you are precious. Worth holding on to, worth chasing down in the middle of the night. You need to fight for your father. I need to fight for you. You run again, it wouldn't surprise me. Just know, I'll be hot on your heels."

Aida peeled off her cardigan, tossed it across the foot of the bed, toed off her shoes, and climbed in wearing leggings and a stretchy tight tank top.

I crossed the room, flicked the light switch, and returned to the bed, making myself comfortable on top of the blankets.

With a huff, Aida complained, "You'll get cold. Get under the covers with me. I won't bite."

Wasn't her I was worried about. "I might."

"I might like it if you bite."

"Aida, please. It's been a long day. I get under there with you, neither one of us will get the sleep we need."

"You're very sure of yourself, Cowboy. What makes you think I'm so easy?" she teased. "C'mon. I promise. No hanky-panky. Sleeping only."

Sighing in defeat, I rolled off the bed. So much for playing the gentleman.

I slid between the sheets. Heat coiled through me.

"Tucker," she whispered, rolling to face me, careful not to touch.

"Yeah?"

"Thank you for understanding."

She found my hand, in the small space between us, and curled warm, soft fingers around mine. That small gesture made my heart explode like the Grand Finale of the Fourth of July fireworks. Hot damn, how I wanted to act on that adrenaline rush.

She yawned.

Right. Sleep.

I stopped fighting the heavy weight of my lids.

The mattress was firm, the sheets warm and soft, and small fingers clung to mine.

I leaned closer and whispered, "Run all you want, Bambi. I'll always chase you."

CHAPTER 9

Aida

I WOKE TO A BRIGHT room, warm, achy, and with a full
bladder. Assuming Tucker was sound asleep behind me, I
slid out of bed, quiet and careful not wake him. Groggy, and
desperate for the toilet, I barreled into the bathroom, never
considering it might be occupied.

Holy hell, was it occupied. By a six-foot-something
naked man roughing a towel over his hair. Muscles taught.
Skin dewy.

A heady citrus scent enveloped me, making my senses
hyper aware of the glorious, sexual male on display.

He hadn't heard me enter the room.

My gaze fell like a lead weight to this erection. I knew
Tucker was big—long and thick. I'd held him in my hand,
through his pants anyway. What I didn't know, what I wished
I'd known, was that he was also grotesquely scarred, from a
few inches below his navel, down to the root and halfway up
his penis, and from what it appeared, with my quick glance,
the entire area surrounding his manhood. Scars resembling
a cracked windshield, crooked arms stretching multiple
directions.

I should have backed away—covered my eyes, turned
around, something, anything. Instead, I froze, horror stricken

by the grim facts clicking one by one into place, filling the last holes of the Tucker puzzle I'd been too slow at piecing together.

No wonder Tucker hadn't wanted to fuck me. Men and their pride.

I'd stabbed and scarred a man, in a man's most prized feature. I'd bragged, laughed even, about doing so.

All these months, Tucker had been hiding a horrific wound, while I'd been proud of inflicting one. What a sadistic bitch.

"Aida." Tucker snapped the towel to his crotch, covering the very thing I could never un-see. "Jesus. You scared the shit out of me."

Funny. He didn't seem embarrassed. Or devastated.

I was mortified.

"I. Um. I'm sorry. I. I. I had to pee ... didn't know you were in here. Oh God. I'm sorry."

Sorry for so many things.

God, he must think me cold and heartless.

I backed out of the small space, pulled the door closed, and dashed to the bed, slipping under the blankets, my back to the bathroom. Eyes pinched shut, I willed sleep, or a massive black hole, to swallow me whole. Take me away from the guilt and shame.

Sleep didn't come. Nor did I disappear into a dark abyss as I'd hoped.

I waited, heart thumping, for the unavoidable, uncomfortable conversation.

So, when Tucker came out of the bathroom, kissed my head, and whispered, "Bathroom's all yours, Bambi," before slipping out of the room, I didn't know whether to laugh or cry.

Laugh, because I'd dodged a bullet, at least for a little while, or cry because I wanted to know the intimate details behind those morbid scars. More so, I wanted Tucker to *want* to share those details, not just with anyone, but with me. Only me. I wanted that. Oh God. I wanted that. To the point my chest ached.

My heart not only ached. The moment the door clicked behind me, it cramped, in protest most likely, of things left unsaid, apologies left dangling on the tip of my tongue.

Or maybe, the sharp pain in my chest was merely, simply, caused by the sudden absence of a man I had fallen for.

Tucker

I'd fallen hard. How did I know? Because when Aida's wide-eyed gaze fell on my scars, my flaws, those incessant reminders of past sins and a future I'd long ago given up on, I hadn't been embarrassed. I hadn't been ashamed. I wasn't any less a man.

Damn, what a great feeling.

It was done. The hard part was over. Didn't go down as planned. But, such was the way of life.

Now, it was up to her to process. I figured she needed time alone to do just that. So instead of forcing the uncomfortable conversation, I walked around to where I'd left her laying, and dropped a kiss on her head. "I brought up your suitcase. I've got something to do. Be back in an hour."

I tucked the nerves away and willed my brain to carry me away from the beauty in the bed, because my heart wanted nothing more than to join her, bury myself in her soft, sweet warmth, seek comfort in her acceptance.

Funny thing, and confirmation that I'd fallen hard, was that I trusted her to process, and question, and work through the shock of seeing my dark and ugly without running for the hills.

We both had flaws, be them internal or external. In exposing my imperfections to Aida, I was free. I no longer had anything to hide.

Whether she could live with, lay with, want a man with my disfigurement, I would wait and see. I would be patient.

Because I had fallen that hard.

When I returned, an hour and a half later, Aida had changed clothes and tied her hair into a floppy mess on top of her head, revealing her long neck.

"Ready to hit the road?" I asked, grabbing her suitcase off the bed so as to keep my hands off those curves, and that enticing olive skin.

She'd avoided my gaze since I entered the room, busying herself with straightening the comforter, fluffing pillows, picking nonexistent lint off her sweater.

"Aida," I said, dropping the luggage and stepping deep inside her personal space.

Her attention remained on the floor between our feet.

Dipping low, I caught her lips with mine in a soft exchange, and hopefully, a reassurance.

Her gasp caught me off guard. Her compliance boosted my ego to the moon.

Too soon, she pushed me away, eyeing me warily, uncertain and completely out of character. "How?"

"How what?" I asked, missing her mouth already.

Her hands raised to my chest, palms flat. "How can you kiss me like that? How can you not hate me?" She stepped back and gestured to my crotch. "You obviously suffered something horrible. I stabbed a man in that same area, and bragged about it."

"What you did to Rafael has nothing to do with my scars. Physical or otherwise."

"Is that why ... Are those ... Your scars ... Are they the reason you haven't wanted to fuck me?"

"Partly," I lied. Truth was, I hadn't wanted her to destroy me.

Aida stepped closer, pressing against me once again, one hand on my chest, the other rubbing the scruff on my jaw. "Were you worried I would be turned off?"

"In the beginning," I confessed.

She hit me with a hard glare. "It doesn't bother me."

"You don't know how happy I am to hear that." I forced a smile.

"I mean, obviously, you're hung like a horse, so there's that. I happen to know from experience that the plumbing works."

"That's the thing. It doesn't work. Not like it should."

"You're sterile," she interjected, not a lick of sympathy in her voice, just cold, hard truth. "How did it happen?"

"Sit down," I said, cupping her shoulders and angling her toward the bed.

I sucked in a breath, for pause, for courage, then released it slow and steady. "You might find this hard to believe, but I wasn't always a nice guy. Ran with a rowdy group when I was a kid. Got into all kinds of trouble. Dad put me in martial arts, hoping to channel my energy, and it did."

Aida leaned back on her arms. "You were good at it, too, judging by the trophies lining your wall."

"Yeah. I was. Got cocky, though. Hurt a kid that'd messed with my girlfriend, Nicki."

"No shit. You? Cocky and overprotective?" she teased.

"After that incident, Dad enrolled me in military school. Shipped me off to Texas. I promised Nicki I would come back for her. When she disappeared halfway through her senior year, I came home and helped with the search. She was gone. Vanished into thin air. Fucked me up good—we'd been friends since kindergarten. She was my first kiss. My first everything. We never found her."

"That's terrible. I'm sorry."

"I joined the Marines fresh out of high school. Barely legal. Recruited into special ops straightaway."

"A Marine? Wow. I had no idea, Tucker."

"I don't like to talk about it. Heavy shit. Did my time, came home, went to work with Dad. His friend in the FBI heard I was home, asked if we'd consult with a local Child Exploitation Task Force he'd help put together."

I squatted at her feet and rested my hands on her knees. "You see, those lot lizards you were asking me about? Many of them are plucked off the streets as kids, forced into the life. So yeah, naturally, Dad and I helped. Let the feds use our trucks. We helped shut down two human trafficking lines. Pulled damn near one hundred women off the streets. Offered them shelter, education, jobs, fucking lifelines. Thing is, most of them didn't know anything better. They didn't have a safe home to return to, or couldn't beat their drug habits, ended up right back where they'd started, knocking on truckers' doors at three o'clock in the morning, offering their services. I couldn't do it anymore. It ate at me like cancer. I wanted to kill every fucker who paid for one of those girls. Wanted to skin the bastards alive who put them on the streets."

"I would've killed them," Aida chimed in. "After I'd fed them their own cocks for dinner. I was damn close to murdering you last night."

"Glad to hear we're on the same page."

"Me too." She reached out and brushed a knuckle down my cheek. Her face softened. "But you still haven't explained your scars."

I sat back on my ass, needing the solidity of the floor. "This is the fucked up part. About a year after pulling out of the task force, I was on a long-haul run, Missouri, about to tuck in for the night, when I watched a girl stumble out of a cab across the lot, clearly high, but also hunched over and having a hard time staying upright. She fell to her knees, vomiting something dark. Looked like blood. I dialed 911 and ran across the lot to help her. When I approached, I couldn't believe my fucking eyes. It was Nicki. Stick thin. Ratty hair. Eyes vacant. Bloody lip. She didn't recognize me. I'm pretty sure she didn't see me at all, she was so far gone. Same time I heard the sirens, girls started scrambling. Another woman screamed at me to get my hands off her friend. She thought I'd hurt Nicki. Started throwing punches, then tried to pull Nicki to her feet. Nicki cried out on pain, vomited more blood. I lost my shit, had nothing but murder on my mind. I headed for the cab Nicki had come out of. Fucker must've heard the sirens and was firing up his truck to split. Next thing I know, I'm in his cab, beating the shit out of him, while he's trying to drive away. Another driver had been shooting up in the back of the cab. Must've hit me over the head. I woke up in the hospital two days later.

"Oh my God," Aida breathed, eyes glassy and wide.

"Fucker was so high, he drove his truck over the side of an overpass. The driver and his partner both died. I escaped with my life and a gut full of twisted metal."

"And Nicki?" Aida asked, holding her stomach, face pale.

"Fucker ran Nicki and her friend over in the process. And it was my fault."

Aida pushed off the bed, knelt in front of me, and grabbed my chin like a mother scolding her child. "No. It wasn't."

"If I'd stayed with her, instead of going after the guy, she'd be alive. She'd be here, with her family."

"Here?" She studied my face.

I dropped my head and mumbled, "Yeah, Bambi. Nicki was Chris and Mama's daughter."

Aida fell back on her ass and rubbed a fist over her heart. "That's why they help the girls. That's why you rescue them."

"It happened by accident, really. My first run, after I'd recovered, I couldn't sleep. Sat up all night watching a couple of girls slither from cab to cab. Fucking killed me. These girls were daughters. Couldn't fathom how mothers and fathers would let this happen to their children, while people like me, could never be a parent. When I watched a young girl climb into a Mack with a man who had to be sixty, I decided to skip the legalities and get that child out of the fucking life. Choked the guy out, carried the girl, who was kicking and screaming something fierce, back to my cab and brought her here. Told Mama, *'You wanna help. Here's your chance. Make sure Nicki hasn't died in vain.'* Mama and Christopher took it from there. Saved thirty-six girls so far. One hundred percent success rate."

Aida sucked in a gasp, pushed to her feet, and towered over me, fisted hands landing on her hips. "You're the Rest Area Reaper they're talking about on the news."

I nodded.

Her gaze trailed the length of me, from crotch to chin, in a torturous perusal. The corners of her mouth lifted, and when her eyes finally met mine, she whispered in the sexiest damn growl I'd ever heard, "So, you're kind of a badass, then."

Swear to fuck, my universe imploded.

I don't know why I'd waited to tell her. I should've known she'd understand.

Aida

I didn't understand. How could Tucker, a man who rescued truck stop prostitutes, all of them children, be so kind to, so accepting of a woman who, in a sense, and not wholly by choice, exploited women. Because that was exactly what I'd done from the time I realized the women on my father's payroll were obligated to obey my every word. Be it directing them on the stage, or behind closed doors, I had been their Madame.

Madame. Nothing more than a pretty word for *pimp*. A pimp like the men Tucker wanted to murder.

In my defense, abuse of any kind toward Dad's women was forbidden and strictly enforced. Dad's girls were clean. No drugs, no alcohol. Freedom to come and go as they pleased. Each and every one of his dancers or escorts worked for Dad of their own free will. Most of them were happy with their jobs. If they weren't, I'd made sure any grievances were rectified, by any means necessary.

Sixteen was a young age to fall into such a position of power. Dad had recognized early on that I had a soft spot for his ladies, and to keep me busy, and under his thumb, he'd given me the job. Unofficially, of course. But the women respected my father, and, in turn, showed nothing but admiration for me.

No matter how I spun it, it didn't change the fact that Tucker and I clearly operated on opposite sides of a blurred moral line. He fought for the good guys. I was raised one of the bad.

Water and oil.

We would never work.

Although, until I'd met Tucker Slade, I hadn't considered myself morally corrupt. Mob life was all I knew. Until being immersed in small town sweet and innocent, I'd never had cause to question whether my existence was leaving a nasty stain, or brightening the world I'd occupied. My only concern had been staying on top of the food chain.

Tucker was cleansing, scrubbing gently at my tarnished pieces.

I only hoped I wouldn't muddy his soul in the process.

"We should head out." Tucker's gruff voice broke my reverie. "Got a lot of road to cover."

Deep blue eyes regarded me thoughtfully, and I couldn't help but feel a little less dirty.

"I'm sorry, Tucker. I'm sorry for sneaking out in the middle of the night. And I'm sorry for almost blowing your head off." I meant it, too. I didn't want to be the cause of grief in that sweet man's life. I'd acted on impulse, as was my nature, putting not only myself at risk, but my baby, too.

I had to trust that my father could handle his business.

Tucker curled an arm around my shoulder and dropped a kiss on my head. "All's forgiven, Bambi. Let's go. Got a surprise for you."

I followed Tucker downstairs and into the crisp, sunny Montana morning. Lifting my face to the vast, blue sky, I drew a deep breath and released my worry to the beauty surrounding me.

Tucker grabbed my hand and pointed to the end of the driveway. Frankie sat, shiny and proud, pinned to a massive, blue trailer.

"We're taking your truck? What about your Jeep?"

"Jeep is in the trailer." He strode with purpose toward the front of the vehicle.

I squealed with excitement when Tucker opened the door to his cab and Lola jumped out, stub tail leading the charge of her adorable butt shake. Ignoring Tucker altogether, the mini black bear wiggled and rubbed against me, nearly knocking me over with her enthusiastic greeting.

"Lola's coming home with us?"

"I was hoping she could stay at your apartment. You could keep each other company while I'm at work."

"I've never had a dog," I said, squatting to scruff Lola's face and accept her slimy kisses. "I don't know how to take care of her."

"Pretty sure she'll be the one taking care of you." Tucker skirted around us and hoisted my suitcase into the cab. He hopped back down and patted Lola on her butt. "She's never warmed to anyone the way she has with you. Dad told me she went ballistic when you left last night. Feels the need to protect you the same way I do."

I ignored that comment. Tucker knew I was well equipped to take care of myself. Still, I couldn't discount the warmth spreading through me. He wanted to keep me safe. Not for a paycheck or out of obligation, but simply because he cared for my well-being.

I rose to full height, fisted the collar of his jacket, then rolled up on my toes, meeting him nose to chin. "I know twenty different ways to kill a man with my bare hands. I don't need protection. But I like that you worry for me, Cowboy. I like it too much."

I captured his mouth before he could respond, moaning when his arms coiled around me and his tongue darted between my lips, making way for a deep, promising kiss. A kiss he broke all too soon by slapping my ass and ordering me into his truck.

I stepped up and shimmied my belly between the captain's chair and the steering wheel. The inside of the cab was large and shiny, mirroring the midnight blue and chrome of its exterior.

I stood between the seats and took in the beauty of his mini hotel on wheels. Stretched across the back of his cab was a full-size bed, covered in a midnight blue comforter. Black, quilted faux leather lined the walls surrounding the sleep area. A mini sink, oven and fridge claimed the wall directly behind the driver's seat. Behind the passenger seat stood a set of cabinets stained in black. Blue light trimmed the entire back interior.

"This is … wow. Gorgeous."

Tucker squeezed in behind me, dominating the small space, and slid his arms around my waist, resting his chin on my shoulder. "Aida, meet Frankie. My home away from home."

"You travel in style. I'm impressed."

Scruffy stubble scratched my cheek, inciting an embarrassing shiver. "We should hit it. Got a good ten hours driving time ahead of us."

I didn't want him to let me go. His strong arms warmed me, his breath in my ear soothed me. His hard body, for reasons I couldn't comprehend, smoothed my jagged edges.

Wrapping my arms around his and lacing our fingers over my growing belly, I tilted my head into his neck and inhaled his fresh, earthy scent. As I rubbed my palm over his knuckles, I felt a tickle, a palpitation, beneath our joined hands.

"Oh my God," I said with a gasp. "Did you feel that?"

"Was that her?" He flattened his hand over my stomach. "I felt it."

The baby moved again, another flutter stealing my breath.

"There she goes again," Tucker said with a laugh.

I choked on the emotion swelling in my throat and turned to catch his dewy eyes—not envious or sad for what he could never have, but completely, selflessly happy.

Tucker

Happiness was a moot point. Holding Aida in my arms, feeling her child move inside her, sharing an intimate moment, I knew deep that, happiness be damned, I would spend every waking moment for the rest of my life protecting that woman and her child. Whether she wanted me or not, I was all in.

Familial obligations weighed heavy on her mind, but I would do everything in my power to show her that family wasn't only blood ties. Family were the people who fought for you, who carried you through your worst, celebrated your best, loved you through the nitty-gritty ups and downs of life. Blood or not, family claimed you, held tight, and never let go.

When it came to Aida, I never wanted to let go.

Two hours into our drive home, conversation had dwindled, and I'd turned up the volume on the stereo. I glanced Aida's way every so often. When her lids closed, and her head lolled to the side, I thumbed through my iPod and pulled up my driving playlist. Old school rock, country, and a mix of Latin pop to keep things lively.

Great music. Open road. Aida by my side. Life didn't get much better.

Half an hour past Billings, I was deep in the zone, belting out the last chorus of Toby Keith's "You Shouldn't Kiss Me Like This."

"You have a sexy voice," Aida mumbled, stretching her arms over her head.

I reached over to lower the volume, but she slapped my hand away.

"No. Don't stop. I want to hear more."

"I'm not used to an audience." I reached forward again and muted the speaker.

Aida huffed. I was certain, if I looked, she'd would've been making a face or rolling her eyes.

"I heard you singing in the barn yesterday. It was beautiful." *Click. Click. Click.* "Before I went in, I thought you were singing to your girlfriend."

Heat rose in my cheeks, not at the memory of her catching my private moment, but at the recollection of the kiss we'd exchanged. "I didn't think anyone was around."

Aida drew a deep breath, then released it with one big burst of air. "I wanted it to be me you were singing to. God, how pathetic is that?" *Click. Click. Click.*

Her confession hit me like a knife to the chest, piercing me with a sharp pain, seizing my ticker. "Aida."

"Nobody has ever sung to me."

I had a hard time believing that story. "No one?"

"No," she whispered.

"That's a shame."

"Where'd you learn to sing like that? Did you take lessons, or is it a natural gift?" she asked, turning in her seat to face me.

"The television was rarely on at our house, but the radio? Twenty-four-seven. The house was never quiet. Mom used to sing me to sleep every night."

Her head fell to the side, leaning against the headrest. "I never knew my mother. Not even her name."

"I'm sorry. I can't imagine how hard that was."

"I always figured she was one of Dad's flavors-of-the-month. Maybe he got sloppy, knocked her up. When I was a little girl, and I'd ask about her, Dad always changed the subject. When I got older, if I dared mention my mother, he'd get angry and disappear with a bottle of bourbon. So, I stopped asking."

I tried to picture a young Aida with shiny hair, round cheeks, and eyes too big for her face. I couldn't imagine growing up without a mother's bosom to cling to, her kisses to make things better, or the sweet, soft sound of her voice sending her child off to dreamland. "Sorry, Bambi, but I think that's bullshit. You have every right to know who your mother is. Fuck's sake. He could at least let you know whether she's buried or breathing."

"I appreciate your concern, Tuck. I do. But you don't know my father. If he doesn't want me to know, he has good reason." Aida turned to face front again.

I didn't know her father. Didn't want to know the man who kept a child from her mother. "Again. Bullshit."

"We grew up in different worlds," she said to the passenger side window.

"I'm painfully aware of that, sweet thing."

"I like you, Tuck. I do. So much that my entire body aches sometimes. But you know we could never work, right? Not long term."

Fuck. She was finding excuses to bolt. "I disagree."

"Tucker," she said, voice oozing conviction.

"Aida. Listen. I see you. I see who you are under those thick layers of self-preservation. You're loyal. You're brilliant, and sexy, and mysterious. But you're also vulnerable. You're afraid of letting people in, of exposing your soft spots."

"Soft spots get people killed."

"Jesus. Listen to yourself." I paused for a breath, heat coiling in my gut. "Aida. You are a mother now. Regardless of your past, every day you have a choice. Every fucking day you wake up, you can choose to go back to that lifestyle, or you can choose better for your child."

"If I walk away, I have nothing. No father, no money, no home."

"You have me!" I yelled, slamming a palm on the steering wheel.

Her head whipped my direction. From the corner of my eye, I watched her chest rise and fall, her spine straighten.

"No, Tucker. I don't." She pointed a finger at her own chest. "I have me. I've always only had me."

"You have me, Aida." I shook my head in frustration.

"I can't have you, Tucker. Not the way I want."

"Why?"

"Because you'll be my soft spot. I let you in, you become a target. My father, his enemies, it never ends. Someone will always be after us, always lurking in the shadows, waiting to strike."

Bullshit.

"What about Rafael? Was he a soft spot?"

"No."

"Why?"

Aida gripped the sides of her chair. Poisonous silence billowed around us. When she dropped her head, I asked again, "Why?"

"Because I didn't care whether he lived or died. He was nothing but a good fuck."

Click. Click. Click.

Those damn nails. I held back the profanities itching to fly. I didn't know if she was trying to convince me, or herself, that we couldn't work. Either way, I wasn't having it, and I was about to tell her so, but she spoke first.

"Rafael lived the life. He knew the risks."

Fuck me, that was a low blow. "And I don't? Is that what you're saying? When you look at me, is that all you see, some small town dumbfuck with a boner for a mob princess? Jesus, Aida. Give me some fucking credit."

"No, Tucker. That's not what I see," she said, her volume rising. "What I see is a man who doesn't look right through me, but into me. I see a man who gets off on making me laugh. I see a man who would spend the rest of his life giving me soul-shattering orgasms while he slowly died of blue balls. I see a man who gave up six years of his life to take care of a sister he'd only just met. Someone who risks jail time to save girls who will never know his name. A man who would sacrifice his own morals, his happiness, to take care of a family that isn't his." Her hand cupped her stomach. "I don't want to be the woman who ruins you."

"Ruins? Aida. Listen to me. I've seen darker shit than you could possibly imagine. I've hiked through hell and back, carrying half-dead brothers over my shoulder. I look ruined to you?"

My cell buzzed, and the Bluetooth picked it up, projecting my call through the cab speakers.

I gave Aida the international signal for "shhh" before answering the call. "Johnson. Hey, bud."

"Slade. Good to hear your voice, man. When you coming back to work for me?"

"About the same time hell freezes over."

"Aw. You're breaking my heart."

"Take it you got my message."

"Yeah, Tucker. Listen, I couldn't find anything under the name Rafael Turner except some rough fight footage. You know me, though, love a good challenge, so I dug deeper. Even made some calls."

"And?"

"Got shut down. Not more than an hour after I hung up the phone, a couple of suits with higher security clearance than mine came for a visit. They were curious about my interest in Turner. Seemed to be fishing as much as warning me off any further inquiries into the guy."

"Shit."

"I don't need to tell you what that means."

"He's deep." I roughed a hand over the top of my head, hoping to dislodge some of the irritation that'd settled there. "Sorry to pull you into this."

"No worries. Sorry, friend. I can't go any further with this. Got a pension to protect."

"Understandable."

After ending the call, I shot a sideways glance to Aida. The glow on her face had nothing to do with pregnancy. I'd guess fury. Outrage. But hidden behind those red cheeks and fiery eyes? Fear. And rightfully so.

She'd connected the dots.

Rafael Turner was a goddamn undercover agent.

CHAPTER 10

Aida

I WAS IN HELL.

Treading lava in the deep end of Lake Hades. Barely holding my head above the spite-fueled flames searing me head to toe.

My family had been infiltrated. Manipulated. Set up. Unbreakable chains had fallen because of one weak link.

Me.

Rafael had played his part to a T. Brutal fighter. Check. Skilled lover. Check. Loyal dog. Check. Dear God, it was terrifying how easily he'd wormed inside the impenetrable Voltolini fortress. But to what end? Why such extremes to marry into a family he was supposed to bring down?

Unless.

Aw, shit. How could I have been so blind. The world blurred. My stomach coiled. The truth became so shamefully obvious—he'd gone rogue. Called to the dark side by avarice, or bloodlust. Or maybe that narcissistic sliver I'd once been attracted to had festered and spread its poison, filling him with fatal overconfidence. The fool had actually believed he had the power to overtake my father's empire.

Using yours truly—his magic cock and eager sperm the weapons of mass destruction.

Rafael Turner had planned to either dismantle or inherit my father's empire through a sham marriage.

Dad had known. It made sense, his eagerness to send me away rather than simply scold me. He'd had a plan for Rafael, and I'd screwed us all with my short fuse and lust for revenge.

It wasn't too late, though. I still had the power to right my shameful wrong. Rafael may have been undercover, his performance may have been Oscar-worthy, but there was one thing he hadn't faked. An innate possessiveness. A weakness all too easy to exploit. All I had to do was wait. He would come to claim his child. If my father didn't kill him first, he would hunt me down. And then?

Rafael Turner would die.

At least, that was what I told myself, while I stewed alone, in a pot of malice soup.

We stopped at a rest area. It was small, but well-maintained, and I didn't feel the need to shower in bleach after using the facilities. While I waited for Tucker to return from walking Lola, I stretched on the small bed of his cab, studying my reflection in the dollar store mirror perched on the wall across from me. The distorted image was a harsh reminder of what my life had become—awry, misshapen, and dark. Or had it always been that way and I'd been too immersed to notice?

Damn Tucker. Damn Whisper Springs and its wholesome horde. Damn my newfound conscience.

A wave of guilt washed over me, diluting the rage. The baby must have sensed my sudden mood shift because a flurry of palpitations erupted in my belly. I sucked in a breath and absorbed the sensation.

Tucker and Lola climbed into the cab. Lola flopped on the floor at my side, and Tucker greeted me with wind-burned cheeks and a mile-wide grin. I'd never tire of the candor lighting that smile.

"Hungry?" he asked, grabbing my coat off the passenger seat.

"Always." I stood and slipped my arm into the sleeve he held out for me.

"There's a bar down the road. You okay walking?" he asked, offering the other sleeve.

"I'd climb Mount Everest for a meal right now." My stomach rumbled at the promise of food, my woes temporarily forgotten.

He stepped right into my personal space, zipped my coat, and pulled the hood over my head, pulling the sides tight under my chin. "Look at you all bundled and cute."

"Cute?"

"Yeah, cute."

"Never, ever, has anyone been brave enough to call me cute."

"Doe eyes, button nose, rosy cheeks. Without all that makeup, you're a freakin' kewpie doll. Sorry, Bambi. No other word for it but cute." He dropped a kiss on my nose, released my hood, and grabbed my hand.

I had no idea what a kewpie doll was. Surely, I should have been offended. But the warm and fuzzies stuffing my insides made any emotion other than ... well, warm and fuzzy, impossible.

Half an hour later, Tucker and I sat near the back entrance of the aptly named and, judging by the crowd, popular, Roadside Bar and Grill. I wiped barbecue sauce from my mouth and dropped the napkin into my empty burger basket. Tucker popped a fry between his lips and leaned back in his chair, studying me with a curious scowl.

"What? Do I have food on my face?"

"You seem happy. Too happy."

"I guess I am. That a problem?"

He crossed his arms over his massive chest. "I expected you to be livid. I figured you would've blown your top by now, after hearing about Turner."

"Rafael is as good as dead. That makes me happy."

"Does it? Is that you talking, or your father?"

"Does it bother you, knowing I would enjoy watching him bleed?"

He leaned forward, hands folded on the table. "What bothers me is that you've been conditioned to feel that way. I believe that deep down, you don't want anyone to suffer. Deep down, you are a normal girl with a big, fat, squishy heart, brought up in a brutal environment. You created layers of bullshit to protect yourself, layers of a false Aida, to fit in, to survive."

My core temperature rose. "Wow. That's deep, Tuck. You're wrong, though. The only thing I love more than my baby are my knives. I love the power they wield. I get a little thrill spilling blood. Want to know what else gets me off? Watching men bloody each other. In the ring, on the street, doesn't matter. I was never more turned on then when those Aryan pricks beat you to a pulp." I ran a finger over his healing wound. "Your face all cut and bruised. So damn sexy."

"I don't believe you."

"Believe what you want, Cowboy."

Twirling his soda bottle between his thumb and forefinger, his eyes seemed to lose focus, then brightened with clarity. "You know why it was so easy for Turner to con you?"

"Well, this should be good."

"Because he pierced your shield, targeted that sweet little girl you try so hard to hide. You want to be taken care of.

You're attracted to fighters because you want a man who will fight for you, not force you to fight like your father did. You want a man who will let you be a woman, let you be soft. A man who will burn away those layers, a man who wants you. Not your name, not your power, but the lonely girl inside."

I fought the urge to jump across the table and rip Tucker's tongue out. My insides heated another thousand degrees. Yeah, I was in hell.

"I've struck a nerve, haven't I?" he asked, too fucking confident for my liking.

"I'm not some pathetic princess waiting for her Prince Charming." I truly was offended. If that was how Tucker saw me, he needed a cold, hard slap of reality across that pretty mug. "Rafael will come for his child. When he does, I will kill him. With a smile on my face. That's the truth. That's the kind of girl I am, and always have been."

The cocky, beautiful, blond beast sat back in his chair and fucking smiled. "Thank you, Bambi."

"For what?"

"I knew you had a plan brewing in that stubborn head of yours. You're going to wait him out. If Papa Voltolini doesn't take care of him, you will."

Bastard had played me. Damn, there was more to his dark side than I'd suspected.

"You're a mean sonofabitch, you know that?" I asked, snatching one of his fries, then throwing it back in the basket. "You could've asked me."

"Would you have told me the truth?"

Absolutely not. "Of course I would."

"It's a good plan. Better than going after him. There's only one problem."

"What's that?"

"I won't let him anywhere near you."

How sweet. I'd let him hold on to that little fantasy for a while. Rafael Turner would find me. I'd make sure of it.

Tucker

Rafael Turner would never find Aida. I'd make sure of it.

I wasn't above kidnapping. If abduction was required to keep her out of harm's way, I was wholly committed. And if I'd learned anything the past couple of months, it was that Aida's life had been a crash course headed straight for disaster. Harm's Way was nothing more than a street sign she passed daily on her way to the intersection of Anarchy Avenue and Doom Drive.

Damn. How did I get here? I'd thought I could keep my life simple, single, drama free? What an idiot. I wanted Aida. No sense arguing that point. With Aida, there would never be simple. Since I'd met her, single had lost its appeal. Drama free was a pipe dream.

Aida wanted revenge. Couldn't blame her. Problem was, she was blinded by her lust for retribution. She couldn't see the obvious. If she took down Turner, she'd lose her child. I'd lose Aida, to a life sentence either behind bars or behind the pearly gates. Either option was unacceptable.

I remembered Tito's words the last time I'd spoken with him. *Keep an eye on my girl, over there. She's got a heart bigger than Texas. Just gotta shovel through a valley of bullshit to find it.*

Bullshit was right.

Lucky for me, bullshit burned. I held the goddamned torch.

I waited at our table, eyes on the restroom door Aida had disappeared behind almost five minutes ago. When she emerged, holding the door open for a young girl, then winking at her, the dark fog hovering over me lifted.

Beautiful or pretty were insufficient words to describe Aida. She carried herself with a regal confidence that, coming from any other, would be off-putting, but on her was seductive, and enticing. Add to that her dangerous, wicked edge, and she was downright charming. No, not charming. Bewitching, in the most dangerous way, because not a man alive could look at her and not think about fucking—mating, in its rawest, most primitive form. Alluring curves. Beguiling features. Seductive voice. Aida was the perfect temptation.

When she caught me staring, and blushed, I damn near blew a load at the table.

She raised a hand to her swollen midsection, let out a puff of air, and said, "I'm ready, if you're ready."

I'd never been more ready for anything or anyone, ever. Only, I was confident we weren't talking about the same kind of ready.

"Yeah. We should hit it," I managed to mumble through my sudden onslaught of disrespectful fantasies.

I guided her through the door and pulled her against me for the hike back to Frankie. When I helped Aida into the cab and her ass bumped my groin, my vision blurred. Suddenly, I was the bullshit. Aida was the damn torch, burning me top to bottom, decimating logical thought.

I locked the door behind me, and before Aida could sit, I grabbed her hips and urged her toward the back of the cab. Fuck me, but the close quarters were doing a number. Everything smelled of her, sugary sweet, like cotton candy. There was no moving without rubbing body parts.

"What are you doing?" she asked, eyes wide, turning to face me.

I shook my head, closed my eyes, gave my brain one last chance to convince my libido to calm the fuck down.

"Tucker?" she asked in a whisper. "What's wrong?"

Dropping my forehead to hers, because her worried gaze weakened me, I confessed, "Everything's right. I feel like a jackass saying this when your world is upside down, but for the first time, everything is right. Everything I want. Everything I've ever needed is right here in front of me."

Aida jerked back, doe eyes ablaze with understanding. Voice breathy, she asked, "Are you saying what I think you're saying?"

"If you're thinking what I hope you're thinking, then yeah."

"If you're hoping that we can fuck, then I'm all in."

I curled my fingers around the base of her skull, gripping that silky hair tight. "This isn't just a fuck. Understand? You and me are so far beyond a cheap roll in the sack."

"If you're trying to get in my pants, Cowboy, I'm more than ready," she said, lips dangerously close to mine. "The whole *everything I want and need* confession, we'll have to discuss later. That's too much for me to handle. Hope you're okay with that."

"I'll be okay as soon as you're naked."

Lola was all kinds of curious with her cold wet nose in my business. I scooted her to the front of the cab and closed the heavy curtain, shutting out the dog, the world, locking my lady and me in the small, intimate space.

My cock was so ready to play, I could feel my pulse tip to root, hot lust pumping through my veins. I bent to kiss her. Aida fisted my shirt, pulled me down hard, lip bruising hard, and moaned when our tongues collided.

When she broke the connection, too damn soon for my liking, she shrugged off her coat and dropped her ass to the mattress. I towered over her, pulse racing, struggling to breathe.

"Take off your coat," she ordered, tugging at my belt.

I obliged, and by the time she had the first two buttons of my jeans undone, I'd removed my shirt as well.

Slow and steady, she worked the denim down my hips, over my ass. When she peeled my boxers halfway down my thighs, my erection sprang free. Aida seemed oblivious. She lifted her cold, soft fingers to my waist and traced my scars one at a time. I shivered, despite the trail of fire left in the wake of her exploration.

"They're not ugly, Tucker," she whispered, raising her face, eyes soft, locking on mine. "You're beautiful. Brutally beautiful."

Words. Mere words, powerless, yet powering the fire growing in my gut, spreading through me, a soul cleansing inferno.

Holding my gaze, she pressed a kiss to my abdomen, then made her way down, moist lips warming my skin. I watched as Aida worshiped my gruesome parts with her mouth. With each kiss, she washed away the shame I'd carried. With each press of her soft lips on my skin, she accepted my ugliness, and I was hypnotized by her beauty, her delicate touch, her hands more healing than the doctors and nurses who had tended to me in the hospital.

God, this woman.

Aida

This man. This man. Perfection. Hard and trembling under my fingers. I kissed him, every inch of his scarred flesh, the gruesome wound that, on Tucker, was more a work of art than a defect. Sweet Papa, he was beautiful. Hard, battle-scarred planes. Marred skin hiding a man of steel—rugged and stoic.

I gauged his responses, the flexing of his abdomen and thighs, his sharp intakes of breath, his sighs. When he'd relaxed enough, I gripped the base of his cock. Tucker's hands slammed against the roof. For a moment, I feared he'd fold.

"How long has it been since a woman has touched you?" I asked, slowly pumping the length of him.

"A long time, Bambi," he groaned, jaw clenched. "Too damn long."

"That's a shame. This body was made to be appreciated."

Gazes locked, I lifted his shaft, and licked him from root to tip, a moan of pleasure escaping my lips as his head fell back on his shoulders. I licked again, with more pressure. Tucker's hips jerked, but he didn't pull away. Thank God. When I reached the tip of his cock, I pulled him inside me, stroking my tongue on the underside of his rigid flesh.

Sweet Jesus, the man was thick and hard, and so damn hot. His musk made me dizzy with want, his salty flavor ignited wicked urges. I pulled him in, as deep as his size would allow, savoring the flavor, the fullness.

My body was on fire. As I worked Tucker with my mouth, I squeezed my thighs together, hoping to ease the pressure. One touch between my legs and I would've come hard. For the second time in my life, I wasn't chasing the release. I wanted our time drawn out, anticipating the sweet agony. I wanted Tucker's touch, his heat, his cock, everything.

He thickened in my mouth, and I knew he was close. I was more than eager to take him, swallow every drop of his release, but I wasn't ready to be finished. I was greedy. Greedy for his grunts, and thrusts, and sweat, and moans. I wanted his face near mine when he came. I wanted his words, his lips, his eyes.

When I released him and slid off the bed, landing on my knees at his feet, Tucker bent to pick me up.

"Give me your boot," I said, pushing his hands away.

He raised his right foot to my thigh. I made slow work of lifting the hem of his jeans and untying his laces. I made slower work of pulling his shoes and socks off, then sliding his jeans to the floor. Even his feet were spectacular, long toes, high arches, strong and masculine. Had my baby bump not been in the way, I might have bent to kiss them.

I drew my fingers up the curve of his calves, then the tight swell of his thighs above his knees. Defined muscle twitched under my fingertips.

The gasp he expelled when I dragged a nail under his heavy sac thrilled me to the core, and I was about to take him in my mouth again when he bent and slid his warm hands under my arms and helped me to my feet.

"Your turn," he whispered, deep and throaty, before pressing a delicious, delicate kiss to my lips.

As he undressed me in the small space, as my skin exploded in tingles and bumps, as I watched his pupils change size with his thorough examination of my naked body, and he caressed my breasts and dropped to one knee to press kisses to my belly, three words bubbled on the tip of my tongue.

I love you.

But that was insane.

Hormones had to be playing with my psyche. Then I looked down at him, cupping my stomach, so adoring, and ... God, I wanted my thoughts to be real. I wanted to love.

I could love.

Who was I kidding? I loved him. I did.

Oh, fuck. I was fucked.

I was fucking in love with Tucker Slade.

I knew the swelling emotions were real, because I knew, truer than the sky was blue, that I couldn't tell him, because telling him would be selfish, confessing would give him hope for an impossible future. I knew my feelings were real, because I wanted to protect him—from me, from my baggage. No. I would never verbally confess my feelings.

The human body, however, could speak volumes, and my body was about to recite a damn soliloquy.

I lowered myself to the bed and laid back, spreading my knees wide. He crawled over me, his cock bobbing between us, the thick, purple head hot and smooth against my skin.

He reached over me and pulled a condom out of a small bedside drawer. I watched, in eager anticipation, as he sat back on his heels and rolled it on. He took his time, eyeing me, stroking his length. So, I played along, running a finger down my moist slit with one hand, rolling a nipple between my thumb and forefinger with the other.

I had to be in love with my cowboy, because it didn't bother me that I hadn't shaved my pubic area in days, that I hadn't a lick of makeup on my face, or that I lay shamelessly splayed across his bed, stroking myself, in the cab of a damn semi-truck instead of a five-star hotel.

I didn't care. Because Tucker was Tucker. Unpretentious. He was stormy, wise eyes, and strong, unyielding arms. He was forgiveness, fun, and sunshine. He was generous, and gentle, and genuine. I didn't have to put on airs or hide behind my mask of vanity. What an amazing feeling.

Tucker watched, frozen, hypnotized, as I worked my pussy. He stopped the teasing strokes of his cock and rolled his bottom lip between his teeth. Rapid breaths, flushed cheeks, muscles tense. Dear, sweet Lord, he was ready to blow his load just from watching me. Hell if that didn't make me wetter.

I removed my hand from the sweet spot between my legs, stretched my arms over my head, and crossed them at the wrists in mock submission. "I'm all yours, Cowboy."

How erotically thrilling to watch his eyes darken, the muscles in his jaw tense, to hear the low groan rise from his chest. And before I could enjoy that small victory, Tucker's heavy body covered mine.

His expression morphed into something I'd never seen before, the hunger and want disappearing. In their place, possession. And as I registered the look as domination, he slid a hand down to my hip, tilted my ass off the bed, and slammed into me, as if he knew a slow approach would be insulting.

"Fuck," escaped my lips, appropriately and repeatedly, as he pulled out and slammed into me again and again. Gone was the tender and giving man I'd come to adore. In his place, a beast, relentless and greedy, taking his sinful pleasure with each savage thrust.

The pounding continued, with ragged breaths and raking nails, *fucks,* and *oh Gods,* and *you're mines* coming from both of our mouths. Bodies slapping, hips grinding, hair pulling. Deep, brutal kisses. At some point, could've been minutes or hours, he managed to sit back on his heels and pull me with him.

Arms wrapped around his neck, heels planted into the mattress, I rode him, his entire rigid length. Up and down, grinding, arching, writhing. I couldn't get enough. I was a woman obsessed, chasing the high that was Tucker. His sweat, and muscle, and erotic woodsy musk. When my thighs tired from the exertion, Tucker supported me with one arm around my waist and the other under my ass. He held my weight while he continued to pump.

I'd been fighting my release, holding off, prolonging the pleasure. But when Tucker gripped the back of my neck, brought his lips to my ear and said, "You're mine now, Aida. I'm never letting you go," I lost the fight.

I lost my fucking mind.

Tucker

I was out of my goddamn mind. Knew it. Didn't care. Aida was mine. I would protect her. Keeping her safe meant giving her the tools she needed to protect herself. Fuck Tango. Fuck Voltolini. Bambi was getting her damn knives back.

"I don't have to tell you those are illegal in most states, do I, Tuck?" Jim, my longtime friend, chided me over the phone.

"Trust me. I'm aware. If we could keep this between us, that'd be much appreciated."

"I might have something to get you by until the others are ready."

"Thought you might. Knew you wouldn't disappoint."

"Only for you, boy."

"Thanks, Jim. See you tomorrow. Owe you big time."

"Looking forward to it."

I ended the call and whistled for Lola. She trotted my way with a stick in her mouth, butt shaking, ready to play. I threw the thing one more time and glanced over my shoulder toward the truck where I'd left Aida sleeping inside, naked, and if I'd done my job right, boneless.

My dick swelled. Damn. This was going to be one helluva long drive.

We got back on the road twenty minutes later. An hour after that, we checked into a hotel. Ten minutes after checking in, I washed Aida head to toe in the small shower. And before we were dry, I carried her to bed, and my tongue was covered in her sweet juices, her fingers tangled in my hair.

"Oh, fuck. Fuck. Fuck. Fuck," she moaned, grinding her pussy against my mouth. So damn responsive. It didn't take long to work her into a frenzy and make her come with an explosion of profanities.

Before she could recover, I hooked her legs over my shoulders and buried myself deep. I'd intended to take it slow, but Christ, with my Bambi, I was out of control, my thoughts consumed with the need to claim her. Every thrust, every touch, bite, kiss, I marked her, made her mine. Fuck if I'd let her walk away. Fuck if I'd let another man touch her. She was mine.

When I reached my breaking point, and spilled my seed, swear to my Maker, I saw stars. Might have lost consciousness for a sec. I rolled off my breathless lady, pulled her tight against me, and listened while her breathing slowed, waited for her to soften and sink deeper into the mattress. When certain she was deep in dreamland, I closed my eyes and let exhaustion pull me under.

The morning sun coaxed me back to consciousness. Muscles protested when I stretched. And when I remembered where I was, and better yet, who was next to me, I rolled over, eager to start my day the way every warm-blooded male should start his day—balls deep in his beautiful lady.

Only, the bed was empty. The pillow, the sheets, cold.

I rolled off the squeaky mattress and checked the bathroom. Empty.

I spun a three-sixty, surveying the room. My duffle lay where I'd left it a mere eight hours before. Aida's suitcase. Gone.

My blood boiled. My heart, though, remained a fucking glacier.

Aida had bolted. Again.

"Fuck!" I tore jeans and a tee out of my duffle bag and yanked them on. I should've known. Should've fucking been ready for it. I hadn't convinced her not to go back to New York. She'd only been biding her time. Waiting for the perfect chance to disappear.

I fumbled with my boots, the tremble in my hands making it difficult to manipulate the laces. God damn, the woman was dead set on getting herself killed.

My vision blurred, rage taking hold, and I searched the small room for something to decimate. Shit. There wasn't time for a meltdown. How many hours did she have on me? Three? Four?

I gathered my bag and stormed out the door, blinking against the bright sunshine.

"Morning, Cowboy."

I skidded to a stop. Aida held a coffee cup in one hand and the end of Lola's leash in the other. Lola trotted up to me and offered herself for a rub. My bag hit the ground with a thud, my heart hit my gut with a splat.

Sweet Mother of Mercy, what a sight.

Aida's long, raven hair framed her face in soft, loose waves. She wore her moto boots and black leggings, a black turtleneck sweater, and my damn flannel jacket. Red flannel was definitely her color. The damn thing was three sizes too large for her, but somehow, it worked.

"You were sleeping so soundly. I couldn't bring myself wake you. I walked Lola. Fed her, too. Brought you coffee. Stole cash out of your wallet, but I didn't think you'd mind. You know, 'cause it's coffee."

When she smiled up at me with her rosy cheeks and nose, clueless to the hell I'd just put myself through, I ran a hand through my hair and laughed.

"What's so funny?" she asked, gifting me with her own raspy chuckle.

I closed the distance between us and cupped her cold cheeks. "God damn, woman. What you do to me."

Her eyes searched mine, brows pinched in confusion.

"When we get home. I'm fucking you in this jacket."

That earned me a smile.

I plucked the coffee from her hands and kissed her forehead. "Where's your suitcase?"

"In the truck," was her simple reply.

"You've had a busy morning."

"I've never slept better. Woke up full of energy."

"Yeah. I know what you mean."

Aida rolled up on her toes and whispered, "A good fucking will do that to you." She slipped my keys and Lola's leash into my hand. "Put the dog in the truck and drink that coffee fast." Her palm grazed my crotch. "We have half an hour before we have to check out. You're fucking me in this jacket now, Cowboy."

CHAPTER 11

Aida

"AIDA. THIS IS MY friend, Jim Calloway." Tucker stood taller than usual, eyeing me with an expression I couldn't read.

"Nice to meet you, Aida." Jim gave my hand a hearty shake. His grip was soft, his voice softer. He studied me through his gold-rimmed glasses and tilted his balding head. "Have we met before? You look familiar."

"No," I mumbled as I took in the magnificent surroundings of the building we occupied, nestled dead center in what may have once been farmland. Blackened anvils and hammers. Steel presses. A machine that resembled a guillotine, a large, brick forge, and various other daunting gizmos and gadgets. "You're a bladesmith?" I asked, barely able to contain my glee. I stepped closer to the small table standing next to us and ran my finger along the cold, smooth steel of one of the many knives laid before me.

"Master Bladesmith for over twenty-five years," Tucker chimed in with a proud grin, patting his friend on the back.

"May I?" I asked, picking up a small fixed blade with flip-flop patterned steel and a handle made of a pale wood. "It's gorgeous." I flipped the knife in my fingers, inspecting the fine workmanship, admiring the hours that went into folding and cutting the metal. "It's light, too." A bit heavier than my babies at home, but those had been custom made for my hand, designed to hide inside my shirtsleeves.

"The scales on that lady are spalted birch. Beautiful, huh?" Jim asked. "The unique coloring comes from fungi in the trees." He picked up a matching pair from the end of the table. "These are my favorite. Six-and-a-half-inch with Desert Ironwood scales. Two-and-three-quarter-inch blades. Made them a few years back. I was playing around with a new folding pattern. I call it crisscross; my wife calls it kaleidoscope."

I dropped the knife I'd been holding and snatched one of the sets from his fingers. Truly a thing of beauty. It had a darker handle, but the steel? Sweet Papa. The steel had been folded into a pattern that, yes, if you held it at the right angle in the light, resembled a design you would see through a kaleidoscope.

I spun the knife in my hand, between my fingers, tossed it gently in the air, tested its weight, pulled my thumb across the edge of the blade. A shiver of pleasure rocked my body, and I hoped to God neither of the men had noticed.

"We'll take those," Tucker blurted, a heady gaze boring a hole through my soul.

He'd noticed.

I turned on my heel to face him. "You're buying me knives?" My heart raced erratically. "But I thought ... But Tango said. I mean. What?" Oh God. Tears were building. If I'd any question whether I had feelings for Tucker, that moment sealed the deal.

He got me. He understood. He knew what I needed. But more important, he trusted me.

"I knew she'd fancy those." Jim smiled wide, his shoulders straightening with pride. "The ladies love those pretty designs."

Lady? If he only knew. I laughed and shook my head.

Jim handed me the second knife and paused before releasing the fruits of his labor into my care. Our eyes met, and, for a second, I feared he had changed his mind about parting with his creations.

With brows pinched, he asked, "You sure we haven't bumped into each other somewhere?"

I blamed the tingles prickling my spine on the pure joy of being surrounded by sharp metal objects. Not the fact that the barista at the coffee shop had asked me the same question earlier that morning.

Tucker shot me a nervous glance before shoving his hands deep into the pockets of his jeans, dropping his head, and rocking back on his heels. "Aida. Head back to the truck. I'll finish up with Jim. We need to get back on the road."

I nodded and looked again to my new favorite person, Jim the Master Bladesmith. "Don't suppose you have any sheaths laying around?"

"Aida," Tucker snapped. "Truck. Now."

Jim cleared his throat, clearly catching Tucker's not-so-subtle hint for me to leave them alone. "Of course I have sheaths. I'll send them along with Tuck."

Not sure what came over me. Gratitude. Joy. Relief. Whatever it was, I threw my arms around Jim and planted a big, loud kiss on his scruffy face. "Thank you, Jim. You've made me a happy girl." And then I whispered so Tucker couldn't hear, "Wrist or ankle sheaths if you have them, 'cause a girl's got to have her secrets, if you know what I mean," and slipped away before he could respond.

I waited for Tucker in the truck, feeling light and airy, and a little like my old self again. The knives were heavier and clunkier than I was used to, but they would do. And they were mine. And as I watched Tucker approach, in all his rugged sex appeal, I thought to myself, thank God *he's* mine. *Thank God.*

Tucker

"Thank God for greasy burger joints." Aida dabbed a napkin to her lips and sat back in her chair while pure bliss settled across her gorgeous, glowing face.

She had coiled her hair in a loose knot on top of her head. She still wore my jacket, and she hadn't stopped smiling since we'd left Jim's place two hours ago.

I was responsible for that smile. No better feeling in the world.

The diner we'd happened upon was small, maybe ten tables, and quaint. A married couple owned the place. They were friendly, and well matched. Jennifer ran the counter, while her husband, Ron, flipped burgers in the back. We'd learned all this from our waitress, Katie, who had an infectious personality and a gift for gab.

"Did you enjoy your burgers?" Katie asked as she refilled our drinks. "Can I get you dessert? Auntie Jen makes a killer pecan pie."

"No, thank you," Aida said, rubbing her stomach.

Katie tilted her head, and lowered her brows, attention fixed on Aida. "Do I know you? You look familiar."

A rosy hue tainted Aida's cheeks. She faked a grin. "No. Sorry. We've never met."

Click. Click. Click.

Fuck. Jim had asked her the same question that morning.

Aida's gaze sliced to mine.

Click. Click. Click.

My chest caved in.

Looking unconvinced, our happy server shrugged her shoulders. "Could swear I've seen you before," she mumbled and headed to her next table of customers.

"That's the second time someone's asked you that, Bambi," I said, jaw cramping.

"Third." The corner of Aida's bottom lip curled between her teeth while she waited for me to respond.

"What?"

"Coffee shop this morning."

A fistful of WTF knocked me in the kisser. "Shit."

My phone buzzed in my pocket. I'd turned it off last night and only remembered to power it back up when we'd sat down to eat. Tango's name lighted my screen.

"Yeah, T. What's up?"

"Jesus Fucking Christ. Where the hell have you been? I've called five goddamn..."

I held the phone away from my ear while expletives exploded from a seething Tango.

"Tucker? Tucker. You there?"

"I'm here. Shit. What the hell, man?"

"Where are you? Aida okay?"

"We're fine. She's great." I braved a glance her way. A wave of nausea hit when I noticed the lack of color in her cheeks. "Just finishing lunch. We'll be home in two hours."

"You in public?"

"Yeah. A diner."

"Get her the fuck out of there. Now." The urgency in his command was palpable.

Pushing from my chair, I motioned for Aida to follow. "Talk to me, T. What's happening?" I tossed a wad of bills on the table, tangled my free hand with hers and headed for the door.

"You haven't heard the news? Looked at a goddamn paper?"

"No," I said, tripping over a pothole and righting myself before taking Aida down too.

"It's Voltolini, man. He's all anyone's talking about. It's bad, Tuck."

"How bad?"

"Explosion. No survivors. They identified Luciano's body. His bodyguard, too. Aida's face is all over the media. They don't know if she's missing, or one of the victims. They're still pulling bodies out of the carnage."

A sheen of sweat covered my body.

Aida's fingers tightened around mine, and when I opened the truck door and motioned for her to climb in, she stood her ground. "What is it? Tell me."

"Let me talk to her," Tango said in my ear. "I should be the one to break the news."

"No," I argued. "I've got this. I'll see you in a couple of hours."

I ended the call and squeezed my cell hard before tucking it back into my pocket. My hands trembled, and I couldn't meet her gaze.

"Tucker. I know that was Tango. What's going on?"

I opened the door wide, taking my rage out on the handle. "Please. Climb in. I don't want to talk out here."

Moisture pooled in her beautiful eyes. She already knew. "I'm not moving until I hear the words."

"Aida." I stepped closer and cupped her cheek, blocking her from view of passersby.

She jerked her head out of my grasp and backed up until she was flush against my truck. Raising her chin, she sucked in a breath. "Say it. He's gone, isn't he? Tell me, Tucker. Just fucking say it."

"Yeah, baby. He's gone."

I reached for her, but she recoiled. Damn, if that didn't make my guts twist. Her eyes glazed, her lip quivered, her trembling hands slid from her stomach to clutch her chest. And then my strong girl crumpled. My knees hit the pavement, and I pulled her to my chest and held her while she fell apart in my arms.

Her grief seeped through my shirt, into my skin, and deeper still, to those parts kept under lock and key. I wrapped my arms around her head, hiding her face from view, and absorbed her screams of anger, her sobs, her violent trembles. When her breathing slowed, and her hands un-fisted from my collar, I lifted her into the truck.

Grim silence escorted us home. The moment I threw the truck into park, Aida climbed out, ignored Tango, who'd waited outside to greet us, and disappeared through her apartment door.

"What happens now?" I asked.

Tango fisted his hands in his hair. "No word from Tito. Christ. I don't even know if he's alive. Not sure how to move forward."

"I do. We keep her on lockdown until shit clears."

His red-rimmed eyes darted wildly from the door, to the sky, then to the ground, where he kicked at a stone, then continued to toe the dirt. "She won't have that, you know. She'll want revenge. She'll fight back."

"We can't let that happen."

"Voltolini's dead," Tango said, voice thick with emotion. "You get what that means? I'm no longer under his thumb. Aida is free to do whatever the fuck she wants, and trust me, that woman is already forming a plan. We can't keep her prisoner. And there isn't a thing you, I, or a damn army, can do to stop her."

I clenched my fists at my sides, wishing I had something to hit. Despite knowing full well Tango spoke the truth, I wasn't going to give up without a fight. "Like hell."

"Listen, Tuck." Tango shook his head, then crossed his arms and settled into a wide stance. "You and I haven't had much time to get acquainted. You've kept to yourself since I came back to Whisper Springs, giving me space to bond with my boy. I appreciate that more than you know. Says a lot about the man you are. So, I feel I owe it to you to say this." He looked over his shoulder then back to me. "I see the way you look at Aida. Pretty obvious how you feel about her. You must know, Princess Voltolini is nothing like you and me. Luciano didn't coddle his child. From day one, she was privy to every dirty detail of his business. She wasn't only a witness. She participated. Her hands aren't clean."

Obviously, he meant well, but I didn't appreciate where the conversation was headed. "What are you getting at, brother?"

"Aida is a chameleon. She's learned to change colors to fit in, to adapt to any situation. She appears to be getting along fine with us, but don't let it fool you."

"She's changed."

"I want that to be true more than anyone. And don't get me wrong, I'm not trying to scare you off. Giving you the full picture here. If Aida decides to step forward, the Voltolini empire is hers. Everything. That woman is in a crazy insane position of power here."

Aida

Power. Wealth. It was mine for the taking. What I'd been groomed for.

My legacy.

Only, it was no longer *my* legacy alone. I was no longer a *me*. I was a *we*. The inheritance I had once been proud of, now hung like a noose around my unborn daughter's neck.

What a horrifying thought.

But not the scariest. What I found most terrifying about being the last surviving member of my family, was the knowledge that my legacy didn't matter. I didn't matter. Not a soul in the world would weep for the extinction of my bloodline. Why? Because in the grand scheme of things, nothing I'd done, nothing my father had accomplished, made a damn bit of difference.

All that power. For what?

Dad was gone. And I couldn't remember the last time I'd seen him smile.

For reasons I couldn't begin to wrap my head around, I didn't want to leave this Earth without making a difference, to someone, anyone, even if only one person. I wanted to know my smile would be missed when I left.

I rolled to my side and wiped my raw eyes. I hadn't a clue whether it was day or night, or how long I'd cried. Tucker had come in twice to check on me. Twice I'd sent him away. I had no doubt his words would have soothed my ragged soul; his arms would have eased the pain. But this pain I needed, no, deserved to suffer. This grief I needed to process on my own.

Only, after countless hours of weeping, the weight of loneliness pressed too heavily on my chest. Only one set of arms could free me from its crushing burden. For the first time in my life, there was someone I wanted to fall into.

I sat up and dropped my feet to the floor, surprised to see a giant dog curled in a ball by my bed. Lola's head popped up, and if I didn't know better, she had a smile on her face. She pushed to all fours and came at me with a ferocious butt wiggle.

"Hey, girl." I gave her ears a scratch. "When did you come in?"

Lola followed me out of the room and down the hall. Although it was no surprise, my heart skipped a beat when I spied Tucker sprawled on my couch.

Lola trotted to his side and dropped on the floor beside him.

Heart pounding an erratic rhythm, I admired the man stretched across my sofa. One arm draped over his eyes, the other across his torso. His denim-clad legs were crossed at the ankles and propped on the armrest. His hair was a mess, his T-shirt wrinkled, and his three-day stubble was patchy at best. He snored. I was sure if I kissed him, his breath would taste of onions and cooking grease.

I'd never wanted anyone more.

I needed, more than anything, to be close to him. I bent down and brushed my lips across his, a thrill dancing through me when he smiled.

"C'mere, Bambi." Tucker rolled to his side to make room. He lifted his arm and waited for me to nestle against him.

An irresistible invitation.

I wiped a tear from my cheek and stretched beside him on the oversized cushions.

When I'd settled tight, my back against his front, he splayed his fingers across my belly, and whispered, "Aida?"

"Yeah?" I whispered back.

"Promise me something."

"What is it?" I asked, rubbing my hand over his and lacing our fingers, the pressure on my chest subsiding. Loneliness didn't stand a chance against Tucker's embrace.

"Promise me, whatever you're planning, you'll talk to me about it. Promise me you won't disappear."

I wanted to offer him the assurance he sought as much as I wanted to devise the proper plan of action. My wound, however, was too raw. I couldn't process anything beyond the blanket of grief that weighed me down. There wasn't room in my head or heart for anything other than sadness. "That's not a promise I can make. Not right now. But you're wrong if you think I'll blindly go after whoever is responsible for my father's death."

He sighed, tightening his grip. "I know you'll do what's right. Tango is convinced you'll want revenge."

"Tango knows the old me. He's only ever seen me at my worst."

He cleared his throat. "And me? Who have I seen?"

Shocking how easily the answer sprang from my lips. "The me I'm learning how to be."

"Aida," Tucker whispered again, his lips close to my ear.

"Yeah?" I asked, turning my head, craving his mouth.

Tucker drew in a breath. His fingers traced a slow, loopy pattern over my stomach. My body exploded with want. He rolled closer and whispered against my lips. "I'm so fucking sorry about your father. If I could bear the pain for you, I would, you know that, right?"

"I know." I nodded, blinking against the pooling moisture. "You have a way of making everything better without even trying. I hate that you have that power over me," I confessed.

I captured his wrist and guided his hand from my stomach to the apex of my thighs. He wasted no time stretching his fingers, a low moan rising in his throat when he found my sweet spot.

"Make my pain go away, Tucker. Please," I begged, voice breaking on a sob.

In a heartbeat, I was flat on my back. Tucker hovered over me, arms boxing my shoulders, fingers brushing hair off my face, and hips nestled between my thighs. Warm, heavy, and exactly what I needed.

"I can't erase this kind of pain, Bambi." He dropped a kiss to my forehead.

I slid a hand up his chest, around his neck, and squeezed tight. "Then help me forget for a while."

Liquid eyes seemed to assess me. With a warm smirk, he pushed away, sat back on his heels, and peeled my leggings and panties down my thighs. I lifted my knees and feet, watching his muscles flex and roll as he rid me of my clothing. My body warmed with anticipation, my heart buzzed at the flush in his cheeks, the flare of his nostrils, the erotic sweep of his gaze.

Oh, the high. I was drunk on his want. Obliterated by his blatant desire for me. And every time that heady glare swept over my body, I fell wholly mesmerized into an alternate universe where only Tucker and I existed.

Tucker dropped forward, catching himself with one arm at my shoulder. With his free hand, he teased a finger between my legs, exploring with a gentle touch before pushing between my folds. I arched into him. He caught my moan with a kiss.

Too soon, he pulled away and helped me out of my shirt, leaving me naked on my couch. Tucker stood. With heavy breaths, he stared down at me, taking me in, like he couldn't get enough.

My heartbeat skidded to a halt when he scrubbed his hands over his face, dropped his chin, and kicked at something on the floor.

"What is it?"

Hands to hips, he huffed and shook his head before raising his pained gaze to meet mine. "You are so fucking beautiful, Aida. Sometimes it hurts to look at you." He pounded a fist to his chest, over his heart. "Right here. I can't take the ache."

I couldn't take the look of devastation on his face. "You say that like it's a bad thing."

"You have the power to destroy me, you know. If you leave. If you disappear on me, I'm a goner."

"Tucker, don't. Please." I sat up, my body coiling to flee, but I was torn between running and desperate to hear what I feared he was going to say.

"Before I make love to you, before I'm inside you, I need you to promise you won't disappear. I get that you have responsibilities back home. I understand how deep you're in. Just promise you'll keep me in the loop. Don't shut me out. Let me do this with you. Because whatever your fate, whatever shit you have to shovel, it's nothing compared to the fucked-up mess I'll be if you leave. Let me carry you through this. Or at the very least, let me stand by your side."

I couldn't breathe past the lump in my throat. I was drowning in emotion. Emotion I'd never dared let in. "Why, Tucker?"

"You really need to ask?"

"Why?"

"Because I love you, Aida Voltolini. I'm so fucking in love with you I can't breathe most of the time. I know you think you can't love me back. And I don't give a shit. 'Cause even if you never admit it, even if you never say the words, I'm gonna love you anyway. I've got no choice. You're in my blood. You're my fucking heart, the voice in my head. So, you see, if you disappear, you'll leave me a hollow shell. That's why I need you to look me in the eye and promise you won't make a move without me. I'll take on whatever shit comes our way. What I can't take is losing my girl."

Painful, violent beats hammered my ribcage. Three words. Three simple words held more power than knives, fists, or bullets. Three syllables disintegrated my indestructible shield.

I love you.

He loved me.

Had he been any other man, I would've laughed in his face. Or used his profession of love as a weapon, bent and twisted his misguided devotion for my own morbid needs, only to toss him in the trash after I'd had my fun. Not because I wasn't worthy of another's love. But because no one had ever dug deep enough to uncover the real me. No other had cared to lift the curtain and see the girl underneath my name, the promise of power and riches that overshadowed all my feminine complexities, all my quirks, my dreams, my hopes and fears.

Tucker Slade had seen through my mask from the very beginning.

Tucker loved me. Deep and true and without prejudice.

I trembled under the weight of his confession. My body shook, tears fell, and I couldn't mask my feelings any longer.

Tucker dropped to his knees in front of me. "You're shaking."

"I'm terrified," I admitted, fingers curling into his shirt.

"Why?"

"Because I don't know how to do this."

"Do what, baby?" His voice broke.

"Love you."

Tucker

"Love me?" I asked, voice trembling like a damn pubescent teen.

Aida fisted my collar in both hands and tilted her face to mine. "I love you."

I. Love. You. Three words used all too often and frequently for the wrong reason. Not in this case, of that I was certain.

"God, I love you," she said again, her body relaxing into mine, as if the weight of the world had just been lifted.

I brushed a strand of hair off her face and tucked it behind her ear. I've never seen so much vulnerability in her eyes. "I know."

And there it was. That damn laugh. My soft spot.

"You did know, didn't you?" She dropped her gaze and lifted it slowly, the uncertainty gone. "I love you, and I fear by admitting that, I'm handing you a death sentence."

Fuck. My heart fucking exploded in my chest. She was worried about me. "If this is death, I welcome her with open arms."

Aida sighed and dropped her forehead to my chest. "I promise I won't disappear. I can't." Her lips blazed a trail of fire up my chest and neck. "I'm terrified of losing you, too."

Aida pulled me in for a kiss. A salty, wet, passionate exchange. A contract, a promise, a sealing of our fate.

I urged her legs around my waist, cupped her curvy, gorgeous ass, and carried her to the bathroom. When I set her on her feet, she snagged the hem of my shirt and lifted it over my head. I reached into the shower and turned the nozzle. While the water warmed, Aida popped the button on my waistband and peeled my jeans and boxers down my thighs.

Her heavy breaths and parted lips filled me with crazed lust. I captured her wrists, raising them above her head, and pinned her to the wall. While I fucked her mouth with my own, I stepped out of my pants and kicked them to the side. Christ, this woman. So soft and pliant against me. Molten temptation and cool pleasure.

On a moan, I broke our kiss and pulled her with me into the welcoming spray.

I took my time, washing first her hair, then her body. My greedy hands caressed every inch, every curve of her olive skin. She returned the favor, paying special attention to my erection. By the time we'd rinsed the lather from our bodies, I was damn near crippled with pain. My cock had never known such torture.

We dried and made our way to the bedroom, hand in hand, naked and unabashed.

Aida loved me. It cost her to say those words out loud, to offer a piece of her soul, but she'd said them. Aida was mine. And despite her grief, or maybe because of it, I would no longer hold back. Maybe the timing was wrong. Her wounds too raw. But I would take what she'd given, and by the time I finished reveling in her confession, there would be no doubt in her brilliant mind that I would be master, protector, and king of her goddamned universe.

She looked up at me through weary, heavy lids, and I damn near caved and ordered her into bed. She needed rest. But she needed liberation, too. Hell, I needed to be the only person setting her free.

"Turn around and crawl up on the bed. All fours."

Her brows furrowed in confusion, or was it warning? I couldn't tell. Not that it mattered. Sooner or later, she'd learn that with me, it was safe to concede.

"Ass in the air, Bambi. That pussy is all mine now. I'm taking it. With my mouth, then my cock."

Goosebumps covered her backside as she turned and prowled to the center of the mattress.

I stalked behind her, my knees between her pretty little feet, my hands on her hips, and planted a kiss on the dimple above her heart shaped ass. "I'm going to help you forget for tonight. But know this..." I whispered against her dark skin. "I'm in charge. And by the time I'm finished, you won't remember your own name."

Aida trembled against me, a moan rising in her throat. As she lowered her face to the bed, opening herself further, I trailed a finger down her crevice, parting her folds. I could've spent the next twenty years admiring the enticing sweetness she offered. However, my cock had other plans, and he was screaming at me to get the show on the road.

I inhaled her heady scent, my erection jerking, eager for relief. But tonight was about my girl. With one hand on each cheek, I massaged her soft flesh. I flicked my tongue across her clit, then sucked it between my teeth. Aida slammed her hips back, grinding against my mouth. Always vying for control.

With lips and tongue, I worked her, worshipped her. With my hands, I held her steady. My heart? Hell. I'd lost that weeks ago. Aida clutched it now, in her powerful fist.

I played, explored, and teased until she came, crying profanities into the mattress, fucking my face. Before she could recover, I pushed inside her. Holy fuck, I nearly came as she rocked against me, her heavenly core a tight, warm vice massaging my cock.

The room was quiet, aside from the sounds of our lovemaking. Moans. Sighs. Skin slapping skin, the fucking sexy sound her juices made while I pumped in and out of her tight, silky heat.

Aida must have sensed that I was close to my release. With a groan, she crawled forward on the bed, and away from me, my erection twitching like a mad dog. She eyed my angry cock, then me, the devil lighting her grin. "Lay down, Cowboy."

So much for being in control. I obeyed.

Facing away from me, Bambi straddled my hips, rewarding me with a glorious view. She reached between her legs and gripped my erection before sliding into position and taking me in, slow and deep, stealing my breath, and, I was quite certain, my soul. And then, heaven help me, she started to move, swaying her hips, gentle at first, back and forth, slow and controlled.

I watched, unseeing, only feeling every slap of her ass against my abs, absorbing the weight of her plump rear as she ground against me on every down stroke, taking me deeper and harder. We were both slick with sweat and hypnotized by lust. Aida lost control, writhing and moaning, bucking, trembling, riding me like a woman in the throes of an erotic possession. Feral, and free, and fucking me into oblivion.

I couldn't breathe. I couldn't see. I couldn't keep up. And when the world started to fall away from me, I bolted upright with the force of the storm raging through my gut.

I came hard, holding her in a vice, my lips in her hair, her round ass still rocking against me. Sweet fuck. Sweet fucking hell this woman was going to be the death of me.

Aida's thighs quivered, back curled, and head dropped, as she rode out her orgasm on the most erotic string of dirty words I'd ever heard. She slumped forward, her hands on my knees, and started to laugh. "Aida. Aida Voltolini," she said with a breathless rasp.

I fell back, bracing my arms behind me, admiring her form. The arch in her back, the dimples above her ass cheeks. I reached forward, pushed her raven hair to the side, then over her shoulder, and traced her spine with my index finger.

Aida shivered. "You promised I'd forget my name. I haven't forgotten yet," she said, glancing over her shoulder, offering a smirk.

Didn't matter that I hadn't recovered. When she rolled her hips, tossed her hair, and reached between my legs to squeeze my balls, it didn't take long for my cock to get back in the game.

By the time the sun peeked through Aida's small windows the next morning, she'd forgotten her name, and I'd come close to begging her to take mine.

CHAPTER 12

Aida

A HEAVY SNOW FELL the day before Thanksgiving, lulling the world outside into a sleepy quiet while my prison shrunk around me.

Still no word from Tito. My father's death no longer made headlines. The media frenzy surrounding the explosion, as well as speculation as to my whereabouts, had fizzled after the first week. Still, I wasn't about to take a chance with my daughter's life. Returning home, revealing to the world that I was alive, was not an option. My father, his bodyguard, his lawyer, and two of his closest associates had been executed along with the staff that had been commissioned to my father's Poughkeepsie safe house. Several bodies remained unidentified.

Chances were high that I had a price on my head, as well.

So, I stayed in my little hole in the ground apartment. Out of the public eye, and halfway out of my mind. I paced my small living room, nervous and agitated, drowning in grief. Had my father been given a funeral? Had anyone claimed his body? I hated not knowing. Hated that a million miles away, my life had burned to ash. And I'd been the one to light the match.

Bereavement, frustration, and rage consumed me, a slow smolder decimating my sanity. I had no outlet.

Pace, pace, turn. Pace, pace, turn. The handles of my blades bit into my palms.

Pace, pace. Lola whined. I ignored her.

I paced some more, this time down the hallway.

The knives were heavy in my hands. I couldn't let them go.

Lola cried again. I yelled at her to shush.

Fuck, I was being an asshole to the dog. I marched over to the mutt and rubbed her tummy with my toes. "Sorry, girl. Didn't mean to snap at you. It's the hormones."

I blamed everything on hormones. Excessive crying. Ridiculous mood swings. House cleaning. I'd never cleaned a house in my life. Now, I couldn't stop. I'd even rearranged furniture twice in the past two weeks.

Tucker had spent every night with me, and Lola had spent every day by my side. We'd developed a routine, me and the cuddly black bear. At seven every morning, I would let her out to do her business, then feed her. Tucker would take her for a walk before leaving for work. I'd work out in front of the television, along with those ridiculous on-demand exercise programs. Eat. Nap. Eat. We'd go outside, to the private side of the yard, and I'd throw Lola's ball for her.

Some days, Lola and I would head upstairs to hang with Rocky. He was on vacation from school for the week, due to the holiday, and I had to admit, the little tyke was growing on me. He had his daddy's exotic green eyes, and no surprise, he'd already learned to work them to his advantage, hence, my newfound affinity for Legos.

I had just decided to head upstairs to add the finishing touches to my princess castle when I heard the scrape of a snow shovel. Lola and I pushed to our feet at the same time and raced for the front door.

I stepped outside and quickly jumped back in, the icy cement biting my bare feet.

Shielding my eyes from the blinding glare of white, I looked to the top of the stairs. Tucker rested an elbow on the handle of his shovel and crossed one heavy snow boot over the other. "Hey, Bambi. Get dressed. Time for you to get out of that house."

Lola pushed past me and trotted up the stairs, marring the crystalline perfection of the snow that had drifted down the first three steps. Crisp, cold air licked my nose, burned my lungs, tightened my nipples to painful peaks.

"I'm not much in the mood, Tuck," I said, crossing my arms over my chest.

"It wasn't a request. Get dressed, bundle up good, and be out here in ten."

I cocked my hip and lowered my brows. "Or what?"

Tucker just shook his head and smiled, then turned his back and continued with the scoop and toss, clearing the walkway like a pro. He'd become awful bossy since we'd shared those three special words with each other.

I stood in the doorway longer than necessary, in awe of his powerful form, and the grace in which he performed such a mundane task.

Twenty minutes later, I emerged from my hidey-hole, bundled head to toe in wool, down, and thermal lining. Tucker had shoveled a path around the house, giving me easy access to the front deck. I found him sitting with Rocky on the porch swing, laughing and wrestling.

"Aida!" Rocky hopped down the steps and barreled toward me, a fluffy, colorful bundle of winter gear. He could hardly put his arms around me, but that didn't stop him from trying.

"Hey, Rockster. You didn't tear down my castle, did you?"

"No way, Auntie Aida. I built a dragon to protect your castle."

Auntie Aida. My heart seemed too big for my chest.

This kid hadn't only grown on me. I'd fallen in love with him, too. My vision blurred and a pesky tear fell down my face. I wiped it away before anyone could notice.

"C'mon." Tucker joined us, holding two large, red, plastic discs.

"What are we doing?"

Tucker quirked his brows at me. "Um. Sledding."

"What? No. That can't be safe." I stepped around him, dead set on heading back into my cave.

Tucker grabbed my hand, halting my retreat. "Let me guess, you've never been sledding."

I shook my head no, suddenly ashamed of my deficiency in the childhood whimsy department.

The smile that graced his face was so full of mischief I couldn't help but laugh.

"You're not afraid to take on drug lords, or angry strippers, but you're afraid of a sled. Well. This'll be fun," he chuckled, pulling me through the snow toward the hill that led to The Truck Stop. He glanced at me over his shoulder. "You can wipe that worried look off your face. You have a bun in the oven so you can't ride one of these bad boys. I just thought you might like to come along and watch."

"Oh." Thank God.

We stood at the top of the hill and looked down over the white blanket of cold. The Truck Stop was closed due to the snow and the holiday, so the parking lot was still barren and pristine, unsullied by tire tracks or footprints. I spun to my left, taking in the serenity of Lake Willow. Across the bay from The Truck Stop, I could see the Rossi Mansion, its sprawling property the boast of Whisper Springs. Tango's childhood abode was half the size of the castle I'd grown up in, but double the charm, lacking harsh security gates and high, stone walls.

Then I turned to take in Tango and Slade's new digs, standing tall and proud atop its snow covered, lakeside hill. A quarter the size of the Rossi estate, quadruple its fill of love and warmth. I envied the small-town charmer. Envied the children who'd been raised in this close-knit community.

A finger hooked under my chin and soft, cold lips pressed against mine, warming me to my core. "You okay?" Tucker asked, brushing a loose hair off my cheek with his wet glove.

"It's so beautiful here," I mumbled, lost in the ocean of his gaze.

"Take my hand. We have to head down the hill a bit before I let the Rockster loose."

I stepped closer to Tucker and lost my footing, not because the hill was steep, but because I couldn't tear my attention from his beautiful face.

His free arm shot around my waist and held me steady. "I got you. I got you."

Yeah. He had me all right.

Tucker

I had Aida right where I wanted her. Outdoors, with a big, fat smile on her face. Her woes forgotten. At least for a little while.

Rocky and I raced up and down the hill. Aida cheered us on from the bottom. Laughing. Clapping. Victory dancing. She even got Lola involved, throwing clumps of snow in the air for her to catch.

Not long after I molded a small jump, Tango and Slade joined us. The races turned into snowball fights, our sleds became shields, and Aida murdered us all with her impeccable aim.

Her laughter was back.

Christ, that laugh.

A siren's call. Leading me to certain death.

Hours passed, and when the sky opened up, spilling giant flakes, we called it a day. Tango carried a snow-drenched Rocky up the hill. Slade hauled the sleds. Aida and I took our time, her clinging to my arm to stay upright on the slippery incline.

I stripped her naked inside her door. Kissed the warmth back into her cheeks.

We fucked. We showered. We fucked in the shower.

I made love to her in her bed.

We ate chili and watched television, tangled together on her oversized couch.

I hadn't heard the click of her nails all day.

Her knives remained untouched on the side table.

When we fell into bed again, I slept better than I had in weeks.

With dawn came immeasurable pleasure. Aida's lips. First on my scars, then my cock. I returned the favor. My lips. Her sweet, sweet pussy.

Lola's barks and incessant knocking cut our morning intimacies short. I scrambled out of bed, wrestling gravity and drowsiness to hurry into my jeans. When I opened the door, an arctic blast forced the sleep haze clean out of me. My mother's rosy cheeks and mile-wide grin took care of my lingering erection.

"Happy Thanksgiving!" She threw her arms around me.

Lola jumped, whined, and wiggled, desperate for Mom's attention.

"Mom." I hugged her tight. "What are doing here?" I pulled her inside and closed the door, shutting out the cold.

"Surprising you. It was Slade's idea. She said Aida wasn't in the traveling mood and that you wouldn't let her spend Turkey Day alone, so, here I am." Her rosy cheeks were a welcome sight.

"Dad with you?"

"He stayed home," she said, squatting to give Lola her greeting. "Bob Riggins was released from the hospital a few weeks ago. Some of the boys are taking turns nursing him. Your dad volunteered for the holiday shift so the others could be with their families. I told him you wouldn't mind."

"Nah. Glad to have you here." I offered a hand to help Mom stand. "Did you drive all night?"

"Flew in. Slade picked me up this morning. I was going to surprise you at dinner, but I couldn't wait that long to see you." She stomped the snow off her boots and slipped them off her feet.

I helped her shrug out of her coat, avoiding eye contact. My cheeks pulsed with heat, and I couldn't help but feel ten shades of guilty for being caught half-naked in a woman's apartment. Didn't matter if you were sixteen or sixty. No son wanted his mother privy to his bedroom affairs.

Aida came down the hallway, hair disheveled, my flannel coat pulled tight around her naked body. "What's going ... Oh. Oh! Lettie." She floated across the room, landing in my mother's arms. "What are you doing here? Everything okay? Where's James?"

Thank God, she'd covered her private bits.

"Mom decided to surprise me for Thanksgiving," I offered, barely holding the laughter in.

"That's. Wow. That's wonderful." Aida pulled my mom to the couch. "Coffee?"

"Love some." Mom made herself comfortable.

"Let me get dressed." Aida looked down, wiggling her bare toes.

Mercy, those legs. So damn tempting poking out from under my jacket.

"Sorry. I wasn't expecting company," she said, not at all bashful, but respectful, and I admired her grace in what could've been an uncomfortable situation.

My mother waved her off. "Please, sweetie. We're all adults here.

Aida retreated to her room. Mom gave me an *oh, we're gonna talk* look. I made myself busy with the Keurig machine. When Mom came around the corner, all smirk and bright, knowing eyes, I made myself busier by stacking croissants on a plate.

"You've got it bad."

That was an understatement.

Mom carried the plate of pastries to the table. "Your father and I know, sweetie."

Translation? *I'm going to spend the rest of my life making you feel guilty for not trusting me with Aida's true identity.*

"I figured the two of you would put two and two together." Slade had filled Mom and Dad in about Tango's relationship with Luciano Voltolini. I'd hated keeping them in the dark, but Aida's identity wasn't my secret to tell. Of course, now that her face had been all over the news, it was only a matter of time before people figured it out. I hadn't been worried about the customers in The Truck Stop. Aida had always sat in the corner table. She'd never talked to anyone other than Charlie and Margie, who, for obvious reasons, were now in the loop.

"Are you in danger?"

I almost snorted. I was danger. Mom didn't know that about me.

"No, Mom."

"If I can help in any way—"

"Absolutely not." I slammed my coffee cup on the counter. "I don't want you near any of this. Between Aida and Slade, I've got my hands full. I can't worry about you, too."

"You can't save every woman you see in trouble, Tuck." She pushed me out of the way and finished filling the last mug. "And it sure as hell is not your job to worry about me."

"Mom."

"No. You listen and you listen good. Aida has been a guest in my home. Any fool can see that you're head over heels. In my book, that makes her family. My family. And we take care of each other. It's not all on you. Understand?"

Sure, Mom talked a good game. She didn't understand the danger, though. She hadn't seen what I'd seen. Lived what Aida had lived. The most danger my mother had been in was helping Slade rescue Rocky from his psychotic birth mother, and only by delivering the little guy, and falsifying the hospital and birth records.

I turned to argue. Aida stood in the doorway, hair pinned up, dark green sweater dress clinging to every curve. Fuck. Those curves. Her legs were hidden in tights and biker boots. She wore lipstick and not much more on her face aside from the look of pure adoration aimed at my mom.

Pierced me. Knife through the heart.

Mom was right.

Aida was family.

Aida

Family.

So, this is what it feels like.

I melted into the melon-colored love seat, and propped my feet on the matching ottoman, allowing another wave of serenity to wash over me. Rocky hopped up next to me on his knees and lowered his face to my stomach, which was ready to pop, because the twelve pounds of turkey, and three gallons of gravy I'd shamelessly devoured.

His small hands flattened on my baby bump, and he pressed his lips into my sweater. "Hello, baby. Hello, baby. Can you hear me?" He giggled and jumped down, disappearing into the family room. What I wouldn't give to have that energy.

From my seat, I had a view of the chaos in the kitchen. Tucker cleared the table, Tango stacked dishes in the dishwasher, and Lettie cleared the buffet of leftover pie and plates full of cookie crumbs.

Slade came around the corner, glowing and happy, and dropped her butt next to mine. Tango's father, Carlos, soon followed, having been shooed out of the kitchen by Lettie.

"She scolded me for putting rinse aid where the soap was supposed to go," he said with an impish grin.

"You did that on purpose," Slade laughed. "So you didn't have to do any more dishes."

Carlos only winked. Damn, the man was handsome. Aside from a few wrinkles, he and Tango were nearly identical. He'd aged more gracefully than my father had, a byproduct of their respective life choices, no doubt.

He crouched next to me, pulling my hand between his own. "How ya holding up, Princess?"

I didn't have the energy to lie. Carlos had grown up with my father. He knew what kind of boy Luciano had been and the man he had become. "I'm holding it together, though it's difficult. Part of me wants blood, part of me wants..." I slipped a glance to the kitchen. In particular, to Tucker, who was now crouched at the cupboard, fitting pots and pans in their proper place. That was until Tango, soapy hands and all, slipped his arms around Lettie, and twirled her around the kitchen. "Part of me wants what you all have."

Carlos rose to his feet, kissing my forehead. He cupped my chin, lifting my face to meet his emerald eyes. "Princess. You decide to go home, there's no doubt you'll have the world in the palm of your hand, to mold, crush, or manipulate however you desire." He stared long and hard at me. "But if you choose to stay here, every person in this house will carry *your* world in the palms of *their* hands. Freely and joyfully. You've got family here, baby girl. Remember that while you weigh your options." His eyes liquefied, holding my gaze again for an uncomfortable spell. "I miss your dad terribly. I know he was rough around the edges, but I can't imagine he'd want that life for you or his grandchild." He kissed the corner of my mouth this time, tender and caring, then sauntered off, calling after Rocky.

Slade's arm slid around my shoulders. "Carlos is wise, for a pompous, womanizing ass, isn't he?"

Wise, yes. His words pierced me something fierce, and I blinked away the sting in my eyes. I couldn't get emotional in front of everyone.

"What's your beef with Carlos?"

Slade threw her head back and laughed. I envied her organic nature. "Oh, Aida. Someday, when we have a few hours to ourselves, I'll tell you the story."

"That good, huh?"

"That long." She rolled her gorgeous blue eyes.

"Has Tango heard from Tits?"

"If he has, he hasn't mentioned anything. I know he's worried. He checks his phone obsessively."

"My guess is, he's shacked up with some clueless, barely legal fitness model, getting his rocks off until all of this blows over." *Or dead. Or being tortured,* I thought to myself.

Wouldn't be appropriate, or productive, to voice those fears out loud. Although, I knew she was thinking the same thing, by the look in her eyes.

"Mom," Rocky called from the other room. "Mom. C'mere."

Slade hopped up, heeding the call, and bounced away, light and airy, to the other room.

When I turned my attention back to the kitchen, Tucker strode my way, six-feet-something of determined and devastating male. He leaned forward, pressing his fists into the cushion on either side of my head and lowering his mouth to my ear to whisper, "I need to be inside you, Bambi. Let's go."

Heat flooded my cheeks.

Tucker helped me to my feet. "Aida's wiped," he shouted over his shoulder. "We're gonna head downstairs."

Everyone shouted goodnights, and I barely squeaked out my response before the door closed behind us. Snow crunched under our boots, and the night sky, clear and twinkling, lit the path leading around the side of the house. Tucker let go of me only long enough to unlock the door. Once inside, he pressed me against the wall and crushed my mouth with a brutal kiss.

One hand palmed the wall next to my head, his other, oh sweet Papa, with his other hand he pressed on the underside of my belly, rubbing gently, before sliding down, and lifting the hem of my sweater dress. He shoved his fingers between my legs, and released a frustrated groan when my tights prevented him from connecting with my naked flesh.

"Fuck," he mumbled into my mouth.

Before I could respond, he pulled away and yanked my tights and panties down my hips.

I gasped, surprised, and aroused by his brutality. Before

Tucker, I'd always been in control. Especially when it came to sex. Fucking had always been about me. About the release, about the high. About power.

Something in Tucker's eyes, his breaths, the tension in his movements, told me he needed control. Something about the way I loved him, allowed me to step outside of myself, to sacrifice my pride, to give the man full authority.

Tucker spun me around to face the wall, dug his fingers into my hips, and nudged my legs apart with his booted foot. Heavy breaths blew in my ear. Strong, rough hands smoothed over my ass, parting my cheeks.

Without warning, he shoved his cock inside me. "Sweet hell, baby."

I hadn't even heard him undo his pants.

I braced myself, hands flat and shoulder high, my cheek smashed against the rough texture of the paint.

Cock buried deep, Tucker bit my shoulder, slid his hands over mine, encasing my fingers, and fucked me against the wall, fully dressed, and one hundred percent in charge.

Brutal and unchained, he chased his release. Breathless and needy, I let him use me. And as fast as it started, he came inside me, his body pressed against mine, his breaths jagged and hot against my neck.

Never had I allowed a man to get off before I had. Never had a man dared to try. I'd never felt such satisfaction, cocooned between Tucker's arms, his sated dick sliding out of me, his semen, hot and sticky between my thighs. I had never felt so coveted.

Forget feeling loved and needed. To be wanted, so desperately, on such a primal level? Well, that was a high I could easily form an addiction to.

Tucker

Addiction was a dangerous thing. I'd had Aida that morning, and several times the night before. Problem was, the more I had, the more I wanted, and the whole damn day had been an excruciating test of self-control. A test I failed. Out of my mind with lust, I'd taken her like a savage against the wall. Selfish bastard.

I'd yet to recover, when she turned, still caged between my arms, and wrapped her fingers around the back of my head. "Cowboy," she nearly purred. "Promise you'll do that again. And soon."

Inside, I was screaming, *yee-haw, let's do it again now.* But I was a man for crying out loud, not a horny teenager.

"I'm no cowboy," I whispered, still catching my breath. "Never touched a horse, or a cow for that matter. Besides, cowboys are gentlemen. And the things I want to do to you are definitely not fit for a lady."

"Hmm." She nibbled my chin, giving it a sharp pinch between her teeth before letting go. "No one has ever accused me of being a lady."

"Damn, right." I dropped to my knees and slid my hands to her waist. "You're all woman." I kissed her round stomach and helped her step out of her tights, then used them to wipe the mess between her legs.

Aida shivered. I stood, slapped her ass, and ordered her to the shower. I waited until she was out of sight to tuck my semi-erect cock back into my jeans. When I heard the water running, I locked up, cranked the heater, and searched my phone for a number I hadn't called in years.

Connor Howe answered on the first ring. "Sweet Jesus. Tucker Slade? That you?"

"Howe." I shook my head, reeling with a flood of memories. His voice didn't match the pasty, computer whiz I remembered from high school. "Need a favor."

Howe was the valedictorian of my graduating class. He'd also been my best friend, and the too-small kid I'd pulled out of many dire circumstances due to his lack of bulk, and his disdain for violence. No arguing, the guy was fucking brilliant, into some deep-web conspiracy theory shit. Conner had planned on joining the Marines alongside me. Instead, he'd been recruited by a private organization. The kind that operated above the law. The kind of agency the United States government denied existed, but called upon when they couldn't get their hands dirty.

"Anything." His voice sounded gruffer than I remembered. I had no doubt his chosen career path had taken its toll.

"It's a big one."

He huffed. "I owe you big."

"I need someone to die. It needs to be brutal. It needs to be public."

"Send me the specs."

"Will do."

"Slade. You good?"

Conner was the guy who'd helped me learn to navigate, and then manipulate the various means in which underage girls could be procured. Social media, deep web, over the radio waves, or via the local paper. The game was always changing.

"I'm good. You?"

"Never been better."

"All right. Happy to hear it."

We caught up with a short and to the point convo. I ended the call, pulled up the file I'd prepared weeks ago, and hit send.

Fingers laced behind my neck, I paced the living room. Inhale. Exhale. Inhale. Exhale.

Would she forgive the liberty I'd taken?

After watching her interact with my family at dinner, and after she'd offered her body so selflessly to me, I had no other choice. Whether she recognized the change or not, Aida was adapting. Hell, she was evolving. Princess Voltolini, no matter her past, deserved a chance. At family. At freedom.

What she needed most was a chance to succeed as a mother.

What I needed most was to keep her alive.

I had the power to give her the impossible.

And so, I did.

The deed was done.

Even if I'd wanted to, I couldn't take it back.

CHAPTER 13

THE HEADLINES READ SIMILAR across all media outlets.

"The Body of Missing Mob Princess Found Dead on Father's Gravesite."

"Pregnant Heir to Voltolini Empire Executed."

Merry fucking Christmas to me.

I tore my gaze from the muted television, mind numb, ears buzzing, heart beating half its normal tempo. Tucker's arm came around my shoulder, pulling me deeper into his heat. Tango's worried face came into view. Slade's blue eyes darted from me, to Tango, then back to me.

I had no words.

The old me would've erupted in a flurry of rage and wounded ego.

The new me burrowed deeper into the arms of the man I loved, staring into the faces of a man and woman who'd welcomed me, adopted me into their family. As I sat in a warm home, on a cozy chair surrounded by shiny bows, torn Christmas paper, empty boxes, and toys, I sighed a breath of relief, and thought to myself, *I'm free*.

Who was responsible? What was their endgame? "It had to be Tits. He's the only person I know who could've pulled this off."

"I'm not about to make any assumptions, Princess." Tango squatted at my feet, rubbing his hands over my knees, hope swimming in his green eyes. "I hope to Christ it was Tito. That'd mean he's alive."

"Who else would benefit from pulling off this ruse?"

"I hate to say this," Slade chimed in. "But what if it's someone trying to lure you out of hiding."

Tango nodded. "Someone who knows you. Knows your short temper. Maybe they're trying to flush you out, hoping you'll come forward to prove you're alive."

"Like Turner, you mean."

He released a loud sigh. "Could be Turner. Could be whoever's responsible for the explosion. Turner makes more sense. From what I remember, the guy was possessive as fuck, especially when it came to you. And now that you're carrying his child? Who knows what the hell we're up against."

"Does he have that kind of clout?" Slade asked.

"We know nothing about him," I reminded everyone. "Except that he wasn't who we thought he was."

"So now what?" I dared ask.

Tucker, who'd remained silent until that point, slid out from under me and pushed off the couch, cussing under his breath. "Now what? Simple. We don't do a damn thing."

A phone buzzed. Tucker shoved his hand into his back pocket and retrieved his cell. After checking his screen, he stormed across the living room into the kitchen, and I assumed, by the slam that shook the walls, out the back door.

"We can't do nothing," I mumbled.

Tango dropped his head. Scratched his temple. Lifted determined eyes to mine. "Nothing is exactly what we do. You hang low for a bit longer. Give it some time. Wait for the story to fizzle."

"I want to go back to work with Charlie."

"Aida," he argued. "We can't risk someone recognizing you."

Slade claimed Tucker's empty spot on the sofa, slinging an arm around my shoulders. "She'll stay in the kitchen. Besides, she doesn't look the same as the woman in those images. Chances are, no one will recognize her. If anyone does, we'll blow it off. Everyone has a doppelgänger, right? Besides, we have proof that she's not Aida Voltolini."

God, I loved her. Like, really, really loved her.

She had my back, and she argued a good point—I'd gained weight, my face was fuller, and when I wore no make-up, I looked like a completely different person than the mob princess who'd arrived in town months ago. And besides, I had proof, in the form of ID and credit cards, that I was not Aida Voltolini; I was indeed, Aida Suarez.

Whoever orchestrated my fake death, I wanted to hug them.

"I don't like this," Tango complained, brows pinched, jaw set tight. "You know I'm no longer under obligation to protect you. You're free to do whatever you want."

"But?" He wouldn't loosen the reins that easily. He'd always been as protective of me as Tito had.

"Fuck." He pushed to his feet. Started pacing, then stopped in front of me again, hands to hips, releasing a frustrated breath. "Stay here. With us. The job. The apartment. It's yours if you want it. I know it's not what you're accustomed to, but you have family here. And you're safe."

"I'm not running back to the East Coast, if that's what you're worried about. I've no desire to put my baby at risk, Tango."

He studied me for long moment, then nodded. "I believe you." He sighed, scrubbing his hands over his face. "You should keep a low profile, though. Those Aryan fuckers haven't come back, but that doesn't mean they aren't out there, biding their time."

"No worries." Slade patted my thigh. "We'll walk to work together in the mornings."

"Better yet, I'll drive you," Tango interjected.

Slade's lips disappeared between her teeth. Her lids closed, and she inhaled deep and slow through her nose before gritting a response, "Sure. That'd be good, honey. You could drive us to work."

Slade lived for her morning and afternoon walks. I hated that she was giving up her sacred time for me.

"Perfect." Tango helped Slade to her feet, then slid his arm around her waist. "Tucker or I can drive you home after your shift when we're available. If we're not, I'll have whoever is on security detail give you a lift."

"Okay. It's settled." Slade flashed her mega-watt smile, rose on her toes, and kissed her man on the cheek. "Can we get back to enjoying our Christmas now?"

Tucker walked back into the room, face red, eyes narrowed on me. It was obvious his phone call hadn't been a happy one. He clapped Tango on the shoulder, hugged his sister, and announced, "We're heading downstairs. Be back up to help with dinner in a bit." He grabbed my hand, and off we went.

He opened my apartment door, moving aside for me to go first, as his chivalrous nature dictated. Only, he didn't slap my ass as I made my way through, per his norm. Nor did he rip off my clothes and take me in the hallway as I'd hoped would happen.

He gripped my hand tight, and with heavy strides, pulled me toward the bedroom. On the bed sat a present, rectangular and flat in shape, wrapped in shiny gold paper with a glittery red bow.

"Tucker. We said no presents."

"I know. Just open it."

I picked up the gift and sat on the edge of the bed. Tucker joined me. Thigh bumping mine, he leaned back on his arms. Thick muscle bulged under his dark denim, pulling it tight across his leg, filling me with longing. I wanted that power between my legs. I turned, planting one knee into the mattress and hoisting my other leg over his lap. At seven months knocked-up, the maneuver was no easy feat.

Thankfully, Tucker was strong, and instead of watching me struggle, he grabbed my hips and guided me into position over his thick bulge. He then laid back, hands clasped behind his head, making room for the baby bump.

I admired his solid form beneath me while I untied the bow. "Did you wrap this?"

"Sure did," he rasped, offering a playful wink. "All by myself."

"You're quite handy with the scissors and tape, I see," I said, struggling to find a way past the wrapping paper.

"I'm a handy guy." Tucker's hand snapped to the side of my stomach, fingers splayed, thumb rubbing a small circle. God, that small gesture did remarkable things to my insides.

I ripped the paper and popped the lid off the unmarked black box, gasping at what lay inside, shiny and sharp and perfect. Handmade fixed blades, carved thin handles that fit perfectly in my palm and would be easy to hide under any outfit. My damn eyes started to burn, and before I could gather composure, tears spilled down my face.

For the second time that day, I was at a loss for words. Words seemed insufficient. And as I stared into the eyes that peered straight into my soul, as the gravity of the day struck me hard, I buried my face in my hands and I cried. Cried for my first real Christmas. Cried for the man who truly knew me. Cried, mourned, and celebrated the me that no longer was.

Aida Voltolini was dead.

Tucker

"Aida Voltolini is dead," Connor announced. "Have you seen the news?"

"Watching it now. What's going on? Wasn't supposed to happen until next week. We weren't supposed to talk—"

"Wasn't me, Tuck," Conner cut me off. "Someone beat us to the punch. This shit legit?"

"No. Fuck. It's not legit. I'm with her right now." I looked over my shoulder to make sure no one had followed me out of the house. "Any way you can find out who did this?"

"Already working on it. Don't like being trumped. I'll hit you up when I find something."

"Thanks, Conner. I have one more favor to ask. Money is no object."

"Fuck that shit. I'm not taking a penny for this gig. If there's someone out there capable of pulling off this charade, I need to meet them. What do ya need?"

"Can you make her photos disappear? If people recognize her, she'll never be free."

"I can do better than that."

"Thanks again, Con. Merry Christmas, buddy."

"Ho. Ho. Ho."

My earlier convo with Conner played on repeat in my head, unease seeping deeper into my bones. Aida had drifted into dreamland at my side hours ago, clutching her sheathed knives to her chest like a security blanket.

Sleep wouldn't come for me. I rolled off the bed, careful not to jostle the mattress, slid the blades from her grip, and laid them on the nightstand.

I envied the peaceful set of her face.

There would be no peace for me. Not until I had answers. I was supposed to be the one to give her freedom. Not some ghost. Fuck. Fuck!

Lola followed me to the living room and curled into a ball at my feet. I'd just settled on an episode of *Ice Road Truckers* when Lola started to growl.

"Shush, girl. Don't want to wake Bambi."

Lola sat up, growled, trotted to the front door, hackles raised.

Lola's nature was to protect her family, a job she'd always taken seriously, and at times, proven a bit overzealous, so I paid her little mind.

Until I heard what sounded like a cough outside.

Lola erupted, growls and barks and gnashing teeth. Mindless of my half-naked state, I crossed the living room and threw open the door. Lola took off at a dead run, up the steps and across the lawn, disappearing in the cluster of trees at the far end of the property.

I saw no one. Heard nothing. The snow in the yard had been trampled from our fun and games earlier, so I couldn't make out any fresh footprints. Must've been a raccoon, another dog maybe. I whistled for Lola to come back and turned to head inside, my feet painfully cold, my nipples hard enough to cut glass, when I spied a cigarette butt laying near the back porch of the house.

"Fuck," I muttered, bending to cover it with snow. There'd been a rash of home robberies around town. Maybe someone was casing the place. Tango had given his security team the night off.

"What are you doing out there?" Aida's silky smooth voice warmed me instantly. "It's freezing. Come inside."

God, she was irresistible, drowning in my flannel jacket, wiping sleep from her eyes. Bare legged and sexier than fuck. I jogged down the steps to greet her, sliding my icy hands under the coat.

"You bastard," Aida sputtered, laughing her deep raspy laugh, wiggling to free herself from my frozen fingers. "Your hands are like ice."

I tortured her for a few beats longer before letting her retreat into the warmth of the house.

I shut the door and watched her fall into the cushions of the couch. "What were you doing out there?" she asked, tucking her legs under herself and my coat tighter around her chest.

"Thought I heard something. No big deal. Probably just a critter." I settled next to her and pulled her into my lap, her back to my front, and wrapped my arms around her middle to warm myself.

We sat, unspeaking, in the dark, Aida warming my arms with her delicate, soft hands. I cherished the comfortable silence, the steady pace of her small breaths.

Aida quieted the noise in my head.

When she laid back against my chest, resting her head on my shoulder, I asked, "Was Rafael a smoker?"

"No," she answered through a yawn. "Why?"

"Just wondering."

She tensed. "Tucker. Why?"

I didn't want to worry her, so I attempted to change the subject. "Why are you out of bed?"

"Lola's barking woke me." Aida stood, stretched, dropped my jacket at her feet, and sauntered, in all her naked spender, down the hall. I followed, and after I'd fucked her silly and we settled under the blankets, she asked, "Why did you ask about Rafael?"

I wouldn't lie. But damn, I wanted to. "I found a burning cigarette outside."

"And your first thought was Rafael?"

"Just covering all the bases."

"It might belong to one of Tango's guys. Or maybe a crow or a critter dropped it in the yard. It's probably nothing." She patted my chest, giving me a good ol' *there, there.*

"Yeah. You're right. I'm sure it was nothing," I said, only to appease her. I didn't mention that fact that whoever had been outside picked the one day Tango's security detail wasn't on duty. It wasn't a critter, and it wasn't coincidence. But I wouldn't mention that to her. Those were particulars I was sure she'd work out on her own.

She hadn't clicked her nails in weeks. I wanted to keep it that way.

Aida snuggled against me, her sweet ass nestled tight against my sated dick. "Tucker," she whispered.

"Yeah, Bambi?"

"Merry Christmas."

I pulled her closer and kissed the back of her head. "Merry Christmas. I'm sorry we didn't get you a tree. We'll have to do that next year."

Aida

Next year. He said, *next year.*

Tucker was talking long term. His words made me ridiculously happy, even though he was confident in a future that, when I tried it on, didn't seem to fit. I couldn't think of next year. I couldn't think past what would happen one or two days in front of me.

I'd never dared allow myself the luxury of planning too far ahead. My life hadn't room for that nonsense. Live for the moment. Live for the thrill. Me. Me. Me.

How wrong I'd been. How single-minded. How self-indulgent and foolish.

I fell asleep between two powerful arms, against a chest that seemed to beat in sync with mine despite the ocean of moral disparities between us.

I woke to the rapturous sound of Tucker's voice, singing above the low volume of the stereo, a soulful rendition of "Hallelujah," from my small galley kitchen.

I freshened up in the bathroom before joining him. He stirred something on the stove. When he turned to greet me, and I drew him in for a hug—a gesture that'd become second nature—he rocked us back and forth and continued to belt out the lyrics, his chin rested against the top of my head, my cheek pressed to his bare chest.

He was singing to me. To *me*. Or maybe he wasn't. Perhaps he was just singing along to the stereo like he always did. Regardless, I pretended his performance was for my ears only. Like a love-struck teen, I allowed every word to seep through my skin, burrow deep, fill my peaks and valleys, and smooth my sharp edges. And I felt no shame in basking in the glow of a beautiful man and his gorgeous voice and the giddiness that accompanied his attentions.

The song ended, and Tucker kissed my forehead, then leaned back and studied my face. "Prettiest damn corpse I've ever laid eyes on." He drew me close again, to kiss my temple, my nose, and lastly my lips.

A corpse. Funny. I'd never felt more alive.

He turned, grabbed two bowls out of the cupboard and proceeded to fill them with oatmeal. I hated oatmeal, but my stomach rumbled at the maple smell, so when he offered me a bowl, I smiled, said thank you, and followed him to the small kitchen table.

"I have a surprise for you today."

I raised an eyebrow. "Where I come from, surprises are never a good thing."

He laughed, drawing my attention to his deep dimples and perfect white teeth. I'd never been so affected by a smile. People who smiled that wide usually had a hidden agenda. Not Tucker. He was truly smiling for the sake of expressing his joy.

I loved Tucker's ear-to-ear, and damn him, it was impossible to resist the pull of my own lips in response.

"You'll like this one, I promise."

I believed him. Hard not to. He hadn't done me wrong yet. And the knives? He couldn't have given me a more perfect gift. Which reminded me...

"Tucker?"

"Hmm?" he mumbled with a mouthful of oats.

"Why the knives?"

"Why not?" was his knee-jerk response.

No buttering me up, no kissing my ass. No making himself look good with some well planned, self-exalting explanation.

"What's the matter?" He laid his spoon down and wiped his hands on his napkin, giving me one hundred and ten percent of his attention. "Don't like them?"

"I love them."

Tucker stared at me long and hard, the crinkle of his eyes softening. "I knew you would." Apparently relieved, he picked his spoon back up and got back to business.

"How'd you fit them to my hand so perfectly?"

"I have my ways," he said to his bowl of oats.

My brain reeled. When had he taken measurements? It had to have been when I was sleeping. Unnerving, really, knowing that I'd slept sound enough for him to size my palms and fingers without me knowing. More unsettling, was the fact that I could fall into deep slumber around him. I wasn't on my usual jagged edge. I couldn't afford to let my guard down, yet I'd done it night after night with Tucker.

I could've pursued the matter. Instead, I ate my oatmeal, which, I'd decided after my first bite, I no longer hated.

"What's my surprise?"

"Patience, Bambi."

I gave him my stink-eye, a look that sent most cowering into dark corners. The bastard remained unaffected.

Tucker's phone buzzed. He answered with a "What do you have for me?" His face broke out in an infectious grin. "Yeah? All good? You're the fucking man. No words, dude. No words."

He ended the call, practically jumped over the table, and kissed me with an air of possessiveness I couldn't wrap my pride around.

"What was that for?" I asked, choking on my food.

"Get your shoes on. We're going for a ride." He shuffled into his Red Wings and grabbed his wool hat off the rack.

I waddled his way, feeding off his excitement. He helped me into my coat while I slid my feet into my snow boots.

Tucker didn't say a word. Only grabbed my hand and guided me to his Jeep.

Twenty minutes and four country songs later, he turned up a private road littered with *no trespassing* signs. The sun disappeared through the thick cover of pines and reappeared when Tucker pulled into a clearing, and next to a two-story, sprawling, modern log home.

He parked, jogged to my side of the vehicle, and helped me down.

I could barely keep up as he climbed the steps to the front porch. Stomping the snow from his shoes, he pulled a key from his pocket, unlocked the door, and gestured for me to enter.

He had a key. And he was smiling like the cat that ate the canary. My stomach lurched. "Tucker."

"Yeah, Bambi." He shook his arm like a mad man, hurrying me through the door.

"You didn't," I mumbled, stepping over the *Welcome Home* mat.

"I most definitely did. Waited four years for this baby to hit the market."

A gasp escaped my lips when I stepped into the open foyer. Straight ahead, a massive, open, polished wood staircase led to a balcony-style hallway with three sets of doors spread across the length of the wall. To my right, a sunken living area, the centerpiece, a wide, stone fireplace surrounded by a leather couch, and oversized matching chairs. To my left, a modern black and stainless steel, open kitchen. Behind the stairwell, a floor-to-ceiling window that opened to a giant barbecue pit. Everything in the space was large. The windows, the furniture, the ambiance.

"You bought it furnished?"

"No. Furniture arrived last week. Come upstairs," he said, already halfway up the open, wide stairwell.

By the time I reached the top, Tucker had pushed open a set of hand-carved double doors, revealing the massive master suite. The window, opposite the door, and spreading the length of the room, overlooked a large yard, snowcapped trees, and in the distance, Lake Willow. I pressed my palms to the glass, awed by the sprawling, pristine, snow-blanketed property below.

A private, mountain oasis hidden mere minutes from town.

Warm hands slid around my stomach. A solid chest pressed against my back. Tucker buried his nose in my hair and inhaled. "Can you imagine, making love, right here, right like this, against the window?"

My knees buckled. My eyes snapped shut at the illicit thrill running through me. "I've never seen anything so beautiful," I rasped.

Tucker backed away from me. "Close your eyes."

"Why?"

"Just do it," he ordered, grabbing my hands and raising them to my face.

I obliged.

With one arm wrapped around my shoulder, he guided me for twenty-three paces, turning right twice. A door hinge squeaked, he pushed me ahead three more steps, then sighed, loud and hard, his chest pressing against my back.

His hands shook as they lowered mine to my sides. "Okay. Open."

My heart beat thunderous and violent against my ribcage.

I stood inside a luxurious, white and pink, frilly and fluffy, airy and bright nursery. I half expected birds to fly through the windows and hang floral garland from end to end. The furniture was white, and clearly hand-carved, and definitely not baby store, mass market furniture. I was staring at furniture that had been designed. Planned. Furniture fit for a princess.

I knew what his gift meant. The finality. The trust. The commitment. The blind faith. I knew what the nursery meant to him. It meant next year, and the year after, and the year after that. It meant forever. A forever I didn't know how to give.

Tucker loomed dangerously close behind me. He let out a long breath. "What do you think, Bambi?"

"I don't know what to say."

Tucker

"Don't say anything." I could feel her slipping away. Retreating.

I'd known it was a crap shoot, building a room for her, for her baby. I'd known it was a risk. Yet, I needed to prove I was in for the long haul.

"Wait here," I told her and ran downstairs to grab my cell out of the Jeep, and to take a breather, also giving her a breather. When I returned to the nursery, Aida was bent over the crib, running her fingers along the quilted bedspread. She picked up the stuffed animal I'd placed in the center—brown with white spots on its back, a butterfly on its shoulder, oversized brown eyes, and exaggerated lashes.

"It's Bambi," she mumbled, clutching the toy to her chest.

"C'mere." I curled my arm around her waist, gripping her hip, and headed to the matching rockers.

I helped her sit, then dropped into the chair next to hers.

"Why two chairs?" she asked, rubbing her hands over the smooth, white stained wood.

I could've admitted that I wanted to be by her side while she nursed, while she rocked her princess to sleep. Instead, I answered, "Why not?"

"This is quite a surprise."

"This isn't the surprise." I fired up my browser and Googled her name. "Not all of it, anyway."

Photo after photo of Aida popped onto the screen. "This is the surprise." I turned the phone to face her, and watched, with baited breath, while she studied the details presented. Every photo was of Aida Voltolini. None of the images looked like my Aida.

"Tucker," she said, breathless, wary. "I don't. I mean." She choked on a sob. "How?"

"You're free, Aida."

While Aida didn't have a huge internet presence, no social media pages, no tabloid scandals, her face had shown up here and there over the years, candids that were unavoidable, especially for the daughter of an infamous crime lord who'd liked to be seen on the arms of wealthy men. However, the pictures were no longer an accurate representation of Aida. They'd been tweaked, distorted, just enough to ensure nobody could match the flat images to the flesh and blood face that sat next to me.

No fucking idea how Conner pulled it off. No clue how I'd ever repay him. We played news footage from when her father had been killed. Those images reflected a different Aida as well. Conner had worked a miracle. Good fucking guy to have in your corner.

"You did this?" she asked, voice breaking.

I nodded. Unease slithered through me at the dark set of her eyes.

"How?"

"I know a guy."

"No more Aida Voltolini," she mumbled, eyes glassy, unfocused. "This is really happening, isn't it?"

"Aida. You're free. Free to live in peace. Free to make whatever the fuck you want out of your life."

"Tucker." She slapped my phone into my palm.

Click. Click. Click.

Not the fucking nails. "You're not happy."

"I don't know if I want to be free. I don't know if I can give up my birthright. My name. My blood. Just like that.

And how can I leave everything so open-ended? Somebody took down my father. Somebody needs to pay." The pink in her cheeks spread. So did the fire in her eyes.

"Why?" Fuck, I was losing her.

"What do you mean, why? That's how it works. You fuck with Luciano Voltolini, you pay. In blood."

No. No. No. No. No. She didn't mean it. "Aida."

"No, Tucker." She rose to her feet. "I know what you're going to say. And you're wrong. I can't put all that behind me. I can't forgive and forget. It's my history. It's my ugly, fucked up life. You can't possibly understand. I've killed people for lesser crimes. I've carved, I've dismembered, I've choked the life out of men twice my size. I'm good at it, too."

Aida paced the whitewashed floor, the heels of her boots loud and rhythmic in the quiet space, her fingers twisting, pulling, wringing the shape, the life, out of poor Bambi.

I was about to speak when she yelled, "God damn you, Tucker," and threw the innocent toy across the room. "And now I'm just expected to play house? Pretend I'm sweet and innocent Aida Suarez? Sit at home, change diapers, bake cookies, while you're off to work every day? You want me to play wife? Is that what this is about?" she asked, gesturing, quite aggressively, around the room. "Did you think I'd fall to my knees and thank you for this? For this room? For the assumption that I even wanted to shack up with you? I don't need a fucking white knight, Tucker." She stopped in front of the big window, one hand rubbing her belly, the other pressed to her mouth.

When she turned to face me, I could swear, her eyes glowed red. I was fucked.

"Oh my God." She shook her head, loose waves bouncing around her face. "Oh my fucking God. It was you. You arranged my fake death."

Fire beat my cheeks. Dread squeezed the blood from my rapidly beating heart. I could've easily choked out a denial. I hadn't been the one to pull-the-plug, so to speak, regardless of my intentions. "No, Bambi. It wasn't me." I pushed off the rocker and retrieved the stuffed animal from the floor. With a long sigh, I confessed. "But I won't lie. I had arranged for it to happen, only—"

"Only what?" she screamed.

"Somebody beat me to the punch."

Her mouth dropped open. Snapped shut. Pursed. Then she shook her head, throwing her arms out wide. "What the hell were you thinking?"

"That you'd be free. To live the way you deserve, the way your baby deserves."

"That's noble, Tuck. There's just one problem."

Yeah. I sure didn't want to hear what was coming next.

"I'm not yours. My life isn't yours. My baby. Is. Not. Yours. These huge fucking life decisions were not yours to make. You didn't give me freedom, you took it from me. I choose my own fate. Haven't you figured that out by now?"

Sure. Part of me knew she was right. Justified as her indignation was, it didn't stop me from unleashing the alpha beast. Especially after the *I'm not yours* comment. 'Cause really, whether she would freely admit it or not, she was mine. Which also made her baby mine. Which, by default, made her life, mine. That's how I was built. Not a damn thing the fiery-eyed, razor-tongued, she-devil could do to change that fact.

I tossed Bambi—the stuffed one, not the knocked-up one—back into the crib and met Aida toe to toe. Tension hung in the air, a poisonous gas, choking rational thought and gentlemanly guise from the room. "Let me tell you something, Princess. When you spread your legs for me, begged me to fuck your uptight little brains out, you gave up any right to criticize my actions, or judge my intentions. I won't apologize for doing what needed to be done. You're my girl. Makes you my responsibility. It's my job to take care of you however I see fit. That's how I'm built. Understand?"

Too late, I regretted my outburst.

"Understand this, douchebag. I'm nobody's girl but my own." Aida rolled up on her toes, which brought her eyes level with my chin. The devil himself couldn't have rivaled the glare she shot me. "You're a good fuck, Cowboy, but I'm done. We're oil and water. It was never going to work."

Like hell.

"You love me," I reminded her.

Without pause, she retorted, "I told you what you wanted to hear. Only because I wasn't ready to give up that monster cock of yours. That's all you are to me, Tuck. A good fuck. A means to an end. Just like every other man in my life." Aida turned and sauntered away.

I stood, dumbfounded, wounded, and breathing through the sting of that awful sucker punch.

Ugly words. That's all they were. A ramshackle wall to guard her tender heart.

"Bullshit." I stormed toward her, rage and pain fueling my nerves. I reached for her shoulder, to stop her, to slow her down, to pull her to me, hell, to just connect.

Wrong move, apparently. What happened next can only be described as hormone-induced fists of fury.

I woke some time later, on the floor of the nursery in my new house, with a throbbing pain in my temple. My Jeep was gone. And so was Bambi, the stuffed one, and the knocked-up one.

CHAPTER 14

Aida

"NEW WAITRESS STARTING TODAY?" I asked, struggling to adjust my bra.

Slade stood in my bedroom door, looking pert as ever. Tall, lean frame. Legs that stretched to the moon. Perfect blonde hair and flawless, peachy, glowing skin. She made even the unexceptional Truck Stop uniform, red T-shirt and khakis, look amazing.

I looked down at myself and wiggled my toes. At least I could still see my feet, if I leaned forward a bit. Oh, who was I kidding? To see anything below my knees, I'd have to bend at a ninety-degree angle. I couldn't even do that anymore. I waddled to my bed and parked my ever-expanding ass on the mattress.

"She's starting today. Her name's Tuuli. You'll like her. Sweet girl." Slade snagged my boots out of the closet and squatted at my feet to help me slip them on.

"You don't have to do this every morning, you know."

"I know." Huge smiling eyes blinked up at me. "I can't stand watching you struggle. You look like an overturned beetle trying to right itself."

I laughed, because truly, it had to be quite the sight, me trying to bend and dress my feet. Hell. Trying to dress at all.

"Tango said your doctor appointment went well yesterday."

"It did. Baby is healthy. I'm healthy. Everything's good." Except my heart. My ticker seemed to have malfunctioned, or aged a thousand years, aching all the time, creaking and moaning while it pumped blood through my rusty pipes.

Slade rose to stand. I followed her gaze to Tucker's flannel coat draped over the end of my bed. Shit. I'd meant to hide that in the back of the closet.

I ignored her eyebrow wiggle, and her infectious smile.

"You talk to him?" she asked, offering her hand to help me up.

I slapped my fingers into her palm. "No." And then I asked the one question I didn't want to ask, but needed answered in the worst possible way. "Have you heard from him?"

"This morning. He just got back from a run."

My pulse quickened. A *run*? Or a *hunt*? A little thrill shot through me. Shameful, really, how the thought of Tucker rescuing young girls, possibly making their rapists bleed, or, better yet, choking the life out of the perverted fucks, made me shiver with pleasure. I'd been obsessively watching the news for reports that The Reaper had struck again.

"You ever gonna tell me what happened?" she asked.

And expose my weakness and fears? Hell to the N.O.

Could I tell her I panicked? Confess that Tucker's gesture, the nursery, the color scheme, everything, was perfect, and the thought of living with him, raising my daughter, with Tucker, scared the ever living shit out of me? "I'm a heartless bitch, Slade. I used Tucker, led him on. He wants more than I can give."

My only female friend crossed her arms over her chest, raised a brow, and stared me down. "You and I both know your story is bullshit." She picked up Tucker's jacket and tossed it at me. "Don't worry. I won't push the issue. He's my brother, but you're my friend, my sister, and we ladies need to stick together."

Slade headed to the living room. I followed, my heart warming at her *friend* and especially her *sister* comment. For the first time, I shared a deep, soulful connection with another female. And I knew, for the first time, that I would do anything to protect our special bond.

"The baby furniture will be delivered today. I told Tango to have them set it up in your room, but if you'd rather, we can move all your stuff upstairs into the extra bedrooms. That way you and the baby can have separate space."

Tango and Slade had been hinting at me to move upstairs to the main house. I suspected it was because they had little faith in my parenting abilities. I understood their concern. I was terrified myself, but I wasn't about to disrupt their lives by forcing my bastard child on them. I'd been enough of a burden.

"Down here is fine. Thanks for the offer. I know you're trying to help, but I need to do this by myself."

"What's this *by myself* crap? You're not raising this baby alone. As long as you're here, you've got family. Understand? Besides, we'll be down here getting our greedy little fingers on that princess every chance we get."

I threw her my best fake laugh, topping it off with a wink. "I am so excited to meet her I can hardly stand it."

Fuck Slade and her sweet little personality, for making me love her so much. Fuck her for making me want to cry again. Fuck me for being such a sap. She'd seen me cry once already that morning, over a damn puppy food commercial. I wasn't about to break down in front of her again. I turned my back and busied myself with the dog's leash.

"Lola upstairs already?" I asked, missing the mutt's wet nose and morning licks.

"Yeah. Rocky's taking his dog sitting duties very seriously. He made up a corner for her in his bedroom."

Tucker hadn't claimed his dog back after I'd rendered him unconscious and stole his Jeep three weeks ago. I was thankful for Lola's company. Now that I'd gone back to work at The Stop, Rocky had taken it upon himself to babysit the mutt before and after school. Which was fine with me, because it gave me more Rocky time, too. The kid had grown on me, and taken root, like a wart. A cute wart.

"Ready?"

"Ready."

Ten minutes later, I stood in the diner, buttoning a special ordered, maternity chef's coat, over my chest. Charlie and I had developed a smooth morning routine. I separated meat from the bone for the chicken soup. Charlie started the chili. We chopped, diced, sautéed, flipped, fried, laughed, told dirty jokes. We danced around the kitchen, a perfect partnership in our knife-riddled ballet.

I passed a burger plate across the service counter when I heard a familiar laugh over the usual dining area racket. The laugh that had become one of my favorite sounds in the world.

My gut twisted and churned. Pushing up on my toes to see over the counter, I scanned the rows of tables. In the far-left corner, in the special table boasting a picture of Slade's mother and grandfather, Tucker sat with his back to me. Tuuli, the new waitress, stood at his side, smiling wide, a coffee carafe in each hand. Tucker's fingers grazed her waist, and in a gesture far too intimate for two people who'd just met, he stuffed a folded piece of paper into her pocket.

Like I'd taken a bullet to the chest, I stumbled backward, bumping into Charlie, who incidentally, and rather unfortunately, had been holding a stack of plates, which then, despite his desperate attempts to stay balanced, tipped over and crashed onto the stack of freshly washed milkshake glasses, causing a clatter that rivaled cathedral bells. The gentle giant tripped over his feet and dropped, like a nuclear bomb, on his ass. The entire building shook.

Of course, profanities erupted from both our mouths. I squatted, to check Charlie was okay, when the baby decided to perform a backflip, causing me to lose balance and land on hands and knees, nose to crotch, in the giant's lap.

Because that wasn't awkward enough, two beefy arms wrapped around my middle, pulled me off Mount Charlie, and set me on my feet.

I was immediately overcome by a familiar woodsy scent. Tucker. Shit.

I squeezed my eyes closed, willing him away.

"I've nothing against blowjobs in the middle of the day, but not in the same room where you prepare my food." Tucker laughed. "That's just not sanitary."

My cheeks could've erupted hot lava. I glanced from Charlie, to Tucker, and back to Charlie, who was now in a fit of hysterics on the floor.

I found no humor in the situation.

I shoved past Tucker and made my escape, but not before flipping him off. "Not fucking funny, Cowboy."

Tucker

Funniest damn thing I'd ever seen? Charlie's face, while Aida struggled to wiggle out of his lap. The poor guy looked mortified. Aida, on the other hand, wore a murderous glare that stabbed me in all the right places.

I should've chased after her, but I couldn't in good conscience leave Charlie alone to clean the disaster. Glass and porcelain shards littered the kitchen, corner to corner, counter to floor. Even picked some out of Charlie's hair.

Slade jumped in to help, and between the three of us, we had everything back in working order in under twenty minutes.

Aida had yet to come out of the office. Damn, how I wanted to be in there with her. Wasn't about to push the issue though. Aida wasn't the type of woman you pushed. Learned that the hard way. Still had a sore spot on my head to remind me. Figured three weeks was ample time for her to come to her senses. Obviously not. Girl was more stubborn than I'd suspected.

I was about to head home when Slade grabbed my arm and pulled me out the back exit into the icy blast of winter. The door barely closed behind me when she shoved a palm into my chest.

"Want to explain that little show with Tuuli?"

"Little show?"

"Don't play innocent with me, Tuck. I saw it. Everyone saw it. You two were all over each other."

I wanted to laugh. Until I realized that Aida might have witnessed Tuuli's blatant, and unconvincing sexual advances as well. And, dammit. That just pissed me the hell off. I loved my sister, but I wasn't about to get ripped a new asshole for something I didn't do.

"Listen. I can see where you might've gotten the wrong idea. But let me assure you, nothing happened. Your new little waitress zeroed-in on me the second I walked through the front door. She even slipped me her number. I let her know I wasn't interested and slipped it right back into her pocket. The only thing I'm guilty of is asking how her first day was going."

"Oh."

"Yeah. Oh."

Slade crossed her arms over her chest and offered a rueful grin. "I'm sorry."

I could've tortured her for a bit, but frankly, I already had one mad lady in my life, I certainly didn't need another. "You're forgiven."

"Should I fire her?"

"No. Not on my account."

"Whew." Slade dropped her arms and slumped in relief. "Thank goodness. She's running circles around Margie today. It's nice to have some fresh blood in here. Gonna tell me what's going on between you and Aida?"

"Not much to tell. She's mad. It'll pass."

"She misses you."

Fuck. I missed her too.

"Don't give up on her, Tuck."

"Not giving up. Just giving space."

She rolled her eyes. "Sometimes, space is the last thing we need."

"Did I just hear you right? Miss I'll-talk-to-you-in-two-days-when-I've-cooled-my-jets."

"Listen. You're right. I'm the kind of girl who sometimes needs space, especially when I'm mad at you. There's a difference, though. My space has always existed inside the protective shield of loved ones. Tango and Rocky. You and your parents. My work family. Aida's space is unguarded; I mean, we're here, obviously, but she doesn't get that, yet. In her world, there's no border, there's no support system surrounding her, and she's just floating around out there in the great unknown, lost and alone. You need to show her that she's not alone, no matter how hard she pushes, or how much she insists that she's doing great on her own. Her personal space bubble will eventually get too big. She'll be lost."

Not quite sure I understood what my sister was trying to say. What I did know, what resonated deep, was that without Aida, my heart was a black hole, sucking all my joy, and sense of purpose into its unfathomable depths. I was done with keeping my distance.

I'd pretended to stay busy with work. Hunted twice. Left two girls at the Compton ranch. Nothing filled the Aida-shaped hole in my soul. Not even beating the shit out of a pimp I'd "accidentally" bumped in to.

"We done here?" I asked Slade. "I kinda need to be somewhere."

"Yeah. We're done." She gave me a squeeze. "Go get her, tiger."

We headed back inside. Slade passed her office door, turned and offered me a wink, then headed to the dining area, calling Tuuli's name.

Palms sweaty, I turned the knob and slowly pushed the door open. "Aida?"

I felt the soft rush of wind pass my face, heard the dull thunk of something hit the wall behind me. Knew what it was without having to look. I ducked back behind the safety of the door. "C'mon now, Bambi. Violence isn't necessary. Just wanna talk."

Thunk.

Another knife embedded in the door above my fingers. Damn the girl had impeccable aim. Couldn't ignore the swell of pride in my chest.

Foolishly, I assumed it was safe to enter. When I stepped back into the line of fire, a third blade landed at my feet, stopping me in my tracks.

"I'm not in the mood for talking."

I threw my palms up in surrender. "Okay. Okay. I get it. You're not ready to see me." When I finally rested my gaze on the beauty standing before me, I stumbled back a step. Fuck. Her baby bump had doubled in size. So had her breasts, but I tried not to focus on those. Not a good time.

Cheeks flushed, chest raising and falling in short bursts, Aida stared me down. "What do you want?"

I wasn't about to back off, but damn, if looks could kill, I'd be dust. "Want to make sure you're okay."

"I'm not your concern."

Christ. How long was she going to carry on her charade? "Okay then. How's my dog? You taking good care of her?"

Aida rested both hands on her hips and took a deep breath. "*My* dog is good. You no longer have a dog. She likes me better, so she's mine."

"Fair enough." I nodded in concession. Choose your battles wisely, I reminded myself. Besides, I had left Lola with her for a reason.

"Anything else, Cowboy? I need to get back to work." Aida waddled past me—and what a waddle it was—and plucked her knives out of the wall and door.

Knowing she wouldn't want to struggle in front of me, I squatted and picked her blade up off the floor. Without meeting my gaze, she held out her palm. When I handed her the knife, she elbowed past me, nose in the air, and headed toward the kitchen.

I wasn't ready to let her go. Damn, how I wanted to throw her on the couch and fuck the attitude right out of her. "I miss you."

Aida paused, her feet squeaking on the tile floor.

Turn around, baby. Turn around.

Aida shot me a glance over her shoulder, a small smirk playing on her face. Damn the girl was stubborn, and killing me.

"I miss you, Bambi," I repeated. Groveling idiot.

Her smirk disappeared, and as I watched her retreat, she shouted over her shoulder, "I know."

Aida

"I didn't know, Aida. I'm sorry. I never would've flirted with him." Tuuli stood a safe distance away, shoulders slumped, nervously picking at the skin of her arm. Hips cocked, her right heel bounced off the floor like it had a mind of its own.

Mousy little thing. Too bad. She was pretty, underneath the piles of bullshit she was feeding me. My inner lie detector was bouncing off the charts.

"Didn't know what?" I asked, clenching my fists at my sides.

Tuuli stared at the floor. "That he was your boyfriend."

"Who said he was my boyfriend?" Why did my voice sound so high?

"Tucker did. And then Slade." She dropped her hands to her hips and sucked in a sharp breath. "I'm sorry. He was so nice to me. He didn't have a wedding ring so I figured *what the hell* and wrote my number on a piece of paper. I tried giving it to him, but he said he was in a committed relationship, with you."

Hmm. The convo shifted from suspicious, to morbidly exciting. "He said that?"

"I can't lose this job. I'm not a slut or anything. I don't go around giving my number to every guy I meet. I just. He just. I don't know. He was so nice, and I'm new in town and my girlfriends said I needed to stop being so shy, and that I needed to flirt if I wanted good tips."

I couldn't be mad. I would've done the same thing had the tables been turned. Tucker was eye candy, the kind that put you at risk for diabetes. Only, had I been the new waitress making the moves, I wouldn't have taken no for an answer. I would've had the man trapped, pants to ankles, in the ladies room, tipping me in other ways.

The old me would've done that, anyway. The new me? Well. The new me choked on the rush of motherly instinct rising in my throat, and instead of giving Tuuli the proverbial pat on the back, I instead said, "Listen. You can't go around giving your number to strangers, especially at work. Besides being highly unprofessional, it's also so, so dangerous. God, what if he was a serial killer or something, or some perverted old man who picks up young girls and sells them on the black market? You have to be careful."

Tuuli cringed. More than cringed. Curled in on herself. All color left her face, which was nearly impossible seeing as she was one of the palest girls I'd ever seen. She rubbed her stomach, gaze aimed at the floor. "I know. You're right," she half-squeaked, half-whispered.

For the first time since she caught me in the hallway, she met my gaze. The girl had beautiful, stormy, ocean blue eyes. Eyes that had seen too much. Eyes that didn't match her demeanor when she asked, "Is he your baby's father?"

Instinctively, protectively, my hands raised to my stomach. "It's complicated." I dropped my protective glare into place. "And none of your fucking business."

Why did I snap at her? Not sure. I was sure, though, that I didn't trust the girl. I'd mastered the art of reading people at an early age, and this girl was hiding a novel's worth of secrets. Tuuli whispered another *I'm sorry*, turned on her heels, and headed back to the dining room, leaving me to focus on my painful heartbeat, and Tucker's haunting words. *I miss you.*

I missed him, too. So much. Too much. More than I missed Tito. More than I missed my dead father. Or my old life.

The baby missed him, too. When he'd been in the office earlier, she had started to move inside me at the sound of his voice. That was why I'd bolted, instead of hashing things out with him like I should've done. I couldn't let him witness me breaking, and for reasons I didn't understand, and certainly didn't one hundred percent believe in, I needed to stand my ground.

Tucker needed to know I wasn't the kind of woman to bow to a man's will.

Although, shamefully, and most likely because of the stupid hormones, I wanted to.

Tucker

I wanted to lock her in the bedroom and fuck her into next week. I wanted my hands, my lips, my tongue, touching every inch of her round little body. I wanted Aida. My Bambi. I wanted us.

I needed her under my roof. In my bed. Smiling at me from across the breakfast table—messy hair, swollen lips, sleepy eyes. I needed that surge of adrenaline I experienced every time she walked into my line of vision. More than anything, I needed her to need me, too.

I watched, from Rocky's bedroom window, as Tango walked Aida down the steps to her apartment door. I waited. Waited. Waited for Tango to come collect his son. I heard the back door open and close.

"Well. This is it, Rockster. Wish me luck." I pulled my little nephew into a bear hug, mussed his hair, and gave him a high-five.

"Luck, Tuck," he said before giggling at his rhyme. Then he hot-footed it down the stairs to his dad singing, "Luck, Tuck. Luck, Tuck."

I followed, calling Lola to come, offered Tango a quick handshake, and headed toward my certain humiliation. A worthy sacrifice, if it meant having Aida back in my arms.

Fuck.

I shook off my nerves, cleared my throat, and strummed my guitar. After knocking softly, I parked my ass on the frozen cement stairs. Then I started to sing, hoping like fucking hell that Tango was too busy with his son to hear me. I belted out the lyrics to Gavin Degraw's "Soldier."

My voice trembled. My long-neglected Martin was out of tune. I forced the lyrics anyway, and urged my rusty fingers to move against the biting cold.

I'd come nearly to the end of the song, the line about never surrendering, when the door opened.

My beauty, my fucking soul, leaned against the doorjamb, and crossed her naked legs at the ankles. Arms crossed, head down. My goddamned flannel jacket wrapped around her like a security blanket.

It took everything in me to stay where I was. To choke out the last lyrics. And to pray she was getting the message. *I'm here to stay. I got you.*

Tear-soaked lashes lifted, revealing those big fucking doe eyes I missed so much.

And when she smiled. God, when she smiled, I was done for. Her gaze dropped to my hands, raked the length of the guitar, and landed on Lola. She tilted her head, her smile turning into a devilish smirk. "C'mon, girl," she said, opening the door wider for Lola to enter.

I was frozen in place, dumbstruck, awed, overwhelmed by her beauty. Aida raised one of her delicate deadly hands to her face and wiped the moisture from her cheeks. Our eyes locked. My heart calmed. Her cheeks flushed.

Like the soul knows its maker, I knew deep and true, that whatever it was that drew us together, however many obstacles we'd be forced to decimate, Aida and I were bound by destiny, and we were going to be okay. We'd been planned from the beginning of time. Our names had been written in the stars.

I would fight until my dying breath to make her understand that, too.

And because I knew she would be my soldier, every bit as much as I would be hers, I whispered, "I need you, Bambi," trusting that she wouldn't let me down.

I pushed to my feet on her sharp inhalation.

"Say it again." Aida gripped the lapels of her jacket.

"I need you."

Her fingers curled around the wool flannel, and slowly, torturously, she pulled the coat open, revealing her naked breasts, the stretched skin of her round belly, her dark, hardened nipples.

Like an animal in heat, I inhaled, craving her scent. I struggled to pull oxygen into my lungs. My cock hardened, and pulsed, and jerked in my pants. And like a switch had been flipped, the dominant me I'd tried so hard to keep at bay, pushed to the surface, and before I could get him in check, Aida was in my arms, I'd pushed her inside the door, slammed it shut, and tore that fucking coat off her body.

So much for groveling.

I pinned her against the wall with every intention of giving that mouth a workout. She pushed me away, lids heavy with lust, lips parted in a *whoa there, cowboy* smirk.

Her deadly fingers curled around the neck of my guitar. She turned, giving me a good, hard look at that heart-shaped ass, and offered her hand. When I linked our fingers, Aida guided me to her room—the siren luring the doomed sailor.

Aida laid my instrument on the bed. I barely had time to take in the small space, now crowded with a crib and a changing table, before she tugged at the buckle of my belt. I dropped my coat to the floor, and pulled my sweater over my head while she worked the buttons of my jeans.

"Lay down, Bambi," I urged her, pulling her hands away from the danger zone. If she touched me, our reunion would be over before it began. "I need to look at you."

With a moan, Aida crawled to the center of the bed, stretched on her side, and teased a finger around the pebbled tip of her swollen breasts. Fuck me. I'd never seen such a mind-blowing display of raw, sexual, female beauty. Round and swollen, and full. Full of desire. Full of love. Full of life, in the simplest, purest form.

I knelt, to loosen my laces, unable to take my eyes off the soft curves spread before me. I scrambled to get rid of my boots and jeans, cringing through the pain of my atomic hard-on, and when fully naked, I gave my cock one good stroke before stretching on the bed, side by side with my eager girl.

Our lips crashed together in clumsy desperation. Arms and legs tangled. Hands exploring. Hips thrusting, bodies gyrating. The baby made it damn difficult to pull her as close as I needed. Aida pushed her fingers through my hair and pulled hard.

I'd missed that wicked edge so much.

Her kiss deepened, and I gave her everything I had—my tongue, my lips, my heart and soul, my strength and fears— and when I moaned in unbridled pleasure, she pulled away and stroked my cheek with a delicate, desperate touch.

Then my hard, dark angel softened, revealing the vulnerable girl I'd known was there all along. "Sing to me again," she rasped, tears spilling freely.

A small request that meant the world.

My heart split wide open. Fuck. Why hadn't I done this sooner?

My dick throbbed with the need for release, but I pushed through the pain, curling my arms around her.

At first, I hummed, because that's all my throat could manage. My favorite song by Terence Trent D' Arby, the song she had caught me singing in the barn. The song that shares the name from my favorite movie, *Frankie and Johnny*.

With her belly pressed tight against mine, Aida continued to cry while I sang softly in her ear. I hated that nobody had ever sung to her. I hated that my precious angel hadn't enjoyed simple childhood pleasures, like singing, like raising pets, like playing with dolls, and learning how to nurture and care for another.

And while I crooned in her ear, bodies pressed tight, I felt a gentle roll across her stomach, and then the firm push, of an arm, or a foot, or a head, I couldn't be sure. I was sure, though, that I felt the baby move. And I was sure that my heart grew ten sizes when Aida's cries turned into chuckles.

Pressing her lips to my ear, she whispered, "She only does that when she hears your voice."

In that moment, one of the top five greatest days of my life, I became a father.

CHAPTER 15

Aida

A FRESH, HEAVY SNOW fell, hugging the trees, and cocooning the property surrounding The Truck Stop in a gorgeous, shimmering sheen of white that had too soon been defiled by the destruction of a snow plow.

I swallowed my last sip of hot chocolate and watched through the service window as Tuuli handed the bill to her only remaining customer. Charlie and I had closed the kitchen thirty minutes ago. He'd left for the night, eager to get to his weekly poker game. I'd promised to stay and lock things up for Slade, who had dinner plans with Tango's father.

The customer, who sat with his back to me, was large, and appeared to be in no hurry to leave. He wore a black beanie and heavy coat with a high collar that blocked his face from my view. He studied the bill, said something to Tuuli, then handed her a wad of cash.

If I wasn't mistaken, her cheeks reddened. Then again, everything made her blush. I waited for the man to ready himself to leave. Instead, he settled deeper into his seat and twisted his coffee cup between his thumb and forefinger.

I released a groan. What was his deal? I wanted to go home.

My new cell phone chimed with an incoming text.

Tucker: Running late. Traffic is a nightmare. Officer
McGuire will drive you home.
Me: Stay safe

Tucker and I hadn't discussed living together again. He
had, however, asked me on a date. I'd accepted, and after
dinner and a stroll through Lakeside Park, I'd invited him in,
and I'd given him dessert with a side of orgasms. Afterward,
he had held me close, singing a tune his mother lulled him
to sleep with when he was a child, "Dream A Little Dream."
I'd heard the song a million times, performed by different
lounge singers in one of my father's classier establishments
on the Upper West Side, but the lyrics had never touched me
like they did when they came from Tucker's lips. I'd fallen
asleep in his arms, sucker-punched by a love song.

The last few days had pretty much replayed on the same
loop. Dates. Sex. Cuddling. Falling asleep together. Waking
together. He'd drive me down the hill to The Stop before
heading to his home office. He'd pick me up in the afternoon,
or whenever I was too tired to be on my feet any longer.

Aida Voltolini was fading into the bliss of small town
simple. Aida Suarez was blossoming.

Funny thing? I was starting to like the new me, despite
missing that wicked edge I'd always loved to teeter on.

A chill danced up my spine as Tuuli slammed through
the kitchen door.

"I don't know what this guy's deal is, but he won't leave.
Says he wants more coffee. Shoved a handful of twenties at
me." She dropped a wadded pile of green on the counter.

"Fuck no," I said, pushing away from the sink. Being a
short girl, I'd been taught, or trained, rather, to carry myself
like the deadly heiress I was. Lithe. Graceful. Confident.
Agile. Intimidating.

My father used to say, "Carry yourself like you own the world, Princess, not like you bear its weight on your shoulders. Imagine the little people at your feet, fleeing, scurrying, praying you step around them rather than crush them under your heels."

His advice had served me well over the years. I'd walk into a room, and everyone, strangers and acquaintances alike, would step aside with looks of reverence on their faces.

Dad had never considered that I would someday be carrying seven extra pounds of human, and twenty extra pounds of whatever it is women gain while growing a baby, and as I waddled across the kitchen, and down the hallway toward the dining room, I had to stop and pull up the waistband of my maternity leggings because they were rolling down my stomach. I also had to catch my breath, which had become more agitating over the past few days.

I took a moment to straighten my shoulders and conjure my *don't fuck with me* face before pushing through the swinging double doors. Unfortunately, my sciatica decided to flair, shooting knee-buckling pain through the left side of my ass and down the backside of my leg. "Ow. Fuck," shot out of my mouth, and I gripped the counter, breathing through the burn.

When I lifted my head, set to scream in frustration, a familiar set of hazel eyes glared down at me, stopping me cold. Massive hands gripped my shoulders. Thick, full lips parted on an exasperated exhale before twisting into a morbid grin.

The Earth disappeared under my feet, and darkness ascended.

"Princess." Rafael's gaze dropped to my belly and rested there, full of misplaced awe. "Seems I've found you just in time."

I tried to pull away. Strong fingers curled tighter into my flesh, holding me steady.

Bile rose in my throat. My vision blurred for a few torturous moments before narrowing back into focus. Razor sharp focus.

I met Rafael in the eye. He leaned close, lips to ear close, inciting a shiver, and not the good kind. "Whoo baby," he whistled. "You're a sight. All round and swollen." He inhaled a sharp breath. "My cock is so fucking hard right now."

I blinked the last bite of shock away, and found my voice. "It still works? Damn. Thought I'd taken care of that bastard."

"Oh, baby. It works. I'm gonna show you just how well." Rafael yanked hard, crushing me to his chest, and forced our mouths together.

I wasted no time pulling his bottom lip between my teeth and sinking deep. He tried to pull away, but I tightened my jaw, gagging on the metallic tang of his blood. The bite earned me a hard slap to the temple. Reflexively, I released his lip and thrust the palm of my right hand into his nose.

Rafael's head flew back, warm spray hit my face, and I turned and sprinted toward the kitchen. Tuuli stood in the hallway, eyes wide, phone in hand. I hoped to Christ she'd dialed 911, for her sake, anyway.

"Run!" I screamed, grabbing her elbow as I passed, and yanking her with me. "Run, goddammit."

We were almost to the back exit when a bullet embedded in the door above our heads. Pushing the small girl behind me, I turned to face two hundred pounds of pissed off, bloody male.

He wouldn't shoot me. That much I knew. Not while I was carrying his child. I sucked in a breath for courage and turned my back to the man. I met Tuuli's frightened eyes and pushed the back door open. "Go. Get out of here. Run like hell."

Tuuli froze in place, her small window of opportunity gone. Rafael's hand came around my throat from behind. Before he could secure me, I dropped like dead weight to my knees, effectively freeing myself and rolling out of the way. I pushed to my feet but a muscle-shredding cramp forced me right back to the floor.

Tears blurred my vision, and I clamped my mouth shut to keep from crying out in agony. Oh, fuck. My insides tightened and twisted, like a giant screw was being hand cranked through my lower back. I'd never known such torture, and I was helpless. Couldn't move, couldn't breathe, couldn't defend myself.

Rafael turned to face me, blood dripping from his nose, chest heaving, eyes blazing. "Get up, Voltolini." He kicked at my feet.

Tuuli screamed, blood curdling, and surprising, coming from her mousy frame, and launched herself up, onto Rafael's back, wrapping around him like a monkey hitching a ride. The poor girl didn't stand a chance against the well-trained fighter. I watched in horror as he twisted, grabbed her small frame, and tossed her like a rag doll into the wall. My would-be savior fell, her head hitting hard and bouncing twice, before her body went limp.

I needed to fight. But the pain. The crippling pain held me prisoner in my own body.

Rafael crouched, brushed hair out of my face, then pulled a rope out of his pocket, and proceeded to tie my wrists together behind my back.

He then lifted Tuuli off the ground like she weighed nothing and hoisted her lifeless body over his shoulder before grabbing a handful of my hair and forcing me to my feet. "Time to go, Princess. No more bullshit. And if you don't come quietly, this pretty little waitress will take one between the eyes."

For all I knew, Tuuli was a ghost already. Blood trickled from the back of her head, weaving a trail through her white hair, following the length of her ponytail, and drip, drip, dripping on the checkered tile.

If she wasn't dead, I had no doubt she would be soon. I didn't want to be the reason for her demise. I wasn't willing to risk even a one percent chance she'd still be breathing at the other end of this nightmare. So, despite the rage welling, rolling, boiling, churning inside me, I didn't fight back. Not yet.

Besides, I had backup. "You won't get two steps out that door, you fuck-twat." I groaned. "I have security detail outside."

"You mean that sorry excuse for an officer in the Chevy out front? He's been dead for hours."

Tucker

I'd been stuck in traffic for hours.

Damn snow. Damn careless drivers. Damn, I needed to get to my girl, fall into bed, snuggle close, and sleep for the next twenty-four hours. The day had been one shit storm after another with the weather. Highways closed. Drivers stranded. Bullshit paperwork.

When I pulled up to the dark house, the first warning tingle hit me. When I opened the door to Aida's apartment, Lola sprinted outside and tore down the hill. The apartment was dark and quiet. My heart hit my gut with a thud.

It took me two seconds to search the place. Living room and kitchen, empty. Bedroom, empty. Bathroom, empty. I sprinted back outside and across the lawn. The thick falling snow played with my vision, but I could see that The Stop was dark inside. The closed sign blared at me like a warning signal, and Lola was barking something fierce at Officer McGuire's Chevy.

"Fuck," I shouted, my legs carrying me toward the diner.

I pulled my cell from my pocket and dialed Aida. The call went straight to voicemail. Then I dialed Tango. His sleepy voice greeted me with, "This better be good."

Skipping pleasantries, I spit out, "Aida with you guys?"

"No, Aida isn't with us. Thought you were picking her up."

"I got stuck behind a pileup. McGuire was supposed to drive her home. Just got to the house. She's not here."

I had descended half the hill, my heart beating harder with each trudge through the white frozen terrain. Tango released a string of profanities.

Through the front window, I caught sight of movement, a shadow, and felt a rush of relief. I wanted to run, but my boots sunk calf-deep into the snow, and it took all my effort to stay upright.

"Listen, T. I'm almost at The Stop. Call you back." I shoved the cell into my pocket.

By the time I reached the truck, I was out of breath, and my lungs ached from the cold. That was nothing compared to the freeze that hit my veins when I noticed the broken driver's side window. When I looked inside and found the new hire, Jason McGuire, laying across the seat, eyes open but lifeless, I damn near fell to my knees.

The cowbell rattled, snapping my attention back to the diner. A large man, shrouded in black, barreled through the front door, gun raised and aimed at my chest.

The air left my lungs, but I coiled for a fight.

The dark figure stopped in his tracks. Lowered his arms. Swiped the hood off his head, and met me with a dead stare.

Tito.

He stepped closer, giving me a full view of his features. He was not the clean-cut, playboy I'd met months ago. The man standing before me was broken. Thick, unkempt beard. Dull, red-rimmed eyes that hadn't seen sleep in days. Red, puckered skin marred the left side of his otherwise handsome face, stretching from his temple downward, disfiguring the corner of his eye.

"Tito. Where the hell have you been? We thought you were dead."

"Tucker." Tito offered nothing but a clap on the shoulder before pulling a cell out of his pocket and thumbing the screen.

"Where's Aida?"

Violent, angry eyes met mine. He spoke into his phone. "T. How fast can you get to The Stop?" He paused, pounding a palm against his head. "No. There isn't enough time. Meet me at Eagle Point Motel. Come alone."

"Where's Aida?" I asked again, my mind, my patience, spinning out of control.

A cop was dead. Tito had appeared out of thin air. There was only one explanation. One outcome to this scenario. Her demons had come back to haunt her.

Tito tucked his pistol away, his eyes focused over my shoulder. "He found her."

"Who?"

"Turner. Fuckin' Turner. I had him. I finally had him cornered, and this damn snowstorm fucked everything up."

My legs turned to rubber. My body numbed. "Turner's here? He found Aida? How? Where is she?"

"Where's your Jeep?"

"At the house."

He pushed past me, head down, gait resolute.

I matched him stride for angry stride, a time bomb of rage, heat, and jagged nerves. We made the climb back toward the house, silent, but roaring nonetheless.

"Eagle Point Motel," he commanded before climbing into my Jeep.

I drove, unsure what I would find when we reached our destination, but one hundred percent certain that when we found Turner, I was going to kill that motherfucker.

Aida

"I'm going to kill you, motherfucker," I snarled, turning to check on the mousy little blonde.

Tuuli lay unconscious in the back seat. Her chest rose and fell in short bursts. Breathing, thank God, but I didn't know the extent of her injuries, and I had no idea how much time we had before Rafael decided he didn't need her anymore.

I could not lose my shit. For Tuuli, for the baby, I had to keep my crazy in check until he let down his guard.

Rafael half-smiled, shifting the ancient sedan, no doubt stolen, into low gear. "Ugly words from such a pretty mouth."

He didn't know ugly. Not like I knew ugly. I lived and breathed dark and dirty. I was about to unleash my tarnished soul all over his ass. "I won't kill you right away, though. I'll start by gutting you. I'll tie your hands above your head, cut you slow and deep, but I'll keep you conscious, so you can watch your innards spill to the floor at your feet. You'll cry. They all do. You'll beg me to stop. I won't. When the floor is wet and slippery, I'll cut you free. You'll struggle to get away. Even try to scoop your rubbery guts off the ground and run for help. You'll try. And because you're a pathetic piece of shit, you'll fail. You'll fall into the pile of your own intestines, roll around, tangle yourself, maybe even try to stuff them back inside your rotting carcass. All the while, you'll be screaming. Screaming. Screaming like a terrified child."

Veins bulged on his hands and forearms. His eyes never left the road, but when he backhanded me, his aim was spot on. "You're crazier than your old man."

I only stopped taunting him because another cramp hit me hard. I faced the window, baring down, breathing through the agony. Tears of pain wet my face, but I hid behind the shield of my hair.

I wasn't naive. The baby was in trouble. Probably stress-induced. It was too early for her to come, so I convinced myself I wasn't having contractions. Mind over matter, or some bullshit like that. I couldn't buckle. I couldn't break. I needed to buck the fuck up and push through the pain so I could take care of Rafael once and for all.

We headed around the south side of Lake Willow and parked in front of room number five at the Eagle Point Motel. The sky was dark as tar, the stars hidden behind black snow clouds. Had I been with anyone else, or not chomping at the bit for blood, I might have enjoyed Mother Nature's artwork. Instead, I plotted the death of my baby's father. Bare hands, blunt weapon, or sharp object? So many options. Whatever I chose, the result would have to come swift, considering my uterus was trying damn hard to turn itself inside-out.

Rafael hoisted Tuuli back over his shoulder, pulled a key out of his pocket, and led me into the small room. My senses were bombarded with telltale signs of bachelorhood. Stale pizza. Body odor. Dirty clothes tossed about. Porn magazines tossed across the counter of the kitchenette.

Rafael had found my knives before stuffing me into the car. He pulled them out of his coat pocket and tossed them on the unmade, queen-sized mattress. Careless idiot.

With a tight grip above my elbow, he forced me into the small bathroom and shoved me onto the toilet, ordering me to, "Sit still" before dropping Tuuli into the dirty tub.

He stuffed a hand towel in her mouth, and pulled another rope out of his pocket, working it around her wrists and ankles.

While he had his back to me, I worked viciously at the ropes binding my hands. He stood, moved to the sink, and proceeded to clean his bloody face and poke at the bruises and swelling around his nose.

I wasn't the only one who'd gained weight since the night I'd sealed Rafael's fate. His once-defined muscles were now more fluff than buff. He'd shaved his head. His hazel eyes remained the same, though, wild and exotic against the backdrop of his rich, dark skin.

"What's the plan, here, Einstein?"

"The plan is simple, Princess. I take care of you until you deliver my child, then I slit your throat." He stuffed a wad of tissue up his left nostril. "You're dead already, so no one will miss you. Especially me." Rafael shot me a wink, studied himself one more time, then squatted at my feet, rubbing his large hands over my thighs. "Then I disappear with my child, and your fortune."

I threw my head back and laughed. "What fortune? Aida Voltolini is dead. I've got nothing."

His head tilted, brows pinching together in amusement, or perhaps dismay. "You don't know, do you?"

"I know you're going to die today."

"That's cute." The bastard tapped my nose, then leaned down, resting his forehead on my stomach. He breathed deep and brought his hands up to cup my waist before lifting his head and continuing. "Aida Voltolini never had anything. Sure, aside from your own substantial bank account, you had access to your father's money, but you were never meant to inherit his wealth. Since the day you were born, Daddy Dearest poured millions into offshore accounts under the name Aida Suarez."

"Bullshit." I stared long and hard into Rafael's eyes, desperately searching for signs of deception. I found nothing but cold, hard truth. "I don't believe you."

"When's the last time you checked the balance on your bank account? The fake one."

My heart dropped to my gut. I'd never checked my bank account. Hadn't used the credit card even once. Between Tucker, Tango, and Slade, I'd had no reason. They'd taken care of every necessity. Food, clothing, housing, even baby supplies. I'd never seen a bill from the ob/gyn. I wasn't even getting a paycheck from The Truck Stop.

I worked viciously at the ropes binding my wrists, every string of willpower I owned stretching to its limit. I would not let him see me crack. I would not give him access to the devastation wreaking havoc inside my iron shell.

Vile, vile hatred brewed in my gut, a dizzying blend of betrayal and revenge. "How do you know this, Rafael?"

"Your father wouldn't crack, but his lawyer, that guy squealed like a pig when I tore his flesh away, layer by layer. It's shameful how easy it was to persuade him. No loyalty anymore."

"*You* killed them." The ropes loosened behind me, and with careful movements, I worked on freeing one hand.

"Killed them both in that damn basement. Then I lit up the Poughkeepsie sky like the Fourth of July." He stretched his arms out wide, proud as a peacock. "It was beautiful."

I didn't believe for one second that Turner could pull off my father's murder on his own. Either he was lying, or someone was pulling his strings. A rival family perhaps? Didn't matter, really. He'd played a part in killing my father, and most likely Tito. It was his turn to die.

The fool had underestimated me again. He'd assumed a vulnerable position, squatting between my legs, his head level with mine, his attentions on my belly.

My hands now free, I leaned away from him, only a fraction, enough to give me some momentum. Before his eyes met mine, I grabbed the collar of his shirt, tucked my chin and pulled hard, slamming his face into the crown of my head. I did it again, and again, releasing him only when his body slumped against me.

Blood covered his face and hands, dripped warm and sticky through my hair. I pushed to my feet, stumbling over his large frame and catching myself on the towel rack.

Blinding pain twisted my insides, the room darkened, and I doubled over. Time was critical. I couldn't succumb to the agony. I pushed through the pain, one hand cradling my stomach, one bracing me on the wall, and forced my legs to carry me toward the bed where he'd dropped my blades.

"Aida," Rafael half-mumbled, half-screamed.

Another cramp forced me to my knees. Heavy footsteps stomped behind me. I could see my blades. They were close. So close. But the pain. My God. The pain. *My baby.*

"Fuck the money. Fuck your baby and that little bitch waitress. You're all dead."

My baby. My princess.

I pushed forward, on hands and knees, diving for my weapons.

Rafael tangled his fingers through my hair and yanked.

Too fucking late.

I curled my fingers around the cold steel of one blade and swung blindly, catching him above his left knee. And then, I lost control. For my unborn child, for Tuuli, I stabbed. And I stabbed. And I stabbed.

Tucker

Stabbing pain clawed my chest, constricted my lungs, riled my thoughts. I drove in silence, ignoring traffic laws, navigating the treacherous roads like a man with a death wish.

My skin no longer fit around my rage-riddled insides.

The air inside the vehicle took on a life of its own, twirling and swirling around us like a demon—taunting, riling, whispering testosterone filled encouragements, infecting us with insatiable hunger for blood.

I would end Rafael Turner. I would steal his last breath. I would choke the putrid oxygen from his lungs. There was no room for moral justification. Only murder. Only pain. Only revenge. My only purpose to protect my queen.

"You sure that's where he's taken her?" I turned a hard left, the backend of the SUV sliding, narrowly missing a parked car.

"Yes," came from under the dark hood covering Tito's face.

"And you know this, how?"

"Tracked him down this morning. Got caught in the storm or I would've gotten to him before..." Tito sucked in a breath and pounded his fist into the dash. "Fuck! He wasn't supposed to find her."

"Listen, Moretti. Not sure what you've been through. Not gonna ask, either. Right now, Aida is our priority, so you need to steady your shit. Got me?"

Clearly hanging by a thread, Tito clasped his hands behind his head and covered his face with his arms, rocking forward and back in his seat, mumbling words I couldn't make out.

Whatever hell he'd survived, the damage was deep.

We reached the Eagle Point Motel ten minutes later. I parked around the corner. The lot was barren, aside from one sedan parked in front of room number five and a new Ford parked behind the office. The hotel sign read, *Closed for Renovations*.

Tito's voice cut through my stupor. "Renovations, my ass."

Tango's Rover pulled alongside us.

I cut the ignition and slipped out of the seat. While Tito and Tango exchanged an embrace, and long overdue words, my legs carried me toward the only room with a light on, my thoughts solely on Aida.

Tito jogged to my side, meeting me stride for stride, and with a pained growl said, "The fucker is mine. His blood, his pain, his screams, mine."

I didn't respond. One way or another, by his hand or mine, Turner would suffer.

Tango came behind us, gripping each of our shoulders. "We bleeding him for intel before ending him?" Tango asked with a snarl.

"I'm bleeding him for pleasure." Tito halted, pointed to the burn scar on his face. "This right here? That's all the intel we need."

While the cousins shared a stare down, a bonding, or reunion, or whatever the fuck they were wasting their time doing, I closed the distance between me and that cheap-ass motel room door with the cheesy gold-plated number five nailed to its middle.

One kick did the trick.

One glance at the room, the bloodbath, cut me to the quick. Stopped me dead.

I'd come to rescue Aida.

Too bad no one had come to save Rafael Turner.

Nothing, not even the hell I'd witnessed during two tours of duty, could've prepared me for the gruesome scene.

Turner, at least I assumed the bloody mess was Turner, sat in a chair in the center of the small room. The only thing holding him upright was a bathrobe belt tied around his chest and the back of the chair. Flesh hung from his body in ribbons, blood decorated all four walls, even the ceiling. His face was swollen and bruised beyond recognition.

Aida stood behind him, blood matted hair covering her face. One of her knives sat on the bed, she held the other to his neck.

"Where's Tito?" she mumbled.

Rafael wasn't moving.

"Where's Tito?" she screamed.

Nothing but a garbled wheeze came from his swollen lips.

"Motherfucker," Tango groaned behind me.

"Tito is safe, baby," I whispered, unable to back my tone with any semblance of strength. "Look. He's right here."

A large body pushed past me. "Princess. It's me."

Aida twitched at the sound of his voice. Her murderous glare stayed trained on the bloody man beneath her hands.

"He'll never be safe," Aida snapped, voice cold and hard. "My daughter will never be safe." Hands trembling, she leaned forward and laid the blade across Turner's throat. "Not while Rafael is breathing."

She pulled the steel across his throat, half an inch, then released a sob.

"I can't do it," she cried, face crumpling. "I can't kill him. I can't do it." Her knife hit the floor at her feet. "I don't want to be a monster. I don't want to be this ugly person anymore. I can't kill him. I can't with my baby girl inside me. I can't bring her into the world this way."

Good girl.

What she failed to realize, what I would never tell her, was that Turner, although still breathing, wouldn't survive the wounds she'd inflicted. No doctor in the world could stitch him back together. Not in time to save his life anyway.

I shot a quick glance over my shoulder. Tango stood in the threshold, gripping each side of the door frame, and taking in the scene wearing a stone-cold mask.

"I don't want this life anymore," Aida whispered, stumbling backward, bumping against the wall.

Rafael's mouth worked frantically, his head lulling from side to side. I leaned closer, straining to decipher his mumbles. "My girl," he wheezed. "My baby."

I met Aida's eyes. Her lip was swollen, her cheek, bruised. Tears cleared a path through the blood on her face. Trembling hands gripped her stomach.

I stepped behind Turner and bent low, pulling his chin up and pressing my mouth to his ear. I offered him the last words he would ever hear. "That's *my* girl, and that child growing inside her, she's mine, too."

"Take care of Aida," came a gruff voice behind me. "I want his last breaths."

Tito took my place at the dead man's back. He dragged the knife across Turner's throat, opening the flesh ear to ear, and held his head while he jerked and spasmed, his body putting up one last fight before succumbing to death.

Aida cried out in pain. I turned in time to watch her crumple to the ground. Eyes pinched tight, she breathed a loud, "Fuck, fuck, fuck."

I dropped to the floor with her, pulling her to me. "What is it?"

"It's a cramp. Just a bad cramp."

Like fucking hell it was a cramp.

"How long has this been going on, baby?" I asked, brushing clumps of sticky hair off her face.

"Couple hours, I think." She grimaced, her face contorting, nostrils flaring, breaths harsh and deep. "Not sure how long I've been here."

I breathed with her until her jaw unclenched, her face unscrewed, until I felt her muscles relax in my arms. "Aida, sweetheart. You're about to have this baby."

"I'm fine," she argued. "It's just cramps."

Stubborn little minx. "You're about to meet your daughter, Aida."

"No. Not here. Not like this. No. No. No."

She was right. I couldn't let our daughter be born in a gore-fest.

Huh, our daughter. I tucked that thought away for later.

"Okay. Okay." I kissed her forehead. "How often you having these cramps?" Maybe I had time to get her cleaned up. I couldn't very well take her to the hospital looking like she'd just filmed a scene from the latest *Saw* movie.

"I don't know." Her lips curled in a snarl. "I haven't had time to find a fucking stopwatch."

There she was, my feisty girl.

"Okay. We're gonna get you cleaned up." I helped Aida into the bathroom and tore back the shower curtain.

A huge pair of blue eyes met mine from the bottom of the tub.

"Jesusfuckingchrist!" I dropped to my knees and freed Tuuli from her bindings.

Blood matted her hair. She groaned, but pushed my offered hand away and slowly lifted herself from the tub.

"Fuck. Tuuli. You okay?"

Tuuli stared at Aida, as if waiting for an explanation, or permission to speak, I couldn't be sure.

"He's gone," Aida mumbled, then sucked in a sharp breath. "Oh, fuck. Here comes another one." She leaned forward, gripping the sink, bracing for another contraction.

"Tango. Need some help."

Rossi was at the door in a blink. He took one look at Tuuli and ordered her to cover her eyes while he scooped her off her feet and carried her through the carnage.

Like the badass she was, Aida breathed through the pain with a litany of colorful words. When she could stand again, I helped her into the shower, stripped her soiled clothes, and washed the evidence, the blood, and hair, off her body. Her contractions were about five minutes apart so the shower took longer than I'd wanted. There wasn't much time. There also wasn't much I could do while she powered through the agony.

Tito brought in a pair of sweats and a Knicks T-shirt. Last thing I wanted to do was dress her in Rafael's clothing. Options were limited, so I stifled my protest and pulled the shirt over her head. I'd burn the rags later.

I bundled her in my coat and headed for the door. "Tucker." Those big fat doe eyes lifted to meet mine.

"Yeah, Aida," I said, combing a finger through her wet hair.

"I'm scared."

"I know, baby. I know. Me, too. Let's get you to the hospital, okay?"

She crumpled over as another contraction hit.

CHAPTER 16

Tucker

I STOOD, HOLDING SEVEN pounds, eight ounces of precious, brand-spanking-new human, rocking and cooing and kissing her dark, chubby face, and doing my damnedest not to go nuclear on everyone who entered the room. We hadn't had a moment's peace since Aida screamed through her last push and collapsed in exhaustion.

"You're the father?" our nurse, Hillary, asked, lowering the blanket to check Aida's abdomen one more time.

"That's right." I dusted a finger over the baby's shiny black hair before hitting Hillary with a challenging glare. The angel in my arms was mine, whether we shared DNA or not. The color of her skin would never be an issue for this proud dad.

The nurses were still wary of me. Couldn't blame them. Aida had been admitted with a fresh bruise on her face, a nasty cut to her lip, and one hell of a bump on the crown of her head. They'd jumped to the natural conclusion, as I would have, that I was a piece of shit abuser.

Thankfully, we'd had Officer Caldwell to back up our story. He'd met us at the hospital shortly after he'd met Tango and Tuuli at the diner. Their statements must've been convincing.

It was now a matter of public record that Aida and Tuuli had been attacked during an attempted robbery at The Stop, where an off-duty officer had been killed. Aida had gone into labor, and Tango and I had arrived in time to chase off the perp, whom, according to Tuuli, wore a black ski mask and had disabled the security cameras. We dialed the cops. I then drove Aida to the hospital. That was the official police report and the story we were running with. Tuuli was about to get a raise. A big raise.

Tito had stayed behind at the hotel to "do what needed to be done," as he'd put it. I was damn happy not to have to clean up that gruesome mess.

Disturbing as the hotel scene was to see, watching Aida suffer through labor and delivery was the hardest thing I'd ever witnessed. If I could've bore the pain for her, I would have. In all honesty, though, I would've folded after the first round of contractions. Aida had powered through, kicking ass and proving to the world that women were indeed the stronger sex.

"All right, I'll let you get some rest," Hillary said, eyeing me skeptically before dropping her gaze to type notes into her mobile computer.

Yes, the baby's skin was darker than Aida's, and on the opposite end of the color spectrum than my ivory shade of pale. I wasn't about to explain our situation to the nurse or anyone for that matter.

"We can take her to the nursery if you two want to sleep a bit."

"No." Hell no. I wasn't letting that baby out of my sight. "We're good."

I heard Aida chuckle behind me. I hoped to God there was a smile to greet me when I turned around. She hadn't smiled in hours, not since holding her child for the first time.

Finally alone, I stepped to Aida's side. Weary eyes lifted to meet mine.

"How you doing, Bambi?" I asked, pressing a kiss to her forehead and tucking the baby into the crook of her arm.

With a sigh, Aida lifted her free hand to cup my cheek. She rubbed her thumb over my stubble. "Rafael killed my father."

"I'm sorry."

"He was going to kill me and Tuuli. He was going to kill his own child."

My own eyes started to leak. "If he'd taken you from me…" I swallowed the sob threatening to break loose and shook that thought away real quick. No doubt, had Turner succeeded with his twisted plan, I wouldn't have survived the aftermath.

"Tucker. He told me things." She tightened her arm around the baby and nuzzled her hair. "Things he shouldn't know. Things about my mother."

"He didn't know shit," came from a deep, gravelly voice behind me.

"Tits?" Aida whispered, eyes lifting to the man in the doorway, face crumpling in realization. "Is it really you?"

I released her hand and stepped away from the bed, allowing room for Aida to have her meltdown.

Aida raised her free arm to accept Tito's embrace.

"Princess." Tito fell against her, burying his face in her neck.

Feeling every bit the intruder on their intimate moment, I slipped out the door, allowing the longtime friends their reunion. I wasn't alone for long. Slade and Rocky bounced around the corner. Tango followed behind, looking as war worn as I felt. Dark circles, messed hair, and a heavy load of shit weighing down his shoulders.

We exchanged a quick embrace before I scooped my nephew off the ground, "How ya doin', buddy?"

Rockster hugged my neck. "Mom says I have to be quiet in here. She said we have a new baby, and I have to be a good big cousin and take care of her."

I kissed his temple. "That's right, little man. You're gonna be the best big cousin ever."

The little tyke turned his head, his lips tickling my ear. "I don't know how to take care of babies. They're kind of yucky."

I couldn't hold back my chuckle. "You know what? Neither do I, kiddo. Neither do I. How 'bout we help each other out? Sound good?"

He wiggled, letting me know he was ready to be back on his own two feet.

We joined Aida and Tito. Passed the baby around. Made small talk, and avoided mention of Turner, or what could've been.

After a round of hugs and *see ya laters*, Aida and I were alone again. Heavy-lidded and groggy, my Bambi quickly nodded off, but not before whispering, "Promise you won't leave, Cowboy."

Yeah, like leaving was even a remote possibility. I simply kissed her cheek, whispered, "I love you," and snuggled into the bedside chair where I had a perfect view of my Bambi. I'd never given much thought to the validity of miracles. However, considering where I'd been a few years ago, and where I ended up, I was damn sure I couldn't deny their existence. The proof was in the pudding, or in my arms, rather. My daughter.

I was a dad.

Aida

I wished my dad could see his granddaughter. Dark hair, dark eyes, had every visitor wrapped around her little finger. She was master of her universe already, like her grandpa.

"Lucia," I whispered, testing the sound of the name on my tongue. My heart palpitated. The baby's mouth fell slack, releasing my nipple. Out like a light.

Tucker pushed through the door, car seat dangling off the crook of his arm, diaper bag slung over his shoulder, and carrying two paper sacks that smelled like greasy heaven.

His eyes lit brighter than a spring sunrise when they rested on my bared breast. "Did she take to the nipple?"

I nodded yes.

"That's great, baby." He freed his arms, bent to kiss me, and with impressive grace for such a large man, transferred my little princess into her own bed.

I watched, dumbstruck by the raw beauty of his nurturing talent.

"You hungry?" he asked, maneuvering the hospital tray over my lap and pulling one of Charlie's bacon double cheeseburgers out of the bag.

"I just fell in love with you all over again," I said, smiling wide enough to crack my split lip. I wasted no time digging in. It hurt to chew. I didn't care. Hospital food sucked. Charlie's burgers kicked ass.

"So, you're cleared to head home. You just need to finish with the paperwork." He took a hefty bite, chewed, then swallowed. "Decide on a name?"

"Lucia," I said. "Lucia Leticia Slade."

"Leticia?" he asked, eyes turning liquid. "Mom will be over the moon. Wait." His head dropped on his shoulders, and it took a few moments for him to meet my gaze. "Slade? You sure, Bambi?"

"I'm sure, Cowboy."

"Does this mean what I think it means?"

"If you think it means I'm going to share a bedroom with you and have unlimited access to that magnificent cock of yours, then, yes."

"Fuck, baby. Just when I thought you couldn't make me any happier."

With great difficulty, I set my burger back on the tray. The matter at hand required my full attention. "I named you as her father on all the paperwork. I wanted it to be on record, you know, in case anything happened to me." I knew he'd die to protect my child. Couldn't imagine anyone else taking better care of her.

Judging by the look on his face, I'd given him the best gift in the history of gift-giving. The man who could never father his own child. The man who had saved me from myself. The man who loved me unconditionally, faithfully, reverently, unwavering in his commitment to me, not my name, but the lovesick girl inside.

He coughed, clearly trying to cover his emotion, then choked out, "You know this means we'll have to get married soon."

"What?"

"I'm not raising a bastard child."

"Tuck. Marriage? I'm not ready for that. I'm still learning how to change a diaper. I haven't even completely settled into the idea of living with you."

"Technically, and dare I say, biblically, the marriage thing should've happened first."

"Are you kidding me with this?"

He laughed, smiling wider than the Grand Canyon. "Relax, Bambi. Not pushing the issue, just giving you a head's up. It's gonna happen. You're giving Lucia my last name, it only makes sense that you own it, too."

"Tucker, please. Slow down. I just want to enjoy my burger for crying out loud. Fuck. You don't even go to church. Why the hell are you dumping this biblical crap on me? I'm about to have a fucking heart attack."

"Whoa. Whoa. Whoa, lady. Language. Little ears," he teased, pointing to the sleeping bundle of chub.

Crap. I was a mother. Definitely time to start talking like one. Not that I knew how mothers were supposed to talk. Which reminded me. "I have a favor to ask."

"Anything."

"Rafael said something to me that I can't shake."

"What, baby?"

"He said my father had been pumping money into accounts under the name Aida Suarez since I was a child. It doesn't make sense, does it? He couldn't possibly know I'd be using that name someday. The money couldn't be for me. What if it was for a real Aida Suarez."

"You think she might be your mother?"

"Yes."

"And you want me to use my contact to look into it."

"I asked Tito. He shut me down. Said Rafael was playing games with me. But I could tell he knows something. He's trying to protect me from the truth."

"Maybe for good reason. Maybe we should count our blessings and let this go." Tucker paced the room, scratching his stubble. He stopped at the window, stuffed his hands in the front pockets of his jeans, and stared at the cloudy sky.

I wanted to push, to beg, but I wouldn't. If he said *no*, I'd leave it be. The man had done so much for me already. He'd saved me from myself. I was selfish to ask another thing from him.

Shame washed through me. "Tuck. Never mind. You're right. Maybe I should let this—"

"I'll do it on one condition," he interrupted, turning to face me once again. "You let me handle this. You don't worry about any of it. You worry about taking care of you and our daughter. You don't question me about the investigation. You trust me completely with the information I find. Trust me to tell you only what you need to know."

"Deal."

"Deal?" His brows shot up. "No argument? That was too easy."

It was too easy. But I trusted him. With my life. It should have unnerved me how easily I conceded. But it didn't. And I liked that it didn't.

"I just want to eat my burger," I said, pulling my gaze from his gorgeous face and focusing once again on my lunch.

Damn, I loved cheeseburgers. I was going to kiss Charlie so hard next time I saw him.

Tucker

I kissed Aida hard before leaving her and Lucia alone in the nursery. My new favorite thing in the world was watching Aida breastfeed, but I'd been hovering, and I could sense that she needed some privacy. Especially after she'd said, "Jesus, Tuck. I'm not going to break her. I need some breathing room here."

Lola moaned, as if saying, *Yeah, dude. Give her a break,* and plopped her ass at Aida's feet. Except to eat, and run outside to relieve herself, the mutt hadn't left Lucia's side since we'd brought her home.

I jogged down the wide staircase and paused when I hit the last rung, taking in the open living room. Stuffed Bambi sat on the coffee table. The pink, frilly bassinet perched in one corner of the antiqued leather couch, didn't match the log cabin decor, but it belonged there, and oddly, it made the grand house feel like a home. Our home. God, my chest could barely contain the swelling muscle inside.

I headed to the kitchen to make lunch when the doorbell rang. Roger Caldwell stood on the other side of the glass door in full police uniform.

He greeted me with an unconvincing smile. "Tucker, good to see you. How's the baby doing?"

"She's perfect, Rog." I stepped aside and gestured for him to come in. "I'm about to make some lunch. Hungry?"

"No. No. Thanks. I can't stay." He rubbed the back of his neck, shifting his weight from foot to foot.

"What can I do for you?"

"Wanted you to be the first to know that Jonas Carver and three of his crew were arrested yesterday morning outside of Seattle. Long list of charges including human trafficking. Fucker had a handful of underage girls drugged and locked in a small room. All blonde and blue-eyed. Making movies. Sick white-power shit from what I understand. He won't be back to bother you or yours. He'll be locked up for a long time."

"Good news," I said, patting him on the shoulder. "So why do you look like you're ready to jump out of your skin?"

Roger inhaled, steeled his spine, and met me eye to eye. "It hasn't gone unnoticed that crazy shit's been going down in Whisper Springs since Rossi came back to town. Lot of it centered around The Truck Stop."

"What are you trying to say, Roger?"

"Now that Carver's no longer an issue, I assume you won't need my help at the diner anymore."

"S'pose not. But it's not my call."

"I have a family. Two girls. One of them special needs. I appreciate the extra income. I appreciate how you and Rossi watch out for your own. I just want you to know, I'm available if you need me for anything. So long as it's above the law."

"Good to know, buddy. If my instincts are right about Tango, he'll keep you under his employ. Pretty boy doesn't like leaving his family unprotected."

"Yeah. I get that." He turned as if to leave, then faced me again, thumbs hooked on his belt. "Officer McGuire's family received an impressive anonymous donation yesterday. I suspect it came from the Rossi family, but if you had anything to do with it, thanks."

I did. But nobody needed to know. Officer McGuire's wife and son would want for nothing. Ever. It was the least Tango and I could do. "How's his family holding up?"

"They want justice," Roger said, dropping his head low. "Hope to God I can give them answers soon. We've got nothing on the bastard who took him down."

And they wouldn't find a damn thing either. Tito had disposed of Turner's body. All evidence of any foul play at Eagle Point Motel had been burned to ash in an unfortunate electrical fire, along with the owner's body, which Tito had found in the bathtub of room number one.

Roger and I said our farewells. I stood at the base of the stairs, aching to see my girls. When I heard Aida's voice, soft and sweet, and a little unsure, singing "Dream a Little Dream," I damn near crumpled into a blubbering mess. How was it possible to love so deeply and keep your cells from exploding?

I wanted to join them. So much it hurt. But hell if I was going to interrupt their bonding time. Instead, I locked myself in my office and made the call.

Conner picked up before the phone rang. "Slade. Starting to think you have a boner for me."

"Hey, Con. Have another job if you're up for it."

"Anything for you, Tuck. Anything."

I gave him the rundown on Aida's suspicions about her mother, and ended the call, confident he'd find any and every buried detail.

Part of me hoped he'd find nothing but dead ends. I wanted Aida one hundred percent free from her old life. No ties. No responsibilities. No loose ends.

I finished making lunch and carried it upstairs. When I entered, Aida stood at the window, her voluptuous hips swinging back and forth while she rocked and hummed and pressed her lips to Lucia's ebony hair, holding her so fucking tight. The queen and her princess.

Our gazes met through the window's reflection. Her lips lifted in a smile. My heart soared.

Chin to shoulder, she said, "I don't want to put her down. I feel empty when she's not in my arms."

I set our plates on the dresser and met her where she stood, snaking my arms around my girls, around my family. I pressed my lips to the top of Aida's head. She hadn't showered in days. Her hair was oily. Unbrushed. Dark circles framed her doe eyes. She wore nothing but one of my white Fruit of the Loom undershirts and a pair of loose fitting sweats.

Breathtaking, soul-gutting perfection.

There was nothing more beautiful than a woman holding her child.

Aida

There was nothing more beautiful than a baby asleep in her daddy's arms. Lucia was snuggled against Tucker's bare chest, guarded by his corded muscles, wrapped tight in his embrace. Her little lips pursed and made a sucking noise.

I bent low and pressed a kiss to Tucker's forehead. His lids fluttered open, gifting me with the sight of those brilliant blue, dewy eyes.

"How was your shower?" he asked.

"Heaven." I sighed, dropping my butt to the edge of the couch, bumping his hip. "She's so content in your arms."

"Snuggle in. I can fit you both." Tucker scooted deeper into the sofa, and offered me his free arm.

Only half of my body could fit on the small edge, but I clung tightly to him, tangling my leg between his, pressing my nose into his chest, absorbing the heady scent of his bare skin.

"Tucker."

"Yeah, baby."

"I'm happy."

His chest rose and fell in one swift, hard motion.

"I'm exhausted. My boobs hurt like hell. I haven't done my nails in weeks. I desperately need a haircut. My skin is dull and dry. I've got twenty pounds of baby fat to lose. But I've never been this happy. And breastfeeding isn't gross. Shitty diapers don't bother me. I haven't had an orgasm in weeks, and I'm still happy. And the best part is, I'm not scared. I'm not worried that all of this will be taken away from me."

"Baby," he said on a breathy groan.

"Thank you." I squeezed him tighter. "Thank you for giving me this. For giving me normal. For giving me peace."

"If I gave you normal, you gave me extraordinary."

"Are you happy?" I asked him. "Do I make you happy?"

"Baby. There aren't words to describe what's happening in my chest right now."

The doorbell rang. Reluctantly, I pushed to my feet. Through the glass door, Tito waved a hello at me. My heart dropped an inch at the sullen set of his features. He'd lost so much weight. He wore a full beard. His eyes, eyes that used to light up at the sight of me, remained dim. His teasing smirk was nowhere to be found. I feared I'd never fall victim to his devilish grin again.

I opened the door and pulled him into my arms, foregoing our custom cheek kiss greeting, reveling in the knowledge that he was alive. God, I'd missed him.

"Hey, Tits."

"Princess," he half-groaned, half-whispered in my ear. He hugged me tighter than he'd ever held me, and buried his nose in my hair. He'd missed me, too.

I dropped my arms, his lingered before he stepped back and offered Tucker a chin nod. "Tucker."

"Tito. Good to see you man. Beer?" Tucker laid Lucia down in her bassinet. She protested with a squeal before passing out again.

I grabbed Tito's hand and pulled him to the couch. He sat, knees spread wide, and threw one arm over the back of the sofa. "How you feeling, Mama?"

"Honestly?" I sat opposite him, in the overstuffed love seat. "I've never been better."

His sad eyes raked the length of me, then hit me with a hard stare. His head tilted, only slightly, before he half-smiled and said, "Yeah. I can see that. There's a different air about you."

Tucker joined us, handing Tito an open bottle of pale ale, and me an open bottle of mountain spring water.

Tito mumbled, "Thanks," and lifted his thumb to his forehead to scratch above his brow.

Our eyes bet briefly before he dropped his gaze to the floor. A storm brewed behind the mask he wore.

"Were you with him when he died?" I blurted, sensing Tito's need to talk, as well as his hesitancy. He was hard to read. I thought I'd changed over the past few months. My metamorphosis seemed minimal in comparison to the man before me.

Eyes glassy, and still aimed down, he nodded yes.

"Did he suffer?"

Another nod.

"What happened, Tito? How did everything get so fucked up?"

"Croatians."

"Marcovic," I mumbled. I'd met the man. Had never considered him a threat.

Eyes glazed, Tito lifted the bottle to his lips, paused, then threw back a long swig. He set the brew on the knotty pine coffee table, rested elbows to knees, and worked his jaw left and right before continuing. "We'd known Turner was an agent from the get-go. Fucker blew his cover the first week. Your pops wanted to let it play out. Get a feel for what the suits had on him. When Turner cozied up to you, I offered to take him out. Voltolini shut me down. Said there was a bigger picture. Wouldn't say much else."

"Dad knew, and still let me fuck around with him. Why?"

"I wish like hell I knew why. He shut me out, too. When I returned from escorting you to Whisper Springs, I started digging. Didn't like the shit your pops was pulling. He should've eliminated Turner the night you stabbed him. Instead, he held him in the hole at the Poughkeepsie house."

"How does Marcovic come in to play?"

"That's the fucked-up thing, Princess. Marcovic had never been a threat. Not until your pops went deep. The last time I spoke to you, Croatians busted through my door. Sent ten fucking men. Busted me up. Demanded to know where Turner was. Didn't kill me, though, which made no sense. So, I dug deeper. Took some time, but I found the connection."

Tito rubbed his hands over his face, took a deep breath, looked at the sleeping beauty sharing the couch with him. "Fuck. I fucking hate this shit."

"Tits. Just say it."

"Rafael Turner's real name was Ricardo Auguste. He was born in Haiti, to a Rachelle Auguste. No father listed in any birth or medical records. However, Marcovic owned several properties in Port au Prince. One of which, where Rachelle Auguste was employed. Six months before Ricardo was born, Rachelle was gifted one of Marcovic's properties. Security tripled around the home. Rachelle started receiving monthly deposits into her bank accounts, Marcovic's visits to Haiti became more frequent."

"Rafael is Marcovic's son."

"Yes."

The facts clicked one by one into place. "Rafael targeted me to join our families."

"To join. To eventually take over."

"But Luciano didn't know about the blood connection," Tucker chimed in. "So why keep Turner alive?"

"That's what I haven't figured out. I drove to Poughkeepsie to give Luciano the information myself. The fucking Croatians followed me. That's why they hadn't killed me. They were banking on the fact I knew where Turner was being held." His voice cracked. "I fucking let my guard down. Now your pops is dead. He's fucking dead because I was careless."

I sensed there was more to the story, but I couldn't stand to watch him breaking. "How'd you get out, Tits?"

"I don't know." His eyes darted around the room. Wild. Unfocused. "One minute, I'm tied up in the hole, watching Rafael tear Mark Norton to shreds. The next, I wake up on the front lawn. Fucking flames everywhere." Tito bent forward and covered his ears. "People were trapped inside the house, screaming. God, the fucking screams. They won't stop." He rocked back and forth, unhinged, and I feared, teetering on the edge of sanity.

I crouched in front of him, pulled his hands into mine, and told him everything was going to be okay, despite fearing things would never be all right. Not for Tito.

His eyes lifted to mine, so filled with pain and guilt, my breath hitched. "I tried to run back inside. I made it to the basement door before there was another blast." He dropped his head to my shoulder. "I'm so fucking sorry, Princess. I couldn't save him. It was my fault."

"Shh." I rubbed his back, stroked his hair. "No, Tits. Not your fault."

"I took them all out. Marcovic. His men. Every last one of his men. I bled them for intel, then killed them all. I'm sorry I didn't get to Rafael in time. Please forgive me."

"There's nothing to forgive." And I meant that.

Lucia started to cry.

Tito lifted his face and looked at me like I'd have the answers to all of life's mysteries. I ran a hand through his overgrown hair, curled my fingers through the dirty strands, and pulled hard, making sure he'd pay attention. "Tell me one thing. And don't fucking lie."

He blinked.

"You behind my fake death?"

"No."

"You know anything about Aida Suarez. The real Aida Suarez?"

"No."

I studied his dark, hazel eyes. I couldn't find a lie through all the pain. "It's over Tito Moretti. You hear me. None of that bullshit was your fault. None of it was my fault. My father chose the life. Lived it. Died by it. I don't want to go that way. I don't want you to go that way either."

Lucia's wails grew louder, despite the fact Tucker was rocking her. My breasts tingled with the familiar burn of feeding time.

I pressed my forehead to my best friend's. "We're free. It's over. Tell me you're with me."

He nodded. "I'm with you, Princess. I'm with you."

CHAPTER 17

Tucker

IT TOOK SOME DISCIPLINE, but Aida and I had impressively cut back on the profanities. Around the baby anyway. In the bedroom, not so much.

Bambi let loose while she straddled my waist and worked my cock, bouncing her full ass off my hips and thighs. Curvy body. Throaty moans. Bad-girl vocabulary, and those damn eyes, dark and heavy with lust. Fuck. *Fuck, fuck, fuck.* Not much more a man could say.

I refused to look at her full, heavy breasts, bouncing and swaying in my face, fearing I'd lose my fucking mind and blow my load before Aida got what she deserved. Insatiable beast, my girl.

She slowed, teasing her short, and acrylic-free, nails along the path of my scars, sending painful waves of pleasure through me. My hips bucked beneath her at the sensation. A salacious grin parted her full, moist lips. Damn, I wanted to hold her against me. Crush those luscious tits against my chest. Meld every inch of her soft curves to my hard planes.

I couldn't hold her. Couldn't touch her. My hands were bound to the headboard with one of my ties, secured with an impressive knot, the kind they didn't teach in Boy Scouts.

"Aida, baby. I know I said I could handle this, but fuck. You're killing me. I need to touch you."

"Shh." She leaned forward, brushed my lips with her own, and stretched her arm under her pillow. When she pulled out her blades, I choked on a whimper.

When she sat up and arched her back, ensuring I was buried as deep inside her as possible, I hissed in agony. Torturing me further, the pussycat dragged the tips of her blades across her rosy pink, taut nipples. My balls tightened. My dick twitched inside her.

"Not yet, Cowboy," Aida said with a slow head shake. She lifted off me and rested her ass lower on my thighs. My raging cock fell heavy against my abdomen. Mother of Mercy, she was doing a number.

Aida teased her blades down her throat, across her breasts, and lower to the insides of her thighs. Cold steel hit my skin, and swear to my Maker, I saw stars. When she drew the tips in light strokes along the path of each of my jagged scars, my jaw clenched, muscles coiled, and my body ignited in a series of shivers and spasms.

My vision blurred. Lungs failed. I couldn't form coherent words, or rational thought. But I could feel. Where our flesh touched. Where her blades taunted me. My skin, my nerves—hypersensitive.

"You're a work of art, Tucker. So beautiful. But something's missing." Aida moaned, set one of her blades across my chest, and lifted her hips to guide my cock back inside her soft heat.

"What's that, Bambi?" I half-groaned, half-growled, overcome by the sensation of her liquid, silky insides gripping me tightly.

Fully seated, she leaned forward and brought our lips a hairsbreadth apart, a small smile playing on her face. "Trust me?" she asked, doe-eyed and sinfully delicious.

"Fuck yeah," I managed to moan through labored breaths.

"Close your eyes," she ordered. "Don't open them for anything. Promise."

I nodded.

"I want you to feel. To smell. To anticipate."

Fuck, I was in trouble.

"Close them."

I did.

Knives in hand, Aida laid her fists on my chest and began a slow, calculated rock, back and forth, sliding her heat up and down the length of my erection.

"Feel me, Tucker. How wet I am. Mmm. I love the way you swell inside me, getting harder," she taunted, still working me with slow strokes.

Her hands lifted from my chest. The rocking continued. My muscles ached with the need to touch her.

"You're going to feel the sting of my blade, Cowboy. Don't open your eyes. Trust me," she said, almost purring. "Focus on how my body feels, focus on the sounds of our fucking, the smell of our sex. Focus on me. How deep I take you."

The tip of her knife, cold and sharp, poked my left side, enough to shock, but not to hurt. Aida, still riding me, manipulating, controlling, dragged the blade down my ribcage, pushing deeper, threatening to pierce my skin, to draw blood between each rise and fall of my ribs.

At the same time, her other blade drew slow circles around my right nipple. She'd circle, then flick my pebbled flesh with the tip of her knife. Circle. Flick. Circle. Flick. Each time I heard the drag of steel across my skin, I anticipated the sting. The burn. I was on fire.

Sensory overload. Aida on top of me, her blades manipulating, teasing. Circle. Flick. Drag. Poke. Heavy breaths. The slap, slap, slap of her body pumping mine.

Throaty moans. Sweat. Sex. That musky tang of naked bodies primed for mating.

The blade at my ribs poked harder and stayed put, painful yet strangely erotic. Aida rose and fell, panted, groaned. Harder. Harder. Lifting slow, slamming back down, twisting her hips, grinding into me before rising again.

"I'm going to come, baby. I'm going to come so hard all over your beautiful cock. Do you feel me? Do you feel what you do to me?" The blade sunk deeper into my ribs. "Tucker." She stopped the rise and fall, now rocking, rocking, rocking, our bodies fused together, her hips thrusting forward and back. I bucked my hips, seeking more, out of control, out of my mind, so close, so fucking close to ripping the bed apart to get to the tiny little spitfire, to get my arms, my body, everything around her small little body, so full of power, so strong, and sensual, and soft, and dark, and all fucking mine.

"I'm coming, Tuck. Oh shit, oh fuck. Oh, God." Her pussy tightened around my dick in violent convulsions, and I was helpless to do anything but follow her over the edge. Aida leaned forward, her breasts smashed between our chests. I felt the binds at my hands fall loose, and I slammed my arms around her back, pulling her closer to me while I jerked, and cursed, and pumped, and spilled my seed deep inside the perfect, dark, wet, and wild woman on top of me. Aida was limp, her full weight against me while I continued to thrust, to fill her with everything I had, until I collapsed beneath her, my mind a fog, my body boneless.

Aida lay on top of me until she caught her breath. I'd never catch my breath around my girl. When she tried to move, I held her steady. "No. Not yet." I needed more time to absorb her heat, her weight, her energy.

I closed my eyes and fought back a sucker punch of emotion. *This woman. God, this woman.* My lady. My Bambi.

So small. So full of life, of energy, of love and lust and danger, and so mine. So fucking mine.

"I love you, Aida."

She laughed. Then pressed a kiss between my pecs, before planting her palms on my shoulders and staring me down.

The smile that graced her flushed face was hands-down, the most playful, proud, and devastating expression I'd ever witnessed. Gutted me. Rooted me. Humbled me. Terrified me.

"I hope so." She dropped a kiss on my mouth, and sat up. "Because I've branded you."

Aida

"You branded me the first time I heard you laugh," Tucker said, voice raspy and deep.

"I know," I replied, the memory of our first kiss warming my insides. "But that's not what I meant."

Holding his gaze, I tapped the dots of blood that'd formed over the wound I'd inflicted.

He winced. I laughed, then held up my soiled finger for him to see.

"What the fuck?" Tucker pushed into the sitting position, eyes wide. He inspected the newly carved letter A and repeated, "What the fuck?"

"Now you're mine," I said, throwing his possessive words back at him.

"What?" He inspected the small carving. "When did you? How the hell did I not feel that?"

"The fine art of distraction. First, I used my mad bedroom skills to turn your brain to mush, then I used one knife to command your attention, while I marked you with the other."

"Fuck."

"That a *good* fuck? Or an *I'm pissed* fuck?" I asked, bending to kiss him, my lips hovering over his in offering.

"You branded me." He slapped my ass hard. Then he gripped the back of my head and pulled me close for a punishing kiss. When he came up for air, eyes burning, cheeks blazing, he slapped my ass again. "I should be pissed, but..." He shook his head. "Damn, that's fucking hot. Branded. Like livestock."

"Well, Cowboy. You are my prize bull. You're certainly hung like one."

That comment earned me a chuckle. God, I loved his laugh.

Lucia started to cry. My breasts did their tingly, burning thing. I loved the sensation. Tucker untangled his fingers from my hair. I dropped one more kiss on his wet mouth before pushing off him and retreating to the bathroom to clean myself. When I came out, Tucker hadn't moved. He lay, sated, and stretched across the tangled sheets with a lazy grin on his face. "I left a bandage and ointment on the counter in the bathroom."

Tucker huffed, pushed to his feet, and pulled me close to whisper, "Fucking branded. You evil, little, doe-eyed nympho."

"I've wanted to do that since the first time you called me Bambi." Whether we'd realized it or not, he'd claimed me that day. Our first tryst. He'd marked me with our first kiss. I wanted to mark him, too, in a way that no one else could, in a way that was permanent.

Tucker's cell phone rang as I made my way to Lucia's room. I heard him answer and shut himself in the bathroom.

My little angel was red-faced and screaming by the time I lifted her out of her crib. We settled into the rocking chair, and, as she latched on, a peace washed over me.

I turned my head to gaze out the window. Daunting gray clouds rolled across the vast sky. The sun made a valiant effort to break through the dismal patches. I couldn't wait to see the property in springtime. Lola barked somewhere below the window. I couldn't see her, but I had a sneaking suspicion she was warning off a squirrel.

Heavy footsteps padded into the room. Tucker kissed my forehead, then Lucia's before settling into the rocker next to mine. He held my gaze for a long spell, as if gauging my mood, before saying, "I need to leave tomorrow. Have some business to take care of. Be gone two days, tops."

"Hunting?" I asked. It was an innocent question. Tucker had worked from home since I'd moved in, and he hadn't gone on a "run" in ages.

"What?" he asked, swallowing hard, then shaking his head. "No. Flying out for this one. Georgia. Securing a new account."

Yeah, right. "Why aren't you catching a ride with one of your drivers?"

He reached over to stroke Lucia's fuzzy locks. "Don't want to be away from my ladies any longer than necessary."

His eyes liquefied while he studied our daughter.

My heart swelled. "Do you miss it?"

"Miss what, baby?" he said, directing his attention to my breast, then my face.

"Hunting."

"Truth?" He leaned back in his chair and folded his arms across his chest.

I nodded.

"Not sure if I miss it so much as I feel like I'm letting the girls down." He offered a sad smile.

"I wouldn't mind if you continued to help them."

"No." He leaned forward, elbows to knees. Sucked in a breath. Shook his head. "Not leaving you and Lucia alone so I can go play hero."

"It's not playing, Cowboy. You're saving lives."

"Look at you, Bambi. You care. You care about those girls as much as I do. God, I love you."

He was spot on. I cared. It sickened me to think about how many girls, hell, women of any age, were forced into the sex trade. Slaves. And had I not had Lucia to worry about, I would've insisted Tucker take me with him on his hunts. "Will you think about it?"

He scrubbed a hand over his face, then nodded at me. "Sure. I'll consider it." He stood, turned his rocker to face me, then sat again. "I asked Mom to come and stay with you while I'm away. Hope you don't mind."

"Of course not." Besides, if Lettie didn't come, someone else would, like Tits, or Slade, or Tango. A day hadn't passed without at least one of them coming by for their baby fix. They were checking up on me, and I didn't mind. In fact, I looked forward to their impromptu visits.

Tucker watched with warm eyes while Lucia feasted on one breast and then the other. When she fell asleep, he scooped her to his bare chest and rocked, and hummed, and stroked her little back.

My heart broke, every shattered piece growing wings then taking flight. I ached from scalp to toes—skin, muscle, and bone—with love for my family. I ached because I knew my little girl would grow up wanting for nothing. She'd have her mother. She'd have a father. And she was loved. My God, she was loved. I ached because I loved her so hard. I ached because I'd loved my father, too, and he'd missed out on the most important, most beautiful, painful, fulfilling thing life had to offer. He'd been wrong, dreadfully wrong, teaching me that love had no place in our world. What a frightening thing, to live without the most vital connection two humans could share. Thank God, I'd fucked up and had been sent away. Thank God, I'd escaped a life plagued with empty promises, false comforts, and black, empty souls.

Thank God, thank God, thank God.

I left my sleeping beauty and her daddy to their bonding time. After a quick shower, I padded downstairs to let Lola back in the house. She bypassed me altogether and made her way up to the nursery. Yeah. Lucia was loved, all right, by man and beast alike.

While coffee brewed, I pulled eggs, onions, potatoes, and parmesan out of the fridge. Tucker joined me shortly after the garlic had been minced. He held Lucia on one shoulder, grabbed my hand, and twirled me until I smashed into his chest. There, he held me tight, and swayed, and sang along to the radio, some song I'd never heard about dollar bills, cheap thrills, and dancing. I laughed, wrestled free, and continued to cook while he continued to dance with Lucia and sing. Soon, I was shaking my ass and singing along, too. Didn't know the words. Didn't care.

Hadn't worn makeup in months. Didn't care.

Hadn't brushed my hair. Messy buns were my new best friend. Didn't care.

Wore Tucker's baggy sweats and sleep T-shirts. Didn't care.

I was loved. More important, I was lovable, just as I was. More important than that? I loved. Sweet Papa, I had so much fucking love to give, it was painful.

Tucker

Painful as it was, leaving my ladies behind, I was grateful they had each other. The three of them seemed happy to shoo me off. Probably eager for girl time. Fucking blew my mind how well Aida and my mother got along. Of course, Mom got along with everybody, but Aida, she was a harder nut to crack. Mom had pierced her shell the first time they'd met.

It'd been even more painful to lie to Aida about my destination. It was necessary, however, because I didn't want to get her hopes up, only to smash them to dust if the intel Conner had sent me was incorrect.

The lobby of the Georgian Grand Care Home smelled of peaches and seemed more a majestic hotel than a long-term care facility. The front desk alone was a hand-carved work of art that stretched the entire length of the entrance.

A tall, curvy, blonde woman greeted me with glowing, blue eyes, and a million-dollar smile. "How can I help you?" she asked.

"I'm here to see Aida Suarez."

The glow extinguished in one blink. "Excuse me?"

"Aida Suarez," I repeated.

She swallowed hard. All color drained from her high cheekbones. Her gaze left my face and focused over my shoulder before she nodded and backed away from the counter.

Somebody cleared their throat behind me. "Mr. Slade."

I turned to meet a set of dark eyes, framed with thick lashes, set in a chiseled face belonging to a man who stood a head taller, and I guessed about sixty pounds heavier than me. "We've been expecting you. Follow me."

I hadn't told a soul I was heading to Savannah.

The man tipped his head to the girl behind the desk. "Thank you, Caroline. I'll take it from here."

I followed him outside, around the refurbished mansion, and across a sprawling property thick with shrubbery, droopy trees, and green. Green everywhere, in every shade and conceivable texture—the grass, the trees, stretching up the walls, and peeking through the cracks of the cobblestone walkway.

We walked in silence, for five minutes, until we reached a wrought iron gate connecting two high stone walls. The man opened it for me, gestured me through, then nodded toward the small, ivy-covered cottage set dead center in the middle of the courtyard. "There are three snipers trained on you right now. Mind your manners ... you should be fine."

The white painted door opened. A heavily armed man, tall, dark, and scary as fuck with a face full of scars and a threatening glare, greeted me. Not so much greeted, as grunted and nodded toward the back of the small home.

French doors opened to a small garden patio. Seated under an umbrella, was a man and a woman, hand in hand, him in a garden chair, her in a wheelchair. I knew him the moment his head turned my way and his dark eyes met mine. I knew those eyes intimately. The smile, too.

Luciano Voltolini pushed to stand, blocking my view of the woman. He was short in stature. Fit. Well-dressed. Full head of dark hair. Handsome fucking fellow for a dead guy.

"Mr. Slade. I trust you had a safe trip." He offered his hand. A hand marred with gruesome burn scars.

"Mr. Voltolini." I gave him a firm shake. Yep. Warm skin. Definitely not dead. "Afraid you've taken me by surprise. That doesn't happen often."

"Understandably." He gestured for me to take a seat. "You came to Savannah for answers. I'm here to give them to you." He moved to sit, giving me a closer glance at the woman in the wheelchair.

Dark hair, pinned up in a neat bun. Wrinkled skin, dark in tone. Thin, white dress hanging loose on her small frame. Head perched on a slim neck at an off angle. Shoulders hunched.

Our eyes met.

My heart sank.

There was no denying the resemblance.

She spoke, but the words came out slurred.

Voltolini pulled the woman's hand once again into his own and leaned closer, listening carefully. He nodded. "Yes, love. This is the man I told you about."

One side of her mouth lifted in a smile. The other side didn't seem to work.

"Tucker Slade. Meet Aidaline Suarez. Aida's mother."

I quickly rose to my feet and offered her a kiss on one cheek, then the other. She mumbled something. Again, I couldn't understand.

Voltolini laughed, tugged at the collar of his shirt, then patted her hand. "She says you're very handsome. And a gentleman."

"How did you know I was coming?"

"It's my responsibility to know everything, son. Knowledge is imperative to my survival."

"You're supposed to be dead."

"And as you can see, I'm very much alive."

"I don't understand."

"You will."

"You faked your death." I studied the mosaic tile under my feet, the severity of the situation crashing over me. When I lifted my gaze, he seemed to be studying me, waiting patiently for me to absorb the truth. "Aida, too? Her death. That was you?"

"She was never built for this life. She tried. Her performance was brilliant, but that's all it was, a show."

I nodded in agreement. I'd seen through her bullshit act from day one.

"You knew from the beginning her life was a farce," he said, then paused to take a drink. He set his glass down and met me eye to eye. "You chipped away her dirty walls. You set the little girl free. The little girl I could never allow her to be. I watched her fall in love, I watched her blossom. I watched her laugh, and smile with you, and I knew it was time to let her go."

Voltolini nodded at someone over my shoulder. Another man dressed in black stepped to his side, holding a tray with a gold-plated lighter, and a pack of Insignia cigarettes, the same brand I had found burning outside Aida's apartment months ago.

"Do you mind?" he asked, pulling a stick from the black box.

"You were there. Outside her apartment."

"Yes." He stuck the cigarette between his lips and lit it, relaxing into his chair.

"Why didn't you let her know you were alive? Why let her suffer? Do you have any idea how she tortured herself, worried that it was her fault you were in danger to begin with?"

"I was never in danger. Aida's stunt with Rafael, although unfortunate, only hurried the game already in play."

"What game was that?"

"The endgame."

I watched him suck in a drag, hold it, blow it out slow and controlled. He was waiting for me to figure it out. And I did. "You wanted out."

He looked to Aidaline, who hadn't stopped staring at me. "I wanted my Aidaline. She wouldn't take me unless I was out."

Punch to the gut? No. More like a sledgehammer to the chest. "Wait a fucking minute. All this shit. All this show. Explosions, and murders, and tears. My God. The fucking tears your daughter cried for you. All that for the one thing she wanted and needed from you more than anything. All this shit for the very thing you taught her to avoid at all costs?"

Aidaline lifted her chin and mumbled. One word. One word I understood loud and clear although her speech was impaired. I understood, when she said, "Love."

Fuck. Me.

I wanted to murder the guy. For Aida. I wanted him to hurt.

"I know what you must be thinking." He squeezed Aidaline's arm.

"Pretty sure you don't, or I'd have a bullet in my skull right now."

The fucker laughed.

He pointed his cancer stick my direction. "I like you, Tucker Slade."

I didn't like Luciano Voltolini. Not one bit. "Why keep her mother a secret?"

Aida

"Why would he keep such a secret from us?" Lettie asked, her little finger being held hostage by a small fist.

"Lettie. I'm betraying him by saying anything at all. And I feel terrible. But I love him. He loves helping those girls.

And I want to do this for him. I want to help. I was built for this."

"I can see you're passionate about his plight. I just don't know if you understand what a huge undertaking, what an enormous responsibility this would be. And have you considered what might happen if things go bad? If God forbid, you get caught?"

Although she knew the truth about my identity, Lettie really had no clue where I came from, or how I'd been raised. "I learned from the best how not to get busted. I've been responsible for my father's women, and that whole side of the business since I was sixteen. I'm good at it. And I have the fuck..." I winced, eyeing the baby. "I have the money. It's blood money, true, but now I can do something good with it. I can help these girls, these innocent children. I want this so much."

"Rest Area Reaper. Wow. My son. I've always been proud of the boy, but this. God, I think my heart might just burst."

"So, you'll help?"

"I'm in. Yes. Count me in. I'll have to tell James, of course. I can't keep something this monumental from my husband."

"I know. I know. Of course, we'll include James." I bounced, clapping my hands, unsure what else to do with all the excitement bubbling out of me. I couldn't remember ever being excited over a business prospect.

Tucker would probably be upset with me spilling his secrets. He'd get over it. Besides, maybe having his family involved would make it easier for him to accept that rescuing children was his calling. As a team ... good Lord, nothing could stand in our way.

Lettie tucked Lucia into her bassinet, turned, and grabbed both of my hands. Liquid eyes met mine. "Thank you, Aida. Thank you for letting me in, for inviting me to be a part of this." A tear rolled down her cheek, and she gave me the most beautiful smile. "Thank you for the beautiful granddaughter. Thank you for not leaving. But most of all, thank you for loving my boy."

"Like I had a choice." I pulled her in for a hug and held her tight. "He's so lucky to have a mom who loves him like you do." To have a mom at all, I left unsaid.

As if reading my mind, Lettie kissed my cheek and whispered, "You have me, too, beautiful girl. You have me, too."

Her words undid me. Hit me in the hard spots, turning them soft. I used to be afraid of soft, worried it would weaken me. Little by little, this new life, my new family, was proving that soft didn't make me vulnerable, it only loosened the tight weaves of my protective skin, allowing light to shine through and scatter the shadows.

The shadows would always be there, of course. As Tucker had said, darkness was part of my DNA. Only now, I could use the dangerous parts of me for something that mattered. I could manipulate my ugly, and make something beautiful.

Tucker

"Beautiful can't begin to describe my Aidaline when we met." Luciano released a low whistle and threw his head back with a giant smile. "When I fell, I fell hard. Lost my mind." He looked me up and down, then laughed. "I'm sure you know what I mean."

I did. Aida had knocked me for a loop the first time I'd laid eyes on her. I've yet to stop spinning.

"I'll spare you the details of our torrid affair and skip to the main points. Aidaline's father didn't like me. I didn't care. She was mine. When her father learned she was with child, he arranged to have her and the baby..." Luciano cleared his throat. "Dealt with," he finished, his voice reduced to a quiver.

Aidaline's shaky hand rose to rest on his arm.

His features softened before he continued. "Her father was a powerful man. Aidaline disappeared. I tore the city apart for months looking for her. By the time I'd found her, she'd already given birth. Aida, *my* child, *my* princess, had been sold to a family in Jacksonville. Aidaline had become imprisoned in her own body. Her father had beaten her to near death. Because of me. She suffered brain damage. Spinal injury." He pinched the bridge of his nose, dropped his head, and took three deep breaths. "He broke my beauty. He stole my daughter. And so, I promised my love that I would find our baby. I swore to find our daughter and protect her, and keep her safe from the monster. At the time, I hadn't the means to take care of Aidaline. She needed 'round the clock care. So, I left her to find our daughter. I murdered the family that had bought her like she was livestock, and, when I'd grown powerful enough, I came back for Aidaline. I murdered her family. I brought her here. Found the best doctors. I kept her safe."

Aidaline made a wet, gurgled noise, drawing my attention away from Voltolini's haunted face. Tears streamed from her dark eyes. Visible tremors rocked her small body.

Voltolini dropped to his knees at her feet, drying her eyes with his thumbs, and whispering words meant only for her ears. I damn near broke down myself. Luciano Voltolini was human. He was soft. He'd suffered a great loss. He'd made it right, the only way he'd known how.

His cold approach to parenting made sense. He'd wanted to protect Aida from the loss he'd suffered. He'd wanted to make her stronger than the beasts and the demons he coexisted with.

When Aidaline calmed, Luciano gestured for the guard, ordered him to take her inside, and kissed her gently on the head. He watched, spine stiff and lips pursed, until they disappeared into the dark shadows of the house.

"When I'd met her, Aidaline was a proud woman, born into a prominent family. Her father was a politician. Dirty fucker. Because of her association with me, because she loved me, she lost everything. It was Aidaline who'd ordered me to keep Aida away. She couldn't walk. Couldn't hold, or speak to her daughter. Would never change a diaper, brush her hair, sing her to sleep, or comfort her when she cried. She was a proud woman. She refused to let her children..." His chest rose and fell. He shook his head. "Her daughter," he corrected himself. "She refused to let her daughter see her in that condition. Was it wrong? I don't know. What I do know is that Aida is where she belongs now. As am I."

Perhaps I was in a state of mild shock. Hell, maybe I was taking longer than usual to process the twisted history lesson. Whatever the reason, I stared, in silence, for longer than respectful, at the man who had molded my Bambi. I wanted to hate him. I wanted to tighten my fingers around his neck and choke the putrid life from his body. But when I looked at Luciano, I saw Aida. I saw Lucia.

And I was thankful.

Because had he not been who he was, I wouldn't have *my* family waiting at home for me.

So, instead of acting on my murderous impulses, I pulled out my cell phone, tapped the photo icon, and sat with one of the country's most dangerous criminals, who, incidentally, was officially dead but very much alive and kicking, and made him look at baby pictures.

He smiled. I counted five smiles and two chuckles.

After he'd perused the files for the second time and handed my cell back, I asked, "What do I tell Aida?"

"I'll leave that decision to you."

"She has the right to know."

"I agree. The question is, will she benefit from knowing the truth, or suffer?"

Okay. I wanted to kill him again.

"Maybe the question should be, will I suffer?" I asked, tucking my phone away and leaning forward, elbows to knees, meeting the man face to face. "Will there be repercussions if I tell her the truth?"

"No repercussions. Not from my end," he said, grabbing another cancer stick from the tray. "I give you my word."

"Now what?"

"It's done," he mumbled, lighting his tobacco.

"You say it's done. You say you're out, but when I look around, I see guns, and goons, and you still have eyes on Aida, you know everything about her, so is it really done?"

"Tell me something, Tucker, or should I call you Reaper?" He quirked a brow at me, a cocky smirk pulling at his lips. "If, for some reason, Aida walked away from you, told you she didn't love you, didn't want a life with you, would you let her go?"

Easy. "No."

"But you'd let her walk away, let her believe you'd given her freedom."

"Hell, yes."

"Why?"

"Because Aida gets in her own way, more often than not. She'd come back to me, in time."

"Good answer, but I want truth."

Fucker. "She's my heart and soul. There is no life without her. I would take her any way I could get her, whether it be hand in hand, or from a distance."

"From the shadows?"

"Yes," I answered without hesitation.

"Aida needed freedom from me. Aidaline needed me, free of the dirty life. I gave them both what they wanted."

Now he was starting to make sense. "But it's a ruse."

"You're a smart man. To ensure Aida feels truly free, and Aidaline feels safe and loved, I need to stay sharp. In focus. In power. I'm no longer in the limelight. But I'm on top of the game. That's the only way I can protect them both."

"From the shadows."

He nodded.

"Aida is no longer yours to protect. She's mine now."

Luciano's dark eyes narrowed, and swear to my Maker, the temperature dropped twenty degrees. "Mind your place, son. She was mine first. She'll always be mine." He leaned closer, his mask of congeniality gone, revealing a demon more frightening than I could have imagined. "You are only with her because I allow it. You are still breathing right now because I believe you worthy of giving my daughter and granddaughter the life they deserve. Mark my words. Any harm comes to them, you'll be the first to suffer."

Two tours. In hell. I'd seen shit that would make most cower. Met evil face to face. Not once had a man made me shiver. Not once had a man given me cause to consider my religious convictions. Until Luciano Voltolini.

I was glad to have him on my side.

For now, anyway.

I rose to stand. Offered my hand, and a brief farewell.

"Sebastian will see you to your hotel." Voltolini nodded over my shoulder.

The man who had met me in the lobby stood in wait. I followed him. Before we turned the corner, I stopped, remembering Luciano's words. "Wait."

One foot in the house, Luciano paused, and turned to face me.

"You said, *children*, earlier. Is there something else I need to know?"

His lips curled upward, slow and calculating. "You came for answers. I gave you the only truth you need to know. Go home. Take care of my princesses." With that, he disappeared.

I prayed I would never have to look into those soulless eyes again.

CHAPTER 18

Tucker

I WOKE TO A PAINFUL boner and an empty house. I vaguely remembered Aida kissing me goodbye, whispering she had errands to run, and ordering me to sleep in. Not sure how long ago that had been. What I did know, was that my body seemed to weigh a thousand pounds, and my head was still stuck somewhere between Georgia and a set of heady doe eyes. I'd carried the secret for over a month now. Every day it tripled in weight, and I was breaking under the pressure.

Aida deserved to know about her mother and father. I just wasn't sure how to deliver the facts, or if I should at all. What would she do with the truth? Let it go? Be thankful? Or would the pain eat her alive? Would all the progress she'd made, we'd made, be for nothing?

Aida and Lucia, their lives, their safety, were my responsibility now.

I slipped my phone off the nightstand, took a quick dick pick, and sent it to my queen, letting her know what she was missing. Then I pulled on a pair of basketball shorts and made my way downstairs to the home gym.

Half an hour on the treadmill helped to clear my brain fog. I stood in front of the weight rack, checking out my reflection in the wall-to-wall mirror. I no longer looked at my scars with disgust. Now, when I looked, I heard Aida's soft moans, felt the burn of her skin tracing each jagged scar. The A she had carved close to my navel, was nothing but a faint scar, but it was everything to me. And, as I stared at the healed wound, I knew I couldn't put off telling her the truth any longer. She'd branded me. She'd claimed me. She'd given her baby my name, giving me all of her. Committing to me for life.

The truth would hurt. But she wouldn't run. She wouldn't seek retribution. The A she'd gifted me was proof. She'd laid her claim, and if I knew anything about my Bambi, it was that she didn't give of herself lightly, and she protected what was hers. I was hers. She was mine. Nothing, not even blood ties, would change that.

I would tell her. I wouldn't wait another day.

I showered, dressed, headed back downstairs to get some work done in my home office. After an hour of hitting the books hard, I sat back, stretched, and laced my fingers behind my neck.

Quiet closed in around me, as used to be my norm. I was alone. Difference was, I wasn't lonely. I wasn't fucking lonely. What a great, goddamned feeling.

My phone buzzed with an incoming text.

A picture message from Aida.

Her swollen breasts, filling my screen.

Fucking beautiful.

My phone buzzed again.

Get dressed. Tango's picking you up in twenty.
Don't jack off to my photo. Save that cock for me,
Cowboy.

Fuck that shit. I ran upstairs and back into the shower to take care of my boner. Wasn't facing Tango with a diamond hard dick. Came down just in time to see Rocky smiling and waving at me through the front door window.

When I let him in, he screamed, "Happy Birthday, Uncle Tuck!"

"Thanks, Rockster." I grabbed the little shit, flipped him upside down, and dusted my floor with his shaggy hair. His giggles touched me deep. I'd never have a son to pass on my name. But I had Rocky, and, in a sense, I'd helped raise the little guy, and part of who he was came from me, and the gorgeous, funny kid amazed me every day. I was honored to be a part of the tyke's legacy.

"Tuck."

"T-man." I clapped Tango's back. "Where we going? Aida gave me nothing but that you were on your way."

He smiled wide. "Meeting the ladies for lunch."

"Let me guess. The Stop?"

"Where else?"

"Ever get tired of that place?"

"You kidding me? It's home, man. Fell in love with my girl there. It's where I met my son for the first time. Slade and I will most likely shrivel up and die together in that place."

I held back an eye-roll. "How romantic."

We drove into The Truck Stop lot twenty minutes later. Roger Caldwell's patrol car was parked out front. So was my dad's truck. Signs on the window said, "Closed for Private Party."

"What's going on?" I asked, turning in my seat to face Rocky. My nephew couldn't keep a secret to save his life.

He smiled a big toothy grin, his legs swinging up and down sporadically, while he clutched his football tight.

"Rockster?" I said, narrowing my eyes.

"Uncle Tuck. I can't tell you. I promised Auntie Aida. I promised I wouldn't ruin her surprise party. Don't make me tell you. Please?"

Tango and I exchanged a glance. He shrugged. I tried, and failed, not to laugh at the poor little anxious dude in the back seat. "No, worries, little man. I won't make you talk."

Tango turned in his seat, giving his son a most serious face. "You know the drill. Run in there. Let them know we're here."

Rocky unhooked his belt. "Do we get to yell surprise now, Daddy?" he asked as he wiggled out of the carseat.

"Yeah, buddy. Soon as Tucker walks in."

He hopped from the SUV and sprinted into the diner.

"Keep that kid away from the poker tables."

"Ya think?" He laughed. "Happy birthday, brother."

"Thanks, T."

"Ready for this?"

"Yep."

We headed into the diner teeming with balloons, and streamers, and smiling faces. Everyone yelled, "Surprise," Rocky the loudest. Mom held Lucia in her arms. Dad held Mom, one arm wrapped around her shoulder. Slade, Roger, and three of our local drivers, stood in the back with Charlie and Margie. Tito and Tuuli stood behind the counter.

Aida slammed against me, her arms wrapping tight around my waist, her chin raised high, fucking kewpie-doll face beaming up at me. "Happy Birthday, Cowboy."

"Bambi," I said, lifting her off the ground. "I can't believe you did this."

"I had some help." She gestured toward Slade.

"Thank you."

She dotted my face with kisses and wiggled free. "Don't thank me yet. You might not be so happy when you see what I got you."

"Should I be worried?"

"No, Cowboy."

We ate, and drank, and danced. That damn sister of mine, always dancing. Had to admit, though, when Tango held her in his arms, and moved her across the checkered tile, there was no denying they were fated. Two halves of a whole.

Aida retired to Slade's office to feed Lucia. I wanted nothing more than to join her, but I was the guest of honor and there were gifts to open, stories to share, and candles to blow out.

When my Bambi joined me an hour later, she handed Lucia off to Mom, and yelled to the partygoers, "Okay, everyone. Me and the birthday boy will be back in about an hour. Keep dancing, take good care of my baby, and wish me luck!" She laughed, held up crossed fingers, then dragged me outside to my Jeep.

It wasn't until she insisted on driving that I started to get nervous.

Aida

Sweet Papa, I was a nervous wreck. All month I'd kept secrets from Tucker. His surprise party, the doctors I'd interviewed, and hired, with help from Lettie. Finding the perfect property.

Tucker had been acting weird, agitated almost, since returning from Georgia. I suspected that it was because he needed to hunt, to help those girls who couldn't help themselves. Every time I asked about his trip, he'd change the subject or turn the tables and ask if I missed my old life. Of course, I told him no. I didn't miss a damn thing. I was content. Happier than I'd ever imagined I could be. Even more so now that Tucker and I were about to start a new adventure together.

That was, if he didn't freak about my gift.

We turned into the long, private road that led through a patch of pine trees half a mile deep. We proceeded through an overgrown field that blended into a neglected lawn, and up to the long-abandoned home that sat on sixty acres of secluded lakeside property. The mansion had been built in the early 1900s by one of the founding families of Whisper Springs and had been passed down through the generations.

Rita Clarkson was the sole surviving member of the family. She had no one with whom to share her wealth, and she had no use for the home. I'd arranged a visit, via Carlos Rossi, and when I'd shared my vision for the property, Ms. Clarkson not only offered to sell, she made a sizable donation to the cause.

"Aida. What is this?" Tucker asked, leaning forward in his seat to get a better view of the *Great Gatsby* style mansion.

"Happy Birthday," I squeaked, nerves getting the better of me.

"Baby." He sat back, turned to me, brows drawn tight. "I thought you loved the cabin. It's our home. I know it's not what you're used to, but—"

I shut him down with a kiss. When I pulled away, he shook his head and resumed arguing.

"Tucker," I interrupted, pinching his lips together. "The house isn't for us. I mean. Not really. It's ours, but we won't be living in it."

He scratched his head and looked out the window again. "I don't understand."

"It's for the girls."

"What girls?"

"The girls we're going to save."

His shoulders slumped. Eyes crystallized. "I'm done with that."

"No. You're not. It's who you are. It's what you need to do. What *we* need to do." A lump formed in my throat, I choked it down, struggling to find the right words. "All that fucking blood money. All the dark knowledge I have stored in here," I said, tapping my finger to my temple. "I can use it for good. My past, my dirty inheritance, I can make it clean by helping those innocent kids, Tucker. I need this as much as you do."

I watched Tucker process. His gaze darting from me to the property. His face crumpling, his jaw ticking. His fingers curling and fisting at his sides.

"It's perfect, Tucker. Private. Secure. I've lined up doctors, a psychologist. And I found this amazing couple who want to live here, take care of the home, the grounds, the girls. They're perfect."

"Fucking hell, woman. How many people did you talk to?" He gripped the steering wheel, knuckles turning white. "What I do, what Mama and Chris Compton do, it's illegal."

He looked damn near ready to blow his top.

I was damn near ready to scream in frustration. "I know it's illegal. Fuck legal. Felonious is what I do best. Tito wants to help, too. He has nothing to go back to in New York. He's broken, Tucker. And I know. I just know, helping these kids will help him heal."

Tucker threw his door open and exploded from the car. He paced. He fisted his hair. He studied the home. It wasn't until he headed for the front door that I hopped out of the Jeep.

He peeked through several windows, then tested the front door knob.

"I don't have the keys yet. Carlos is helping with the financials, to keep our names buried."

His shoulders stiffened.

I stepped in front of him, palms to his chest, and as I'd hoped, his arms snapped around me. He didn't make eye contact, but there was contact, and that was good.

"Tucker, listen. If you can look me in the eye and tell me you don't want this, fine. I'm good with that. No hard feelings. I'll turn this place into a vacation rental home, or a bed and breakfast ... or something."

His gaze stayed fixed over my head.

"Or maybe a high-class brothel. One thing I've noticed this town lacks is quality whores. What do ya think?"

That earned me a laugh. And a smack on the ass.

When his glassy eyes finally landed on mine, he sucked in a sharp breath and whispered, "It's perfect, Bambi. Goddamn perfection."

All tension left my body in one head spinning rush. Solid arms held me upright.

"There's one more thing."

"More?" he asked with a sigh. "Not sure I can take much more."

"The couple I mentioned?"

"Uh huh," he mumbled, chewing his bottom lip.

"They're your parents."

Tucker let me go, stepped back, and scratched his forehead. "Jesus, Aida. Is there anyone you haven't told?"

"Tuck. Don't be angry. Please?" I reached up, curling my fingers around his shoulders. "If I've learned anything from all you crazy small town hicks, it's that family sticks together. Takes care of each other. James and Lettie are so proud of you. They're excited to help. Living in the home was actually your mom's idea. They want to be closer to you, and Slade, and their grandchildren."

"Baby. Dad can't just up and leave his business," Tucker argued, but I could tell by the quiver in his lip, he knew he was fighting a losing battle.

"It's already taken care of. Your dad promoted Bob Riggins. He's the new CEO of Slade Trucking. James can do his thing from here, and you'll be free to do your thing."

I didn't want his gift, or his day, sullied with worry of the details. I wanted us to celebrate. "And the thing you do," I said, rising to my toes, pulling him down to meet me with a firm grip on his collar. "The illegal thing," I whispered, teasing, nipping his ear. "Is one of the things I love most about you."

I fell into him, soft curves against hard planes. The thrill of his arms wrapping around me, possessive and grateful all at once, hadn't diminished over the months. The anticipation of his sigh, the rise and fall of his chest, his low, throaty moan, had become an addiction more than a comfort. Tucker's reaction to me—his acceptance, his desire—was unfailing, and I craved it. Loved it. Devoured it.

He'd given me a life brighter and lighter than I'd known possible. He'd given me peace. "We should get back. I have one more present for you, Cowboy, but it's at The Stop."

It was my turn to give—the only thing I had left to give.

Tucker

She'd given me the world already, and then some. Her love. A family. A child. Freedom to continue rescuing girls, without guilt and worry. What more could there be?

Trembling hands pressed against my back, then slid down my waist and squeezed my ass before she pulled away from me.

Those damn too-big-for-her-face eyes. I'd always known they'd be trouble. My kryptonite. I stared into them. Watched them sparkle, then liquefy. Her full lips parted on an exhale, causing the unruly organ in my chest to pound something fierce.

Her cheeks turned crimson. Her smile wavered.

My heart dropped three inches. "Aida. What is it?"

She'd never looked so unsettled.

"I just love you," she said, voice cracking.

I cupped her cheeks, leaning down to bring our faces closer. "I just love you, too, Bambi."

A crow squawked overhead. A cool breeze whipped across the lawn. Her gaze dropped to my lips and she blurted, "I know you went to Georgia. I know you visited a long-term care facility."

Fuck. No need to ask how she knew. She'd been a criminal longer than I had. I couldn't fault her for keeping tabs. I'd have done the same.

I brushed a wayward hair off her lip before releasing my grip. "I've been trying to find the right time. The right words."

When I tried to put space between us, she only moved closer. "I told you I would trust you with the truth. And I do. You'll tell me what I need to know when the time is right. I just wanted you to know that I knew. I don't want secrets between us."

"Ask me anything, Bambi. I'll tell you. We'll do this on your time, okay? Not mine."

"Is she alive?"

"Yes."

Her features crumpled. She quickly recovered. "Is she safe?"

"Yes."

Aida maneuvered back into my embrace, pressing her cheek against my chest. "Does she know about me?"

"She does."

My strong girl shivered. "One more question. For now. Then we need to get back to the party."

"Okay," I breathed, exhaling a month's worth of tension.

"Does she have a good reason for staying away?"

I didn't think so. I did, however, believe that Aidaline had believed her reasons for abandoning her child were noble. "She does, baby. She does. And Aida. There's more. So much more. When you're ready to hear it—"

"No more. Not today," she interrupted before raising on her toes and pressing a kiss to my jaw.

I turned to catch her mouth, thankful that I no longer had to carry the weight of my knowledge alone. Grateful to have the trust of my deadly beauty. I bent, cupped her round, firm ass, and hoisted her up.

Aida clamped her legs around my waist. I walked until her back hit the front door of our new house, and I kissed her, slow and deep, savoring her moans, the weight of her arms around my neck, and her tremble when I rocked my hips between her thighs.

Fuck. The way she melted against me. Steroid injection straight to the ego.

I broke the kiss. Pressed my forehead to hers, panting, willing my erection to calm down. Aida's hot breaths hit my face, adding fuel to my fire. "We should go."

"Right," she mumbled, pressing her lips again to mine, then burying her face in my neck and squeezing me tight.

The door at her back creaked in protest when I set her down. I slapped a palm against the chipped paint. "This shack needs a shit ton of TLC."

Aida laughed. A confident, *already got it covered* laugh. She slipped under my arm, tangled her fingers in mine, and pulled me toward my Jeep. I opened the passenger door. Before climbing in, she turned, and gave the mansion a long, hard perusal. I studied my girl. Watched the corners of her eyes crinkle in thought, then the almost unnoticeable curl of her lips.

The gift was as much for her as it was for me. She needed to be part of something good. Not a doubt in my mind, she'd take the ramshackle castle, mix it with our dirty deeds, and build something monumental. Something that would leave a mark.

I was no longer ashamed of my affliction, my need for hiding in dark shadows, stalking my prey.

I was a caged eagle set free.

I pitied the fuckers we were going to bring down. Together.

Aida

Together. Hand in hand. Side by side. In unison.

Partners. Family. Lovers.

Tucker and I were going to kick some serious ass.

All my shit, all his shit, had been necessary. Early on, we'd suffered alone, so that we could become the strongest halves of the whole we now made.

Indestructible. Inseparable.

Except for one tiny detail.

A detail I intended to fix before another day slipped by.

We exited the freeway, turned onto the pothole-riddled street that led to The Stop. The parking lot was empty. The lights shut off.

"Tucker." I turned in my seat to find a deep set of dimples. "Where is everybody?"

That devilish grin came out to play. "Gone home."

Oh, fuck. His birthday present. My heartbeat tripped. I'd planned so well. Slade had helped. How could she leave? "What do you mean, *gone home*? I need to feed Lucia. I haven't given you your last present."

"Aida." Tucker reached across the console and pressed his palm over my mouth. "Everything is fine. Trust me?"

He rolled up to the back door, still silencing my protest, and were I not a bundle of agitated nerves, I would've sunk my teeth into his palm and demanded he spill the beans.

He raised a brow, his cocky smile spreading wide. "Trust me?" he asked again.

I nodded. He dropped his hand.

I followed him through the back door of The Stop, through the dark hallway, past the kitchen, and into Slade's office.

Champagne-colored candles burned on Slade's desk, casting a warm, romantic glow through the room.

"Tucker. What is this?"

I tried hard to ignore the devil dancing in his eyes, but fought a shiver nonetheless.

"You marked me with your knife, making me yours," he growled, his voice a low rumble, thick with desire. "Now it's my turn."

All hints of playfulness evaporated from his face. He stalked forward, half-beast, all man, tearing his shirt over his head. I barely had time to wrap my head around the turn of events before my sweater was dust, and my bra was tossed across the room. Tucker's strong hands curled around my shoulders, backing me into the couch, pushing me down. He dropped to his knees, spread my thighs, and settled between them.

"Fuck yeah," he groaned, lifting a breast, and pulling the tight, sensitive bud between his lips.

With his free hand, he worked at the button of my jeans. I tried to help, to hurry the frantic pace, the need to mate stronger than I thought possible, but he shoved my fingers away.

"You," he ordered, "sit still. Don't move."

Sweet Mother of Mercy, I wanted to throw him to the ground, ride him hard, maybe carve the letter *I* into his skin. Hell, my whole name. I could have. But I couldn't wait to see where he was going with his sudden shift to alpha beast.

"Lift your hips," he said, moving to my other breast for a quick taste.

I planted my feet on the ground and raised my hips. Tucker tugged my jeans and panties down my thighs, off my ankles, and shoved them aside.

Oh God. The feral heat in his gaze. So damn intoxicating.

His lip curled up in one corner. He slid his hands over my thighs, then under my knees, pushing them up, opening them wide. My breath hitched, our eyes met, he lowered his head, and fucked me delirious with that sinfully talented mouth of his.

In no time at all, I was holding my own legs, bucking against his face and fingers, while he worked my clit with his tongue, and my pussy with his talented hands. I was almost there—that point of ecstasy where your body coils, about to split into a million brilliant shards of pleasure. I was so close, dizzy from the high, when he stopped.

The bastard sat back on his heels, evidence of my arousal on his face, lust in his gaze. "Stand up. Turn around."

I was a mess. Loose limbs, throbbing clit, heavy breaths. The old me would've clawed his eyes out for denying my orgasm. The old me would've used any means at my disposal to make him finish the job.

The new me. The me who loved Tucker with ridiculous, syrupy sweet fervor, rose to stand, turned around, planted my knees into the cushions, and curled my fingers around the back of the sofa.

The leather scent only heightened my arousal.

"Fucking hell, Bambi. You're beautiful."

I heard the slide of his belt. The thud as his jeans hit the floor.

"Give me your hands."

Oh God.

Slow and steady, I moved my hands behind my back, and lowered my cheek to the back of the couch to steady myself. Shivers racked my body when he tightened the belt around my arms at the elbows. And shit. Oh, fuck. Oh, shit, when he dragged a finger up the crack of my ass, I moaned and shivered, and bit my lip to keep from begging for more.

"I've wanted to make love to you, right here, just like this, since the first time you kissed me."

"Mmm," was all I could say.

"Do you remember, baby, how you teased me? How you climbed on my lap, fucked my mouth with your tongue, pulled my hair?"

He dropped wet kisses on my shoulder when I nodded.

"You owned me, even then. Hard as I tried to deny it. You fucking owned me."

More kisses on my neck, accompanied by shiver-inducing nibbles.

He massaged each side of my ass cheeks, lifting and separating them. I moaned, anticipating what was to come. His cock. Oh, God. His cock.

He teased his tip at my opening.

"You've thought about fucking me on this couch, too, Aida, haven't you?"

He pushed inside me, just a fraction. I was speechless. Mindless.

"I know you have. I've noticed how your cheeks get rosy, you chew on your bottom lip, every time we're in this room together."

He wasn't wrong. Every time I was in Slade's office, I replayed that moment. Fantasized a hundred more.

I'd planned on proposing to him, on the red leather couch where we'd shared our first kiss. The rings were hidden in the bottom drawer of Slade's desk. I was his gift. Me, taking his name, marrying him, becoming his wife, his lover, his best friend, legal and binding. Giving the last part of me to the man I loved, starting our new life together, free and clear of the Voltolini name.

That had been the plan, anyway.

The proposal could wait. The need to have Tucker inside me could not.

"It's my turn to own you, Aida." He thrust hard and deep. Fully seated, he grabbed the back of the couch, sliding his hands under my head, no doubt to protect me from the pounding I was about to receive. There was no slow build-up. Tucker dropped his head to the back of mine, and he fucked me hard, heavy breaths in my ear, the loud smack of our bodies colliding.

Rough, loud, unapologetic.

Grunts, thrusts, *fucks*, and *you're mines,* moans, and cries.

One of his hands left the couch, found purchase on my hip, then moved around to play with my clit. That familiar rush of lust stole through my body, my insides coiling tight, my body buzzing with the promise of glorious relief.

Tucker pulled out. His hand leaving me wanting, throbbing, damn close to crying.

"Fuck!" I screamed, frustrated and obliterated.

Tucker tangled his fingers through my hair and pulled tight, sliding his cock back inside me. Slow. Calculated. He pushed all the way in and stilled.

The belt came undone. My arms dropped to my sides, and I grabbed the back of the couch.

He started to move again. Slow and gentle, his right arm bracing my body just below my breasts, the other hand sliding over my left arm, then lacing our fingers over the back of the couch. This time around, his movements were slow and sweet. With each thrust, each roll of his hips against me, I felt more loved. I countered his movements, arching my back, grinding against him.

Sweat, leather, skin, the scent of our arousal—all of it became too much to bear. I fought back tears; I fought the urge to crumple into his arms, or crawl inside him because I never wanted to be separated again.

One tear rolled down my cheek, then another.

And then, when I thought I couldn't take another breath without falling apart, Tucker leaned into me and whispered, "Look at your hand, baby." He untangled our fingers, revealing the ring that, at some point during our lovemaking, he had slid onto my finger. The ring I had purchased. His birthday gift.

Tucker pulled out of me again, then urged me onto my back before settling between my legs. He didn't move right away. He studied me, studying him, with his cocky grin. "You didn't think I'd let you propose to me, did you?"

Dumbfounded, I nodded.

"I'm a gentleman, remember?"

I nodded again, brushing a tear off my face with the back of my hand.

He reached between us, grabbed his cock, and guided it home. Then, he leaned over the side of the couch and pulled out the ring I had bought for him to wear. Platinum, with two inlaid rows of diamonds. One row of black rocks, the other row, clear and perfect stones. Oil and water, side by side, creating a beautiful masterpiece. He slid the band on his finger. It fit perfect, like I knew it would. "Marry me. Please, baby. Don't make me wait any longer."

My ring matched Tucker's, only a feminine version. I didn't care that my surprise had been ruined. Didn't care that Slade had obviously double-crossed me. I just wanted to be Mrs. Tucker Slade. Small town hick. Off-the-rack clothing. Flannel shirts. Greasy burgers. I just wanted to spend every day of the rest of my life loving Tucker, spoiling our daughter, building a family and traditions.

God, I had so much love to give.

And so, on the couch in my best friend's office, naked, crying, and ready to burst with unfathomable joy, I said *yes*.

I finally got my orgasm.

And our tryst, in The Truck Stop Diner, became a monthly event.

ACKNOWLEDGEMENTS

Once again, thank you, thank you, thank you, to my readers. I appreciate every single one of you. It never fails to blow me away that you chose to read my book out of the millions of awesome stories out there.

Debra, Dru, and Helena at Buoni Amici Press (http:// buoniamicipress.com). You ladies rock!

Julie Trisolini. There aren't enough sweet eyes in the world for you, my beautiful friend.

For all the kick-ass bloggers out there, my deepest gratitude and respect. Nichole Hart, I adore you the most! Shh ... don't tell anyone I said that.

Mom. Thank you for always encouraging my love for storytelling.

Share-Bear. Thank you for saving my honor by kicking those pesky boys in the balls. I couldn't have asked for a better sister. There's a little bit of you in Aida.

SexyBoyfriend. Gah. There aren't words. I just love you.

My babies who are bigger than me. Stop growing up. And thank you for not having me admitted to the looney bin yet.

And above all, thank you Jesus!

OTHER BOOKS BY
Krissy Daniels

TRUCK STOP SERIES
Truck Stop Tango
Truck Stop Tryst
Truck Stop Tempest
Truck Stop Titan

THE APOTHEOSIS SERIES
Aflame
Aglow

How To Kill Your Boss

If you enjoyed *Truck Stop Tryst*, please share the book with others and don't forget to leave a review.

CONNECT

www.krissydaniels.com

Facebook: @authorkrissydaniels
Instagram: krissydanielsbooks
Twitter: @kdanielsbooks
BookBub: @KrissyDaniels

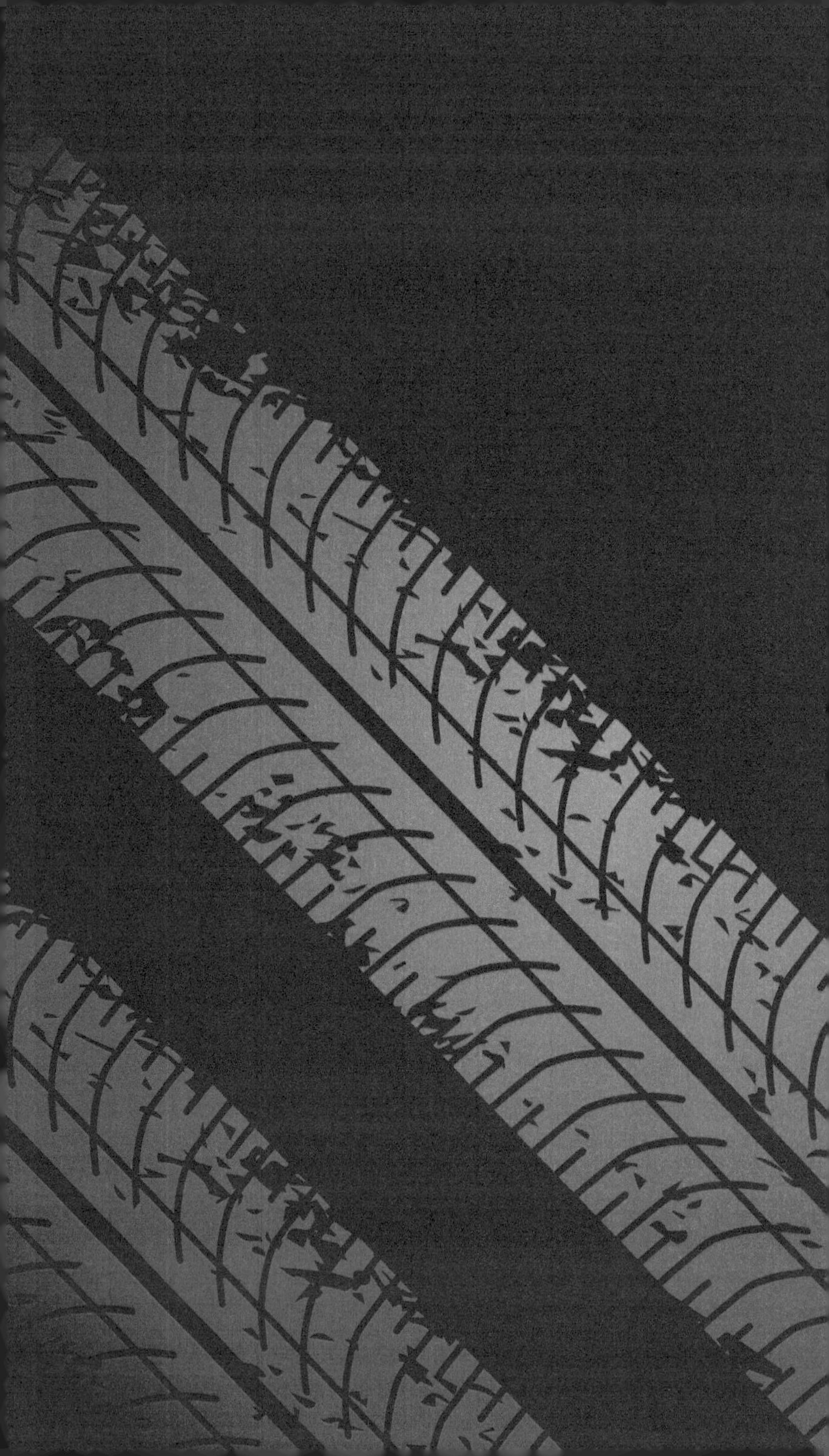

www.ingramcontent.com/pod-product-compliance
Lightning Source LLC
Chambersburg PA
CBHW021057110726
47900CB00007B/1921